THE NOONTIDE SUN

To Harry,

onetime classmate

and great organiser.

THE NOONTIDE SUN

Deirdre Chapman

Mad Pomegranate

Mad Pomegranate
Glasgow

This is a work of fiction set on a fictitious island. All characters and events are of the author's imagining. Any resemblance to actual people, alive or dead, or to actual events is coincidental.

ISBN 978-1-910256-26-8

www.madpomegranate.co.uk

For my sons Christopher, Lucien and Dorian, their wives Jane, Harriet and Tara, their children Julius, Christian, Helena, Louisa, Corinne and others to come, and, still, for Mike, Hellenophiles all.

I have bedimm'd
The noontide sun, call'd forth the mutinous winds.
And twixt the green sea and the azur'd vault
Set roaring war: to the dread rattling thunder
Have I given fire, and rifted Jove's stout oak
With his own bolt: the strong-bas'd promontory
Have I made shake, and by the spurs pluck'd up
The pine and cedar: graves, at my command,
Have waked their sleepers, op'd, and let them forth
By my so potent art.

Prospero. Act V, *The Tempest*

1

It happens often. A car slows. Pulls half in to my gateway. The engine idles, muffled by eucalyptus. The driver talks, in Greek or in English. Out on the road, window down, he talks to himself. Reading on my terrace or weeding among the olive trees I half listen. A half-life in sound bites. It's enough.

It's a hot day with a light breeze. The sea swooshes onto the strip of sand behind the corn stalks across the road, a goat bell tinkles and there is a shifting of small hooves among dry pasture a long way off. A hen lays an egg in the farmyard on the hill. The afternoon hums. A driver talks his half conversation and I half listen.

I'm weeding under the olive trees and the driver is speaking in English, English with an accent. Ours is an island that likes to be visited and ELF is its dialect.

Then kill him, says the driver.

Crouching under an olive tree, a tuft of rye grass in my right hand, I spot a pottery shard edge-up under a mandrake. The last piece I found had a streak of glaze on it. Archaic period, the archaeologist at the museum told me. The driver is listening. To his caller, I hope to his caller. Under the tree I listen to him listening.

The olive tree I'm weeding under is in the second row back from the windbreak tamarisks which themselves have a windbreak of myoporum. The eucalyptus is inside the tamarisks. The theory of a windbreak is that it has gaps, that it slows the wind rather than stop it stone dead. Mine is a stone dead windbreak.

The driver listens. My crouch unravels and I hit the ground sitting. It's hot and dry, the light dappled and twiggy, and there's an oily, wine-y smell from last year's fallen olives.

The driver laughs. Could this be banter? I don't do banter, possibly because I was an only child. The car engine is cut. A plane crosses the sky, north west to south east, very high.

The driver speaks. His tone is flat and bloodless, synthesised almost. I hear names, the names of someone I know, of someone I don't, and of someone I know of, know by sight. The name of a boat, emphasised. The voice has begun to sound familiar.

Another car passes and slows, its driver calls a greeting – Greek greeting, male bonding, obscene, more or less reconfigured to include the old, the halt and the asexual, amongst whom, on a hunch, I would put the driver. He answers, quite amiably, in Greek. Greek Greek? I'm not sure. The second car moves on.

It's quiet. He's listening, I'm listening. The sea

climbs the tiny slope of the beach and falls back over and over and the breeze stops at my windbreak. In the parallel world where he is not listening but simply no longer talking it might be prudent to stand up. The first car is right there, close enough to smell. I stand very still, smelling it.

It's metallic blue. Everything is blue here, everything that isn't white. Let us be off, then, says the shallow person in my head, to drink off-white coffee from a blue cup under a blue sky while lounging in a white or rather an ecru deckchair, unbleached canvas, sun-faded, all shades of white being permissible, white on white particularly good. Standing here is **not** good.

The driver clears his throat. I catch a movement where the sound was and now he's real. When I **can** move it's backwards, my eyes glued to the impression of a man sliced and laced together with branches and twigs.

I would like to turn round so I do that and walk towards the house. This now, though, this jars. Wrong colour music. I stop walking. In The Hall of the Mountain King from the Peer Gynt Suite. The driver answers his phone.

Look, my friend . . .

At the steps to the terrace I turn and reconsider. On this island, in this country, *my friend* voiced with such sterile courtesy is not a good greeting.

Inside the house the phone rings. I go up the steps but stop short of opening the door. The phone is on answer, it will stop after three rings and a lot of my calls are wrong numbers, and of the calls I am expecting – the garage, the courier service again, the electrician – two at least will leave a message, but if it's an impulse call from someone I care about the impulse will pass. I have put myself beyond all but fleeting impulses, exiled myself into a place of hedonism to sit forever on the terrace of traitor-trash beneath the sun that never sets clutching the wineglass that never empties. How it really is, the embedded thorns beneath the perma-tan, the limited understanding when evening comes of the anyway navel-gazing television news, Greece engaged always in an argument with itself, seldom looking up to see the others in the room, and before the evening the afternoon, the long disquieting afternoon when something starts to build out there beyond the planted perimeter . . . I have chosen this.

Hesitating with my hand on the door I unlatch it. It swings open. The ringing stops. Someone is leaving a message. It's Nico, Mr. Fixit to the foreign community. At length and at some volume he invites me to a party tonight at his new house. I don't know whether to close the door on his voice, which itself will make a sound and flag up the sound of Nico modified by human agency or to let him speak – through, plainly, an open door – to the garden and the road. Sound travels up from the road and even from the beach beyond, from where on Sundays when local families gather I can follow whole conversations. It shouldn't, I think, travel as clearly from the house to the road, but how would I know?

And does it matter? I am good at living alone but I do know that I have lost judgement. I am hyper-attentive, like the feral cat that steps out from behind the geranium and freezes, blanking out what's there and useful while it rakes the air for signals. A sixth or seventh sense has been telling me that the driver has – or had – excluded the possibility of there being anyone within earshot, and that this is not only because there is no car in the driveway, and a house this far from the village would need a car, but also because if he is local – and he is, I know the voice – he might know that this is a foreigner's house and so habitually discount it.

Nico has stopped talking. The door is ajar. Before I accidentally opened it the driver had repeated the name of the boat.

Apollon Express. Nineteen thirty. Be there.

No sounds now but I'm picking up quite a heavy stillness from the other side of the hedge. Or inventing one. It stops. I sense it as being switched off. I am standing on the terrace, screened, but perhaps not in outline, possibly, even in outline, discernibly alert, unnaturally poised, brain circuits on full siren-screeching alert for the slightly familiar voice while telling myself again that all this signifies nothing, nothing at all.

The engine starts. The car crunches softly out of the gravel verge sounding . . . muted? Can you do that with a car? It climbs a gear and moves off in the direction of the village, the direction where I cut back the windbreak to allow a young agave a clear gap to grow. From the terrace steps I swivel to watch. Blue, newish, mid-size, I don't do makes of car. One occupant. It brakes for a moment, a long moment, then accelerates away.

An egret flies over like a nazgul. I remember the pottery shard. I remember coffee. I remember the rear view mirror.

As the heat thickens and the air grows too heavy to stir itself I go down to the beach. There are two people there, women, the usual women. The unclothed one is stretched as always across the narrowest stretch of sand between the sea grass and the water's edge so that I have to step round her. The other is in a blue bikini under a blue and white umbrella where the beach widens. I walk beyond them and spread my piece of Indonesian batik in my usual spot under the tamarisks. We ignore one another. None of us swims. When I close my book I find it's still at the page where I opened it.

The Greek people in my experience are intelligent, courteous, possessed of incomparable dignity, generosity, good looks, talent for dancing and rhetoric, intuition and family values, but they are not good at waiting.

The quayside at 19.00 is crowded with Piraeus-bound Greeks waiting badly. Unable to switch off – the off switch is altogether missing from the Greek parts list – they slump behind the bars of the passenger cage because a sea that, when they raise their eyes, has nothing on it, is too depressing to contemplate. Their boat will be coming from the south, from Santorini, in parallel with the southward-headed Piraeus boat bringing the person whose extinction I plan to subvert.

The chalked-up departure time of the Apollon Express on the south-bound passenger shed tells me it's due to leave for Santorini at 19.45, and so expected from Piraeus around fifteen minutes earlier. There are a few rucksacks in there but no people. Only foreigners are going to Santorini and they're all outside lolling on their backpacks in the sun. The punctuality of backpackers – a tiny victory for Western upbringing – has quite disrupted Greek travel habits. Now the boats are on time and this evening the islanders waiting for the Highspeed to Piraeus, departure time 19.20, can no longer look out of their windows and leave the house when the boat is in sight.

I find a place at one of the café tables opposite among the older, smarter, been there done that, several times actually, travellers who are sitting over *frappés* and ouzo. Since I have no admitted purpose in being here I have brought a book. I order a fresh orange juice and open it. I can't, though, take my eyes off the locked harbour gates where the touts with their ROOMS signs are grouping and where the disembarking Apollon Express passengers will stream through, heels grazed by ice cream pantechnicons and cement lorries and the motor bikes of the Athens party set, currently girl up front, guy on the back. I'm looking for the owner of the voice or more likely the recipient of his call while hesitantly awaiting the arrival of the person I know slightly and/or the person I know by sight. Hesitantly because . . . well, because I hesitate. Because not to hesitate would require me to act.

Any good?

The voice, southern English, startles me. A man at the next table is watching me from behind reflective glasses.

The book?

I don't know which book I've brought. I look at it,

open at Chapter 1, early for an assessment. I do the shrug that tells him that, and turn back to the sea.

Only I thought his last one was disappointing.

Really? I look at him again, finding reasons to dislike him as much as I already do. Slightly too well turned out casual sports presenter look, need to impress, intention to dominate, and not that into reading or he'd be doing some now instead of using my book to get attention. Which isn't going to happen. I'm focusing, watching the quayside cluster for a homicidal non-traveller who may not speak Greek. This takes concentration. But he is not to be put off.

Holiday over then?

A boat has rounded the headland.

Oh, I'm not travelling.

Meeting someone?

Possibly. You?

He doesn't bother with that. *You live here then?*

He is both less and more interested in me now, chance to impress zeroing but then I may have contacts. And I can't just blank him. It's the effort of getting here you have to respect. No-one just fetches up here except perhaps a small but growing colony of single women wafted here on propitious currents from beyond the Pillars of Hercules to rescue and redistribute small homeless animals.

Meanwhile. Yes.

There's a ripple amongst the Greeks in the passenger shed, and at the café people are counting out euros and reaching for their bags. The backpackers haven't stirred. No-one fits my profile however roughly I sketch it.

I pick up my glass and turn to face him. *You too?*

Not yet. The plan is for an eight/four split. Eight months here, four there.

A second boat has rounded the headland. Without leaving my seat I can tell that the first boat is returning from the Southern Cyclades, headed for Piraeus. The man who is just an acquaintance and/or the other should be disembarking from the second.

A screech of brakes in front of us halts the traffic circling the windmill. Horns blare. A small white car, soft top, French, iconic, name escapes me, *deux chevaux*? has stopped right in the carriageway. One of those stick-thin arms loaded with bangles comes out to open the driver's door from the outside. A woman gets out, unhurried, very feline, long tangled grey-blonde hair, spectacularly scrawny deep-bronze midriff looped around with antique chains, ankle length tie-dyed skirt. Her companion, a decade younger, maybe two, clambers across into the driver's seat, kisses her and screeches off as one of the little cluster of port police detaches himself to come across. Ah, the port police, so reliably, so sleepily menacing in their Ton-Tons Macoutes shades and shirts that leave their glinty blonde forearms and serious watches exposed.

This one saunters across, looking amiable. The drivers who had to brake yell at him for a bit, letting off steam. He listens, leaning on a roof, in languid, girl-pleasing mode while checking out the backpackers, then loses interest. The drivers shout on, approaching drivers lean on their horns, the policeman blows his whistle, all of it reflexive, to be ignored, the Greek normality that

I'm attuned to, that fixes me here. The constant throbbing baked sea smell. The headache-y din of wind and waves and people shouting across streets or into mobiles. Then the hiatus, the empty afternoons when nothing moves, no cars, no people. The swing of climate and people from never quite convincing inertia to practised hysteria. Life as performing art, the arguments rehearsed but the kindnesses improvised, the big issues offstage, deferred, not happening, the set a shadowless sugar cube village, loomed over by mountains and perfumed by coffee, hot paving stones and freshly baked bread. In contrast to the analytical edginess of foreigners, imported anxieties, the practice of rationality.

The woman from the *deux chevaux* finds her sunglasses in her hair, puts them on and crosses into the Piraeus departure shed from whose seaward end people are now erupting. As they race one another to the first boat its car deck jerks open to robotic snatches of *Für Elise* which someone – stoned, anarchic, disaffected – chose as the music of Aegean arrival, and which right now is being reprised along the quay as the second boat reaches its mooring. The backpackers stand up and the ROOMS touts converge on the exit gate which the Ton-Tons Macoutes have begun to open.

I put some money on the table and close my book. He's still there, chair slanted my way. Behind the shades I feel his eyes pale and beady and still on me and dress him in the polished shoes and the blazer he'd be wearing over his fully fastened honeycomb polo shirt had he not decided to leave his native land. He's the type of bad traveller who leeches onto someone else to suck up what he's missing. That's part of it. The rest is straight antipathy.

The first boat is disembarking. A loose load of tourists fresh from a small island sojourn stroll down the ramp in company with half a dozen dusty cars, a cycle group, shaven-headed and in gloves, and a French tour bus. Against these the boarding passengers hurl themselves pursued by a revving horde of cars and empty soft drinks trucks ready to take out anyone who stands between them and Athens. The café patrons amble studiedly behind. The second boat completes its ponderous reverse routine, a formation dancing or perhaps an about-to-mate turtle. Its upper decks are crowded with passengers and its scale dwarfs everything in town, even the Byzantine church.

I stand up, nod a curt goodbye to the man at the next table and stroll across the road with an unconcern that is only partly affected. The ramp ends its jerky descent. The passenger stampede will narrow and converge on the exit gate. Like wolves sizing up a caribou migration, the rooms touts and the restaurant touts and the car hire touts slide through, thin, predatory, focused, but in the end almost obliterated by the sheer press of bodies and of growling, revving, lorries pushing behind them.

I stay outside the gate, a little to the right of it, and concentrate. He is one of the last to disembark, the man I know slightly, the other not to be seen. I go through the gate. I'm hesitating still, asking myself what I'm doing here, when I spot my erstwhile café companion edge up on the other bank of the passenger stream.

Something separates him from the crowd. An agenda. And now he has all my attention.

I step forward into the thinning crowd. I animate. I look surprised. *Hi*, I say to the man I know slightly. Are you going to Karistos? Can I give you a lift?

Equally surprised he says yes and I match my pace to his and walk back through the line of touts, scanning their faces and the faces of the people waiting outside the gate, past the waiting taxi drivers and on along the sea front, conversing awkwardly, towards my car which I have just collected from the garage and which is parked so far away that I have used up every vestige of our common ground before we get there.

2

A phone is ringing. Mine? Could I have chosen that as a ring tone?

Its number is held mainly by plumbers and joiners, people who expect not to show up and for me not to have waited in anyway, but so far no-one has used it or I would be reconciled to the Sugar Plum Fairy.

Is that yours?

Because it certainly isn't mine, he means. We have travelled out of the port town along the road to our village and I'm passing up prompts to explain why I have apparently turned up to meet him in the hope that he'll hand me something.

I know him as a gallery owner, which is to say he has converted one of the most picturesque ruins in the old part of the village to host summer exhibitions, and now that the island pulls artists the way it used to net fish he is spoiled for choice. But you don't make money from offering wall space and, every couple of weeks, a glass of wine, and so, really, I know nothing about him except that he is American and has another source of income.

I should answer it. I pull up in front of a cypress-shrouded chapel set back from the road and winkle it out of my bag. It's the girl at the garage to tell me my car is ready. I know it's ready, I'm driving it.

I thank her and ask my passenger where he'd like to be dropped. At the track turn-off for Aghios Konstandinos, he says. I know it, it's a monastery on a hill just outside the village, recently closed down, its few remaining monks relocated. He has only hand baggage, he says, and he'll enjoy the climb. That's good news as I'm anxious to terminate our non-conversation.

Approaching the track end I check the mirror and register that the car behind is one that has been tailing us all the way from the port, that passed us when I stopped, and which I don't recall overtaking, which means that it stopped too, and, remembering suddenly why I'm doing all this, brake sharply and skid off right onto a donkey path with low thorny bushes left and right that graze the bodywork. My passenger is astonished beyond speech. So am I. The car behind brakes but doesn't blast, sinister behaviour here, and continues on towards the village. It's new, rakish and silver.

In silence we climb through a couple of slack hairpins and slow at a traditional farmhouse, single storey, very converted, blazing white, with a perfectly trained bougainvillea in one of the less obvious colours and an immaculate white geranium in an amphora set on the paved courtyard.

Here?

He nods and gets out, searching for his keys.

I reverse with some difficulty. Though the area round the house looks impeccably tended the track above leading to the monastery is engulfed in crown daisies, mallow, poppies, wild carrot and convolvulus.

I have churned through a three-point turning, the dizzy scent of crushed camomile competing with the giddy sea view which has opened up below, and am ready to head off with a wave when he lays down his bag and signs to me to stop.

Look . . . Alice, isn't it?

Anna.

Marcus.

I know.

The sun is slipping down behind the mountains across the bay, casting long shadows. Traffic passes sporadically on the road below. A wasp is whining.

I'm grateful, he says, *but, you know, bemused?*

I switch off the engine and open the door.

I think we'd better talk.

It surprises me every day that I'm here on this island. It takes, as I said, purpose. But to stay here or rather to go on staying here takes a great lack of purpose, a suspension of rationality, an ability to live in the present that I hadn't suspected in myself and which I still don't trust myself to maintain. And so my assessment of other people is coloured by the idea that they are naturally of a disposition which for me is acquired and perhaps temporary. Also not entirely honest.

I have been incurious about the other foreigners

here. I should fix that. Now as Marcus undoes a series of complicated locks and stands back to wave me across his threshold I find myself in an uneasy parody of intimacy. But then his décor takes over.

Off the tiny entrance hall is a long pale room with a tile floor that seems neither terracotta nor marble but something the colour and texture of slightly overbaked meringue. There is soft pale seating. Someone has been in to open the shutters and let in fresh air and there are fresh rose petals in a glass bowl on an antique painted dowry chest. A floor lamp made from a wind-bent and peeled olive tree dangles a milky glass globe behind an armchair, and there are two amazing paintings, one a haze of cracked gold, an impressionist Byzantine icon, the other dark red and smoky, something being sacrificed, or someone.

But then, standing in the far corner with its back to the wall, looking towards us but also slightly past us, as if something that has been happening there for a long time is still going on despite our arrival, is an Archaic *kouros*. I stare at it. Its half smile slides beyond and above me. I find myself trying to catch its eye. I feel slightly giddy.

It's a copy, says Marcus's voice behind me. He has shed his bag and linen jacket and is carrying a tray with glasses and a jug of swaying clinking iced liquid.

Melon juice. Despina's welcome back.

Despina I take to be a housekeeper. Everything about Marcus says unattached. As, I suppose, does everything about me.

He nods me towards the sofa. We sit and raise our

glasses. The melon juice is translucent, pale green and delicious.

I angle myself away from the peripheral stare of the *kouros* and look down into my glass.

Do you know of anyone, I say, *anyone who might*, this is ridiculous, *want to kill you?*

For the first time I look him in the eye. He lays down his glass and does not look surprised. The rose petal, melon and beeswax scented air grows stiff with plots thickening.

He gets up and goes out into the hallway and standing at the still open front door looks down the track. He closes the door. He comes back into the room, sits down, takes out his mobile and turns it off. Then he looks at me.

Tell me, he says.

Driving back through the fading light I smell illicit wood smoke – we are in the close season for bonfires – and feel a weary slackening of tension and the beginnings of an anti-climax headache.

I acted, but of course nothing is resolved. Resolution would, anyway, be out of place here. If things were ever resolved what would we all do? Marcus listened intently, I think that's the word. Sustained eye contact, overt concentration, though that may be just his style. He questioned me as keenly as politeness allowed and at no point suggested I was a hysterical fantasist, but he gave me little in return.

His attempts to pin down the driver and the blue car – *You truly have* ***no*** *idea of the make? Was it a* ***recent*** *blue?*

You know, more grey-blue than blue-green? You really didn't notice whether it had a Greek number plate? You know, with Greek lettering? – made me feel like a crap road accident witness, but also left me with the feeling that he could have contributed more.

As I take the bypass round the back of the village then begin the long loop of the bay that will bring me home, I wonder why I didn't ask him about the other man whose name I heard mentioned, Thanasis, *éminence grise*, developer, a man who is on every committee on the island. Did he know him? Know him well? But then, better not. Concerned, yes. Curious, no.

And at the time, as we switched from melon juice to coffee, coffee, rose and beeswax scents now mingling in that unearthly room and the sky outside changing from indigo to mauve, I noticed only that he was charming, and deeply, unsettlingly, practised in that charm.

I'm sorry, I'm sorry, he said at one point, waving towards me a cigarette packet he had been replacing on the table on the assumption that I didn't smoke. When I shook my head I left him with the impulse to offer me something else. He went out of the room and came back with a bowl of pistachios and some thinly sliced marble cake arranged on a translucent porcelain plate. He laid it before me as if it might tempt out the spirit of buried recall. His hair was slightly damp at the front as if he had held his hand under a tap then run it through his hair while checking himself out in a mirror. I ate some of the cake and continued failing to plump up my story. His hair was the bleached well-conditioned yellow with gold stripes of expats who live in the sun. Also his eyes were very blue.

I don't smoke either, he said. *Normally.*

A death threat **is** *unusual then?*

He smiled and did that habitually charming person's re-setting of the face muscles, angle of presentation, boyish droop, elegant sprawl, the only clue that he was very consciously under control.

Coolly assessing as I was I badly wanted to dabble in the charm after a day of introspection and indecision.

I expected derision, I said. *Instead I get cake.*

Well, you know, it's a dangerous world.

I guess so. Since you haven't put forward a candidate for your hypothetical killer. I've told you the voice was slightly familiar. A name or two might clinch it.

He shrugged.

From which I take it that there are several possibilities?

I was being facetious, trying to lighten things up so that I could take my leave, but he said, perfectly seriously, *I mean, it's a dangerous trade.*

Running an art gallery? I had picked up my bag and got to my feet.

Amongst other things.

Oh I see. Drug trafficking? Prostitution?

Antiquities.

Ah, I said. Which gave far more weight to our parting remarks than either of us intended.

Back at the house the answerphone light is flashing. There are three messages: the garage to say my car is ready, my husband, unheard from these two years, asking me to call him back, and Nico's party. I have the car. I don't have the time right now – in a day or two, a week perhaps, I will certainly address it, return that call. Adrenalin through the roof, though, so no option but to go to Nico's party.

3

So it is in first-off-the-rail dress, adrenalin already running low and a bottle of 2012 Kryptos Reserve leaping like a caged salmon on the passenger seat beside me that I take the unmapped road to Nico's house.

The track lurches tirelessly between pitch dark fields and there is no moon, no landmark, no habitation, and no point to this but the rigour of a decision made and acted on. I hate parties. The headlights are all over the place as we dip and sway, the car, the wine and I, across baked ruts and loose rocks, the open window drawing in smells of hot stone, thyme, lentisk and goat, a muted drumming of cicadas and at last, in the distance, a bubbly passage of *nissiotika*.

I hear the party as I spot a cluster of lanterns set among boulders beneath a bank that is cluttered with crashed cars and motorbikes. OK, not crashed, parked. Parked imaginatively, so Greek cars. Because level ground is a whole sixty seconds walk away. And sometimes that **is** unreasonable. I reverse back to the bank and tilt my car in with the rest.

The house is small and stone-built and barely shows up in the dark. The voices and more low-tech lighting come from behind it. And when I've picked my way around over loose paving and some new planting the scene is another of those puzzling perspectives of the village and its bay.

Below and beyond antique black barley fields it glows and twinkles in all its profligate and tourist-seducing up-lighting, copying itself in the still waters of the bay. Two fishing caïques, dimly lit, make their way back towards the harbour and, far out, the flowing necklace of an inter-island ferry vanishes, bead by bead, behind a headland.

Taking in all this and adjusting to candlelight and the scented smoke of mosquito coils I am grasped by hands, kissed by faces, greeted by voices, German, English, French, Greek, while a disembodied grip releases a wineglass into mine. It's always like this. Sometimes I'm charmed by it, always disconcerted, trying not to reprise the question of what I'm doing here, for we connect stageily and patchily all of us rag-bag foreigners. We greet each other effusively in over-articulated English, enquire after one and another's seldom impaired health, then talk like actors marooned in Act 1 of a bad play as we lack the common references and prejudices to move on. Everyone is rather beautiful, not over-weight and dressed in natural fibres. But the set upstages the actors every time.

Out of the dark comes Nico. *Welcome. Welcome to my*

new home built with my own hands and also the hands of some Albanians and, I think, one Bulgarian and a Serb.

Nico is a stonemason also gifted in trouble-shooting and creative planning applications. Single and fluent in the languages of summer holiday Kryptos after working his way through a European community of fourteen-day girlfriends, thereby making himself unmarriageable, he has matured into everybody's good friend.

Hallo? Girl in a green dress. *I think we know each other. A little?*

Something about the long neck and heaped-up hair strikes a chord.

On the beach? I think we go to the same one. Today for instance.

Are you . . . ?

No. I'm the other one.

She has a pleasant complicit smile.

You live in that house just above the beach, don't you?

That's right. You?

Inland a bit. Up the track by the dovecote.

I know it. I walk up there sometimes. I don't recall a house, though, apart from the farm.

And the goat shed. I rent the goat shed.

Really?

I was up there one day painting the goats. It was afternoon and there was no wind. For once I couldn't see the sea. I felt – she studies my face – *there's something here. Something happening or about to happen. Do you know what I mean?*

I look around me. People in party poses are balanced on a crust that might, if a few things come together, shake them off or swallow them up. It's not what she means but it's close.

I thought, if it lets me stay I'll try to paint it. Panayiotis finally agreed.

He did or . . . It?

I don't think he could have unless it had. Do you?

The place she's talking about lies hidden by a rise in the ground as I sit on the roof terrace with my sunset glass of home-grown past-season rosé. It's a stretch of corn stubble separating the mountains from the sea, pure space, oddly empty. Something holds off the developers who are so busy elsewhere. But I would hesitate to make it concrete or give it volition. She is gauging my reaction.

I don't do sea. No boats, no windmills, absolutely no bougainvillea. It's the interior I want to capture. It feels . . . older.

You're a real painter then? You sell?

Enough. By the way I'm Rebecca.

Anna.

Next time you're passing drop in.

And now I'm being introduced to someone I can hardly see. A trailing vine waves its tendrils back and forth between his face and the candlelight. His name is Peter, Petros translated or true Peter I don't know.

Ah yes, he says gripping my hand. *I have seen you before.* An accent. Greek with some adulterant in it, slightly nasal, Dutch? He stands very still, still holding my hand. It is the stillness that sets off alarm bells. I want to ask where, where has he seen me? Instead I let the pause trail on.

In the supermarket, he says at last, relaxing his grip.

Really?

Almost certainly. Yesterday it was. You were in front of me.

Little vine patterns flicker across his hollow cheeks. He is tall with a receding hair line.

Which supermarket was that?

With the difficult parking on the corner near the post office.

Ah yes. I don't usually go to that one, because, as you say, of the difficult parking.

But yesterday I believe you made an exception.

I don't think so.

Could this be the voice? Something about its flat insistence rings a bell. This is a maximum avoidance party guest, yet I'm hanging on his every word. He turns his head as if to call up further proof of my shopping habits, giving me a glimpse of a profile hacked out of basalt. But we're on this weird domestic tack. Perhaps he will itemise the trolley contents. Or is he working out how to pin me down to my front garden this afternoon – hours ago, though it feels like a week? The profile blurs back to hazy full face with vine tendrils.

Where do you live?

I hesitate. He notes my hesitation.

You live here? On Kryptos? Where please?

Is it just the English or does he really need to know?

Anna! Anna! How are you darling? Come and meet . . .

Excuse me, I murmur, and recede like a child from the midnight figure behind the door, a figure which, still motionless, featureless and without speech or body language, watches me go as I let myself be led to another terrace by Birgitte, big-boned, big-hearted, one of the dog re-cyclers, who has found a newcomer, English, with a greyhound silhouette, hard, sleek hair and an assessing gaze even in these challenging conditions.

Pleased to meet you Anna. And where do you live?

So we go through all the tedious information swapping – she has been here for all of two weeks in her new house on a development which she bought without ever having visited the island – when all I want to do is pick my way back into the darker dark where the cars are upended along the bank and look for a metallic blue one.

In the same spirit in which she will have ironed out the complexities of house-buying in a crazy country she sets about evaluating me in a few brisk questions. To the last – *you have family here?* – which means a husband imported or a locally sourced lover, I answer *no,* at which, deciding I am no threat and no competition and unlikely to be of use to her, she is done with me.

Nice to have met you, Anna, she says, and takes off her person in the direction in which her eyes have already wandered, to Marcus who has just arrived. We nod to each other and I head off to find another drink which will take me to a terrace close to the parked cars. Before I go down there I need to locate the man with the basalt face. He is no longer where I left him. And now Nico and a couple of girls are carrying out platters of food to a plank table set up on bricks in a far corner under a gnarled Phoenician Juniper.

Food! he calls. *Fagito!* He has hung a little bunch of cherries over each ear. He looks like Keith Richards or a Byzantine icon.

People drift towards the table, disengaging easily, an advantage, I suppose, of Society Lite. The tree is shedding needles onto plates of octopus, *kalamares*, aubergine salad and *horta*. I heap my plate and move out into the darkness at the top of a sloping stubble field, darker than ever in contrast to the dim light behind. I perch on an unsteady dry-stone wall and am quickly joined by a few people who have in common mainly that they don't like to eat standing up. I know them slightly, perhaps even more slightly than I know most people, a couple of English painters, a French estate agent and a German entrepreneur who has built a huge house on a clifftop not far from mine which he likes to pretend is a simple cottage.

Have you heard the news? he asks me. *They have agreed the plan for the new airport.*

Now that **is** news.

When did this happen?

This morning they announced it. Just imagine, in three years, maybe four, I may fly from my office to six, maybe seven, kilometres from my cottage!

You mean an airport that can take international flights?

Indeed. We can't think small, you know, in these things. We must look into the decades after this. Most problems are caused by short term thinking.

Then you're cool with package tours?

We have all been tourists once. If money brings change and change brings money we should not resist it. Without tourism we would, all of us, be still in the dark ages. You, of course, are afraid that this will spoil the island.

The hypocrisy test. I think of donkeys in beaded

headdresses carrying bales of straw, long-skirted women with distaffs spinning in shadowy doorways and in the early morning washing sheets in the river, hens scratching on the fringes of the beach and the man in the post office on a hot day wearing two slices of cucumber stuck to his forehead and slicing four more for my father and me while we waited our turn. Once upon a time.

Of course I'm afraid, I'm a parasite, parasitic on the ambience. And, however I trim my shadow and practise my Greek and welcome the prosperity and the reverse migration and the school building and the infinite hospitality of the people and remind myself I am a net contributor to the problem, I still hate change and fear the airport.

Excuse me. I stand up as Birgitte comes past with a plate of something pale and wobbling. *I'm going to grab some of that dessert.* But when I get to the table I lay down my plate and glass and pick my way across towards the unlit side of the house that stands above a steep cutting where the ground below has been terraced. Stretching from here to the far-off lights of the village are black fields, cultivated or not it's impossible to tell, but no builder has yet made his mark. A dog barks a long way off. A shooting star flashes and dies. There are no traffic sounds, just a plane high up and a hum of conversation muffled by the house.

I have a sudden longing to be down there in the dark, to vault over the frame and climb right out of the picture. So I do that.

The projecting stone I try to use as a halfway step

comes loose and I slither down and come to rest with my back against a vertical slice of the grit and limestone bank. It's good. No nettles, no cowpats, no cows. No trickling ditch or rustling bracken. No sticky willy, no rusting barbed wire, no scent of rain. No conifers, no pylons, nothing of the homeland. Not much of Greece either but the blessed baked earth.

I try to stand and discover I have twisted my ankle. That's all right. I sit down again and the pain goes. I'm absurdly happy, Alice, after all, down the rabbit hole.

Behind and above me music starts. People raise their voices talk over it, and become audible. Right above me at the dark end of the buffet table I hear Marcus talking to, I think, the French estate agent Michel. They are talking about Mavra Vrahia, Black Rocks, a part of the island where the coastal plain vanishes to reappear on the other side of steep cliffs and offshore rocks, not really black – islanders use the word for everything that's depressing because not a God-give white – just darkish and glistening with spray. On the other side of the cliffs the arable land reasserts itself and broadens as it turns the corner to become the eastern coast of the island before another buttress, equally fearsome, closes it off. I once tried to walk all round the island. This was the part that defeated me.

Mavra Vrahia, Marcus is saying. *Why?*

It's the new place. We always need a new place.

Where would they swim?

That has been addressed.

Isn't it rather turbulent?

It is fresh. In these too-hot summers we are having now

that is good. They will make terraces in the rocks, here and there. Some will have pools. It will be private I think.

You think they'll get planning permission?

Thanasis has taken care.

Thanasis. The second name, the second familiar name, mentioned by the drive-in death-dealer. But here Nico's voice intrudes. He is singing a snatch of the tune that's playing and topping up wine glasses.

Ah my good friends. My handsome French friend who is selling our island piece by piece and my smart American friend who is selling bad pictures of it and I don't know what else. Let me fill your glasses. Have you heard that we are to have a new airport?

How did that happen? Marcus's voice. *Surely the majority were against it?*

You are talking about American democracy my dear friend, English democracy, maybe French and German democracy. This is Greek democracy. We invented it. We know how to make it work. Not one rule for everything, black and white, very boring . . . a little different every time.

Nico's voice, singing, drifts away.

Terraces in the rocks, right, Marcus, also receding, repeats to himself. And now over a clatter of spoons on plates come two new voices female, unfamiliar.

And of course I was overweight again.

Home counties voice. Older.

You were bringing so heavy things then?

German. Much younger.

Tea. Custard powder. Lea and Perrins. The usual things.

You bring tea?

Well you know how it comes here. Individual sachets. For a tea bag?

I do not drink tea.

Ah. Lucky for you then.

One of the Lea and Perrins sorority, sometimes post-colonial, sometimes just made that way.

The voice of Dimitris cuts in. *Ladies, ladies. How are you? I am Dimitris.* Delightful Dimitris, craftshop owner, mainstay of potters, weavers and jewellers.

Pleased to meet you, Dimitri. I'm Joyce.

Elsa.

Joyce, Elsa. Please, continue. What were you talking about?

Elsa, distancing herself, *tea.*

Tea. This is like English film, old style. Please, I will listen. You make English film.

It was only with reference to being overweight.

You? My dear lady, you are perfect.

No no, not me. My luggage.

Excuse me. Luggage?

Baggage then.

Baggage. I know what means baggage. Young peoples here, always with the big baggage. You go to buy maybe some bread and you can't get in the shop. Two, three young peoples in there with the baggage. They turn round, poof poof, their baggage hitting peoples. They make to pay, they take off the baggage, put it on the floor, we must step round it. Why? Why all this baggage? Dear lady, explain me.

Well, I suppose if they'd just come off the boat, and they hadn't found a room . . .

Hadn't found a room? Please. All this island is rooms. Every house, the big sign. ROOMS. All peoples here, maybe they don't speak English, old peoples, peoples from farming, little children, babies, they don't go in school yet, they all know this word, ROOMS. Please tell me, how they not find a room?

I have come here with a rucksack. The voice of Elsa.

Rucksack. That is the word. (Dimitris)

Oh. I thought you lived here. (Joyce).

I am here since two days. I don't like to sleep in rooms, me. I find this nice beach.

You mean you're sleeping on the beach? My dear, don't you know that's illegal? They stopped all that years ago.

It is not a problem. I transport my refuse. But everywhere I must take my rucksack.

Well I see your problem but frankly that is the sort of situation the legislation was brought in to prevent. Backpackers everywhere, sleeping bags all over the jetty, nobody spending money, the local economy seeing no benefit. It's not the sixties now you know.

I think I would know that. In nineteen eighty-nine was I born.

Ladies, ladies. Here we are happy, yes? Like family. Sometimes we like to talk about tea, sometimes we like to sleep on beach. Which beach are you sleeping on my dear?

Fuck you.

Panayia mou.

Footfalls. Dimitris proclaiming himself innocent before God in thought as in deed, calling on the Virgin to second that. Enough of this. I've heard it all before, endless exhausting Euro-pidjin. If eavesdropping is not to become my default mode I need to get a life. Starting now.

My ankle takes the weight as I start to hobble round the base of the bank, looking for footholds, dialogue pursuing me, the cast up there changing slightly with every twenty degree shift. I'm listening out for the bleak basalt voice, glancing up as I go in case that exaggeratedly Permian profile inserts itself between me and the stars.

Yia sou Dimitri. The unmistakable husk of the lovely Meriel. Flick of a lighter. Whiff of her Gauloise.

Meriel, tell me, am I a bad man?

No worse than a few hundred others I suppose. Nowhere near as bad as that little creep Yanni.

Yannis is my friend, Meriel.

The little shit was my friend too I thought.

You have quarrel?

Quarrel? That double-dealing little low-life doesn't stretch to quarrels. He does deal on, deal off, phone off, over and out.

Ah.

***Months** of faffing around which is not my way but I can do self control, then this guy comes from nowhere, Holland, Heraklion, someone said, I don't know but he's here, I just saw him, and deal over, the house is his.*

I am sorry Meriel. What house is this?

You know the old church by the road just before you turn off for the monastery on the hill? Aghios Konstandinos?

Of course.

Opposite and along a bit, up on the hill, by itself on a little plateau? An old house? Tiny? All shuttered up? There's a fig tree on the terrace.

I know it. Once the Roussos place.

And now mine. Should have been.

But . . . you are sure he was going to sell to you Meriel?

I tell you it was a done deal.

But it is not his, Meriel.

He was acting as agent for the owner.

The owner is in Australia and Dubai and some other places. Many sons, many owners. Yannis, he is not in real estate. Everyone now is in real estate. Yannis, I don't think so.

He could sell it to this other guy, he could sell it to me.

Meriel, don't ask me about this, Yannis is my friend, but I think there is something here, something not about real estate.

You're shitting me. Everything not squeaky clean and above board. Yannis not a saint. Give me a break. We're talking about two rooms with a seaweed and clay roof. Bamboo ceiling. No electricity. No mains water. A well, a fig, a lemon tree, some vines and half a dozen olives that no-one has looked at in years. I already transferred the money from my bank back home.

You put it in the account of Yannis?

Of course not. He wanted cash. It's in my account here.

I think you must look for other place Meriel. That one no good.

The no-good place, then, must be just around the shoulder of the hill from the all-too-good place I visited this evening with its icons and its aura. Is there a connection? I hope so. With which unqualified reaction I realise I have just stepped out of the audience. I no longer wish to embroider all this on my death shroud.

I have to exit the rabbit hole. But the bank now

looming above has gone from steep to vertical. I start to work my way along to where the slope will slacken and I can bypass the party, get to my car and head home to process all this. The sounds above are now jumbled and sporadic, the music muted, the bank climbable and I can see the glint of a car. It's blue. Then I remember that my car keys are in my bag and my bag is back up there by the dry-stone wall where I left it in search of dessert.

I grab at a bush to haul myself up then slither back down as its thorns tear my wrist. As I reach out again it starts up, twice now in one day, In The Hall of the Mountain King from the Peer Gynt Suite.

I freeze: brain frozen, breath frozen, action frozen; icy subterranean tune repeating, mocking its own tinny rendering, milking it for chill. Down here in the dark it gambols manically through the chambers of my one functioning sense. This afternoon it drifted up to me, rising incongruously on hot air through a screen of eucalyptus and tamarisk, now it falls on cooling air, holding me immobile in this pit. Again it starts. Then a hand comes down out of the higher, thinner dark. Marcus's voice says *just passing?*

I grasp the hand and am hefted up in one economical heave, muscle behind it, the surprise of this jolting my brain back into action but screwing up my chance to pick up . . . what? A Norwegian holiday maker with a phone to his ear? I'm staring around, not focussing because the dark is different up here, listening for a one-sided conversation but not hearing anything because Marcus is speaking.

I've been looking for you, he says, dabbing at my wrist

with a white handkerchief, real, not Kleenex. *I wanted to ask you . . . to keep this thing just between ourselves.*

I think about that. What it might mean. And how, if he had known it, he had no need to say that, as I have no possible confidant anywhere on this island. And I wonder if that is quite the good thing I have always judged it to be. And I decide to be careful, creative even, in my response.

Marcus is tying the handkerchief round my wrist. It has a curly monogram in the corner. I step away, lay a reassuring hand on his shoulder.

Apart, of course, I say, *from my husband.*

4

I waken thinking about Raffy. I try not to do that so I put him on hold and go out into the garden to gather peaches for breakfast.

They are not without flaw but they are mine, hanging sun-ripened and sun-warmed three paces from the table under the palm tree where I will eat them with yoghourt and honey and the new issue of the Athens News which has a fresh scandal on the front page, a bishop and real estate scandal replacing the bishop and icon scandal of last week. A gangland chief doing time for murder has been scooped by helicopter out of a prison exercise yard, and professors and students striking against education reforms have been joined by high school teachers and pupils. Primary school teachers and pupils are debating whether to join them. With everything normal in the wider world, then, and the peach glut lighter by five – anything but watch them drop to the ground and lie there shrinking into grubby felt retro lingerie – I take stock of where I am. In the ditsy sense.

Where I am in the literal sense is trapped in the almost unvarying idyll, blue sky, blue sea, still no wind but the humidity negligible, a lot of wasps hanging about the lantana bush making a noise that could get irritating, and now the phone ringing.

I am not inclined to answer it. Though it could be the electrician. Something may have happened. I'd rather not know what.

Gravel crunches and beyond the drooping fronds of the palm tree a red van hurtles up the drive. It brakes noisily and a voice shouts over the engine *O manaaaavis!* The greengrocer. He locates me under the palm fronds and kills the engine. *Kali mera, Kyria mou*, he shouts, throwing open the door to reveal two sorts of green beans, courgettes, beetroot and a mound of dew-fresh *horta*. I resign myself to a week of serial vegetable eating and buy a kilo of everything. Sometimes I try for half a kilo but he makes such a drama of disentangling leaves and fronds, farmer's fingers plucking at wisps while he glances up to check that I know what my solitary and unnatural state is making him do. He crams all this into blue plastic bags, starts the engine and reverses while I go into the house to hunt out change. While I'm doing this the phone rings again.

I hand the money through the window and, as he drives off, he tells me my phone is ringing. Because of this I feel obliged to answer it. Fortunately it stops before I get there. Since last night it is not on answer.

Where I am in the fluffhead sense is unsettled, so I

whitewash the long wall between my house and that of my new as yet un-met neighbours, scrub the spatters off the paving stones, wash the brush, put on a fresh T shirt, cook up all the vegetables, make some *skordalia* from the sack of potatoes the *manavis* presses on me every spring, eat some of this and, now that I have structured a morning and placated the thing that guards the threshold of the afternoon, go down to the beach.

Rebecca is not there. Neither is the other. Two men are. They swim. So do I, but I stay closer to the shore.

This evening when the sun is starting to go down I shall walk up the track past the dovecote, past the farm, to visit Rebecca in her goat shed. But first I have to phone Raffy. The number he left me is on the answerphone. I have a problem with this. How to access that number without playing back everything in the voice mail. I am not at ease with my answerphone. It is a negation of chance. Also choice. I do recall seeing a SKIP button – it **was** there but this no longer seems to be the case – so I settle for listening to all the voices and messages that together form a commentary on my recent life, and out of this not very involving pageant create for myself a strange sense of unease, so that when I arrive at Raffy's voice I am too edgy to take in the words. I run it all again and this time find myself too distracted to get down all of the number. Then the plastic skin of the malevolent memory box reveals a secret door. Behind it is the SKIP key. I write down the number but it has the wrong grouping of digits to be British. There is no country code. Only then does it come to me that it's an Athens number. What does this mean?

I don't know that I can handle this right now with the sky turning golden after another hot airless day in which I have painted, swum, cooked, pinned up some bougainvillea, and put off calling Raffy. I can't be indoors when such a sky is out there. So I put the phone back on answer, head out into the glare of the lowering sun, and take the track that turns away from the sea and climbs to the slightly higher ground of the jutting coastal plain which here extends for barely a mile before it reaches the eastern shore of the island overlooking the narrow gulf between our island and its bigger sister.

Between the sea and the start of the mountains is a thin scattering of small farms, crumbly icing sugar houses nestling amongst their produce. Close by the track is the farm of Panayiotis with a herd of goats and two cows, hobbled and roaming but kept out of the rows of beans, peppers, onions, tomatoes. There are lemon and fig trees, exuberant unwired vines and an olive grove with hens scratching in the rich red soil between the trees. A turkey keeps guard from the roof of an outbuilding and a dog goes into a killing frenzy as I pass, then switches off once I am twenty metres beyond the gate.

Where the track runs out at the far shore windsurfers have built themselves a fragile settlement, limestone rubble and plaster walls, lean-to pallet extensions, palm leaf pergolas, geraniums in pots and blue-painted zinc tables. The sand there is creamy pale and the island across the gulf rises like a mirage from a desert floor, spinning, hallucinatory, out of it. I understand why Rebecca has placed herself in the gap between the two seas, where the wind slackens or dies and the loudest sound now the dog has stopped barking is the buzzing of bees.

The track takes a loop after the farmhouse and in a shallow dip I see the freshly whitewashed goat shed with Rebecca seated at her easel outside. The dog when it stopped barking must have given her the precise time that a walker coming this way would appear in her view. She looks up and waves as I leave the track and crunch over the stubble following my shadow towards her.

The painting is of a goat standing on a rock, its four hooves bunched together on a flat summit the size of a plate, not tapering down from its head and spine – I can see that – but coming up out of the rock. Its head is in profile, its facing eye yellow as the sun or perhaps hollow with the light coming through from beyond and its posture one of huge indifference. It is pre-human, pre-animal, animal evolving from mineral, god evolving from both. She has caught it, the beginning of things whose echoes underlie everything here. I recognise it and shiver. And the shiver too I recognise. The *kouros*. The *kouros* in Marcus's house.

I was painting the landscape, she says, *but the plants were wrong. Too new. Except the fig. And the olive.*

And the vine? We look across at the next island rising sheer from the sea, birthplace of the putative starter-plant. Dionysus, bored, playing with the seedling, planting it in a bone, the vine fusing with the bone to make it less plant, more animal, Dionysus fusing with everything to make it less itself, more a possible something else. It's what happens here. You merge.

Rebecca goes into the goat shed and brings out a jug

of the farmer's wine. It's the gold of the goat's eye, translucent and astringent. A breeze stirs the air, the first real breeze for days, warm, but with an odd chill in it. We sit on a rock and drink the wine – a blood-tinged gold now as the sun slides into a fire-pit between two peaks and commands our attention. But the indifference of the goat is in everything in this landscape, and as we sit here in silence the coincidence of our both being human tips the balance and inclines me to think I might confide in her. The Marcus murder-plot or the Raffy re-emergence. No need to saddle her with both. I settle for the olive-grove incident and am choosing my words when the dog starts to bark.

Two passers-by in one evening? That's a record.

I thought the surfers would pass this way.

Sometimes. Usually they go along the coast track. Anyway they have vans and bikes. The only people who walk here are, well . . . us.

The dog stops barking and after a measured interval two men appear. They see us, hesitate, then walk on without the customary nod. They are twenty-ish and well developed – to be picky, over-developed – and look Greek. And if surfers don't walk, far less do Greek alpha males.

Curious, says Rebecca. *I saw those two this morning in the field behind your house.*

Doing what?

Hanging about. I was afraid they might be surveying it for a villa complex or something, but no, they were just hanging about.

I've seen them too. They were on the beach.

I feel a fresh sense of foreboding, resist the reflex to shrug it off, and commit myself now to telling Rebecca everything.

Inside the goat shed she lights candles, finds a canvas chair for me and perches on her folded-up futon. I start my story under the olive trees and continue to the end of Nico's party. She sets a kettle on a primus stove and makes instant coffee, adding milk from a tin. We're at the other end of the spectrum from Marcus's place, yet in its pared-down, chalky ambience, not so far away. I wonder if I am betraying the secrecy promise I didn't quite make to him.

I think, says Rebecca, *you have a problem. How much of a problem . . . ? Well.*

Beyond the goat shed door the sky is dark. *I don't get it. Any of it. I don't even get what it is I'm not getting.*

Then let's go over what you **do** *know.*

An overheard remark.

Remark?

Order then.

Death sentence.

If it was serious.

Marcus thought it was?

I believe so. Though he didn't seem too concerned.

And you thought that was normal?

I'm a little out of touch.

From outside comes the crunch of returning footfalls. Rebecca offers to make me up a bed on her floor.

Nothing has actually happened, I point out.

That you know of.

She's right of course. Time has passed. But if Marcus remained quite sanguine, why should I be worried? Perhaps because now I've put myself in the picture. With him.

He gave me his number. Do you have a phone?

Of course she hasn't. And thinking of phones I have to stop blanking out the call from Raffy of whom I have told Rebecca nothing.

I must get back. I'll be all right.

Then I'll walk you to the track end.

We set off by star and torch light, cicadas electrifying the air around us and the dog signalling our passing. The turkey on the barn roof roosts against a spangled sky, and where the track ends a brief run of faint street lights makes a stab at civic order, gives up, and leaves the stretch to my gate in the usual sub-Stygian gloom. I promise to contact her next day and we agree on the beach as our connection point. If I don't turn up she'll come to the house.

Alone again my head is full of Raffy. Why did he call? Why did I not call back? And why is he in Athens? Perhaps because – only now do I let it strike me – he is coming here.

The smart-ass answerphone light is flashing up more missed connections and botched responses. I press the play button without pausing to close the door or turn on a light as if I may yet catch up on my caller. Whom I assume to be Raffy. Raffy **is** there behind two callers who don't leave a message, only the sinister withholding *duh duh duh*. He tells me he is catching a boat. The sound of his voice scrambles my brain. Boat, I think. Boat to where? Here of course. Now. Tonight. This blankness I feel is pathological. Does he expect me to meet him? Of course. That's why he phoned. But did I pick up the time? Of course not. And so I must play back all the messages.

And again I'm apprehensive. Something in there scares me.

There's just enough starlight and distant street light to let me locate the SKIP button. In the dark, finger pointing like a gun, I run these people past me and take aim, SKIP SKIP SKIP then SKI . . . my finger aiming before I can call it back. The voice. **That** voice. It was there. I've gone past it and people are inviting me to lunch weeks ago, passing on numbers of plumbers and carpenters, reporting bad weather back in Britain in the bleak voice that solicits an invite. Raffy tells me he is arriving at ten tonight. Then I go back to the beginning to nail my nemesis, SKIP SKIP SKIP, hold the SKIP. Hold my breath. Sounds outside. In the garden. Sometimes there's a hedgehog out there. It rustles. And there are cats. They're silent. This was the sound of a twig snapping. Snapping under a foot. One of two? Four? Digging out the car keys, slamming the door, switching on full beam lights and revving noisily, I set off once again in the direction of the port.

5

That first year we flew to Athens on a charter flight from Gatwick, my father in a light blue chambray jacket, unshaven, beginning the beard he would grow on holiday and also – I was ten and already observant – his personality shift.

He ordered brandy. My mother in a new short haircut raised her eyebrows and declined to join him. It was morning.

He sat in the aisle seat, our interpreter to the world of the plane. I had the window seat, the start of something for me too. My mother between us, unrelaxed in that crisp hairdo and easy-care blouse, leafed through the newspaper, the in-flight magazine and, at last absorbed, the Blue Guide to Greece, while I began my love affair with Out There: the Thames Estuary, the coast of France and, after a lot of cloud castles and moats, the Alps, still snow covered, diagrams in black and white, but enclosing deep valleys, diagrams coloured in, sometimes in heart-stopping detail. My discovery of the fragility of human settlement.

In Athens we stayed in a monster tourist hotel, not quite finished. I remember it in selective detail: the salami-coloured terrazzo reception area, the bank of lifts, the cake for breakfast. The discovery of a button marked ROOF above Level 12 in an empty lift when I'd gone to fetch my cardigan. Pressing it. Rising. Door sliding open. Vertigo swooping, howling, tugging at me, swinging me left and right between a view of Gotham City and a great red sky. I clung to the wall of the box the elevator lived in, a box perched on an unfenced, unfinished roof, swept by gusts of wind, peopled with bricks and cement mixers but no people and at my feet the great yawning abyss of the yet-to-be-tiled swimming pool. I felt my lack of body weight, my lack of supervision, of permission. I saw neon signs with the names of other hotels. I saw the Parthenon on its rock. My legs gave way and I grabbed a cement mixer for support and noticed that the Athens beneath me had iron-railed balconies crowded with plants and people eating dinner and alien sounds of traffic, music and voices. Slowly, exchanging handholds, I retreated backwards into the still open, still empty lift and descended to my room where I picked up my cardigan then went down to join my parents at the outdoor terrace restaurant for dinner.

They were deep in private-seeming conversation and I said nothing, but when I looked at the other parents and start-of-the-holidays children they seemed less interesting, chattering as if they'd never left home. And so I confirmed the boundless possibilities of going it alone and spotted a tendency that I chose not to nip in the bud.

We had two whole months of holiday and no set plan, so after the sights of Athens and a side trip to Delphi and Epidauros we started to check out the islands. Aegina, Poros and Hydra came and went. We returned to Piraeus. Then early next morning, sunbaked and crumpled, stripes starting in our hair and *bouzoukis* lodging in our heads, our eyes now forever adjusted to intense blues and whites and our ears to the Greek language, we boarded a boat for the Cyclades, sized up two consecutive islands from the deck class rail, and got off to take our chances at the third.

First we stayed in the port town with its salt-encrusted sea front, secret inner streets and high wild hinterland. But every departing ferry reminded us that our stay was temporary. We caught a bus to another village by the sea, identified it as the one that the gods had assigned to us, found a house to rent, and returned to the port only to collect our things. And then, on a beach, Raffy.

But before I met him there were his brothers.

Michael was sixteen and scornful. He had heavy dark blonde hair that reached his shoulders and a red bandana. He stood on the prow of the caïque that ferried us across the bay and performed a mighty and, I thought, unnecessary leap onto the jetty. He tied the ropes in the sort of loopy obsessive knot Girl Guides fixated over and I knew he was not my type. This was as self-protective as it was dismissive. He carried a harpoon and his T shirt was more often off than on.

Gabriel, twelve, was more geeky though I didn't know the word then. He wore glasses and collected hermit crabs for which he made a little pool, and chased lizards across the rocks.

Michael and Gabriel were allowed to go to the beach on their own. Raffy, six months older than me, was not. He had been ill, or his mother had, but finally they came, he and his mother, and everything changed.

She stepped off the boat, tall, blonde, disengaged, wrapped in something white and fluttering, a goddess amongst mortals, and through the holiday families scattered along the beach there spread a wave of self-abasement. Raffy came behind, picking his way across the rocks, plainly even from a distance caught up in his own world, which was just as well as his mother never looked back.

As they came up to where we were sitting, my mother and I, my father was touching down in the shallows, toned and already tanned, beard now trimmed to designer stubble, his already interesting face surprisingly enhanced by his experiment. My mother, a little confused by the emergent look, no longer commented. She and I were finishing a sandcastle which Raffy's mother, beginning the swerve that would bypass it, correctly identified as home base for the approaching swimmer. She stopped and smiled at me.

Taj Mahal? Acropolis?

I was embarrassed for her. Plainly our castle resembled neither. You can't make Doric columns out of coarse-textured sand and anyway she meant the Parthenon.

My mother began to answer but by that time my father was alongside us and Raffy's mother was turning her attention to him.

Your daughter is an artist, she said. She was American and that was somehow not a surprise. *And what's more*, she said, glancing back for the first time, *she looks about the age of my son.* Then, turning to me – she knew to do that – *How old are you my dear?*

Ten.

I knew it. Raffy is badly in need of company. The others tend to leave him behind. Will you be here for long? This time talking to my mother. *By the way I'm Claudia.* At which she held out her hand to my father who after some hesitation took it in his wet one, my mother meanwhile scrambling to her feet with a forced smile.

Ruth, said my father indicating with his chin but without turning his head in my mother's direction. *Anna. I'm Evan.*

And this is Raffy, said his mother as he covered the last few yards with a look of well honed resignation.

In the days that followed, enchanted days in which I fell in love forever with the island, days on which Raffy was allowed to come with his brothers to the beach so long as he then came under the care of my parents, we discovered a mutual disaffection. We did our own thing, swimming or reading, but companionably.

The evenings, at least until Lucas got there, were another story, for Claudia, never again seen on the beach, had decided in that first moment to appropriate my mother as child-minder and my father as after-dark companion, tolerating my mother as a necessary part of the deal.

Nothing was said – it was a learning curve for all of us I think – but my mother, sidelined and addressed with a false sisterliness by Claudia that often involved a strategic step-down as if implying that she couldn't handle grown-up conversation, grew distracted and helpless as evening approached and she changed into one of the two striped dresses she had brought and we went to the taverna where it was understood we would always meet Claudia, sometimes smouldering under heavy eye liner in a fringed Flamenco shawl, sometimes with gold on her cheekbones and gold sandals on her feet, her hair looped up like one of the statues in Athens and in the same sort of over-the-shoulder white dress.

Of course none of this would have been more than an amusement – I could see that even then – if my father had not turned out to be so susceptible. For just as I was turning my back on the places I had loved, my bedroom under the eaves, our bookshelves, the plum tree, the path to the lake, the lane to my grandmother's, her conservatory, its grapes and frogs and orchids, in favour of this scorched, bone-dry underfurnished landscape, so my father appeared to be rejecting the people in his life – my mother, me, also no doubt those at home – for a Claudia configured society.

One evening when his treachery got too much for me I blurted out *She got a first, you know.* ***He*** *only got a second.*

A what, dear?

My mother. At university.

As Claudia looked nonplussed and my father did his distancing thing, Raffy's eyes met mine.

How about we go get an icecream?

We carried our blue glass shell-shaped dishes, our long spoons and our glasses of water to one of the tables under the plane tree. It felt cool and lightly done. I was outside it, watching us. So was he.

Raffy picked up his spoon and looked at me.

That was good, he said.

What was?

What you said then. About your mother.

It was because . . .

I know why it was. My mother was bugging you. She bugs me too. All the time.

I didn't know what to say to this so I said nothing.

It's all an act.

What do you mean?

She doesn't know jack shit. It's a cover-up.

She's very beautiful.

Yeah. That's why she gets off with it.

I hadn't known that it was possible to be detached about your parents, but now that Raffy had shown the way I thought about it and began to do some off-loading.

My dad is bugging me, I said.

Yeah, well. That's the way it goes. When **my** *dad gets here it won't be so bad.*

What's he like? Your dad?

Lucas? Fine.

Where is he?

Looking for angels, I guess.

He's an . . . I thought a bit and, my father being an archaeologist, tried . . . *angelologist?*

Kind of. He writes books about icons. Saints and angels and stuff. That's why we're all called after archangels.

Archangel. Nightmare image from way back. Book of animal skin with moths' wing pages, pages falling open, freeing the angel, its wings stiffening, shoulders hunching, all of it coming for me till I snap it back into the book. Archangel phobia, hard to kick. Raffy was watching me, waiting. We didn't go to church, I didn't know angel names.

Michael, Gabriel and Rafael, he said.

Your real name is Rafael?

Sure.

Then why does everyone call you Raffy?

Because no-one can say Rafael.

On the day that Lucas was due to arrive I was expecting a man with a fiery countenance, but he was dark and slim and graceful and not as tall as Raffy's mother. Where Michael was like Claudia and Gabriel like neither of them, Lucas might have been Raffy's older brother. He was, in fact, six years younger than Claudia, but I was not to know that until Raffy and I were man and wife, Lucas my father-in-law and Claudia . . . still Claudia.

Not so many people at the port this time. This is the last boat of the day. Where the sea sparkled there is now a black void, industrial wasteland you might imagine, the harbour railings turned to factory gates and the people, without sun, to matchstick men. The meeters and greeters are fewer and less into it, smoking more, chatting edgily, backs to the void, ready to call it a day.

The parking place I find this time is closer to the jetty. As I lock up I see the *deux chevaux* of the other day or one like it parked two in front of me. Across the road the café now looks bleak and uninviting and, under its harsh lights, almost empty, the strengthening breeze flapping the awning and clearing the quayside of casual strollers.

One of the port police is listening to his walkie-talkie. When he passes I ask if the boat is on time. He nods towards the sea and indeed from behind the dark bulk of the headland comes a lengthening ribbon of lights with gaudy diagonals. That boat is bringing my husband. I have no idea why.

It occurs to me that I have come straight from a stroll three hours ago without passing a mirror or pausing to pick up a sweater. I feel chilly, naked and unprepared. I cross the road to the café and walk past the sign that says Toilets For Customers Only, past the owner who ignores me, leaning his elbows on the counter and watching a football match. The place smells of ashtrays and cheese pies. I squeeze into a tiny cubicle, back out, find a light switch, then peer into the dim freckled mirror. My face looks raw and unsure of itself. I put on some lipstick and a slash of eye liner. Hunched forward in this awful light and sharing a cupboard size space with an overflowing loo-paper bin I now look like a soon-to-be murder victim in a middle-America fifties motel. And that, I think, is much how I feel.

Back outside the boat has begun its docking

manoeuvre and there's no time to collect my thoughts, to think about how Raffy might act or look and how I might present myself after all this time.

The exit area is badly lit and I'm not confident I'll pick him out immediately. I see a few single men but they look too swift of foot and spontaneous to have come from an international flight. I don't expect Raffy to be so unencumbered. But then might he too be travelling just from Athens? He could be living there. The last I heard of him he was in London, but that was two years ago.

There. Carrying a weekend bag, hair ruffling as always in the wind, head inclined to listen to a woman walking alongside him, height, shoulders, his whole outline sparking deep memories. They are coming down the ramp, pausing and moving aside as a car comes through from behind, blocking my view of them, but in that moment I recognize the woman as the departing ferry passenger from the *deux chevaux*, she of the crinkly, jangly sixties look and the toy boy companion.

And as if on cue a familiar voice comes from behind me. *We meet again.*

I turn and see last night's man at the next table. I am slipping into a crack in time in a black and white movie where random events are poised to wind up not so random, perhaps not random at all.

This time of course he is not wearing dark glasses. He has small light blue hazel eyes, eyes which are weighing me up too closely for comfort.

Travelling this time or just meeting?

Oh . . . meeting.

I disengage carefully, keeping him in my radar, and

turn back to pick up Raffy or the Raffy look-alike and his female companion. They must be on the other side of this line of disembarking cars. Then I notice that people are also coming out of the other exit gate which is usually locked against backpackers trying to busk it. I understand suddenly that the script for this has already been written and that I must not panic or, if panicking, not show it. I fight that as I go along with it, not rushing like a Maenad to the place where I last saw him, but wanting to. I decide to stay at the gate I've chosen and then, when they don't appear, as they surely won't, saunter casually down to the other.

The last car has passed. There are a dozen people to come and none looks like Raffy. Now I run to the other gate. There are just half a dozen stragglers there and he is not one of them. Two or three guys are hanging about outside the gate, all huge, hormonal, gap year. I cross to the windmill, landmark for missed arrivals, but the people here, trying to get their bearings, are too young, too pale, too gauche, too logo-infested to merit a second glance.

Missed the boat, has he?

I turn ready to zap him with my off-the-scale adrenalin surge. His fault, all of this. If he hadn't distracted me Raffy would be here now. Then I get a grip. People who want to be seen seldom disappear.

He is hovering still, staying in the shadow of the passenger pen. I calm myself and search again, this time taking in the whole harbour area, now almost clear of people, the room touts done for the day and retreating towards the brighter busier core of the town glowing with yellow light behind the palm trees, a town full of wives cooking and children being called in for dinner.

I'm sorry. I have to go. And still he lingers. I recall my suspicions – he may, after all, be somehow relevant – and as I head off along the dimly lit sea front I'm listening for following footsteps. There are none but, rummaging for my car key, I see the *deux chevaux*'s lights come on up ahead as it pulls out into the roadway, does a U turn, and speeds off along the exit road that leads in the end to any point on the island.

I get the car open, climb in and sit there until the interior light goes off and I can hide in the dark then compose myself while I try once again to make sense of a world gone mad.

The sister I was going to have who didn't quite work out and the brother before that . . . we were going to draw a line under them. That's what my father said. And my mother finally agreed. That's what I heard, clinging to a shutter on the balcony with the shaky rail outside my parents' bedroom, on the night I heard them rowing, the second last night of our holiday, and, with hindsight, the first day of my decision to detach. Those were their problems. I couldn't help.

We had eaten *souvlaki* wrapped in *pitta* from the little cabin in the square – after Lucas came we didn't always eat with the Hollanders – then we'd gone to the café for cakes and coffee and rather a lot of Metaxa for my father.

I wondered if anyone else could hear. The village was only small then with no street lights. Our house – single storey with our two bedrooms sharing a balcony and downstairs a living room with a bead curtain so that you could leave he door open – was built out over the rocks.

Across the bay the lighthouse flashed out its beam. I counted to sixteen between the flashes. The light ran across the water towards me on the balcony before it disappeared.

In a while my mother stopped crying. It was OK for me to feel happy now which was good because the warm dark air and the lighthouse and the sea crashing on the rocks below were making me feel very glad to be alive.

On the last night we had dinner with the Hollanders and told them we would be back next year.

When we went home my mother went back to teaching. In the spring my father wrote to Kyria Drossoula to book the house again and this time my mother had different clothes and longer hair, and my father had shaved off his beard and I understood that parents were also people, people who would be forever changing.

Michael wasn't there – he was staying with friends in France – and Claudia was less in evidence. When we did see her she seemed preoccupied.

Lucas didn't come until the last days and Raffy was . . . different.

He, Gabriel and Claudia had already been there for a month when we arrived. They were now living in Athens – Lucas was doing some work with the Byzantine Museum and finishing a book – and their school terms seemed enviably and exotically flexible.

In the afternoons Raffy was now allowed the right to

roam as long as he stayed away from deep water, and he exercised it to the max, going off for long treks in the hinterland. He spoke some Greek now and didn't much want to hang out with the foreign holiday kids on the beach.

But something was wrong with the Hollanders. Even Claudia had lost some of her shine. I was troubled for them, but more than that I was curious.

One night Gabriel came to our house, Gabriel who didn't talk to a person if there was a cicada or a lizard around. It was quite late and I was already in my nightdress.

Raffy is lost, he said.

Where is Claudia? asked my mother.

I don't know.

Hang on till I find my sandals, said my father. *I'll help you find her.*

No. No. I'm supposed to be looking after him.

He told us that Claudia had given them money for *souvlaki*s and cokes and had gone off with some guy to a party at the other end of the island.

He looked at my mother and read her expression. *No, it's cool. She does that. We're fine. Generally.*

He had last seen Raffy when they went down to the harbour on their way home to watch a fishing boat come in. Raffy and he had gone on board to help the men carry the fish boxes. *We do that. They know us.*

My mother and father exchanged glances. My heart thudded and stopped. Again Gabriel read our faces

He didn't fall in. People saw him after that.

Gabriel had missed Raffy during the fish box

unloading and had quizzed the other guys. One of them told him he had gone off with a man who had come looking for him. The fisherman had seen them turn off along one of the labyrinth of passages that radiated out from the harbour and when Gabriel went looking he found a Greek boy he knew who had seen Raffy and a man pass that way. Gabriel had gone on looking for nearly an hour – *good man*, said my father, clapping him on the shoulder – but now he'd run out of ideas. He'd gone back to their rented house but he wasn't there.

Maybe he's looking for ***you***, said my mother.

Could be. I thought he might come here.

My father went off with Gabriel and quite soon they found Raffy sitting on a wall near their house. He couldn't or wouldn't say where he had been.

When we were both fifteen and starting a sort of dating – walking out to the lighthouse, sitting at a separate table in the café, sussing out the limits of our empathy, not sure yet where this was going – I asked him if he would tell me about that night. It was, I suppose, a test.

He chilled me out. *Off limits*, he said. And walked away.

Sitting here now in my car on the deserted sea front, the wind rattling the shop signs and a cat picking its way along the litter bins, I think of that first disappearance.

Question: How well did I ever know my husband?

Answer: How well does anybody?

Answer to answer: Better than this, you can bet on it.

Question to question: Why ask this now?

Time to be practical. If ours was an on-going relationship I might be able to second-guess his movements. As it is, the possibilities are surely not unlimited. They can be narrowed down to:

Possibility 1. He missed the boat or changed his mind.

Outcome: he has phoned to say so.

Objection: the message should have come before I left.

Mitigation: with no response to his other messages, why bother?

Possibility 2. He arrived but didn't see me.

Outcome: he has gone to the house. Qualification to Outcome: if he knows where it is.

Objection: he didn't look for me.

Mitigation: he thinks I'm not here.

Conclusion: the possibilities **are** unlimited. He could be anywhere. But at least I can narrow them down by going home.

As I start the engine I see him again, the man at the next table, standing watching me from the shadow of a palm tree.

Back on the road, tugging the car at speed round familiar bends whose dark and fuzzy verges can secrete halogen-blinded tourists plodding into town, I turn at last into my own unlit and still unfrequented drive and go straight to the answerphone. It is on. It is not winking. Why do I allow this thing in my house?

So, what now? Chill. Analyse. Deploy logic. All beyond me. I feel draggy, laden, thick, defeated, and under the weight of that my personality is splitting.

I should do something. Have a shower.

After the shower, though it's now close to midnight, I put on a fresh top, raspberry pink, with matching lipstick, a splash of O de Cartier, my silver ammonite necklace, a present from Raffy, and a jangly bracelet or two, then plump up the outdoor cushions, throw on some music and pour myself an ouzo. Then I cook some pasta, make an olive, caper and basil sauce, open a bottle of wine, switch on the palm tree up-lights and sit down to eat in the leisurely style of a second home owner in a property brochure while waiting for my divided selves to reconvene. The outcome of which is that Possibility 3 comes to mind.

Possibility 3. The memory is full.

I check. Possibility 3 is correct.

So, Outcome 3?

He guesses that and takes a taxi to the house.

Stumbling block: then where the hell is he?

Mitigation: how could he guess the laid-back person I've become, a person who fails to return calls and lets the memory fill without checking?

Laid-back? Sitting at my outside atmospherically lit table for one, bats circling, cicadas chinking, a mosquito whining, I wonder again what I'm doing here. The house . . . the garden . . . conceived as a shared project. A shared dream project on our shared dream island. The island that, after we married, he took care never to come back to. Hence my inability to grasp that he was coming here tonight.

I empty the last of the wine into my glass, bring it indoors and tackle the answerphone. ERASE, ERASE, trigger-happy now, ERASE, ERASE. I hear a sound in the unlit front garden, ERASE, ERASE, the sound of a twig snapping, ERASE, ERASE, and recalling its recent predecessor the other twig, snapped during my last run-through of the messages, a whole Hammer Horror sound effects studio out there, I realise I have erased The Voice.

Sometime in the night I'm wakened by the wind rattling the shutters and the wine I drank. As I get back into bed I hear what sounds like the grating of chair legs on the roof terrace above me. I turn over and go back to sleep.

6

Next morning the phone starts ringing early. The courier service wonders why I have not collected the parcel I am not expecting and which they have been calling me about all week. I tell them I'll pick it up this morning. The electrician says he may come this afternoon but more likely not. Then Gabriel. **Gabriel!** He's on Mykonos.

I'm at the port and there's a boat going your way in half an hour. Lunch?

Well yes.

Talk later.

Gabriel. What does this mean? Names and updates, two years of news from a very tall relative by marriage. Why he's here, though, and why now, I can't imagine. But the answer to that may shed some light on Raffy.

I tidy up proactively and drive once more to the port town where I collect and sign for a bulky and completely puzzling parcel addressed to me. The sender is given as

Byzantium Books. I lock it in the car boot and take my seat at the harbour café to await the boat from Mykonos.

Cappuccino ordered, book deployed, Chapter 1 again fails to hook me. A brisk wind is keeping the sea and sky that dazzling scoured blue that the white town feeds off, blue blood coursing under its blue-white skin, casting long blue shadows when the sun goes down. Across the road two police cars are parked. Four policemen – real, not port – are standing talking. Real talking. The port police are also busy, today preventing drivers from dropping passengers near a taped-off rectangle by the railing, while the drivers are at full stretch preventing that outcome. They brake and argue for the time it will take their wives and mothers to unload the boxes, babies and bird cages that are needed for boat travel in Greece.

I would follow this through but the catamaran from Mykonos has rounded the headland. I close the book and cross the road.

I spot Gabriel right away, hair like the burning bush, absurd height, geeky stoop, tinted glasses in coloured frames, that whole thing he has going, the contradictions and counter-contradictions he needs to show. That's good with me, cautionary even, as I remember how mood-altering other people can be, particularly people who carry an alternative version of your history. We hug, then hug again.

Well. Do we have wheels? He is anxious as we always were, all of us, to get away from this jittery milling point of arrival and departure to **our** place, the village where our families met, whose shops now feed me, whose post office holds my mail when I have any and on whose streets I have not set foot for several days now.

In the car we stick to catch-up chat. He is in Mykonos *on business*, this in heavy quotes. *Earning the pink dollar. Spending the pink euro.*

In Karistos we head on autopilot for the oldest and once the only taverna in the village, awkward with each other, the wrong two people in what was once the right place, but Maria, spying him, has no such hang-up and rushes out to embrace him – at groin level, he checks a wince – pink shades, then, no disguise against the pure in heart. He holds her away and studies her.

You're dyeing your hair.

So are you.

And heels! You used to be a ***widow****.*

My little Gabriel, I am a widow still, but now it is possible to be also fashionable, come, come, all this in Greek, grabbing me with her free hand and drawing us inside to see the dishes on offer, which are the ones she always made plus lettuce. So . . . hair, heels, a more demonstrative health awareness for people with a limited vegetable repertoire . . . I see Gabriel bring himself up to speed on Karistos.

With a carafe of house wine on the house – *wine from us*, she says so that he can sample her recent English – we head for the corner table that was always ours where Gabriel, unshipping the carafe, halts abruptly and looks around him. I know that feeling. That lurch into then out of the past. Ease, unease, alternating. He shakes his head and sits.

So, he says. *Life story. Precis.*

It's not a life you can do that with, Gabriel. You know how it is here. I just take the days as they come.

And how. But you? I never took you for a drop-out.

Though of course we all knew you were going to be a fashion photographer. I recall just the one T-shirt. Grey, I think. You were a geek.

Yeah, well, it's a great way of being obscure.

You were all of that.

Oh I'm still obscure. I accessorise it now, that's all.

And I'm still not a drop-out. Though I would have to study that. *Anyway . . . the Doctor Doolittle thing? What became of that? You wouldn't even let us kill mosquitoes.*

I guess I found I didn't have to turn my back on the whole human race. Just half of it.

Was it that bad?

Back then Claudia constituted half the human race. At least it felt that way to me.

I should ask how she is?

Strategic memory lapses. Otherwise undiminished. Living in Cape Cod, complaining about the cold and young people nowadays. Not so many willing acolytes in Cape Cod.

And Lucas?

So much better on his own. In fact right now he's on sabbatical. Travelling. A new book, I guess. He's not that communicative. Perhaps he'll turn up here. I did email him to say I was coming.

To Mykonos or to Kryptos?

Just Greece I think. The Great Satan perspective.

And Michael?

Ah. Well. Michael. The incredible hunk.

Do you see him much?

Look, when I came out Michael took it personally.

Personally?

That whole swim/drive/drink further/faster/more . . . the fuck'em'n'leave'em thing? That was **not** *what I had been trying pathetically to emulate all these years. Duh.*

So you don't see him?

Oh I **see** *him. But* **communicate***? Forget it. Which brings us, I think, to Raffy.*

Yes. Well.

Any idea where he is?

Do **I** *have any idea? I hoped you were about to tell me.*

We haven't been in touch since Easter. We had a family reunion of sorts then I think he was going back to London.

You mean you didn't travel with him? To Athens?

God no. Two models, the fashion editor and half a dozen hangers-on to iron the frocks, that's our little troupe.

I can't believe it.

Well, I did start out as a wild life photographer, but in, you know, sea otter currency – one published sea otter a month to, oh I don't know, a couple of shoots in Port of Spain or Mykonos, though last year I did drag the whole circus to the Okavango Delta and they were right, the background was too busy for prints – on those terms that's a trade-off and a sacrifice I find I can make.

I mean I can't believe it's a coincidence. That you and Raffy are here at the same time.

Raffy? Raffy is here?

And so I tell him a rambling tale of phones fixed and mobile, of encounters improvised and botched. I linger over the olive grove incident enjoying its cool and impersonal qualities before I start to skim over the Raffy no-show, but he scents evasion, leaps across and wraps me in a bear hug. I distance myself – people are watching – but he keeps it up until he squeezes out a tear. I reach for a napkin to mop the tear, and see that it still has the taverna name printed in blue in not quite the right place on an outline map of the island. I show him. We're done with being grown-up. It's good.

But this is serious, says Gabriel finally. And, I can see, it is. He sits back and re-runs what I've just told him as if a separate take on it needs to be scanned and saved. And it's into this blank that Nico arrives.

Anna mou! He pats my shoulder then turns to Gabriel with an unctuous smile and an outstretched hand.

This is your boyfriend?

Brother-in-law.

How are you, brother-in-law? Nico.

Gabriel.

It was Nico who gave the party I was telling you about. I'm afraid I never called to thank you. It was . . . I consider and veto the things it was . . . *wonderful.*

Wonderful for me also, but now a not so wonderful thing has happened on our island. Have you heard? Last night a man was killed. A foreigner.

A road accident? There are a lot of those in a place where driving is an expression of personality.

But Nico is looking portentous. *I am sorry to say this, Anna mou. Killed with a knife.*

That **is** a shock. I flick through likely causes: family squabble, guest worker grievance, drunken tourist. Violence is almost unheard of here for the good reason that emotions are seldom suppressed. Then I remember the police cars and the taped-off rectangle. The unusual number of police. Their unusual sense of purpose. Slowly the significance seeps in and with it the implications.

Where was he killed?

At the port.

Gabriel is looking at me, both of us now getting to our feet. *Raffy.*

Just the one police car now, the officer sitting over a *sketo* at the café, but keeping watch nonetheless for when we walk up to the tapes and stand there he puts down his cup and crosses to join us.

Can I help you?

I would very much like to think not, says Gabriel, towering over him and taking refuge in obscurity, not a good course. *We have just heard a man was killed last night. Who was he?*

The policeman studies him, size, peachglo hair, rigorously camp glasses. *We don't know yet. A foreigner. Maybe English. Perhaps you have something to tell me?*

He may be my brother.

A quick almost amused flicker in the policeman's eyes tells me he has seen the body and finds this unlikely. He looks at me – it feels like having my irises photographed – then back at Gabriel. I'm clinging to that flicker. In the benign lethargy of the island's law-enforcement practice – the car in front stopped, the driver affably ticked off for speeding, maybe once or twice a year and always under a shady tree – it's a new experience to be under scrutiny. I react by scrutinising back. Modest height, light skin, intelligent blue-grey eyes, more than average curiosity. I take in everything, feel nothing, sidestep the reason we're here. He motions to us to sit at the table he has just vacated at the café where my life is currently playing daily, evenings and matinees, and talks into his mobile. A second car arrives, two officers nod us into the back and we are driven at speed through half-naked throngs of holidaymakers to the Health Centre. I have been here before, the Health Centre, on the day I picked up the stone that was home to a scorpion. We follow them to a basement room, and here too I have been, though in another country. I am blocking that connection quite successfully. I breathe in and out and look pleasant as I did the other time. On the threshold one of the officers stops us and holds out a hand.

Passports please.

Bureaucracy smites us, the humble bereaved, at our lowest ebb. This too is part of the package, the cue for self pity, and this too I can do, albeit with detachment. Again I arrange my face. We find our passports, each with the surname Hollander.

You are to this man here perhaps brother?

Gabriel nods.

Sister? Turning to me.

Self-pity is not a good look. Wife, I say, switching to non-committal. And just as those women captioned *wife of the victim* on Greek TV news channels are seen to crumple without awkwardness or restraint, as if they knew this role would one day be theirs and they must now embrace it or negate it, I start to sway. Gabriel grabs me. *No*, I gasp. An officer reaches for a chair. I want to explain that it is the shock of hearing my voice identify myself thus that has made me lose my composure, but the officers are looking at me now with the elaborate respect due to a widow in this country, one of the greatest things about this country, real respect and real compassion, respect and compassion to which I do not feel entitled. I am out of touch with my married identity. I would need to rehearse it, that feeling of being married, before I could be a widow. It doesn't fit and so this cannot be Raffy.

We are led into a room that retains some of the panic-dampening fresh pine and lemon scent of outdoor Greece in contrast to the brutal hospital version. There is an iron bed covered with a sheet. Gabriel takes my arm. I re-set my noncommittal face. One of the officers, his eyes on mine, grasps a corner of the sheet. I fear an abracadabra moment. I dig my nails into my palms and clench my teeth. I remember to breathe. The sheet is pulled back

It is not Raffy.

It is someone much more recently encountered.

It's the man at the next table.

The man at the next table, which is how I continue to think of him, had had his pockets cleaned out before the police found him. Marks and Spencer boxer shorts account for *perhaps English*.

His face in death has lost the power to irritate but still fails to stir up anything approaching empathy. I try to make amends for that by telling the lead policeman all

I know. That he **is** English. Or was. That he bought a house recently on the island. That he used the first person plural when he talked about this house. That we met for a second time last night. He sparks up at that and wants to know the exact time. The time the boat got in I tell him.

He is no more than formally interested in me now and when I suggest the café owner might know more he takes my phone number and house details and they let us go.

Back out in the sunshine, suddenly light-headed, a genuine reaction at last, I sit down heavily on a low wall, feeling the stored heat on my thighs, everything sharp and strong now, a sweet sickly smell, jasmine, from the flowerbed behind me, and a strong clean salt smell, the smell of the scrubbed decks of fishing boats. Gabriel sits beside me and we take stock, trying to recover our sense of the world as it was an hour ago. The sun is further across the sky, the afternoon older, the passers-by as unconcerned as ever.

Coffee, says Gabriel turning towards the place of many meetings, but I want to get away from the harbour, so we walk up through the bustling square to the café in front of the Byzantine church, where Gabriel orders a *metrio* and I have a latte with two sugars and the biscuit.

I don't want to start another panic, he says, *but it's odd. Way too odd for Raffy. Until we know what was bringing him here and what stopped him – and for all your disclaimers you're the best placed to guess that one out – I don't think we can relax.*

If you mean might we be getting back together you can rule that out.

On your side or his?

Both. Neither. I mean there was no formal split. I still don't know why it happened.

But you left London. You came here. He had moved from New York to London to be with you.

That was his decision. I didn't mind where we lived. But the university job came up and he'd had it with the museum, he wanted to be back in the field.

Hunting Greek artefacts in the cabbage fields of England?

Didn't you ever talk to each other?

We're a dysfunctional family, remember.

He enjoyed teaching. In the summer he took the students to – well, it was mostly to Greek sites outside of Greece – Sicily, Turkey, wherever. I came here to Kryptos after my parents were killed. You knew about that?

Anna I'm sorry. I heard, but I guess I passed on the condolences via Raffy. Not good enough. You know I was crazy about them. So sweet and so straight. I don't communicate enough largely due to my uncompromising self-centredness. A Hollander trait.

Don't apologise. Sweet and straight, eh? In contrast to what? *I have it too. It's being on your own and living in your head. You* ***are*** *on your own I take it?*

Yeah, the past two years. And yeah, I like it.

So do I. But I didn't leave Raffy. Raffy . . . changed.

Look, I'd forgotten Greek coffee came in thimbles. Another latte?

Cappuccino.

While we look around for the waiter I spot a familiar face at the table against the wall – Michel, the French estate agent. His companion is a good-looking blonde boy, also slightly familiar. Toyboy. Not with his *outré* friend whom I imagined talking to my imagined husband. I'm trying to extrapolate something from this but Gabriel turns from the waiter and back to our saga. My saga.

I rather think you did some changing too, Anna.

I came here after the car crash. I wanted to think about my parents in the place where we were happiest. I wanted Raffy to come with me – it was largely thanks to my father after all that he fixed on archaeology – but he found reasons not to.

Such as?

Exam marking. Something like that. Something reasonable but not entirely convincing.

Gabriel's expression has gone not-really-listening. I stop. He comes back from wherever that took him.

Well, I got here and I just flipped. I'd never been here on my own and never outside of the summer months. So yes, I changed. I let the place get to me. But none of that is relevant. Something happened. Something he wouldn't talk about.

Our coffees arrive. I look round at the café patrons to get some distance from this potential wallow-fest, not, I think, of my making. I am quite clear-headed, but the tradition of the confessional threatens. Michel and Toyboy have gone. Gabriel is watching me intently.

Could you date that to an event? Someone he met?

No. It's a complete mystery.

Again he looks over my shoulder and again it's clear

he's doing some lateral thinking. Whatever that is it brings a mood change.

Right. Anyway. You came here after your parents' death. Satyrs were cavorting in the thickets and nereids working round the clock. And then real estate reared its slimy head.

Ye-es.

In the person of a guy with a winning smile and, let's see, a tucked-in seersucker shirt, shades on a cord and a clipboard.

Your estate agent, Gabriel, not mine. A girl. And the house happened first, the agent took some finding. I was walking round the bay one evening when I saw it. Very simple. With a garden. One of two. A For Sale sign at the gate. Remember how we used to freak out when we saw a For Sale sign?

And how. That pink house in the village? With the goat hitched to the pergola? He's back on board. *A pink house with a complementary goat, I mean does it get better? I used to climb in a window and sketch room plans. I had holes in the floor for an indoor wall-cover bougainvillea and a fish pond. Bring the outside in, I thought, and perhaps the inside out. There may have been a fountain. Once I took a bottle of retsina and fell asleep in there.*

I remember. Your mother was frantic.

My ***mother****? Are you sure?*

Definitely.

Hmm. Well. Go on.

I was going to have a house to sell in England – I was an only child, remember? Quite a big house. So . . .

The no-risk, guilt-free unilateral house-shopping orgy.

A small risk. The risk of de-fantasising the thing you were going to ask the fairy godmother for if you ever ran into her. And could such an overwhelming desire ever be guilt-free? *And not unilateral. I called Raffy right away.*

And?

He was horrified.

Because you would be leaving him?

No. No. We were happy. I had my job. A holiday home, that was all. His reaction was completely off the scale. He wanted me to come home immediately. I should have realised he was seriously disturbed.

Disturbed . . . meaning what? Depressed? Paranoid? Screwed up somehow?

Disturbed that I wanted to buy the house. That I wanted to be here – that I was here at all, I think. But in a way yes, he was beginning to act strangely.

But you went ahead and bought it anyway.

I won't let him get to me. *I went home as planned. I told him if it was upsetting him that much of course I wouldn't buy it, but because it meant a lot to me I had to know why. He said I was pressuring him and walked out. He came home later and behaved as if nothing had happened, but when I tried to reopen the subject he just blanked me out. It was frightening but I thought then and I think now that maybe* ***he*** *was frightened. But naturally after that I became wary of him. There were these no-go areas. Maybe some were there before. They* ***were*** *there before. The time I suggested we came here on holiday. He just switched off. Then he booked for somewhere else without consulting me. I mean how odd was that? He* ***loved*** *the place.*

So, the split – his tone is still accusatory – *how did that happen?*

The estate agent phoned when I was out. Discursive,

self-justifying, the way I didn't mean to sound. *She told Raffy the price had been dropped.* I need a break here. I'm in the room with him, his face set, his voice hard. *He thought I'd gone behind his back. He wouldn't believe I hadn't been in touch with her again. He was furious.* And so, again, am I. *I took twenty-four hours to think about it then booked a flight and came here. I left him a note telling him I hadn't married a control freak, I was buying the house, we'd talk about it when I came home. When I came home he'd gone.*

Good God. I had no idea. I didn't know he could be like that.

No? Well I wish I'd called you. I began to think there must be some childhood history. Some behaviour pattern he'd learned to hide.

None I can think of. Except that time, you know, when he went AWOL? Whenever I tried to ask him about that . . .

A clang – sonorous, slightly reproachful – ends the sentence. The church bell recalling us to the here and now. The here, a café table more or less in the force-field of an ancient church in an almost wholly practising orthodox country. As long as we've been sitting here people have been going in and out. The now? I don't really have a handle on the now.

Could we go inside? I never used to want to.

Sure.

He pays for the coffees and we cross the marble-paved gulf between the secular illusion and the spiritual reality.

Although Gabriel has not been inside the church for years for me it's a familiar time portal. I did set foot in it that first summer but, unlike my parents, found it confusing, uninvolving, intimidating even. I loved the insides of the tiny white chapels dotted all over the island with their three bare chalky walls and one fabulous one, all carved gilded wood and smoke-blackened icons with the infant Jesus a mini grownup, perched incongruously on his mother's knee. But the next time we came, a couple of summers on from there, we were with Lucas and Raffy, Lucas so that he could give us the in-depth tour and the informed overview.

He was talking about the timescale, what was happening in the Byzantine world at the time the church was being built, and so I wandered off on my own and came face to face with the Archangel Michael. Life size, taller than that, terrifying. Utterly amoral, shockingly attractive, half man half bird.

I didn't know who he was, only that, like the picture of the archangel that had scared me when I was small, I could find nowhere to place him on my scale of good and evil, so I stepped back and examined him, body part by body part, starting with the feet which, bound in gold, were casually trampling a man with a moustache who lay expressionless on the ground beneath him.

His clothes were amazing, a short slashed leather kilt, a gold embroidered shirt, a gold headdress and a scarlet cloak that hung behind him – behind his shoulders that is to say, but forward from the place that was beyond imagining, the place where the wings began. Just as they had been in the book illustration these wings were fearful to me, overlapping tiers of stiff vertical black and bronze feathers. He held a sword pointing upwards.

When I finally dared to look at his face it was confusing because unlike that other angel he was looking away. His complexion was dark and his expression blank. Mindlessly, without emotion, he used his weight to pin down the man on the ground while he looked off into the middle distance as if admiring himself in a full length mirror.

I was standing right back now, taking in the whole figure, when a man in ecclesiastical robes, bare-headed and carrying a brief case, came down the aisle, stopped beside me, looked at his watch and took out a Yale key which he inserted into the angel's left wing. The angel became a door which swung open. The man passed through and closed it. The angel, back in his carved and gilded niche, continued to look in the mirror and to trample the man and Lucas came up behind me.

It's Michael, he said. And it was. No yellow hair, no red bandana, but Michael nonetheless watching himself, watching other people watching him, not seeing what was beneath his feet. I saw then that Lucas was merely labelling the angel, but my first impression stayed. I saw – but I knew this – that I had not been immune to the attraction of Michael but simply repelled by the mathematics and the mindlessness of that attraction.

Michael is here, I say now as Gabriel and I enter the church. *Are you?*

I don't think so. I'm all over the Italian Renaissance of course, me and my lily and my thrilling piece of news.

What about Raphael?

I have no idea. I don't think I've ever seen him depicted.

Me neither. But I looked him up. Do you know what his task was? That he was famous for?

Tell me.

His task was to bind the demon in the desert.

I don't like to think these words let alone speak them. I don't know what they mean. I look at Gabriel but he has problems of his own.

Well someone had to do it, look, am I OK in shorts?

You'll do.

There's quite an aura. I forgot.

An aura indeed. Gabriel goes off to explore and I flop, suddenly exhausted, into a back seat. But, as the spirit of the place begins to make itself felt, my problems – missed connections, unanswered questions, not enough sleep – start to feel alien and anachronistic. The others in the seats – an elderly woman in a much washed, black cotton dress, a sharp suited woman of about my age, two separate frail and elderly men and a pale young woman with a sleeping child – are plainly in need of urgent intercession. Heads down, lips moving, hands coming up occasionally to cross themselves, they are locked into an intense exchange with one who might help.

She who might help is separated from them by a circling line of icon-kissing believers as well as tourists with open guide books and nylon day packs. Separated and elevated on the iconostasis between two others who might also inhabit their portraits. Separated, elevated and ultimately – as if out of some instinct to contain her – walled up behind a sheet of engraved silver that covers all of her image but her face. And, after all that finally placated with a hoard of gold bracelets, diamond rings, pearl earrings and sapphire necklaces that supplicants have brought her. Above her looms Christ Pantocrator, below her, seen through a slice of glass let into the floor, a column of an earlier pre-Christian temple. Whole aeons of intervention at work in this place.

Gabriel comes back and signals he is ready to leave. We walk out into the bright courtyard.

I'd forgotten. How relevant it still is. How it divides . . . well, them and us.

Quite.

Did you ever believe, Anna? As a child even?

Perhaps if they'd picked a different god? The jewellery, though, I get that. Whenever I just avoid something, or someone close to me avoids something – I'm thinking of Raffy not under that sheet – *I want to thank someone. Pay a debt. You know?*

Some people would say that's belief.

The someone I'm trying to thank looks very like Apollo.

You're scaring me.

And these past few days one of them has definitely been on my case. Dionysus perhaps. Possibly Poseidon.

Just so long as Zeus doesn't come calling.

The intermittently comforting presence that is Gabriel has, I remind myself, a will of its own.

I didn't ask you. How long are you staying?

Tomorrow they're sourcing local accessories. They don't need me. I have to be back by the evening.

Great. You'll stay at my place tonight?

I was kind of assuming.

Then let's buy dinner.

When we get back to the car with fresh bread and

steaks to grill I open the boot to find the mystery package taking up most of the space.

Ah. I forgot about that.

What is it?

I have no idea.

We put our shopping on the back seat and head out again on the road to Karistos.

Who sent it? The package?

I don't know. A courier company called to tell me it was there. That was a few days ago. I thought there must be some mistake but it's got my name on it all right.

Is there a sender's name?

Byzantium Books.

Sounds like some outfit my father might have dealings with.

Do you know of them?

No. But then I wouldn't. There's nothing you ordered yonks back and forgot about?

Zilch.

Birthday coming up? Surprise present?

My birthday is in January.

Right. In that case I think we have to be suspicious.

You think it might explode?

In light of everything else it has to be . . . thought-provoking.

Come on. It was posted before all this happened. Anyway, nothing that's happened directly concerns me, so how could it be connected?

Raffy does.

Does what?

Concern you.

Gabriel is working on something, I realise, an inner private reference file. One hand mangles his disconcerting hair, a gesture I recall from when it was flat and boy-coloured.

Something stopped him, something kept him in Athens. He is very sure that my imagined Raffy was a product of exhaustion, adrenalin and, though he doesn't quite say so, hysteria.

I've been telling myself he just changed his mind.

That's the sort of self-protective schmaltz we lard up our partners with when we can't figure out what's happening. He was coming to see you. OK he didn't come, but he had a reason and that has to date back a while.

And be connected to the parcel? He's really losing me here.

Perhaps. I think you have to not open it. Hide it.

Hide it where?

We'll work that one out once I've seen your guilt-free little hideaway.

The breeze has dropped and the landscape gone slack and sensual. Gabriel, getting out of the car, shades his eyes and groans.

Oh Anna. Oh my. I didn't know you were right by the sea. Let's swim.

It's the golden time when the sea turns to syrup as if it had been boiled with honey and cinnamon and you might emerge from your final dip coated and sticky as a stack of *loukoumadhes* and the sand where it sticks to your caramel coloured skin has the look of gold dust, but right now I have no time for that.

Tell you what, you swim and I'll fix the salad. Then I'll come and join you.

We unload the food and there, again, is the parcel. I feel like a thwarted child in front of a Christmas tree.

Don't you think you were over-reacting?

No I don't. Look at it sitting there. It's got entrapment written all over it.

So what do you suggest we do with it?

He takes in the bougainvillea, the hibiscus, the olives, the palms and the geraniums, all rooted in baked grey-brown soil.

Bury it?

Have you ever tried digging in concrete? Because that's how the ground is at this time of year.

Let's just leave it there for now. Can I grab a towel?

He heads off to the beach and I start to assemble things for a marinade for the steaks. I go out into the garden to pick a lemon from the tree and something flutters in the corner of my vision. A sheet torn from a sketch pad and weighted with a stone lies on the terrace wall. Rebecca. Her sketch shows the beach with the nude in situ, Rebecca under her umbrella, and two men with impressive upper body development swimming strenuously. Under my tamarisk she has drawn a question mark.

So. The guys were back at the beach. And while she honoured our agreement I forgot all about it. I should go up to her place right now to explain and apologise. If I take the car and skip the swim I'll be back before Gabriel returns.

Leaving the door unlocked in case he gets back first I

turn left, then left again where the track leaves the road, and bump and grind up the shallow gradient between the fields, raising dust, slowing for some hens, but not, I note, setting off the farm dog which must be programmed for pedestrians only.

Rounding the bend, slowing, ready to pull in at the verge above Rebecca's place, I see two cars already parked there. One metallic blue, the other silver. I see Rebecca – hands on hips, hair billowing, back turned, flanked by goats – deep in conversation with two smartly dressed men. And, keeping the speed steady, I drive straight on, warm and friendly impulse coolly converted to performance.

I continue straight to where the track meets the sea at the surfers' shacks. Then, there being no point in stopping there, turn right and continue on along the winding and bumpy cliff-top track for a couple of miles until another track goes off to the right and I can complete the circuit back to the house.

Gabriel, wrapped in a towel, has just turned in at the gate. I pass him on the drive and park alongside the house. I sit there at the wheel, window down, engine off, mind still revving.

Well, he says as he comes up alongside. *What now?*

I tell him about Rebecca's sketch and what I just saw.

Well?

They were in suits.

So?

I'm scared.

Why? Because you thought she might be in danger?

Because I thought she might be in the enemy camp.

And that was why? Because of the blue car?

And the silver one. It was a silver one that followed me and Marcus.

Gabriel stands there in sandals, magenta underpants and scarlet beach towel. Water sparkles in his mass of loose curls and the drops pick up the colour from the setting sun. The first bat of the evening swoops above his head. My fingers sticky with oil and lemon grip the wheel. My head is filled with a snapshot. Rebecca, two cars, two men. Come to look at her paintings or just stopping to ask the way – why not, she has a life – but to me irrefutably clandestine because sharply dressed, urban and wrong, their highly polished highly suspect cars parked by a goat shed. Gabriel comes out of his trance and slaps the car roof.

Back in over there, he says, pointing to the olive trees. *Out of sight of the gate.*

You believe me?

No. I think you're turning into a small-island busybody. But after dark we'll bury the parcel on the beach.

Having someone else make decisions is a novelty. You think *OK, sorted*, and just tag along. I remember this, but do I remember it with nostalgia? I would have to think about that. No I wouldn't. But I let him light the barbecue and we shower and I put on a seldom worn dress, then he lifts the package out of the boot while I fetch a spade and my piece of Indonesian batik because, if we're going to ham it up, we may as well ham it up accurately. We cross the empty road and walk down through the stubble to the little beach hidden under the raised lip of the sloping field.

Where?

Under the tamarisks.

Why?

Because that's my place. No-one else will sit there. And I'll know where to find it once this charade is over.

He digs a hole in the dry sand slicing through the roots of the marram grass, far enough from high water mark for it not to grow itself a pool. We bury it under eighteen inches of sand and when it's covered I stretch out my batik square and lie on it, impressing the textile print onto the sand, then turn over and dig inn my elbows, resting my chin on my hands in reading position. I stand up and dust myself down and we return to the house and open a bottle of wine.

Anna, what do you do for money?

I turn in the odd piece on Greece for travel supplements. Some book reviews. I still have contacts. Then there's the interest from the house. Why?

Just wondered.

Where did you get my phone number?

I dunno, I guess from Raffy sometime. Why?

Just wondered.

The charcoal is getting past its peak and he throws on the steaks as I set the outside dining table for two with candles and hibiscus flowers, then lay out my hoard of beans and *horta* and beetroot with garlicky *skordalia*. Soon the air is scented with charred meat and *rigani*. It's a long time since I lived this way. *À deux.* And it hits me as I seldom allow it to how much I miss Raffy.

We take our seats. It's awkward, not convivial. I'm trying to work out why when Gabriel raises his glass.

To absent friends. His words hang there fleshing themselves out and the table for two becomes the table for eight it was built to be, the long cold cement wall seat stretching out beyond the candlelight as if to tempt the missing and the dead to shuffle in out of the shadows and join us. An owl shrieks from the darkness and I reach for my wine.

Your parents. The car crash. How did that happen?

They were going away for a weekend. Just out of Oxford they came off the road and hit a tree. My father was killed outright. My mother died just before I got there.

Shit. I didn't know that. I guess you were in pieces.

I wasn't though.

Raffy identified them. If I'd done that I'd never have got over it.

I'm holding it all away from me, the details I don't let myself think about, the questions that didn't get asked. How much harder it was for him. How unnatural that was.

He was so there for you, as my fashion editor would surely say. A bit of a shape-shifter, my little brother.

All of you, really, except maybe your father. Inscrutable or terminally laid back. Hard to tell. It kept you interesting.

But Raffy . . .

Yes, I think I may have invested him with more of that than he actually felt. Perhaps you too?

Anna, I'm tough. Through and through. But Raffy . . . well, you know, you have it too, the private thing. With Raffy you didn't probe. I guess because it made you seem uncool. When he went missing that time he was just a kid, someone should have grilled him. But no. We respected his privacy.

Lucas was closest to him?

Yeah. But Lucas wasn't there. Claudia was, and she would have been on a guilt trip. She was at a party, remember. So she wasn't going to be asking.

Which left you. Michael not being there.

Embryonic solipsist and grudging child-minder. But yeah, I was worried. Very. Once he was safe I was only too glad to drop it.

But still curious?

I guess. But we're not one of those families that have to follow through every thought. It was never that way.

You must have wondered, though, subsequently, what it could have been that would make him clam up that way.

I guess I thought it might be something from the seamy side. Maybe that was my embryonic sexual identity that thought that, so of course I would suppress it.

Sexual but not reciprocal?

Precisely.

You never found out who the man was? That came for him?

Didn't try. There seemed no need.

And Lucas . . . did he have any ideas?

I don't suppose anyone ever told him.

Because . . . because it begins to seem, does it not, that whatever came to haunt him started from that night?

When I look at it – because I kinda shoved it in the back of the attic – then yes.

And I don't think sex comes into it.

Anyone he needed to sort out he would have . . . sorted.

But this . . . person . . . thing . . . whatever he blanked out . . . the way I see it he was enraged at his impotence to do something about something. So he blanked it out. But he was just eleven that year. How potent could he expect to be?

One hundred per cent as I recall, speaking as a guy, more or less from birth. No I don't think he was beating himself up. I think it involved someone else.

I agree. He couldn't speak out because someone else was involved.

And that would account for his frustration where you were concerned. He owes it to you to be honest. He **is** *honest. But someone else's fate is on the line.*

So. Whose?

He shrugs. We sit in companionable discomfort thinking our different thoughts.

OK. Now you can help me get through half a ton of simultaneously ripening peaches.

Gabriel picks peaches while I clear up and fetch another bottle of wine. It's properly dark now, and quite still. A cicada, volume lowered to night time level, keeps up a persistent hum, and two cats who've been schmoozing Gabriel fall on his steak trimmings with purrs that seem unnaturally amplified. Peaches sliced, glasses filled, into this racket Gabriel says

It's on the island, isn't it? It's here.

What is?

The thing. That he can't sort out. It's here. That's why he wouldn't come with you before. That's why he tried to stop you coming. That's why he's coming now. Or was.

I have been trying so hard not to reach this conclusion that I can't answer him. And as it happens I don't have to, for now car headlights are lighting up the palm tree, the lemon tree, the scarlet hibiscus and the coral one, the cats and the expiring charcoal. Tyres crunch, an engine revs and fades, lights are cut and doors slam. Voices fade round to the front of the house and someone knocks on the front door. Gabriel raises his eyebrows, I shake my head, and we go through the house to open the front door to our friends the crime scene cops, cop the first, cop the second and two others.

I lead them through the house and out onto the back terrace where they have all too obviously interrupted the conclusion of our meal. They apologise. I offer wine which they decline and the two younger men take themselves off to perch on the terrace wall. I ask the senior two if they have managed to identify the man at the next table.

The spokesman, the second cop, the one who took us to identify the body, has a counter-question. Did he give me anything?

Give me anything? Like what?

This seems to throw him. I take pity on him and say of course not, I didn't know him, but he asks me to take him through our conversation.

He asked me about a book.

A book?

The book I was reading.

This book, he gave it to you?

Of course not. I brought it with me.

Why?

To read of course. I was waiting for the boat.

Why was I waiting for the boat? Why indeed. I have managed in the past few hours to forget all about

Marcus. He is watching me, waiting for an answer, so I tell him I was half expecting a friend.

Half expecting? This friend, has he a name?

Gabriel, says Gabriel suddenly, rustling up a dimple or two. *I was coming here from Athens but, you know, Mykonos beckoned first.*

The officer gives him a long look and returns to the book. Do I have it still, this book? Can he see it?

I march inside without answering and stand beside the bookshelves, fuming. This is absurd. I could pick any book. I **will** pick any book. Protruding from my bag on the coffee table I see the likely volume and drop a cushion over it, then carry a dog-eared Muriel Spark out to my inquisitor.

He takes it, looks at it, it's a book. A book in English and a paperback at that. He tosses it onto the oil-spattered marble table without a care for its cover and asks if I have been given or been sent anything recently, anything at all. I say that Gabriel kindly brought me some wine, and last week when I went to the post office to pick up my mail I found amongst the bills a book of poetry from an old friend. The first policeman glares at the second. His look says *cut the good cop crap now or I'm out of here*, and the second policeman, our first of this afternoon, embracing the role of bad cop, tells me he wants to search the house.

I should act shocked or indignant. I **am** a little shocked. *Adeia?* I say with just the hint of a question mark. An *adeia* is what you need for pretty much anything in this country. In theory of course. Bad cop smiles and shrugs.

OK. I smile back and see his smile vanish. A Greek would have argued interminably, conclusively, whereas this aberrant knuckling under leaves him with no choice but to nod his partner into the house from where there comes there comes the protracted click and thud of cupboard doors opening and closing.

Gabriel pours wine and we return to the peaches while the other two sit on the terrace wall, smoking and playing with the cats. In the hiatus where we wait to pick up the question he left hanging in the air everything has become disjointed and absurd, mechanical and cute, like the plot of a Greek TV soap. On cue the senior guys come back from going through my baking trays and T-shirts, reproachful and bored. They have a word with the others who get to their feet and stamp out their cigarettes.

The garden also we must look. They will look. Endaxi? Also I must ask for the keys of your garage and your car.

Of course. I fetch the cars keys, *The garage isn't locked.* As the men are swallowed up in the darkest reaches of the garden to contemplate the outlines of agaves and yuccas or to look at the stars and have another smoke, the others sit down with a game-over expression. I get two more glasses and fill them.

Can I ask what you're looking ***for****?*

A light washes the highest fronds of the palm tree and our eyes follow it as it skims across the sky, the garage wall, the sky again, to rest like a searchlight aimed at the terraced field behind and above the garden, the field where Rebecca saw the two men. I watch it stupidly and try to work out where it's coming from. There are voices, male and female. The light dies and another comes on across the high dividing wall between my house and the house next door.

Neighbours, I tell Gabriel and the cops. *Yeitones.* They had twigged that. Only I, neighbourless since the Athenian family sold up back in the winter, am surprised.

Bad cop, though, while using the intervention not to answer my question has also noted my surprise.

You know these people?

No. Not at all. Never met them.

You are new to this island then?

No. They are. And I tell him about my childhood visits and Gabriel's which usually charms local people but only makes him thoughtful. Why, he asks. Why this island? Chance, I tell him.

I think he is no longer trying to link me to the dead man. I think he is preparing to close my file altogether when the two younger men return lugging a giant terracotta *pythos* and a small Cycladic figurine. They place them on the paving within the farthest reach of the terrace lights. Good cop yawns. Bad cop looks weary. Where, he asks, did I get these?

Where everyone does. Garden centre. Craft shop.

How do I know this?

You take my word for it. Cretan pots, I imagine, look very like Cretan pots always did. The figurine might have marks of an electric drill, but who knows, perhaps the guy did dig it up from a burial site and decide just to sell it for just eighty euros. I take it you think the dead man may have been connected to an antiquity scam?

Bad cop looks shocked. There is bad karma attached to voicing such suspicions in a place where every family owns a piece of land and every piece of land overlies traces of early habitation. Pieces of marble pediment project from old house walls and fragments of column are used as door stops.

Bad cop gets to his feet and tells the men to put back my garden ornaments. He gives me his card.

If you hear anything you think I should know please call me. He takes another look at Gabriel, nods to us both and they leave.

What was all that about? We are nursing coffee cups on the roof terrace above my bedroom, the terrace from which in the dead of last night I heard sounds of human movement or at least of chair movement. The dark road to the village hugs the darker sea, the lights of the police car dwindling along it, and from the garden next door comes an oblique cypress-framed glow, a glow I'm going to have to get used to.

Your surprise package of course. They had a tip-off. A second or third hand tip-off since they had no idea what they were looking for and didn't much care. Presumably you had to sign for the thing? And yet there was no mention of the courier company.

I thought it was about the man at the next table. This label is wearing thin.

Yeah. You assumed that from the start which let them off having to give a reason for being here. Nice move though. The poems too, from the friend. Only your parting shot was a bit knowing. Where did that come from?

Something Marcus said. Also an overwhelming urge to lock horns with tonight's bad cop, this afternoon's rather pleasant guy in charge, who has a name now, Stelios Kritikos.

Well whatever it was all about it was not about him.

I heard what I heard.

But they don't know about it.

No. Thank you for that.

And I think you can also discount your late friend.

Gabriel and his parcel fixation. Concrete and inanimate. Two feet under. The practical alternative to my hovering abstract menace. We are not after all, it seems, returning to the secret of the island, the *it* that is here. Alarmed at his own logic, I sense that he now wants to file away what he cannot finish.

Out on the lagoon in front of the house a small boat is circling. Further out the lights of a passenger ferry swim into the gap between headlands. From the farmhouse on the hill comes the unwinding silver thread of a departing car, wakening a goat that jangles briefly as it changes position, the pool lights are still on at the ship-owner's house, turquoise water twinkling between the tall stems of the fan palms, and from the beach below comes a muffled laugh and a passage of quickly hushed *rebetiko*. For a long time now such things have been both the setting and the narrative of my life. Tomorrow when I say goodbye to Gabriel I will try to remake it that way.

All the same, Anna, he says, after his own protracted pause, God knows why, but I guess **you're** still in the picture.

7

I sleep late and waken to find Gabriel fixing breakfast on the terrace. He has amassed a commendable haul of peaches and is making coffee. A few bars of island music have surfaced inaccurately in his head and he is humming them, while from across the wall come further sounds of human encroachment. The charming, mostly absent Papadakises – Easter, August, the odd weekend – may not, in selling up, have passed on their habits with their house. I will shower, I will dress, I will go there and ask these people their intentions.

Anna? Gabriel passes coffee. It's in a soup bowl and needs two hands. *How are we placed?*

His hair is flat and fluffy and he is wearing a table cloth as a sarong. He has dribbled a heart in tinned milk on the surface of the coffee.

Placed?

Timewise. Could we do a, you know, tour? Round the island? I'd like that.

The neighbours can wait. *OK then.*

When we're set to leave – I'm going to drop him at the port in the late afternoon – he hovers by the car. I toss him the keys. *Relax. I assumed you'd want to drive.* Which will give me time to think. For Gabriel's thinking is, as I expected, threatening to eclipse my own. A man standing six five in his hand-stitched loafers is not about to exit the action with a dragon still on the loose. A dragon, moreover, of his own conjuring. All through breakfast he's been tidying it away. Last night was last night, today is for nostalgia and touring. But the roar of the dragon is loud in my ears. I will reminisce, I will tour, but when the giant leaves the island the dragon roams free.

We have pulled up at a crossroads. *Left, right, clockwise, anticlockwise?*

Depends where you want to eat and swim.

I'm in your hands there.

I think you'll find the beaches haven't moved, but the road has.

Clockwise then.

To me, the island in reverse. The settled shore, more agreeable, more historic, more built and for all these reasons more spoiled is where I take visiting friends first, to return by way of the stark, steep and scary flanks of wind-scoured limestone that form the underside of the island. Green from a distance but green only with ankle-stabbing scrub, much of it scented. The *phrygana*. Lately, our island being currently in vogue and its beaches barred against development, some of those flanks are being sliced into to build studios – studios for people who don't paint facing views that can't be framed. Views of rock and scrub, of hazardous coastline and open sea that will at best unsettle them, possibly unnerve them, and then, if they're lucky, send them home before they're totally unhinged. People should not live where other people have been careful not to.

Gabriel wants to divert down every winding track and stop at every isolated church, but after a couple of dead-ends in people's backyards I've had it with detours. The threatened heatwave is setting in and we need to be at a beach by lunchtime. But another chapel catches his eye and we weave off through the scrub along another seaward path.

It stands on the cliff edge, a tiny chunky basilica, 17th century by the look of it, lime-washed, its massive door wedged open, its treasures being spruced up for its saint's day by the farmer's wife. We back off when we see her but she straightens at our approach, smiles a welcomes and waves us inside. Brass candelabra gleam with reflected virtue as we step around the tomb slabs, Gabriel struggling with the engraved skulls and crossbones in the floor that have spooked him since childhood. Left of the iconostasis I spot another Michael, winged and sword-bearing, fabulously decked out, similarly untroubled by self doubt. Gabriel nods to the farmer's wife and ducks back outside but she beckons me on towards an icon in a recess.

I follow her pointing finger and go closer. A duster and a bottle of lamp oil sit on a shelf next to a lamp which throws flickering shadows onto the icon above. The light it gives is dim and the icon is darkened by time and smoke, but presently my eyes adjust and through the murk comes a pale countenance. A woman, quite tall and rather homely, is holding it together with pious *sangfroid* while round her feet scrawny black demons scuttle like cockroaches.

Demons. Small ones. In a pack. I stand for a while digesting them, then my brain makes the leap. Raphael in the desert. **Binding** a demon. Binding **the** demon. Next to whom these will be as vermin. I see his face and through it an eradication of personality and a stony concentrated will. Then something clicks. I'm recognising, not imagining. The Raphaels, divine and human, are merging into one, an onset of horror I must extinguish before I see their wings. The beeswax smell, sickly and when mingled with Brasso unendurable, evokes Marcus's house, the *kouros* behind his chair, the sacrifices on his walls and, by association, the goat on Rebecca's easel. I feel dizzy. I lean forward and find I'm face to face with a skull set inside the V of its crossbones, fitted into the V between my feet. The farmer's wife grabs me. Her embrace earths me. I straighten up, thank her, feel something more is called for, pat her shoulder and get the hell out of there.

Outside, letting my pulse slow, I stand ankle-deep in springy scrub with a shred of breeze still blowing and the sun shining and the waves frothing at the cliff foot while a two-masted yacht makes steady progress across the strait to the next island. The world bright and simple. Gabriel is already turning the car.

Our next detour is to a hill village for coffee, and here we come upon Marcus. In linen shorts and a lawn polo shirt striped in hazy blurred blues he steps out of a craft shop in the square ahead of a pair of fiercely glamorous women. The owner of the shop is bestowing greetings for a good day and a long life on the women who are in couture cruise clothes and jewellery, carrying a stack of parcels wrapped in crackly white paper tied with dark blue ribbon and garnished with bougainvillea petals.

Marcus looks surprised but friendly. Gabriel, I sense as I make the introductions, has already guessed who he is.

We rearrange the café's chairs and snatch two more for the parcels then crowd into the shade of an acacia. The girls are Texan – vivacious, voluble, mid-way through an Aegean cruise on a friend's yacht. Their hosts are diving today, they tell us, and when Alicia and Diane happened upon Marcus's gallery he kindly offered to take them shopping. Not a hardship, I'd guess. And their quick interest in Gabriel suggests a happy affirmation that the world in all its beauty and diversity is peopled mainly by Ivy League shoppers. They are soon swapping place names, moving on to people names, giving me space to think back to the Greece I just glimpsed where demons co-exist with angels, kept in line by a mortal housekeeper and monitored from the opposing headland by a fragment of a temple of Apollo.

Trying to ground myself I look around the square and see that it has sprouted a new shop. A sign in hybridized Greek and Latin script says *Byzantiana*. When we've ordered coffee I excuse myself and cross to look in the window which is crammed with curiosities, mainly icons on old wood – door panels, shutters, driftwood – one of them depicting the lady with the cockroach demons. Here on neutral ground I can look at them dispassionately, or rather with the passion that says pardon me for not believing but I love your art. Guilty lust objects for rationalists, icons are, deprived as we are in the visual department. Here is Saint John attacked by woodworm on a piece of gnarled bark. I picture a hermit wild of hair and beard, marooned on a rock pinnacle, subsisting on roots and berries, enlisting what comes to hand – ochre, lichen – to paint his image, although I suppose it might be a nicotine-fingered hack in an Exarchia basement. **Is** icon painting policed? Practised only in continence and obedience? And how enforceable is that?

It's hard to see into the display beyond the icons. I glance back at the table. They're deep in conversation and the coffee hasn't arrived. The door jangles as I push it. When my eyes adjust to the dark interior I see leather-bound volumes of Greek mythology and artefacts of many kinds, marble bowls, some fine hand-embroidered woven pieces yellowed at the folds, pewter goblets; a chromium plated toast-rack; a marble fountain with a vine and peacock motif, some very ugly ceramics and an old typewriter. Byzantiana in the looser sense, then.

There's a sound from the back of the shop, someone putting down a cup, and a curtain twitches. The light from the crowded window barely reaches back here and my eyes are still set for sunlight. I await with curiosity the keeper of such objects, a wraith with cobwebs in his hair or a scarlet-lipped woman in purple chiffon and lace. There's a sharp intake of breath and the curtain drops behind a head of girlish hair, blonde-grey and crinkly, ethnic silver earrings, some adolescent cheesecloth, and a pair of cornflower blue eyes set in a very knowing face. I haven't seen her in close-up before. The eyes are remarkable. Watching from the port café as pretty-boy in the *deux chevaux* kissed her goodbye and she left the island to return next evening perhaps in the company of my husband I could not have guessed at the transformative power of the eyes.

She smiles, the smile chasing away the ghost of something that looked like recognition.

If you want to know about prices, just ask. I'm discounting some things to make way for new stock. And she goes back quickly behind her curtain.

I pick things up and put them down, too taken with that look to feel properly covetous, so while I'm casting an eye over ceramic roof tiles and embroidered silk wall hangings I'm re-running the night scene at the port. The woman, left profile, talking, the man, left profile, turning my way but with head bent, listening. Not listening intently, was my impression. Listening as you might to a fellow passenger who has remarked on the toxic carbon monoxide levels as the cars disembark alongside you, on the pitch black night, on the wind getting up, the rumour of a heatwave, the transport strike in Athens, the plans for a new airport on Kryptos.

A snap impression of Raffy based on what? On all the times I've seen him listening. A clip from the ordinary choreography of married life, one's partner in a crowd scene.

And if my impression was right, then what? There

are no postal addresses on the island, no letterboxes in the house doors, no postmen on bicycles working their way round the farms with the killer dogs and the housing developments with their new and mostly absent owners. And so, having failed to spot me, he heads off with a hotel tout to spend a night in town, planning to catch a bus to the village next morning and ask around for my whereabouts. But of the shopkeepers and café owners, so friendly, so large a part of my life and who know me so well by sight, few, I'd guess, would know my name let alone have a clue as to where I live. A tragic outcome. And completely unconvincing.

Scroll back to the harbour. Raffy coming down the ramp. Cue fellow-passenger, skirt billowing, cornflower eyes sparkling, breezy isn't it but there's a heatwave on the way, just look at that queue, not a taxi in sight, I'm being met, can we drop you somewhere? The *deux chevaux* moving off as I returned to my car.

I'm holding a figurine, the Keros lute player. At the back of the shelf where he was sitting I catch a glimpse of milky-white slightly pitted curves. That figure is half hidden, was wholly hidden till I picked up the lute player. I turn the over-immaculate copy in my hands to give myself thinking space. In my head I'm picturing Raffy, bound and gagged, huddled in the corner of a small stony room. She knew me. And hid that. Why?

There's a sound behind me.

It's lovely isn't it? It's the lute player from Keros, an island not far from here. She's English, I think, but with a hint of mid-Atlantic in her voice. If she knows me, knows I live here, this is too patronising by half.

It's normally 120 euros but I could let you have it for 80 if you're interested.

The eyes are so disconcerting, a sweet colour in a hard face. You stare at the colour and avoid the contact. She must see that all the time, astonishment and withdrawal.

What a lovely shop, I burble at her. *When did you open?*

In April.

I just love that rug, pointing to a harshly dyed vermillion runner, *I believe it might be just right for my bedroom. Can you tell me the dimensions?*

She looks at me squarely. She isn't taken in by my enthusiasm or my taste, but she goes, anyway, to fetch a tape measure. When she comes back I'm holding the other figurine, the hidden one from the back of the shelf. As I reached for it a tingle like static leapt the gap to my fingers. Picking it up I waited to be struck dead.

Aaah . . . this is ***glorious****. How much?*

No need to cook up the reaction. In my hand it looks and feels ancient.

Uhu. That is ***not*** *for sale.* She takes it from me and returns it to the shelf, then pulls out the rug and crouches beside it with the tape measure, manoeuvring me back towards the door while she measures the hideous thing.

One hundred and twenty centimetres by forty six, she says getting to her feet.

I start to look for a pen but she forestalls me, reaching for one of a pile of cards on the counter and writing on the back of it.

Thank you. I'll measure the space as soon as I get home. Hopefully – I flash her an artless smile – *I'll be back.*

The card says only *Byzantiana, Objets d'Art* with a mobile number.

What is your name?

Lisa. Lisa Dunmore. And you are?

Anna. Anna Hollander.

The blue eyes are averted as she holds the door for me.

There you are! Gabriel turns from the café table. *We thought you'd gone anti-American on us.*

Lisa Dunmore looks across and, sharply, back at me. *You know Marcus?*

He's a dear, dear friend, I tell her and crossing back to the table feel her eyes bore into my back.

There's quite a party vibe now, a lot of hair tossing and throaty laughter, reigned in somewhat when I join them. Gabriel is in black aviator glasses which bring out his metrosexual look, and the girls are on easy arm-stroking terms with Marcus who today signals that were one to break off the arm it would have STRAIGHT written all through it like a stick of rock, not my first impression of him, but then again certainly my second.

Gabriel is in performance mode, milking his Mykonos colleagues for laughs. Marje the fashion editor, he says, has spent hours stalking Petros the Mykonos pelican, hell-bent on conscripting him as a model.

A model, not a prop. I mean it's a fashion shoot. Retro. She's got matelot tops and Capri pants. Canvas totes with rhinestones. Bikinis and one-pieces. A lot of stud earrings. He pauses, checks we're with him. *Finally she gets practical. A pareo. She tries draping him. He backs off. He won't let her near him but along the way he's taken a fancy to Sondra, one of the models* . . . he checks again – the girls are in there, Marcus less so – *so Marje passes her the pareo and Sondra holds it like a bullfighter's cape. And he charges. But Sondra doesn't have the moves. She's shouting* **get your damn beak out of my crotch** *and Marje is yelling* **here, come back** . . . **here nice penguin** . . .

Under the hysteria Marcus turns to me.

I tried to call you.

Yes?

I wanted to thank you, which I signally failed to do. Dinner this week?

To chase up my suspicions I shall certainly have to put myself about, and if Lisa knows Marcus, Marcus presumably knows Lisa.

Tomorrow OK?

Fine.

A second round of coffee arrives. I look at my watch. It's going on twelve and by the time we leave here it will be seriously hot and my unvoiced plan to drop in at Mavra Vrahia, the site of the development I heard Michel mention at the party, will be hard to engineer. But Alicia's phone rings. The yacht owner has had enough of diving and wants the girls to join him for lunch at a new taverna he has just heard about. Coffees are downed quickly, bill paid, Gabriel hugged, my hand shaken.

When they've gone Gabriel glances across at Byzantiana.

That looks fun. Mind if I have a browse?

Not worth it. Anyway we don't have the time.

No more detours. Gabriel too needs to reach a beach

and the best beaches happen after we round the southern tip of the island with its boat-impaling outcrops and convulsing inlets.

The road demands concentration as it twists down then sharply up high above the sea. The air hanging outside the open windows has lost its ability to cool. When Gabriel brakes for the second time to mop his forehead with his tee shirt I say *Here. Have this.* Marcus's handkerchief has stayed forgotten in my bag. We must be close to Mavra Vrahia, but I'm guessing Gabriel has lost his taste for diversions.

Now we're on a freshly engineered stretch of road, widened and with a lay-by. We round a bend and see below us a tiny perfect crescent of empty sand backed by a row of tamarisks. On our left a track descends steeply towards it. Just before the start of the track an arresting billboard, hand painted, spectacularly so, shows a mermaid with blue and green scales sitting on a rock, one hand combing her yellow hair while the other steers a giant pink prawn on a fork towards her open mouth.

TAVERNA GORGONA, says the sign. PSARIA. FISH.

Gabriel brakes sharply and turns to me.

It must be a mirage. The beach too. I've never seen it before. Right, let's go.

One other car is parked behind the taverna. It's silver. So, OK, half the cars on the island are silver. I haven't told Gabriel about the Lisa encounter or the scenario I cooked up using my intuition and ten minutes away from him. I don't want to be talked out of it.

The taverna turns out to be no more than an outdoor

terrace with a roof of palm leaves attached to a newly built, surprisingly hi-tech kitchen. Tables and chairs painted ice blue are planted in ground cover of blazing white marble chips. We crunch our way over to an end table, our best chance of catching any breeze, close to the sea whose surface barely wrinkles in the slack air.

The group at the one occupied table glance up without interrupting their conversation. They are seated deep in shade close to the wall. As we sit with our backs to them I run over who I just spotted there. Michel, Thanasis, a woman I don't know and someone who from the back appeared to be Yannis, Meriel's hate figure.

A man is already heading our way carrying a tablecloth, a proper ironed linen table cloth, and two menus. The mermaid portrait fronts a slim and very bespoke folded card but no more slim and bespoke than the man who carries them.

He greets us in RP with a hint of RADA. He has a fetching fall of hair and is easy on his feet in a way that could be Marine Corps, could be corps de ballet. Gabriel looks smitten. He compliments him on the setting, the ambiance, the menu. *My sister-in-law*, he says, establishing that we are not a pair, *tells me this is new.*

That's right. In fact you're only my second customers.

So today is your first day? Well you're really brave. Presumably you're relying on word of mouth since you're miles from anywhere.

A sudden whine drowns me out, then there's a rasp of heavy machinery coming from behind a rock buttress. A rock-breaker starts up and doesn't stop. He smiles.

My first wave of captive customers. Building houses for

the second.

Mavra Vrahia?

My you **are** *in the know. Anyway, what we have today is, take it or leave it,* melanouri *– that's bream – caught half an hour ago from just over there, plus of course salad, Greek or green. There's* tzaziki. *And I could fry you some zucchini or eggplant. Then there's the cheesecake I made yesterday. As I say we've just opened. An hour back I was hammering in the sign.*

It's a fabulous sign.

Thank you.

You painted it?

Only way to make the mermaid eff off. She's been hanging around here for weeks.

I'm quite smitten too. *All these customers already*, I say, glancing over at the other table. *Well done.*

Ah well. That wasn't so difficult. The captive customers? Their execs. Some of them. For which reason we do have rather a good wine list. Ostentatious, but good. He points to the second, densely printed, page of the menu, the first being scant and hand written.

So, says Gabriel, *if I come back in a year's time you'll have what . . . twenty tables? Hired help?*

Fifty. A couple of chefs. Once they've built the marina, who knows?

Marina?

In three years max if you're sailing in the Aegean you'll be laying it on that you tied up here . . . the Port Grimaud, the Costa Smeralda of the Cyclades.

But smaller.

Much.

In fact, I say, *it's hard to see where they're going to fit in any boats at all.*

Oh they're fixing that. Blasting away at the rocks like the walls of Jericho. Anyway that's all way off round the corner and no concern of mine, thank God. So we're having the fish, are we? And we **do** *do a house wine. From the barrel. On the yellow side of white and about as dry as a British summer but it has, you know, a taste. Call me old-fashioned but I like white wine to have a taste.*

We order and sit back. Gabriel is enchanted, I'm confused.

This shouldn't be here.

The word investment comes to mind. For whatever reason someone is putting a whole heap of loot into this weird locale.

The least propitious, the least accessible place on the island.

So the land would be cheap.

But would that be such a consideration in the long run? The building costs must be phenomenal. And the views are nothing to speak of. I can see an islet that's just a big rock. Next to it another – this with a sprinkle of topsoil and scrub – vanishes behind the rock wall.

It's a nice beach.

That's another thing. Why have I never seen the beach before?

Because you couldn't see it from the old road? Because they blasted some rock that was hiding it?

I suppose. I sound unconvinced.

You're not suggesting they just made it? On an island that's full of beaches?

They make sand beaches in some parts of the Med.

Anna come on. Why would they do that?

I don't know. I know I'm being obsessive but I want to go and tug at the tamarisks to see if they were planted yesterday.

The fish is delicious, the wine eccentrically fruity, and the cheesecake better than a dessert option next to a building site has any right to be. We lick clean our forks which are small, exquisite and probably Swedish, and decide to swim before we finish off the wine.

Oh Anna . . . Gabriel turns back on the point of shedding his shorts. *Can you,* in loco maternis, *reassure me I'm clear to swim? Safely? On this full a stomach?*

Claudia had views on that?

I've no idea. Maria at the taverna did. Loads of women on the beaches did. They said we should give it two clear hours.

I know. They may have had a point. I try to give it half an hour myself but sometimes that's not possible.

I go in search of a loo to change into my bikini and find a Turkish tiled grotto with a marble basin on a slender stalk and hi-tech hands-off plumbing. *Remarkable*, I tell the owner on the way out. *It* ***is*** *a mirage.*

I know. But don't tell anyone.

The sand continues some way into the sea, rather confounding my suspicions, but once I'm in there I forget everything and just swim and float, float and swim, with the mindless absorption of a piece of plankton. The water is on the warm side of tepid, warm enough to stay in till you're bored. That takes time. Floating, looking back at the taverna, its newness starts to nag at me. There's a gouged-out look to the rock walls on either side as if someone had happened on a perfectly nice cove and decided to modernise it. Also the track leading down here has had no time to develop ruts.

From further out I can see a little chain of islets running parallel to the shore and vanishing towards what must be the north, the biggest of these right opposite the place, still hidden, from which the sounds of machinery are audible.

Michel, Yannis, Thanasis. Michel who knows Toyboy. Yannis of the recently honed property instincts. Thanasis, name-checked by The Voice, a major player in island politics, particularly the preservation of island culture and the philosophy of development. So. A Frenchman and two Greek businessmen having lunch. And a woman. I shall try to get a look at her when I return to the table which should be about now, I think, now that I'm calmed and cooled and critical, and before they leave.

Gabriel, always a strong swimmer, is not in sight as I step out onto dry sand and pick up my towel. There are no free-standing rocks to change behind so I collect my clothes and head back inside just as the woman stands up and moves in the same direction. She hesitates when she sees me. I smile and wave her ahead of me.

No, please, she says, taking in my wet hair.

Go ahead. I'm going to take some time.

I go back out into the sun to wait. She is Greek, fiftyish, stylish, good looking, with her dark hair left dark, unusual in business women here, and a pleasant expression. I shall remember her.

When she reappears the group get up and leave.

By the time I've changed Gabriel is already at the table, dressed and finishing the wine.

Well . . . he breaks off as our host comes with coffees and a couple of foil-wrapped chocolates . . . *that is one big motherfucker of a villa complex.*

You swam there?

I did not. That place is swimmer-friendly like Alcatraz. They've got barb wire strung out so far from that buttress that from the end you can hardly see the shore. Sharks will get snarled. Oil tankers. OK, I exaggerate. But it's big. And kind of pretty, I have to say. There's a lagoon round there, cutting back quite deep, facing up along the coast.

So it **would** *have a view.*

You're still thinking holiday homes?

You're not?

For oligarchs maybe, with that infrastructure . . . were oligarchs likely to snatch a holiday en bloc. *One answer to the cost-effectiveness, though – they've built a jetty.*

So they'd be bringing the stuff in by boat.

You said there's going to be a new airport?

So I hear.

Where exactly?

I've no idea.

Goodbye Kryptos, hallo Benidormos.

We unwrap the chocolates, cold from the fridge and misting over, peppermint creams, alien treats, I suppose, for an atypical clientele. Then the sound of an approaching speedboat breaks in, coming very fast from the opposite direction to the building site. It loops showily, points at the beach, then, its engine cut, drifts in like a suddenly disabled seabird. Loud laughter comes with it.

Two guys – ripped, tanned, shades on cords – jump out and do guy things with ropes, then stretch out a hand to Alicia and Diane, still hung about with precious metals but now in bikinis and sarongs.

Well hi there! They're matey-er to me this time, not so hands on with Gabriel, as they introduce the men, Gregory and Steve, and explain our earlier meeting.

This *is the taverna you were coming to?* asks Gabriel, amused. *Two hours ago?*

The guys glower at him and go inside.

Alicia looks reproachful. She nods towards the rock wall that hides another inhospitable stretch of coastline, and off it, presumably, a yacht. *It took Greg a while to find a mooring.*

Enjoy your lunch, I say as they go to find a table.

We wait till the newcomers are greeted, charmed and settled with menus then go inside to pay the bill.

We don't know your name?

Simon. Yours?

Names swapped, compliments repeated, we snatch another look at the kitchen, wave to the girls and hit the road.

Round the first bend Gabriel pulls over. We're above the site here but a high rock wall backs the lagoon and entirely obscures it. As we move off again the road veers sharply inland. We're back, I think, to the old road, widened and resurfaced, levelling out now on a plateau with higher ground shutting off the sea, but with a view to our right that takes our breath away. A wholly a fresh view of the interior opens before us. The inner slopes of the hills we traversed this morning form the backdrop, with two valleys cutting steeply into them, green with cultivation, and on the crag between them a cypress-flanked monastery.

Gabriel brakes and slows to a crawl as we take it in. *It looks like it's just been put there. We never came this way, did we? Stuck to our own end of the island, I guess.*

Well we didn't have cars. And the roads weren't here. Just tracks. People walked. And there were donkeys, remember? Now there are school buses and everything.

But this view, I realise, comes courtesy of a chunk taken out of a hill – taken out, it would appear, to let a new road from those valleys join the road we're on. A bus turns out of it as I speak, and then we're overtaking a man on a mule, trotting briskly, one hand to his ear.

Is that a ***phone****?*

Now that ***would*** *be deprivation – if there was a man, woman or child on this island without one. Talking of which, we should swap numbers. And while we're onto future planning, how long do you think – you're the expert on this – I should leave the books in the sand?*

You really think it's books?

That was my impression. Probably because it said 'books' on the label.

Well it's up to you but I would say indefinitely.

Now we're at the first of the west coast beaches, the beaches that were always there. A hamlet Gabriel remembers is now three streets deep – taverna street, shopping street, business street – with its own garden suburb, all bougainvillea, banana plants and balconies.

Prosperity, he says. *Is there a catch?*

Water shortage. The fear that the tourists will suddenly stop coming.

Why would they do that?

Usual reasons. No money. Some other country more in vogue. Some other island. Perhaps they'll turn into warring city states again.

But if that doesn't happen then it's good?

In the high season everyone's exhausted. And there's nothing to spend on but cars and phones. They already have the boat, the grape vine and the terrace with a sea view.

And that's a problem?

There's not enough parking space, but yeah, I'd say that people seem as happy as they always did. Which is a couple of levels above anywhere else I know.

He smiles a sign-off smile and brakes for the windmill. *Good.*

Right answer then. And now we're parking once again at the port. We swop mobile numbers, Gabriel readjusts the driving seat and, out on the quayside, turns serious.

Anna . . .

Yes?

You are rather trusting. You know?

You think so?

We're not all as straight as you think.

We meaning . . . ?

People generally. Hollanders especially. Just a thought. Be sure to call me.

Oh I will.

So, I am where? Standing on this shitty quayside with a fresh invitation to rethink the past.

As the ferry pulls out of the harbour and the wake curls and flattens towards the sinking sun I feel a brief flutter of abandonment. It's an Ariadne thing. Which, if I chill for a moment, will be kicked into touch by the other Ariadne thing. Clean slate. New rules. Fresh start. Not that I'm looking for that level of diversion. Just the fresh start and nobody getting between me and my fertile imagination. Then I'll make my own entertainment.

8

But not yet. Rebecca sits on the front terrace, sketching.

Hi, she says, not looking up. *Long time no see.*

I take her in, bare feet, thin white legs crooked to support her sketch pad, frayed dusty pink denim cut-downs, arms an auburn haze of freckles, scribbling, spilling chestnut hair, testing me.

I hover, bag, wet swimsuit, car keys in hand, recalling my suspicions.

It's a long story . . .

With you it usually is.

OK, tea first?

I carry the tea tray across to the pergola at the far side of the garden, the front terraces being now in sun and the back, though shady, radiating heat from every paving stone. We slump into the plump futon under its bamboo shade where I slice a home-grown lemon onto an antique plate and pour tea, Darjeeling, another conceit. The food foibles of the temporarily deracinated are, of course, odious, but I did, one day, when on Amazon, type *tea*, and his was the outcome. And if you can sort that out what else might you not have to settle for? So I emailed the storage company to send on my considerable bequeathed (orphaned only child of only child) china collection, including my great-grandmother's Crown Derby tea service, into one of whose cups I am pouring Rebecca's loose-leaf brew. I offer sugar cubes from a Georgian silver sugar bowl. With tongs. The intention, I told myself, was to help preserve or recover, possibly even to invent memories of my childhood, which has lately been calling to me from wherever I buried it. Rebecca, being female and being here, a caller in the Jane Austen sense, though one who would surely provoke a seizure in Mrs. Bennett, is the first visitor who has given me an excuse to use them.

We settle back with our saucers inexpertly balanced and our cups rattling.

I think you need straight-backed chairs for this look, she says.

There is tension between us. Her stiff pale shoulder next to my salty tanned one exudes righteousness and hacked-off muscle tone. So I absolve her for the moment from double dealing and tell her about Gabriel, the surprise of his visit. I mention Raffy, but only as a link. Then I loosen up a bit and tell her about the man at the next table for whom I realise I have felt little compassion and less curiosity, and while I'm at it about Marcus re-met and about the taverna at the end of the world. She is rather incurious about that. Finally I decide to come clean and tell her about my aborted visit to her goat shed.

But you were busy. Two cars were there.

Yes? Ah, OK. The hotel guys.

I wait.

Other side of the bay? Like a concrete tent? Quite voluble suddenly. *Actually once you get inside the outside starts to make sense. The foyer and the lounge are supposed to be the inside of a cockle shell, so they tell me. Anyway when it's done they want me to do murals. Modern takes on classical themes.*

Well, great. My congratulations. Hollow-sounding, even to me. *Had you met them before, the men?* Sincere, now, with self-interest.

Nope. They just turned up. They'd seen my work in a magazine and then discovered I was, hey presto, here on Kryptos.

Which I doubt, though possibly she does not.

Glass of wine, then? To celebrate?

Thanks but no. I just wanted to check you were all right.

And now I do feel bad. *Dinner then, some evening?*

I haven't said I'll do it yet. Sounding sulky and defensive. *What I really wanted to tell you was that there was a guy asking for you in the village today. At the café in the square. And then I saw him again at one of the harbour cafés. At least I assumed it was you. Anna Hollander? He was asking if anyone knew where you lived.*

The scene I sketched. And deleted. *Did you tell him?*

In light of what you told me, no. Rebecca, it occurs to me, shares or at least indulges my paranoia.

What was he like? Did you get a proper look at him?

American, middle-aged, medium height, dark, quite fit in a preppy kind of way. Nice hair. Thick.

Mmm. I wonder. Age apart, close.

You have an idea?

Not a clue. But thank you.

I did right?

You did. But the commission – why is it so hard to sound genuine – *do you get to choose the themes?*

I'd rather not talk about it now if you don't mind. You got my message?

The sketch. Yes. They were back on the beach, then? Doing what?

Guy things. Squat things, neck things, leg things – you know, like footballers? And earlier they were back in the field. She aims a thumb above and behind where we're sitting.

That's it then. They're Panathinaikos strikers on a wild-flower weekend.

Right now, though, it's Rebecca I'm interested in. She has form, I'm guessing. Art world form. So what is she doing here and why the low profile?

Well thanks for the tea, she says, relinquishing her cup and saucer combo. *I'm glad you're not dead.*

Me too. Look . . . I'm really grateful. If you want to talk or something, any time, well . . .

She's on her feet and sizing up the wall that backs the pergola and separates my garden from the field behind, the usual farmer's haul of loose heaped stones above the crumbling exposed limestone of the terracing. Above that the field rises and flattens out of sight, only the top of the giant landmark tree visible from here, the tree that shades the turn of the path to the farm and her goat shed. *Could I take a short cut?*

Sure. Here is as good as it gets.

She steps into her flip-flops, hooks up her sketch pad and scrambles up the wall, dislodging some of the small stones, her pale legs freakily long and vulnerable, more chestnut hair escaping. She turns at the top and looks down at me.

OK I'm off.

Oh, Rebecca?

Yes?

Did you catch the names of the men who commissioned the paintings?

Course not. They were Greek. Anyway they left a card.

And she's gone.

Another sunset is coming up, a hazy one, heat and humidity already clogging the sky, stirring white into the colour mix so that everything looks acrylic. A stagey synthetic afterglow will follow. I'll have a shower then watch it from the roof terrace while I mull over the events of the day. Or take my book to the beach and not mull over them.

This late I have the beach to myself. Swimming in the red-gold water of my personal land-locked lagoon engages all my senses and extinguishes troublesome thoughts. Two white egrets are hunched on the little isthmus that connects the beach to the almost-island that shelters it from the deep waters of the bay. On the inland side of the island there are traces of an early settlement, sporadic courses of partly dressed limestone projecting from the scrub, reminders of Cyclopean walls, a nudge to posterity. Build here, they say. Out of sight. Out of the wind. But what my exposed and unsettled patch lacks in shelter it makes up for in the depth of its soil. The people on the islet would, I like to think, have grown their crops in my garden. I find things: a handle, pieces of rim and base, once a chert blade. Floating now in a lazy arc, encircled by every phase of civilisation, the island settlement, the chapel on the headland, the farm on the hill, the ship-owner's pad, I'm hit by a real-time memory. The shard under the olive trees . . . the rush of connection – they handled this, they ate off it – the urgent need to know what else is there. Before the light fades I'll look.

But when I flop with my book in my usual place under the tamarisks, flattened, I can see, by large footprints now hazing over and turning sugary, I remember what lies beneath. And now, thanks to Gabriel, I am less aspiring beach babe, more loggerhead turtle. I slide a hand into the soft sand beneath me. There's nothing. I lay down my book and try again. Using both hands I unearth a corner of brown cardboard. And since I'm not and never was of Gabriel's thinking I dig up the parcel and carry it back to the house.

I lay it on the back terrace to open later and go inside to shower away a long and taxing day, but when – clean but still a mess inside – I see a message light on the answerphone and a tray full of tea things that don't belong here in this foreign land, don't go with built-in cement seating and blue and white cushions, things that belong in my great-grandmother's glass-fronted display cabinet with curly legs and a golden key in a lock too high for me to reach, I stop dead. Stop running. Run hot water. Let myself shrink to where I'm reaching up to help her wash these glowing, tinkling things a bowl of soap bubbles. Disconnection . . . loss . . . I let the wave catch me. Let it carry me. But keep my head above the surface.

My great-grandmother . . . silk stockings, tall chairs, ornate tableware . . . my grandmother . . . monogrammed powder compact, chiffon scarves and the ghost of her perfume, L'Air du Temps . . . my mother . . . and my father . . . my mother and father . . . who are connected to me by no objects . . . who are unconnected in every way, whom I strive not to remember because they ought to be alive and are not. Not allowing myself to think about the car crash has, I realise, meant not allowing myself to think about them. Almost not at all.

There's more to it than that.

Raffy, at times, seemed closer to them than I did. At times? Often. To my father at least. And now that that's out there's a for instance looming. Not a powerful for instance but a puzzling one. For instance, once, when we were visiting them . . . I'm there now, opening a door in search of wine for my mother to deglaze a sauté pan for the Sunday lunch we are about to eat, opening a door seldom closed, but closed today, Raffy and my father behind this door talking, breaking off when I walk in. I remember the hurt. And see that the hurt deflected my surprise. I could remember few private conversations with my father. Thinking about that now, being dispassionate, harder still, honest, I can see that I might not have encouraged intimacy. Somewhere in the course of that first Greek summer – the Claudia effect compounded by my mother's sobbing – I took her side.

There were few enough occasions to do that. My

parents were not at war. My father was not a serial philanderer, just easily flattered, and my mother, rather a beauty herself, recovered her equilibrium although never a total confidence in her identity, which led to a decade of bewildering style experiments and hair colour changes, an inconsistency that made her not the stolid rock some of my friends' mothers seemed to be and probably hastened my emotional self-sufficiency.

I remember what I told Gabriel – that I came here after their deaths so that I could think about them. If that was my intention it is not what happened. What I did was master the art of forgetting.

And where is this taking me? Nowhere.

I dry the cups and saucers then tackle the answerphone. It's Nico.

Anna mou. Nico here. There is a man, he is American, looking for you. In the café they tell him I know you. So I say yes, I know her, but right now I don't have my kinito *with the number. I tell him* give me your number and I call her later. *I am careful, you understand, always I have my* kinito. *The number, it is . . .* here a rustle of paper then a mobile number, the code Greek. *He say tell her . . . tell her it is Lucas.*

Lucas. What next? Michael? Claudia?

I'm only a phone call away from possible enlightenment and so, of course, I can't make it. Not yet. I put away the cups and saucers and go out onto the terrace to water the geraniums, sadly neglected these past days, and hear across the wall the sound of what must be my new neighbours moving garden furniture.

No time like the present when the task is not

essential so I hunt out a basket, fill it with peaches, and set off to pay my respects.

Wrestling with their front gate I'm thinking how much I'm going to miss my old neighbours, how much I don't want to break in a new set. The Athenian family were handsome, generous, noisy in conversation, quiet in habit. They were what neighbours in Greece ought to be. Greek. They were also security obsessed, and as I wiggle the third bolt out of its rusty slot, swing back the crossbar and still can't open the gate, it occurs to me that their successors are more paranoid still. I lay down the peaches and crouch to examine the sticking point. A small new padlock without a key is hidden behind an upright. I climb over, spilling peaches, and crunch noisily up the path. The furniture shifting noises have stopped.

Hallo? Voice lifting on the second syllable to show the soft-footed and empathetic neighbour they're really getting, effaceable and deniable in a heartbeat. As they, I hope, will be with me. *Hallo?* Louder this time. *Hallo!* (*Look*, I want to tell them, *I only picked peaches, I didn't cook a* blanquette de veau *or a bake a carrot cake, I won't be dropping in, so stop this and show yourselves.*) Their car is in the drive, a vanilla Nissan Micra.

I continue up the side of the house to the paved and shaded back court whose space is now filled with a very large and very new hardwood dining table surrounded by eight matching chairs. The Athenians, I note, have generously left them their pot plants which are dead.

I hover, feeling less the slighted neighbour, more the menacing intruder. There are no sounds from the house. I retreat to the front terrace and ring the door bell which has the same demented Avon lady sound as my own. This does nothing. I step back and scan the windows. I think I see a face vanish, but then I would. Perhaps they have gone for a walk. In the dark . . . padlocking the gate?

I don't really want to be here any more so I climb back over the gate, go home, fix a salad, and carry it out onto the dark back terrace where I trip over the parcel. I prop it against a chair, turn on the terrace lights and sit down to eat, ears pricked for sounds from next door. There are none. But the parcel is slouching there, challenging me, and pretty soon I lay down the fork and use the knife to attack it.

Not books after all. The thing, whatever it is, is encased in many layers of bubble wrap, separately taped.

As it diminishes in volume it begins to have a shape and a nature. Elongated, dense, pale. Through the last layer of wrap I can see what's coming, but only when I pull it away and hold the thing in my hands can I see its flattened, all-knowing features, its assertive shoulders, its tapering torso, its folded arms and conjoined legs. A Cycladic figurine.

I am dizzy with disbelief. Stronger, far stronger than the questions surrounding its presence here on the bed of bubble wrap on my marble table is the thing itself. It is genuine, it is ancient, it is undamaged and, for the moment, it is mine. I drink in its every detail, its slightly pitted oxidised surface, its style, whose name – *dokathismata*, *chalandriani*, one of those, I'll look it up – evades me, but which is haunting, compelling, earthily unearthly. It is magnificent. It is hot. I could get twenty years just for looking at it.

Entrapment. I see how Gabriel's mind was working, but wonder . . . why?

I'm out of ideas. I lift it from its wrappings, stand it upright on the table, pour myself a glass of wine and sit there finishing my salad, totally spooked.

And with the salad finished, the wine finished, no ideas arriving and the figure still pushing out vibes across the table, I feel an unease verging on dread. Might someone be watching? Watching with intent?

I place it in its bed of bubble wrap, bubble wrap with something opaque among the folds. A piece of paper. Paper with writing. Raffy's writing.

I weight the paper with a marble bowl, wrap the figure loosely in its packing and carry it into the house where I tuck it up safely in a single divan in a guest bedroom, its head on the pillow, its body childlike under the ethnic bedspread.

Then, with stagey composure, because now that I've thought of it of course I feel watched, I go inside, make coffee, carry it out, sit down, take a sip and read the note. Just a sentence. *Hide this. I'll call you.* No signature.

When was it posted? Long enough ago to explain the first phone call. The call I didn't return but coolly made use of – a notional husband conjured up as notional protector – when Marcus revealed his darker side.

Nothing I think of can relieve my culpability. Nothing elucidates. Everything confuses. Then I remember Lucas.

I call him. His phone is off. And so, now I think of it, is mine, although I promised Gabriel I would keep it charged and with me. Not just charged and with me but on.

I find it, turn it on. Gabriel, back on Mykonos and retrospectively solicitous has texted to say that when he's not shooting he will be contactable and only one island away. Hollanders all over the place. But where is Raffy? And do I any longer want to know?

I sleep late and waken with a sense of purpose. I am harbouring an antiquity, my husband is missing, my father-in-law and brother-in-law are separately in orbit somewhere in the Aegean and tonight I am dining with someone who, I fear, will provoke more questions than he answers. Oh, and a man is dead.

Stress demands diversion and I am in active housewife mode when I hear a car turn into the drive. At last. The electrician.

But the man who gets out of the car, a blue car, metallic blue, as I come round the corner of the house and who, not seeing me yet, stands looking around him, is not the electrician. I watch as he turns back and reaches out a clipboard from the passenger seat. When he sees me approaching he takes up a formal business stance and holds out his hand. *Good morning*, he says. His expression changes. *We have met before.* He waits for a reaction. *At the party of Nico? Peter.*

He is the one, the man with the granite profile and the marathon handclasp who questioned me persistently in that flat, accented, possibly familiar voice and filled me with such foreboding and yet such fascinated indecision that my feet would not leave the ground, and whose hand is once again reaching out to shake mine.

I take it. He tells me he has come to advise me on an extension to my house.

It takes me some time to separate light from dark, mundane from extra-sensory, this man with bad breath and a clipboard from that energy-absorbing void, but, when I do, I see a possible reversal. Whatever brought him here he is at present that lowliest of creatures, the provider of a service I do not want. I bite back *extension? . . . what extension?* and smile encouragingly. If he's checking me out then I can check him back.

He has turned about and is casting rather a disparaging eye over my modest cube house with its blue shutters and small windows. He tells me he can see at least two possible places where an extension would be both harmonious and feasible. Is this a genuine cold-call or am I being targeted? The voice I heard in the olive grove is no longer sharp in my memory, but he came, after all, in the death wagon, a metallic blue car.

OK, I say, *talk me through it.*

So he walks me round to the back terrace where last night a marble Cycladic figurine sat propped against the wall and outlines a rather banal boxing in of the terrace to make an office.

But I like it as a terrace.

He makes a sound that I think is a non-native English speaker's sneer, vocalised. A true cold caller would surely be trying to charm me. *Then perhaps it is time to discuss the other matter.*

Other matter?

Your connections. I am beyond clueless. *Your religious reproduction marketing network has been highly recommended to me. I see great potential for Christmas cards.*

It's 29 degrees. And Greeks don't really do Christmas. I can only stare.

Very well. He changes tack. *We shall consider the second location.* He is walking towards the side of the house and I'm following, trying to listen as he suggests an extension that would involve demolishing the utility room and the staircase to the roof.

Why would I do that?

His immobile face and colourless eyes convey controlled exasperation, the tedious waiting for less ordered people to get in line with his thinking. *If you want another room you must be prepared for some disruption.*

The voice on the answerphone, the voice I erased, matched so absolutely the voice I heard in the garden that I had no doubts. Is it being able to see the speaker that makes the difference?

Well thank you for your trouble but I believe I'll just stick with the house as it is.

And now he animates. *But you requested that I should call.*

Did I? I don't think so.

I understood it was pressing. That you had just bought the house and wanted to proceed without delay.

Ah. I think it might be my neighbours you're looking for. Over there. They've just moved in.

Now he looks both annoyed and mortified, a hard thing to fake. *The directions were not clear and of course there are no house numbers here.* Annoyance is winning. *I'm sorry I took up your time.*

Not at all.

Let me give you a card in case you ever think of an extension. He brings out a wallet and hands me a slim blue and gold card. I promise to bear him in mind.

As he backs out of the drive and slows at the neighbours' gate, presumably now with its drawbridge arrangements down, I look at the card. *Thanasis Aliprandis Partnership*, it says. *Yannis Tsanakopoulos, Carolina Alifieri.* Handwritten at the bottom *Peter Karpodinis* and a mobile number.

Thanasis again. Yannis too. Why is the last name not printed? Is he using this as a card of convenience?

As I slump again into the anti-climax zone that's becoming so familiar, triumphalism ebbing as another inconclusive episode comes to an end, I realise that the voice in its expressionless phrasing, its absence of vivacity and above all its tenacity is indeed familiar. It is, as I first recognised, a background voice in the daily life of Karistos. His is one of the voices, Greek-speaking, fluent Greek-speaking, of the group of men who sit every evening playing *tavli* at the corner table of the café in the square. A small triumph but a triumph nonetheless.

And now I must think outside the box. I must phone Lucas.

But with voices drifting from across the wall, muffled by trees and interrupted by bird-song but speaking, I think, English, another idea comes to mind. I take out my mobile, both with me and on, and dial the handwritten number on the card

From across the wall I hear it. In the Hall of the Mountain King from the Peer Gynt Suite.

9

To life after death threat, says Marcus raising his glass and releasing one of his locked-on smiles.

I look down into my own glass where a fly is drowning in a fruity local red. I hook it out with my fork, leave it to dry off on my napkin, raise my glass and still can't avoid meeting the blue killer gaze.

May it be a long one.

You're accusing me of hubris?

No. Just picking up on your confidence.

He ignores my invitation to expand. *I don't believe life is ever without threat, but in this case . . .*

I thought perhaps you had identified the killer and – oh, I don't know – given some money to his favourite charity.

Hmm.

A giant shadow falls across the table. *Ready to order?* The waiter looms, shorter than his shadow but with stock sculpted profile, tumescent pigtail and designer stubble, pencil poised, weight carefully distributed, a starched white chef's apron fluttering from his waist.

We are, the three of us, balanced on a plank above dark water that sighs and slurps and rattles at the newest, most outrageous restaurant yet in a village of escalating pretentions. Stavros has taken over the disused boatyard and set out his tables on a concrete jetty, some small rocky outcrops and connecting boardwalks, along which the waiters must sidle and balance with trays held above their heads like celebrants at a mystery or collective farmers bearing home a Soviet harvest. Tonight is the opening night. Diners cluster in a gloom lit by sporadically flaring candlelight and cling nervously to their tables. We order *mezedhes* of *zucchini keftedhes*, *tzaziki*, prawns and rocket and chicory salad followed by lobster ravioli and octopus *stifadho* and try to relax.

I think, says Marcus evenly, *you are giving me credit for too exotic a lifestyle.*

I raise my eyebrows and spread my hands to embrace the balancing waiters, the channels of moonlit gurgling water, candles fluttering in sand-weighted highball glasses, yachts rocking at anchor, an up-lit Venetian ruin, and on an elevated ridge three restored windmills. Two ornamental geese – a municipal conceit – are paddling like gondoliers along the canals between the tables, foraging for crumbs of aniseed flavoured artisan bread baked in wood-fired ovens.

Point taken. But that applies equally to you. What brand of exoticism do you practise?

Nothing that makes people want to kill me. I read, I write, I swim, I cultivate my garden.

And your husband?

He's in London just now. I wonder if it's such a good idea to distance my hypothetical protector, but I guess he always knew that this was a dinner invitation for one.

What does he do?

He's an archaeologist.

So . . . is he involved in excavations on the island?

Not at all. His interests lie . . . elsewhere.

I don't think I've met him. This is more than an observation, and it's true that this would be unusual.

He's away a lot. Tell me, do you know Lisa Dunmore?

Not by name.

She has that shop, Byzantiana, opposite the café where we met yesterday.

Ah yes. I believe I met her way back, I mean way, way back, but not under that name. She tells me I'm mistaken, but there it is.

Where do you think you met her?

Here. The person I'm thinking of had dark hair but she did have those eyes. It's the eyes. They're unmistakable. Though I have to say the argument against my version would be her age. I was eighteen. Gap year. This person was a lot older. Which would make her older now than seems likely.

But she **is***. Older than seems likely. Do you remember the name, her other name?*

Donnelly, Donnachy, one of those. First name . . . Debby, Patty, Mandy. Something like that.

I didn't know you'd been here that long ago.

Well, it was on the trail. How about you?

Still in ankle socks. Debby-Patty-Mandy . . . she was living here on Kryptos?

I don't know about living. She was working. In a taverna I think. She and her boyfriend. It's the boyfriend I especially remember. He was an operator.

In what way?

Just, you knew to watch out for him.

How exactly?

Usual bad vibes. You know how it is when someone is sizing you up instead of just sussing you out.

And when he'd sized you up . . . what?

Well, I was island hopping. I guess I hopped, so I never found out.

Do you remember his name?

That I do. Zac.

As in Zachary? Or Zacharias? Was he Greek?

English. Or if he was Greek he was brought up in England. Why? Did you know him?

Something rings a bell. Oh look. Food.

Our starters are weaving towards us through the night sky, hovering briefly as the waiter drops off menus at the next table, where sit, I now realise, Dimitris and Thanasis, delightful Dimitris, last overheard at Nico's party and eminent, enigmatic – to me at least – Thanasis. They nod to us across the channel and when our plates have been delivered I tell Marcus how often I find the people I meet here have a history, an ancient history, on the island.

The island doesn't let us go, does it?

It's true. And it strikes me that if I carry that thought through, many things may be even more complex than they presently appear. People too.

Rebecca . . . is she another?

I've no idea. She's a bit of a hobo.

But talented.

Very. I would have liked to give her an exhibition of her own but she doesn't let her stuff go easily. The things I have shown always attract a lot of interest. In fact I've just pointed a commission her way. For the new hotel.

She told me about that. ***You*** *were behind it then?*

Thanasis has . . . projects. He was looking for someone with her sort of versatility. Was he indeed? Rather than spotting her work in a magazine.

He *is building the hotel then?* I glance across at their table where they have turned away to watch a woman tread the springy catwalk towards them like a high wire *artiste* in heels.

He and some others. Loose consortia are the norm here.

I'm familiar with him of course but I don't think I've ever met him. What does he actually do?

Come on. This is Kryptos. The question one never asks. *He's an architect, but how often he puts pencil to paper now I couldn't say.*

A peal of laughter from their table allows another glance. A goose has clambered onto the walkway, stopping an approaching waiter in his stride. The waiter hovers, hip extended, abs engaged, arms high, very Ballets Russes. He holds his balance as the goose glares up at him like a small floored ballerina and, when he side-steps, mirrors his movement. They hang there, goose and waiter, rising and falling as the plank settles. The waiter lowers his tray, the goose rears up and spreads its wings, the waiter freaks, and on the outer islands of our archipelago diners stand up, or swivel to watch, producing a Mexican wave effect and a hint of motion sickness.

There is madness abroad. And right now three things coincide. Marcus grabs a piece of bread and leans across to distract the goose, I discover that the woman now sitting with Dimitris and Thanasis is an almost unrecognisable Rebecca, and someone touches me lightly on the left shoulder. There is no-one to my left as I turn, only an empty table and another boardwalk trembling slightly from the passage of someone now out of sight, but next to my plate is an extra napkin, white with an outline map of the island and something handwritten on a corner. I scoop it off the table onto my knee.

When the goose, lunging at the bread, topples off the plank, soaking us all but freeing the waiter to deliver our main course, Marcus picks up a napkin to dry his arm and Rebecca says *Hi!* She is wearing an iridescent shot silk blue-green dress and pendant earrings. Her hair is up. She looks drop-dead fabulous. They are drinking champagne.

I guess Rebecca decided to do the mural, I tell Marcus, noting that the napkin he is holding is red, as is mine. Under the table I put the white napkin into my bag and help myself to ravioli and *stifadho* as he tops up our glasses. *Talking of which, how's business?* I'm gratified to see he takes a moment to decide what I mean by that before telling me that he has sold three paintings this week.

I've always wondered who would buy paintings here. You can't just stuff them in a suitcase.

Oh we ship them when asked. But some people do take

them home. We keep miles of bubble wrap. At the worst the glass needs to be replaced.

What sort of painting are we talking about? I'm thinking of Nico's jibe.

For the holiday-makers seascapes, chapels, windmills, what you'd expect. They're looking for atmospheric alternatives to photographs. The better stuff stays on the island. With a good exhibition I can sell half the paintings on the opening night.

On the table our plates judder as someone heavier approaches from behind. Marcus shoots off a token smile as a matching couple pass us headed for the empty table on my left. A familiar voice says *I told Stavro he was making the walkways too narrow. In Britain you'd never get off with not having a hand rail.* Joyce from Nico's party. I see Dimitri look up.

Into the pause I say . . . *and the antiquities business, how is that going?*

Marcus takes a moment to consider before me looks me in the eye. *I don't really have anything to do with that.*

No?

It's dicey.

But you did?

People sometimes brought me things they'd found.

Found here? On Kryptos?

Sure.

What sort of things?

Small.

Nothing intact?

Not often.

What about Cycladic figurines?

He is jabbing at an octopus tentacle, head down, shoulders tense.

They belong in burial sites. They would only turn up if an excavation was going on.

And there's nothing left to find.

One lives in hope. If you're a developer, I guess, in the hope of finding nothing. The rest of us, I imagine, dream of digging up an intact Aphrodite from under the roots of a wilting hibiscus. Don't you?

All the time.

And wouldn't your husband be the one to ask?

This is not a good tack to pursue. Marcus is looking closed and charm-withholding. Soon he'll send out bored end-of-evening vibes to put a stop to my questions. Which would be unfortunate. Except for the Lisa Dunmore discovery – and what was that all about? – I feel no more enlightened than at the start. If I'd hoped he might open up about the threat behind our first meeting, or show a glimpse of the unprotected place in his set-up or his make-up that made him take it seriously, I'm not going to get it. If I'd hoped to connect this to Raffy's whereabouts – and for no sensible reason I had – that isn't going to happen either. I should find another opening before this bizarre evening comes to an end.

But before this can happen we have a distraction.

Out along the walkway comes a big man in a tight white suit. A spotlight picks him up as he reaches the end and steps into a small boat. The boat lists, skids, recovers. From the tables there comes the slackened vibe of many people no longer eating. At the oars of the boat sits a smiling Nico, now also bathed in the light that follows them as he rows the short distance to a rock platform. The big man rises, becomes enormous, steadies himself, and lunges. For a moment he hangs, straddling the gap, then, as he throws his weight onto the rock, the spotlight is joined by celestial grade floodlight to reveal a white upright piano which just about fits the surface of the rock and lets the pianist insert himself without pulling back the stool.

The silence that follows is the un-Greek sound of mass hysteria, controlled. At last someone claps and then we all do. One of those Greek rearrangements of the law of probabilities has taken place allowing the pianist to lay out his music with dignity. Nico rows back the few metres to the walkway and, passing our table and spotting us, pulls up a chair and sits down, beaming. There is an alerting micro-second of amplified crackle then the pianist launches into an explosive rendering of, I think, a Beethoven Sonata. We're avoiding each others' eyes, smiling the insane smiles of people who have not had time to process their reactions. The volume subsides. Palpable relief gives way to palpable delight. Nico's smile broadens.

Is my cousin, he says. *Teacher of piano in Athens.*

Marcus signals for another glass and we all relax.

The applause has Nico purring with pleasure. His cousin stands up cautiously to acknowledge it but a move towards a standing ovation is aborted quickly as planks turn to springboards. The cousin goes into a music-for-foreigners selection, Zorba and Never on Sunday, and conversation restarts. Nico turns to me.

The man who was looking for you, Anna mou. Did he find you?

I tell Nico that Lucas's phone has been off or out of range but that I hope to reach him tonight. He still looks concerned.

The man, the foreign man who was killed, you knew him?

I had forgotten how urgently Gabriel and I hurried away when Nico gave us the news.

No. Well, I had met him. But it was not . . . who we feared it might be.

No? His curiosity, understandable, is hard to get round. *The other man, the man who was looking for you, he is friend of the dead man?*

No.

Marcus, no longer bored, is hanging on every word.

Tell me please, Nico continues, *about this dead man. I have heard he is famous English man.*

They've identified him then?

Please?

They know who he is?

Yes. His name is John. He is very famous journalist I think. You know him?

Well certainly not by sight. John what?

Someone is dead? Marcus has lost his cool. *Dead as in no longer alive?*

Murdered, yes, says Nico. *Murdered with a knife. At the port. You don't know this?*

I think, but do not say, *you believe he was mistaken for you.*

For him the evening looks to be over. I chat with

Nico as Marcus starts the long process of catching the waiter's eye. This will not be easy. Boats are missed trying to get the bill.

Finally he arrives. Marcus asks for the *logariasmo*. The waiter brings a complimentary plate of halva, the Greek version, a moist semolina and almond dessert topped with almond slivers and candied lemon, and three silver forks wrapped in fresh scarlet napkins. Nico's cousin goes into an Elton John medley.

Nico tells us how his cousin was visiting, staying with their grandmother as is his custom every summer, when, over coffee one morning, Stavros the restaurant owner, Nico, his cousin and his brothers, all of whom went to school together, hit on and developed this idea. Nico's older brother laid out the walkways. His younger brother did the lighting. The boat is Stavro's own which he uses for fishing in the off season. Stavros is very pleased as he needed cheering up when his wife left him.

I ask for and am given details of this and we finish the halva. Marcus signals again and the waiter arrives with three glasses of *souma*, the spirit distilled from grape skins and seeds. Out on the rock Nico's cousin breaks into a Bossa Nova.

At last the waiter brings the bill, Nico excuses himself to go off and mingle and as Marcus and I get to our feet Thanasis leans across and invites us to join them for coffee. I look at Marcus. He has turned away quickly to hide any naked display of indecision, but turns back with an *OK?* to me.

As the waiter fetches chairs and a hovering French

couple storms our table ahead of the Germans advancing from the right, I excuse myself to go and hunt out the boatshed loos. But at the first street-lamp I stop and take from my bag the white napkin with the scribbled message in Raffy's writing. *Behind the harbour loo. 10.30.* Romantic, eh?

It's ten minutes after that. I push through the crowded waterfront towards the old harbour whose quayside at night is as crammed with tables as its mooring is with fishing boats. Out on the end in the darkness by the seawall are the original hole-in-the-ground public toilets, now enclosed in rough-cut marble walls. The air stirs and suddenly I'm a ten-year-old. It's the smell, hanging on in there, clobbering what it must concede to the *madeleine* in subtlety with the slam dunk of enforced recall. All my childhood summers are here in that smell.

I walk past the entrance, look along the seaward wall. He's there, leaning on the wall, staring out to sea. He looks like the man I saw stepping off the ferry. He turns, and I'm scared.

Hallo Anna.

I don't know what I expected. What I see is a man I used to live with playing a part. He has been watching me, I suppose. I don't want to think about that.

He smiles, and comes towards me.

Behave like a casual acquaintance.

As distinct from what?

Otherwise you may be in danger.

You astonish me.

We'll talk later when it's safe for me to come to the house.

Ah. You know where that is then?

I've been there.

I digest this. It tells me nothing.

Your father is here. Did you know?

That's why I had to see you. There are . . . he has . . . issues.

Issues? Late onset dyslexia, anger management, one of the phobias?

When you meet up with him don't tell him anything.

Like what?

That I'm here. That I'm in contact. Use your judgement. I have to go now.

I'm only on a toilet break myself.

He steps round the far side of the building, fails to look back, and vanishes. I watch the place where he was then go inside the building which, with its cracked tiles, rust-stained basin and distorting mirror looks comfortingly constant and dependable. Nothing in here has changed, the gents still identified by the boulevardier with soft hat and cane, the ladies by a person with a pageboy, a poodle and a parasol. When I check myself out in the mirror I'm unsurprised to find my face not quite as I remember it.

We almost called air rescue, says Rebecca. Thought you'd taken a tumble.

I reach for the glass of champagne Thanasis pours me, which he won't relinquish until I look him properly in the eye, and acknowledge Marcus's introduction.

There was a queue at the boatshed loo, I tell them, *so I went to the old harbour toilets.*

They look at me with variously disguised expressions of disgust.

Don't worry. I washed my hands.

10

The boatyard taverna by daylight makes last night an illusion.

Unsettled by the encounter with Raffy I turned in late not expecting to sleep and, expectation confirmed, got up to numb my brain with small hours TV. Finding the channels hijacked by zombie people with no clothes or dialogue, Scandinavian soft porn with Greek subtitles, mildly soporific but contentious on a couple of counts unlike, say, camomile tea, I switched off one and went for the other.

On a terrace washed by moonlight so lavish I thought I might read by it, I sat with an open book, saw the hedgehog, heard the owl, heard mosquitoes, saw a glow-worm, and gave up all thought of sleep. Finally, with the sun rising, I decided, now that he had been fingered by Raffy, to phone Lucas. But with the phone in my hand thought again.

Use your judgement, Raffy said. Based on what? If he

was not to know that Raffy was here, how did that play with Gabriel? Thoughts of Gabriel triggering my *check messages* reflex, I put down the phone and reached for my mobile. Which was not in my bag.

I hardly expected to find it, twelve hours later, lying on a table top, but I did expect the table still to be here, one row out from the waterline, second island from the left. Instead there is a surreal shore-scape of bare planks and rocks with towers of stacking chairs and tables lined up by the boatshed, now home to the restaurant kitchen and servery, whose huge double doors are still, at this early hour, locked and bolted.

I walk the plank to our platform of last night. To the left sat Joyce and her husband and over to the right was Thanasi's table.

The channels between the planks are all a-flutter, shoals of wispy glassy fish roughing each other up for last night's crumbs. I kneel and peer into the clear water which seems at first to offer a staggering choice of phones, clunking and glinting in shades of Nokia grey. Reaching down into the water, warm even at this hour, reaching almost to my shoulder, my hand still far above the smooth shapes, dappled and magnified, hypnotic and serene in their lack of function, I forget why I'm here. When I stand up, dry my arm on my shorts and look back towards the shore, I find I've lost my bearings. This view is right off my compass. I wonder how it looks from further out.

From the farthest joined-up rock, lapped, I see, by water deep enough to drown an incautious diner, I discover a vista that's quite new to me. I can see across a headland to the monastery of Aghios Konstandinos above Marcus's house. In fact I can see the house. And taking that as a fixed point I can skim over the tawny lower slopes to the old farmhouse Meriel wanted to buy.

Over at the boatshed someone is opening up. I pick my way back there like a lone traveller zig-zagging through airport security on a slack day.

It's Stavros. I congratulate him on the originality of his concept and he tells me he is already fully booked for the week ahead, but no, he does not recall a *kinito*. He opens a wall cupboard. On a shelf still smelling of wood preservative sits last night's closing-time haul: two pairs of sunglasses, a pashmina and a copy of The Iliad. Scents of engine oil, paint, and old timbers are here along with last night's garlic and tomato, while the slice of sunlight falling through the door illuminates a framed sea view that only old caïque captains will know.

It's the time of morning when fishermen mend their nets. Yards of mesh in a rather shockingly fashionable deep aubergine spool across the quayside colouring the space between the white walls and the blue water. Tourists tiptoe and take pictures, watched by a group of moustachioed *kapitano*s in braided caps who sit over their doll's house coffee cups not feeling the need to talk. I find a table near them and when the waiter comes order a *metrio*.

Last night as I rejoined the others I was aiming for this sort of communal solitude. Fresh from the Raffy encounter I had no taste for small-talk. Cool with Raffy, not cool about him, I was trying not to scan the passing faces but doing that anyway, leaving my first impression of Thanasis unexamined. A pocket Olympian, I thought, perhaps consciously so, whose shadow falls across everything here but who keeps his face averted. Fine with me. As he leant past Marcus to shake my hand, I was acknowledging him rather than responding to him. He noted that. And I noted that, while Dimitris deferred to him and while Rebecca, now perhaps indebted, was unusually subdued, Marcus seemed immune, suggesting that, however island politics works, he was not in the loop. It took me longer to realise that I, holding the outsider's card, owing him nothing in the way of gratitude or self interest, had become, for that reason, the focus of his attention.

The talk was general, eased by Nico joining us, and I was only dimly aware of Thanasis watching me, angling to open a line of conversation. Finally he said

I believe I saw you recently at another extraordinary eating place. Taverna Gorgona?

Rebecca looked at him sharply, then looked away. His English was impeccable with hardly a trace of accent. I nodded.

Gorgona? Gorgona? cut in Nico. *Where is this please?*

Thanasis explained. Marcus looked interested. Thanasis, trying to draw me out, was now stuck with a food conversation. I said nothing, and presently he tried again.

What did you think of it?

It was remarkable. Considering. I stopped myself elaborating.

He was not enjoying my reticence.

You are on holiday? Or are you one of our growing foreign community?

Oh. ***Is*** *it a community?*

Your – er – companion that day – he glanced carefully at Marcus in case he and I were presently an item – *does not, I imagine, live here?* Because Gabriel could never pass under anyone's radar.

He doesn't. No.

While Thanasis may have been irked by my lack of response, Nico of the harmonious impulses could not bear it. *He is brother-in-law of Anna,* he explained.

Indeed?

While he watched me with a 'why am I not hearing this from you?' expression, I was asking myself whether his interest in Gabriel stemmed from natural curiosity or whether he thought he recognised him.

He is a strong swimmer, I think.

I guess so. I haven't seen him much in recent years.

And is he still here, on Kryptos?

On Mykonos. Meanwhile. Again my thoughts skidded off to Raffy. Did **he** know this? And mention of Gabriel brought me subliminally to the phone. I should have given Raffy the number. Had I known it.

Whether Thanasis saw my remoteness as a wearisome feminist refusal to be impressed or as a failure to recognise his place in island hierarchy it was proving surprisingly effective, although, as I began to realise, it was not an effect I had intended.

Is your sister here too?

Sister? What was he on about? Ah, the hypothetical wife of my brother-in-law. He was going the long and devious way about finding out whether Gabriel was the brother of my husband. I felt a first prickle of alarm. Once again Nico broke in.

Is Anna's husband who is brother.

Thanasis showed a frisson of pleasure that I was being outwitted.

Your husband then. He is here?

Ah, said Marcus, *Anna's husband*, *the empty place at the table, the shadow on the stairs.*

Rebecca looked sharply at him. So did I.

Raffy was now the centre of attention. I had forgotten that obfuscation is simply not tolerated in this society.

I have never met, said Nico sadly, re-humanising him. Nico does love a family group.

Nor even glimpsed, said Marcus.

Ah well, I said, winding in some faceless frequent flyer to serve as my spouse because the shadow-creature of the harbour toilets was never going to be joining us. *Perhaps some day soon.*

But last night, lying awake, listening for sounds outside that, now I hoped to hear them, didn't happen, I re-thought Raffy's words. *When it's safe.* An affirmation that it was anything but.

So, OK. Nothing is clearer. And as ever I take refuge in the beauty of the surroundings to put it all out of my mind. I pay for my coffee and decide to walk out along the coast road towards what I think of as Meriel's house. As the road runs clear of the sea-front buildings I see across the bay the concrete curves of the new hotel, aspirant cockle shell, blank canvas for Rebecca's murals, meanwhile a concrete tent.

Thanasis and someone else commissioned Rebecca to paint the murals. Dimitris? Craft shop owner, encourager and mainstay of a couple of weavers, a potter, one or two designer jewellers – a sweet-natured man, and serious. His name was not on the card. Or not on the card Peter Karpodinis left me. Loose consortia, Marcus said. Perhaps Rebecca's card has other names.

The village, straggling far beyond its old boundaries, gives out now as the bay it's been stalking comes to an end. The track to its far shore branches right while the hills that have been amassing on my left step forward, separate, and edge down closer to the continuing main road. These close bare hills, I've never really looked at them. This morning they are far more compelling than the endless scene-stealing sea. Raffy would walk in these hills. There were no roads into them then and there are none now, nothing ascending into the hinterland but the odd footpath to an isolated farm, a short cut for a donkey or a motorbike. The villages back there in the interior are reached by roads that pass through friendlier valleys.

Here by the roadside bleached corn stubble shimmers in the heat, hypnotic and time-twisting, slowing my pulse, glittering in the corner of my eye. The hill above curves treeless, scrub-free, tawny gold then tawny brown and, higher still, grey-brown then grey-white as the marble it's made of comes to the surface.

What did Raffy find up there? Buzzards. Buzzards and rabbits. Gabriel's thing, not his. Ahead the slopes curl back towards a narrow tree line, the track that leads to Marcus's house and the monastery.

Traffic is sporadic, only an occasional speeding car forcing me onto the verge. Rounding a bend I hear voices and see cars parked, pennants looped between the pine trees of a roadside thicket. A blue-domed roadside chapel is having its saint's day. As I pass, people call greetings. A trestle table is laden with plates of food and a woman signs to me to join them, smiling and beckoning, pointing to the festive fare. I smile back and gesture to the road ahead as if something urgently awaits me up there.

Past Marcus's track a low ridge grows out of the fields on my left, interrupting the slope of the hill, then as the road bends again I see above me a signal cypress, the side of a low house hanging just below the crown of the ridge, facing towards the valley that carries this road to the port town. On the other side of the valley the stark walls of another deserted monastery, the Monastery of the Archangels, rise out of a steep incline.

A dirt track leads up to the house. I stop and consider. A crested lark hangs above it, dipping and climbing as if writing on the air. I'm so in the moment I forget why I'm here. The conversation . . . the conversation I overheard at Nico's party. The track looks private but neglected, with weeds growing between tyre ruts, but I am after all of a nation that believes such bosky paths were designed by God for us to walk on, so I leave the road and set off up the track which starts right away to zig-zag, turning me to face the house nestled between its neglected vine arbour and its lemon tree. Its tiny plateau opens out to reveal the well and the spreading fig tree and, coming down the track towards me, Lucas.

Painfully slowly recognition kicks in. He gets there first. Well he has been looking for me.

Anna!

Lucas.

He pulls me into a hug before I have time to focus on him and so my hyper-interested gaze lights instead on a flash of white over his shoulder as someone steps back round the bend of the track. But then he's there in front of me, virtually unchanged, smiling his quirky deep-set smile, white edges to the thick hair, deeper smile lines, weathered skin, haze of fine shadow.

He's wearing chinos and a white T-shirt, a canvas bag slung across his shoulder with just enough of an ethnic look to disguise its practical stiffened A4 frame. An outside pocket holds a half litre of water. On his feet are Greek sandals. All this I take in while he tells me of his efforts to reach me, the people he asked, his surprise that no-one seems to know me.

He slides an arm round my shoulders and steers me back down the track as if, combing the countryside, now that he'd found me he was taking me home. As we rejoin the road he stops.

Anna. I'm sorry. You were going somewhere.

Was I? I'm reluctant to oblige him. *Then it can wait.*

He takes that at face value and we walk on, Lucas doing the talking, until we're hailed from across the road by one of the women celebrating the *paniyiri.* As we cross towards her another woman then a few of the men look round and fall upon Lucas with cries, hugs and handshakes. He introduces me. My hand is wrung, my shoulders patted. A handsome white-haired woman puts plastic wine glasses in our hands, someone else gives us plates. It feels good and safe, more than that, uplifting, to be embraced and included in their celebration.

All the same as I sip retsina and nibble at the saint's special biscuit I move back from the table, further into the thicket of pine trees that surrounds the chapel, the resinated air twanging memory chords as I try to work out where we are in relation to known landmarks. Across the road the hill rises. We are midway between Marcus's house and Meriel's. Marcus's house is out of sight beneath the curve of the hill but the monastery above it is clear and imposing standing out from its thicket of green, flanked by its attendant cypresses. From beside the monastery a footpath crosses the hill and descends towards Meriel's house whose roof is just visible. Far above the track the hill is scarred by an old quarry. Below the quarry, ascending the track, I catch a glimpse of a man in a white shirt.

Lucas rejoins me, apologising. I tell him I'm delighted he is so well loved and remembered. *When were you last here?*

Ten years? They have long memories, do they not?

Only adult males, I tell him, stay recognisable. Children, girl children especially, do not. Only a handful of people like Maria from the taverna know me from my childhood visits. I don't say how much I have enjoyed that anonymity. He says that a couple of the women he was speaking to asked him about me. They said they knew me well by sight but not by name.

If only Raffy was here, he says, *I'm sure they'd remember you.*

So. The elephant has entered the room. We take time out to consider. Lucas tells me how sorry he is that we're no longer together, but I'm off on a more urgent tack. He doesn't know Raffy is here. Or he doesn't know that I know. There's a world of difference. I'm going for the first.

I've always liked Lucas, liked him and trusted him, felt good in his company – although in that there may have been an element of taking sides. Claudia automatically confers sainthood on a partner. I listen to him tell me how he quizzed Raffy on our parting, but got nowhere. He is not so indiscreet as to ask for an explanation but the hope hangs in the air.

Days ago I was more than happy to tell Gabriel all I knew of the lead-up to our split, but now I am constrained, not just by Raffy's cloak and dagger message but by Gabriel's cryptic parting shot. I am too trusting. Well, if that means do I believe that people generally do not have a hidden agenda, then yes. And if that belief is now open to revision then that is also true.

He is watching me, waiting for more, waiting very reasonably for me to expand, embroider, seek his understanding, if only for the loner's need to use words. It doesn't happen. Perhaps he thinks I'm too hurt to open up, or that I've remade my life in a way that precludes looking back. But my instinct says not. He knows. He knows I'm not playing straight. I feel him pull back and reconsider as if he's scanning my file, ready to update it.

We finish our drinks, thank our hosts and, heading once more for the village, I ask where he's staying. He tells me he hoped to find a room with Kyria Sophia, their landlady from the old days. When he knocked on her door she was surprised – startled even. His eyes re-run his surprise at her surprise.

But then we hugged. She could not, however, offer him a room. She suggested a friend in the upper village and he is very comfortable there.

And you Anna? What are your plans?

I tell him about last night's dinner and how I came back to look for my mobile which I lost or failed to protect due to not having a bag with an interior pocket designed to stop one's phone falling into the sea while dining on a plank. I'm projecting guileless. Possibly over-projecting.

As we enter the network of streets a man comes towards us, young but with an older man's hunch, hands in pockets. He slows and looks closely at Lucas who is talking and doesn't notice, but as he passes us he glances back. And spits. His meaning is so clear that I turn and look after him. He waits for Lucas to turn, sees me watching him, and continues on his way. Lucas walks on, oblivious, heading for Maria's where custom dictates we will lunch. I think the man is Vasilis, Kyria Sophia's son.

Over lunch I start to relax. Raffy's garbled warnings are surely not incompatible with a thaw towards Lucas. Perhaps it's his resemblance to Raffy, maybe I'm just in need of company. And this is not just company, this was – is – family.

Maria brings us artichokes and *papoutsakia*, 'little shoes' made from halved aubergines with mincemeat, and Lucas fills me in on what's happening across the Atlantic. Claudia, having worked her way through several messy liaisons with, I gather, younger men, mostly in the music business – *after all she was born for unsuitable relationships, I just led her astray* – has emerged more or less unscathed to embrace the senior life. *I think she's embracing it. She texts me from time to time.*

And Michael?

Big changes there too. OK , it's Michael, small changes. There was a bad patch way back when he didn't make the Olympic swim squad – well you'd know about that – and he never really took to coaching. But now he's into wind surfing and doing well I hear. He hopes to make the Olympic squad on that and meanwhile he's preparing for the World Championships.

Gabriel didn't tell me. Ah.

Lucas keeps his head down, eating. When he looks up he says *he tells me your house is charming.* Fine. So we know where we are again. *I'm hoping I'll get to see it.*

Of course, of course. Overdoing it now that I'm revealed as devious, not having mentioned him in the first place. *We could go* – compensating now – *after this? I thought Gabriel was looking great.*

Yeah. So are you.

Well I kind of thrive in the sun you know. I don't know that I could live in London again.

But that brings us geographically to Raffy, or where

Raffy is supposed to be, so I divert seamlessly to island developments, the endless building programme, the burgeoning boutiques, the changes he must be trying to get his head round if he really has been absent as long as he says.

We're finishing up, saying goodbye to Maria, preparing to head off to the car park when there's a familiar shout. *Anna!* Nico is hurrying towards us, hand outstretched, beaming, in his hand my phone. I hug him and introduce Lucas. *My father-in-law*, I say, which delights him, now holding, as he thinks, almost a complete Happy Family set.

Was on chair, he says. *We find when we leave.*

Unlocking the front door, Lucas on my heels, I remember the figurine and, still talking, open the door of its room and toss my wrap over its unsurprised face. We're on the roof now, hanging over the parapet to take in the endlessly seductive sweep of the lagoon, the islet with its pre-classical settlement, the backdrop of larger islands and, framed by all that on its tiny shattered promontory, the sugar almond chapel, church of sea urchin, octopus and mermaid.

Ah, says Lucas. *There it is. Home of the unfathomable icon.*

The what?

You don't know about it? Well now.

A Lucas story. I settle against the parapet. But as he starts to talk something changes, the light I think. The sea churns. At least I hear it doing that. I miss his first words, then pick him up at . . . *looted by a pirate from somewhere in the Levant.* The icon, he means. *A storm blew up off the north of Kryptos and his ship went down. He alone of the crew was washed up alive. Onto those rocks.*

His voice comes from far away. *The sun came up. He saw the icon floating towards him.*

I grip the parapet and his voice is again beside me. *So he built it a church right there on the rocks, and to this day no-one knows who the icon depicts.*

I didn't know, I hear myself say.

No, because the pirate was non-Greek, probably non-Christian, people didn't talk about it. Later they extended the church and re-dedicated it to Saint Nicholas which is how it's known today. But as far as I know the icon is still there.

The sea is calm.

Any time I've passed, I tell him, going for practicalities, *the church has been locked.*

Find out who the key-holder is and tell him you'd like to see it. Better not mention what I told you. It's a sensitive issue.

Still disorientated I suggest coffee in the shade of the pergola and as Lucas starts down the steps ahead of me I glance back at the chapel, but instead catch sight of a touching cameo. Two slab-shouldered men are contemplating the bank of wild flowers opposite my gate.

In the kitchen, making coffee, getting a grip, I check my recovered phone. There's one message. It's from Gabriel.

Urgent you come here Mykonos today. R. in trouble.

11

So I'm on deck drinking *frappé* from a polystyrene cup. Behind me Kryptos has shrunk to a white-encrusted rock in a widening pool of blue, and the wash foaming hypnotically below is bringing me down to ambient deck mode. Zonked. In all its manifestations.

Two languid boys in bead-and-thong necklets play chess in the lotus position, two nuns gaze out across a table strewn with cake crumbs, a boy lies asleep with his head in the lap of a girl reading a guidebook who strokes his hair as she turns the pages and a young couple smooch while their baby snoozes in a nest of fleeces. We churn through the lavish nothingness with a sound that might be our hearts, amplified, beating in unison.

I'm slumped against the starboard rail, feet propped on the chair in front. Feet a dusty lacquered chestnut, chair a standard deck class white. My pulse is back to normal and I would be taking stock but my fellow passengers are far too distracting.

At the forward rail stands a Roma woman with her little girl, each in long patchwork skirt, earrings and bracelets, black hair hanging heavy under fluttering back-knotted scarves. Their presence here means that down in the hold is a loudspeaker van loaded with Cretan ceramics, basket work or crates of live chickens.

Twice, maybe three times a year the gypsies pitch up on the island, spread lengths of vivid cloth on the ground by their vans, invest that area with a sense of home, and sleep through all the night noise of the village. The women wash clothes in the stream and the men drive their vans in a never-ending circuit of the island, snarling up traffic and broadcasting their wares at a volume and with a persistence that in Britain we keep for election campaigns. One day they're everywhere, the next they're gone. And today here they are, going.

Lucas easily accommodated my change of plan. I'd forgotten, I told him, a promise made to a friend. As he witnessed my reaction to the text he would not have doubted its urgency.

I glanced at my watch – a Blue Star would be leaving for Mykonos in just under an hour – and sent Lucas off to pick peaches while I crammed a nightdress and toothbrush into my shoulder-bag. That left time to talk. He talked, I listened.

He had been looking at icons in Romania, he told me. He averted his eyes as he said this and when he looked my way again the irises seemed to be dimming, and in the shade of the pergola I played with the notion that he'd turned away to avoid blinding me, his eyes discharging energy stored from gazing too long upon the excess of gold that in icons represents the celestial presence.

Before that, he told me, he had been in Syria visiting the Monastery of Maalula, where prayers are still spoken in Aramaic and where they have an icon of the Virgin said to have been painted by Saint Luke . . . *my namesake?* . . . and while he was there he had heard tell of another Saint Luke icon lost in a storm somewhere in the Aegean on the way from Constantinople to Mystra in the Peloponnese in the closing days of the Byzantine Empire. Rumour had it that it had recently turned up on an uninhabited islet not far from the Turkish coast where it was poised to cause a diplomatic incident.

I drank my coffee, fought my way back from these purple depths, made him promise to look at some of the island churches with me later – he was going to be on Kryptos for a few more days – then dropped him on the edge of the village, and put my foot down.

Only then did I have time to digest Gabriel's message. Trouble? What sort of trouble? And on Mykonos, an island that Raffy, at least in his earlier incarnation, took great care to avoid.

Since there were no night boats he must have left this morning, either on a regular ferry or on one of the day-cruise boats that go first to Delos, in which case he would have had three hours there before arriving at Mykonos. This was the extent of my reasoning as I responded Girl Scout-style to the command of my phone.

I had texted Gabriel with my arrival time but when I

tried to call him for more information his phone was off. And it's good to get off Kryptos whatever the reason, to slouch here like the others deep in the moment, my bag with its overnight decency kit slumped at my feet, the sun glinting on the dried salt spray of the deck boards as Naxos rushes towards us, the white stacked tiers of the town easing to a human scale as we approach.

At Naxos the nuns leave us. A Greek family and a French one appear on deck and rush for the nuns' chairs. The Greek family wins and gives the chairs to the granny and the slob son. The French family go off to buy drinks from the deck bar as we pull out of Naxos and turn north towards Mykonos, already in plain view, with Delos beginning to stand out in the channel between it and Tinos, when up the iron stairs from the lower deck come two familiar figures in T-shirts with sawn-off sleeves, lumpy tattoo-infested shoulders swelling, medallions glinting, scalps pink under shorn dark-rooted bleached stubble.

I keep my head turned but I'm still assuming it's a coincidence when they start to stroll along the starboard rail towards me, stopping occasionally to lean over the side, then coming on again slowly but persistently, not starting the swerve that would take them round my chair. There's no-one behind me, just the shuttered section of the bar. Everyone in front not sleeping or reading or playing chess is facing the way we're going. I'm still in my prone position, shoulder wedged against the rail, legs up on the chair in front, stiffening as I grasp what might be coming, and even as I flex my legs and using the chair for leverage up-end it in their path before sprinting across the deck, hurdling the chess players and diving into the ladies', I think I might be over-reacting. The Greek woman who freezes before the mirror, lips pouting, lipstick in hand as I dash past her into a cubicle certainly thinks so but probably puts it down to something I ate.

Inside the cubicle I lean against the partition till my heartbeat slows. This puts everything in doubt.

I hear the Greek woman leave. Time passes. Someone else comes in and goes into the cubicle next to mine. It's not unknown for a Greek man to use the women's loo when the men's are taken. In the old days it happened all the time.

I crouch down and see sandals and a coloured cotton hem. The gypsy child. I flush the loo and open the door. Her mother is standing waiting by the basins. I wash my hands, taking my time, and the child comes out. As she stands beside me figuring out which of the many new varieties of tap we have here I smile and lean across to help her. Then I muster my Greek and ask her mother where they're going. She answers in an unfamiliar accent I can't make out but I keep smiling and trying, reciting with an inflexion the names of islands in the group as I hold open the door for them and we exit together.

They're there, standing to one side of the door as we walk past, but with the announcement coming over the address system in Greek and in English that we'll shortly be arriving at Mykonos my new friends go straight to the stairs to the lower deck and I go with them.

Down the iron staircase we go, across the deck, through the lounge, past the ranks of airline seats, people standing up now, pulling out suitcases, unfolding buggies, handing out babies, helping old people, shouldering their way out into the crush. The next companionway is crowded as passengers converge on the last descent to the hold. The gypsies are way ahead of me now, a dozen people between us. I don't know where the men are but for the moment it doesn't matter. In the gloom and clamour of the hold I spot my elected saviours again, their brilliant colours lifting them out from the off-whites and faded denims of the mass. They are making their way towards the stern where their destination is unmistakable, a brightly painted truck, its framework covered in tarpaulins. The husband is already at the wheel. He opens the passenger door and takes the child from her mother then helps her up, while I slip unseen round the back and find that the tarpaulin hangs half-open like a curtain.

I get one foot on the crash bar of a Mercedes, grab the tailboard and haul myself up. It's chickens. I did hope it wouldn't be chickens. They set up a startled cheeping but probably not enough to be accounted suspicious chicken behaviour. I cling to the nearest crate as we roll off onto the quay and hope they won't peck my fingers. Sun shines through the thin nylon weave. The smell is awful. I'm safe, sort of.

My hope is they'll stop somewhere before they start their round of the island, chanting their pitch through a souped-up loudspeaker, *I have chickens, chickens I have, little birds, many little birds, little chickens, come, fine chickens, come I have chickens*, the spiel I hear so often when this van heads out to an area of upscale holiday homes whose owners, visiting for three weeks from the finance desks of Frankfurt and Zurich, seem unlikely customers. I often think the gypsies could use a marketing consultant.

We're heading out of town, but soon we're braking and the tyres crunch over loose ground. The engine stutters and falls silent, and over the snap and crack of cooling metal there are voices, women's and children's as well as men's. When my family have climbed down I wait for a moment then raise the curtain. We're parked in a field beside two other vans whose occupants have turned from watching two horses grazing.

My family joins the others and as they cross together to look at the horses I drop to the ground. Smells of earth, lentisk, hot metal and fresh manure replace chicken pee. We're just off the road that circles the coast. Stooping, I skulk behind a dry stone wall, then straighten up and step out onto an empty road, a road which stretches off between tangled gold-brown verges back towards the town. I set off walking quickly and only when I'm out of sight round a bend do I ask myself where I'm going and why.

I'd like to call Gabriel but I've rather gone off my phone. When at last I locate it at the bottom of my bag it comes up smeared in toothpaste. This ought to humanise it, awaken my nurturing instincts, and I do tackle it with antibacterial wet wipes, but it's alien and capable of anything, like giving away my position. Osama bin Laden, Radovan Karadzic, were tracked by their cell phones. At the touch of my finger the sky could fill with stealth bombers and the fields with men disguised as trees dragging themselves towards me on their elbows. I should ditch it. Or calm down and make my peace with it and with the spirit of this place between places, because I have quite lost my hold on the Greek way of being.

So. I'm on a parched bank by an empty road. There are scents and sights to calm and to stimulate, overdoses of each, aromatic wafts from the *rigani* I've just sat on, stands of sculptured acanthus across the road stiffly silhouetted against the sea and sky, a bank of fennel, a ship leaving the harbour, behind me bare hills and over there the stark white cubes of the town, its perfect outline fuzzed and broken by new building, but hot, hard, Cycladic, real. I'm still holding the phone. I turn it on. Nothing happens, not even Gabriel, still lost in space.

Aversion therapy. Examine the phone. Consider the wonderful invention it is, listing for instance, one's CONTACTS. Not a triumph of lateral thinking, but a stumble in that direction. I have the breakdown service on Kryptos, the Health Centre, the garage, my dentist, the bank, a couple of friends back in Britain who visited me here. I have Gabriel but not Lucas, who is in the notepad back home with my house phone. Nor Raffy. The number he left me was a landline number in Athens.

So it's Gabriel or nothing. Gabriel who must, surely, be expecting me? I could text him. And say what? *Hi Gbrl, on rdsd smwhr on Mkns, poss U pick up?*

It might be more constructive to analyse my predicament. Did someone want me off the island, off the boat, off the face of the earth? If so, who from my stainless past and tangled but blameless present could that possibly be?

For answer comes a soporific chomping. A donkey is chewing an acanthus leaf as it watches over my shoulder a cruise ship gliding to its mooring in the strait. I tuck the phone back in with my toothbrush and walk on towards the fun capital of the Aegean.

Which is where, an hour later, I am, in their *patois*, at, although not of course having fun. Any leaning that way would have had to be aborted since we're in the chilliest of chilled bars in Little Venice, and my companions are as vivid and life-affirming as a row of sucked popsicles, the models, dressed to out-goddess Greece, contriving in flesh and blood a blankness that few sculptors achieve in marble. Marje the fashion editor is another thing altogether. Not blessed with symmetrical features she has dyed her hair blue-green to match her eyes which are on the swimming-pool side of swamp. Her garments are creature-of-the-deep things, round her neck cockle shells are strung on a rope of dried seaweed and from her ears hang mummified seahorses. Gabriel is wearing a scrunchy shell-pink shirt with mother of pearl buttons, a tiny pearl earring and dawn pink shades planted in his now rather coral-tending hair, while the rest of the crew, though not working the mollusc thing, are unarguable frigid style statements.

Gabriel called me. Right on the edge of town I was stopped in my tracks by plink-plink Christmas ballet music coming from my bag.

He had just picked up my message, he said, and was

at the port looking for me. We were still talking when he came into view, a moving landmark. Safe for the moment and grounded, I made him stop at the first on-the-quay, all-day tourist joint we came to.

For fuck's sake, Anna. He scowled at the day-trippers around us. *Five minutes and we're in a garden with upholstery* ***and*** *mint tea. Canaries. Cello concertos.* But to me at that moment trashy and crowded spelled safe. And I needed to know: did he send that text message? And no, of course he didn't.

So I started to tell my story and right off, before I could get to my brush with death on the tourist deck, he stopped listening. The phone. That scared him. He couldn't get beyond the phone. Who would use his name in such a way? I couldn't help there. I wanted him to focus on the why rather than the who, but he was at least bringing himself into the picture and this was productive. So I listed the possible *dramatis personae* – Marcus, Nico, Thanasis, Rebecca, Dimitris, a waiter – all the time thinking my end – and only then thought, uh, his end? Which was where he'd been all along. And then I told him about the guys on the ferry and he looked sceptical. And I became rather fraught and we both fell silent and he sat scowling at a lady stroking a small dog on a basket chair who looked at him nervously and picked up the dog, although he wasn't seeing either of them, and I thought that maybe I was wrong about the guys on the boat.

I've seen Raffy, I said finally to give the dog a break.

So have I, he snarled, dog now cowering in its owner's skirt folds while his hand came up to mangle his hair.

And *Lucas.*

Ah. Hair still getting attention. It was for him, I thought, to open up.

On the boat, he said at last. *Raffy was on the boat coming back from Kryptos.*

He had come up to him at the deck bar. It had been like just a regular meeting of brothers whose paths cross occasionally by happy accident in the free-wheeling style they'd grown up with.

Gabriel told Raffy that he'd been with me and that I'd told him he was in Greece. Just the sight of him seemed to confirm normality so he waited for Raffy to tell him an everyday story of island-hopping, looking up old friends, even the start of a rapprochement. But Raffy told Gabriel he was lying low and also – a side issue, he thought – that he'd seen Lucas in circumstances that confirmed a suspicion he'd had. He told him not to tell their father, should he be in touch, that he was here. When they got to Mykonos he added a caution. Not to tell me they'd met. First he had something to check out. Then he was going back to Kryptos to try to see me.

Try to? He's been watching me. He's been to the house.

Yes, but he said you weren't there and it wasn't safe to hang about. The house was being watched.

It made sense. That was the day before we met. *OK. You've had a boat trip's worth of conversation to my quickie behind the harbour loo. What's it all about?*

Much like we guessed. That incident. That day. I waited. Gabriel was reverse-mangling what in another person might be a quiff. *He'd ballsed it up then, he said. Played safe. It hadn't worked.*

What had he ballsed up? What hadn't worked?

For Christ's sake Anna, I don't know, he's as tight as a cat's ass. My guess is he's decided to play boy detective. He said in case he didn't see you I was to call you a week from then and tell you . . . well, just tell you he was trying to put things right. And that he sent his love.

Great. That makes me feel . . . patronised.

Then let's get the hell out of here. You can take it out on my colleagues. Patronise the fuck out of them – they won't notice – but at least give them credit for their choice of hangout.

But they had moved on from the cello and canary joint by the time we got there and for the past half hour I have been trying to find common ground with people who order cocktails to colour co-ordinate with what they're wearing – coral, aquamarine, pistachio, aubergine. Soon we're going to have dinner somewhere that their on-the-spot fixer knows about. He'll be coming shortly to pick us up.

It's heavy going. And since I haven't been on Mykonos in a long time I would like to have a look round. Besides I could use a change of top being still in the grubby T-shirt I pulled on a lifetime ago. After all, nothing's going to happen to me in these crowded streets.

I tell Gabriel I'm going to look in the shop opposite, then exit from its side door and walk along the market street past the gold shops lying in wait for the wealthy cruise ship clientele and the tourist shops festooned with Mykonos T-shirts. In a side street I spot a doorway display of white cotton and inside find a few things to try on, settling for a loose top with shoestring straps. I tell the girl I'll keep it on and while I'm near the mirror put on some lipstick and let down my hair, then in the next shop buy some bargain-bin earrings. I'm heading back to join the group when I spot a shop with a news stand. I spin the foreign news section, past *Le Monde* and *Frankfurter Allgemeine* to the English papers, one, two, three days old. I see a face I know and a headline, British Journalist Stabbed on Greek Island.

As I hunt for change someone comes up on the other side of the stand and starts to turn it forcefully. Headlines in Albanian, Serbian, Russian, French and German whizz past and leave her unmoved. The asymmetric fringe and the pistachio halter top I have seen before. She's one of the fashion assistants. From the other direction comes a familiar mophead object of desire, looking noticeably older. I step back behind a magazine rack. They kiss. They've done this before. She has something to tell him.

She's here, she says. I snatch a magazine and turn pages while a silence lengthens.

Alone?

Gabriel says they're not in contact.

Between copies of *Hello* and *Côté Sud* I can see his face twist into an unbecoming scowl. She lays a hand on his arm. He plucks it off. He turns and walks away.

Once he's out of sight I go to the counter and pay for the newspaper. The girl is still there, staring into space. I tuck the paper into my bag in case Gabriel sees and reacts to the headline – think furtive, everyone else does

– and get back to the bar just before her. She looks briefly at me and sits down. Then we all stand up again because Toyboy – his name is Kurt – turns out to be the fixer, and he's come to lead us off to dinner. He does not or is careful not to notice that a new member has joined the group.

At the restaurant I'm seated between Marje and the girl in the pistachio top whose name is Shannon.

So, honey, says Marje, *you've gone native Gabe tells me. Give me half a chance and I'd be here too. Me and the goat. Chickens maybe. When I'm through being Über-Leutnant to these airheads perhaps that's just what I'll do. Tell me, what did you pay for your property?* She wants to know all about Greek property law, the taxes, the things to look out for, the risk of coming unstuck. *Maybe I'll have a look-round while I'm here.*

I tell her Mykonos might not be the best place to look as it has some of the most expensive real estate in the Eastern Mediterranean. She takes the point and starts to question me about Kryptos. If there's time to spare, she says, thinking, I imagine, on the hoof, she might come over and check out the situation there. She asks for my phone number. When she turns to talk to the models about tomorrow's schedule I try to break the ice with Shannon.

Is this your first time in Greece?

She bristles, ready to refute that then hesitates. *Yes*, she says unconvincingly.

And what do you think of it?

It's neat. The windmills and that.

Will you be going anywhere else?

She looks around anxiously as if she'd rather consult someone before replying, and indeed Kurt has heard this. He leans across, meets my eye, lowers his voice in practised just-us-two style and tells me that the girls don't know it yet but when the shoot is finished he is borrowing a friend's cabin cruiser to take them on a quick island whirl. *Though we may only get as far as Kryptos.*

Neat, I say. I'm sure now that if he knows who I am and if that matters – if I am the she who is here – he did not previously know me by sight. When there's a move among the fashion crew to head on somewhere else I'm set to opt out, but fortunately Marje vetoes their plans.

You know how you are without sleep, she tells the models. *Holocaust victims in beachwear is not a good look.* And as she shepherds them away Kurt strides off on his own.

Gabriel and I find a café in a little boxed-off square with flowering yuccas and a French tour group being briefed on tomorrow's schedule.

I called the hotel, Gabriel says.

Hotel?

You know. Place for sleeping in? I booked you a room.

Ah. Thanks.

So . . . tomorrow . . . how are you getting back? You haven't gone off boats?

These are islands, Gabriel, there's always going to be a boat. I spoon foam off my cappuccino and watch the tour group. I'm trying to think outside the box. *I know – I don't have to go directly to Kryptos.* I'm thinking holiday travel, island hopping. *I could go to Tinos then pick up the*

Sea Jet from Rafina and get back that way. They won't be watching these boats. By 'they' I mean person or persons unknown, with or without tattoos, real or imaginary.

A decision. Halfway house to being back in control. We finish our coffee and walk down to the seafront where we find a still-open shipping office and I buy a ticket for the morning boat to Tinos. Which leaves just the Gabriel conundrum.

Ever since the group broke up I've been on the point of telling him about the overheard conversation at the news stand, but against that I've remembered that Kurt was at the café on Kryptos where I sat with a strangely abstracted Gabriel who showed no sign of knowing him

Eight o'clock breakfast, says Gabriel as we reach the hotel. *Remember to lock your door.*

I double-lock it and stare at the bed with its crisp single sheet and bedspread with naive fish motif. I'm supposed to **sleep**?

I take off my cheap earrings and lay them on the chest of drawers, take off my new top and put it on the chair with my other clothes, take out my creased nightdress and get into it, take out my toothbrush and clean my teeth. If only I could clean space enough in my head to invite drowsiness. I need a book.

The newspaper. I dig it out of my bag, stack the pillows and settle back to scan the front page. John Burnham was his name, one-time chief crime reporter, later tabloid columnist, recently retired. The slightly familiar name gives way to a slightly familiar biography. His column was a platform for faux-benign questions, questions about asylum seekers and people he is careful not to call benefit scroungers, questions it plans to answer once it has broken down the resistance of its readers. His most recent claim to fame was to be pelted with used nappies by a group of single mothers as he left a sports club dinner where he was guest speaker. But before all that he had a decent history of pulling off some major exposés. He has two children from his first marriage and it is his second wife Elaine who is pictured standing at the spot by the harbour where his body was found.

Paradise Lost, says a subhead over her lament for the idyll that is not to be. Police inquiries are centring on illegal immigrants, most likely a simple mugging strenuously resisted.

John hadn't an enemy in the world, says Elaine.

I yawn. I turn off the light. I sleep.

The fashion crowd don't eat breakfast in public. *It's gross*, Gabriel mimics. They have fruit juice and vitamin pills in their rooms.

He and I are consuming croissants and coffee on the hotel terrace, set into the hillside like a dress circle overlooking the sweep of the harbour below and cueing a wider view of things than I've managed lately.

The pink euro? Where does that come in? Unless I was very much mistaken those were female models.

In his off time, he explains, he is taking some mood shots in key locations using guys he finds in the street. *I'll sell them to a men's mag or maybe to go with a travel piece.*

Isn't that complicated? With the magazine paying your expenses.

Not at all. It's a straight fee and I pay my own way.

Still, a grey area there. I monitor him now for grey areas. For instance, he hasn't told me that he spoke to Lucas.

He waits while I check out then walks me down to the harbour. En route I remember the newspaper story. We sit on a wall and I dig it out of my bag. Gabriel is unexpectedly affected by the face of this man he has seen so intimately and only in death. I who saw and reacted to him in life am more detached. For me the picture of his wife standing by that section of pavement, the sea alongside, the ferry terminal behind, the café opposite, is much more affecting, the prospects they shared, the beauty all around untouched by her loss, but more even than the untouched beauty and her loss I am affected by my reaction to the port area. The idea of disembarking there fills me with dread.

Change of plan. I'm not going to Tinos. I'm going to Delos.

Delos? Why?

First I love Delos and second I can hop on a different boat there that will bring me back to Kryptos. And not to the port. Straight into Karistos.

Straight back here first, however, being the excursion boat it is and Mykonos being the second leg of the excursion.

If I fake an attack of sunstroke they'll let me stay on board. I just want to avoid a welcome committee. It's the port on Kryptos that really spooks me.

It's a thought.

It's a decision.

There's an excursion boat already boarding. As

Gabriel stoops into my private space for the parting double air kiss I have an impulse to clean up one of those grey areas.

When I get back I'll be seeing Lucas . . .

Give him my regards, he says walking away.

I go up on deck and find a seat in full sun. A deck, strangers, the sea, an island I'm leaving behind and another coming up where no complications can exist. So no worries. Like who got at my phone. Gabriel's phone. Both phones. Worst case scenario, neither.

A breeze swings my way wafting high factor Ambre Solaire. The smell of other people's holidays. I go with the flow.

12

In pairs and in clusters many older than average people dressed as white hunters are boarding with cameras and day packs. Small sleek French and Japanese, soft-skinned Anglo-Saxons, taller, huskier Americans.

There's a hush here on deck as if the space enclosed by sea, sky and islands is getting the same going over as the nave of a Gothic cathedral. A sussed, not a slack-jawed, going-over. And there's something else. Maybe it's because they're not that self-involved that they give out an oddly admonitory sense of working to a fraction of their capacity. A shout of *man overboard* or perhaps a fouled propeller or a snatched bag, and they'd be swallow-diving, hurling life jackets, nailing the poor bastard in an arm-lock. It's competence I'm picking up. And basking in. The under-used competence, I think, of people who are never going back to work.

Two American seniors sit next to me after checking whether I speak English and if the seat is free. Martha and Bill are from Phoenix Arizona, on week eight of their golden wedding holiday of a lifetime. *We call it that now*, says Bill, *but we already talked with the company about next year.*

Mykonos receding, they pry politely into my circumstances. I tell them that for now I'm living on Kryptos.

Then you can be our guide, Bill says as we tie up in the island's little harbour.

I'm sure Anna doesn't want two old-timers trampling on her heels.

I'd be glad to, I lie, *if I was, you know, half-way reliable? But I'm rocky on dates. Not a numbers person.*

Bill's silence tells me he is that person.

I **can** *tell you that the Roman era villas with the mosaics are up there on the way to the theatre, and the Sacred Lake and the Lion Terrace are along to the left near the café, and if you want to see the museum as well you'll have your work cut out.*

Lizards dart out of our path as we make our way along towards the oldest part of the site.

Just give us the gist, honey, says Bill, fanning himself with his hat. *What were those Romans doing in that crowded quarter?*

Goodness. I'm sure you've read the guide book.

Sure we've read the guide books, France, Spain, Italy, San Marino, Mozart's Vienna. At Athens we finally packed 'em all up and mailed 'em off home. I mean we're busy. We're travelling. We're taking it in through the skin. The folks who write those things, they're talking to their tribe. For me it's like if I gave them a cost projection and asked for a quick reaction. With the guide books it's like OK, I don't expect to know everyone's name here, but the ***things*** *they tell me I need to know . . . ?*

We're passing the first of the Culture Ministry's signs.

OK. The Agora of the Competaliasts. I know what an agora is but what in hell's name is a competaliast?

I haven't the faintest idea.

See? So if you could just give us the drift?

We are walking along the Stoa of Philip V which we all know because it says so in the general direction of the Sacred Lake.

You know about Leto? The nymph? Who gave birth to Apollo and Artemis here? Which is why the island is sacred?

Is Leto the one with the bull?

Bill, you know that's Europa.

Leto is the one that Hera pursued to prevent her giving birth to Zeus's children. Poseidon summoned up Delos from under the waves and anchored it just in time. She gave birth by the Sacred Lake which is just along here. Holding onto a palm tree which I think you'll find is also here.

If only I'd had a palm tree to hold onto when I was having the twins.

You have twins? Well, there you are. This is your place.

If that's the lake where's the water?

It got to be a malarial swamp. They filled it in. And over there is the Lion Terrace. If you visited Venice you probably saw the lion outside the Arsenal they nicked from here.

My voice reciting second or third-hand facts is losing out to the narratives of the professional guides.

It was small, it was sacred, then it got to be about money.

And politics. Religion, politics and banking. Everything you're here to get away from. If I were you I'd attach myself to an English-speaking tour group then split when you've had enough. Their eyes, still on mine, turn polite. I'm killing the magic. *Look, it's the birthplace of Apollo and Artemis, the most spine-tingling place in the Aegean. Don't waste too much time thinking.*

That's just fine, honey. You go off now and do your thing. Nice to meet you.

I head off, happy to be on my own, passing the Lake House and the Temple of Anius to the Agora of the Italians. I'm walking down there, lingering over the chiselled names, the craftsmanship, the unsettling line breaks, the self esteem, the eye to the future, rewarded daily as we children of barbarians pause, aeons later, to puzzle them out, when I hear ahead of me a French tour group with a German one coming up behind. A language sandwich threatens. I veer off swiftly and glance up at the slopes of Mount Kynthos. A climb would clear my head. But, passing the refectory, I spot an empty outside table, park my bag and go inside to order a latte and a muffin. The duty Adonis tells me he'll bring them out.

When he does he wants to talk. He is one of the pony-tailed, sleepily attentive welcome-to-my island guys who account for most of the marrying out that keeps the Cycladic bloodstock refreshed and provides a steady supply of resident English, French and German teachers as well as instructors in yoga, Pilates and feng shui. He welcomes me to his island. I tell him I live on Kryptos. Ah, he says, so does his friend Vasilis whose mother Sophia runs a guest house in Karistos. Sophia, the Hollanders' landlady, who had no room for Lucas. And whose son spat after him in the street.

Big trouble on Kryptos, he says.

My heart skips a beat but it turns out he is talking about the dead journalist. I ask him where he lives, expecting him to say Mykonos. The old tradition that no-one must be born or die in this sacred place is strong in my head.

Up there, he replies, jerking a thumb towards the slopes above the stadium. *Every morning I see the sun come up over this beautiful island and every evening I see it go down.* It crosses my mind that he may not always do this alone. An unexpected night on this island might be an offer no girl could refuse.

Two English girls arrive and he goes off to welcome them to his island. I drink my coffee and pick at the muffin, distracted from my hazy plans by the background hum and low key euphoria of a lot of good people let loose in the past. Break over, I'm hesitating outside the museum, squinting up at Mount Kynthos, when some people come out, one of them familiar. It's Raffy.

I step back into the shadow of the wall but he has seen me. He hesitates. He saw me move away. Are we kosher here? His call. He makes a decision and moves towards me.

Hallo Anna. Minimal inflection in his voice.

Business trip? I nod towards the museum.

Are you alone?

I am. You?

How long have you got?

Two hours before the boat leaves.

OK. You walk up there, nodding towards the path that leads up Mount Kynthos. *I'll follow you.*

I climb in silence, following the path, a certain frisson in this. A man passes, coming the other way, not looking up or greeting me. At the Sanctuary of the Syrian Gods I stop and look out over the baked, arid, and but for the lake palm, treeless site, the honeycombed roofless merchant houses below, the glinting marble columns around the lake area, the archaeologists' stark quarters, the quay with its moored cruise boats, the craggy outline of Tinos beyond. The frisson is wearing off. The view seems more compelling than anything we might have to say to each other.

Raffy far behind has stopped to talk to the man who passed me. By the look of it they are exchanging more than pleasantries. This feels tedious and married, so I look away, obeying the imprecation in the book of marital etiquette to give one's partner space. Etiquette now made redundant, I remind myself, and not by me. I look again. He's older, I can see that. The outward things – grace of movement, thick dark straight hair, look of purpose, possibility of distraction – still tick the boxes. I no longer know what I feel about him but I haven't gone off him. I don't know him though, and that, bizarrely, is the most familiar thing of all. When in our life together did I begin to realise I had married a stranger, a stranger I had known since childhood?

The man is continuing his descent. As Raffy starts to climb towards me I look away, and when he comes alongside me he acts the part of a person perusing the ruins, perhaps for the benefit of the man below, perhaps for some other watcher – a thought that sets me scanning the people filing along the level ground and picking their way up through the streets of the Roman quarter. When I turn to face him his expression is unreadable.

I have something to tell you.

A buzzard is circling in the thermals above the summit of Mount Kynthos. I pull back from that but when I look at him he averts his eyes.

It was because of me that your parents were killed.

A buzzard or a vulture. There are vultures in Greece, but perhaps not in the Cyclades. He is facing me now but I won't look at him. My eyes settle on the slope above. I feel dizzy. I focus on a wall and a lizard looks back. If only there was a flat field or a brick wall I might be able to concentrate. How clever of Raffy to tell me this where I can't take it in.

He's fingering something, a pebble or a pottery shard, preparing to expand.

I confided in them. In him, rather. Evan. He must have followed it up or told someone. So they silenced him. Them.

They hit a tree.

Do you believe that?

And no I didn't, at the time, believe that. Except that they did. They hit a tree.

I look down at the streets of roofless houses, streams of people weaving in and out as if in some archaic dance ritual. I try to think about the owners of the houses, the merchants. I try to think about the people down there visiting the houses. In commerce too, some of them. I try to think about commerce. I think about people dying. The house owners died two thousand years ago.

I finally focus on what he said and face him with it. *They?*

This would seem to be the crux. But it strikes him as unreasonable. *I can't . . . I don't . . .*

Why can't you, why don't you? More to the point why didn't you? What the fuck is this all about? I look round to call in on my side the sweet reason of the wider world. I see vultures, voids, ruins, strangers, ghosts.

He is looking reproachful. *I couldn't risk you acting on what you would have known.*

You might have let me make up my own mind on that. Life is dangerous. There are other risks. I've been dealing with a few.

What do you mean?

Where would I start? *It was the afternoon and I was weeding under an olive tree.* Perversely I start to experience it again, the painful crouch, the tannin smell of crushed olive leaves, the sinus-zapping eucalyptus, the fleck of glaze on the shard I've just spotted, the voice as banal, initially, as a radio in the background. With the three people I've loved best in the world all now screaming for my attention my brain opts to go for the diversionary jackpot. It was him. The man who came about the home extension. He and the mystery driver, one and the same. And I've done nothing about it.

Raffy is waiting but not watching me. He too has gone off somewhere in his head. I return doggedly to my thought train. I'm an observer, not a doer. A doer would have passed on what she overheard. A fully-functioning busy-body would have risked death rather than live with uncertainty, whereas I have rather feasted on it, using it both to stimulate and to satisfy all my senses. And is this the time for self-analysis?

I look again at Raffy. His role as sightseer is wearing thin. He moves off then turns back, paces on the spot. In his eyes he is the one with the problem. He looks strung out, edgy, out-of-here. As Gabriel said, we are two almost of a kind. And where is all this getting us? I long to talk facts but know that for now I'll only find evasion. And then I remember the marble figurine and feel a rush of healthy anger.

How can you be so disingenuous? In light of your surprise parcel . . .

My what?

But a shout – *Anna! Hey there!* – makes us turn. My companions from the boat are struggling towards us up the path, Bill raising his voice to hold us here until he can complete the climb. It's the shout that drives away the unicorn, the rifle click that startles the stag.

Like they say, he shouts, *it's a small world.* He saves his breath and comes on. *We took your advice, honey.* He stops again. *We're going for the big picture, and my what a picture!*

I move across to meet them at the top of the path. *Martha, Bill . . .* I start the introduction over the sound of Bill's laboured breathing but already I know what's happening. I turn and he has melted into the hillside. *I was about to say 'meet my husband' but I guess he had a date.*

Under her visor Martha looks politely incredulous. I follow the line of her gaze towards the empty skyline. Even the ruins run out here. *What does he do, dear?*

Who's to say what an archangel does? One moment off

about his dark doings in the bad places of the world, then, suddenly, ubiquitous.

The vulture, griffin, whatever, wheels out over the sea as if there's sulphur in the updrift and Martha is assessing me. *Honey . . . are you Adventists?* She turns and looks at Bill, catching his breath while he pretends to examine a wall, his breathing the loudest thing around, and asks me *sotto voce* if I'll take his arm to help him over the loose stones of the descent. She can manage just fine. And this uncomplicated interdependency gets to me and I have to fight down a couple pang. So I turn my back on another failed meeting and in the cosy embrace of their assumptions, that we're all headed the same way, descend with them to the theatre and beyond to the houses of the merchants.

The mosaics of Delos. Dionysus riding a panther, what else would you have on your floor? How much easier to empathise with the citizens of 3rd century BC Delos than with the 21st century laminate layers of suburbia. I'm OK now. But it's here at the House of the Masks that a part of my brain finally twangs loose and starts to act normal. My parents were killed. How doesn't matter. Why is unimaginable. If he's right then the whole now you see me, now you don't performance may not only be justified, it is surely to be respected, and possibly even right. Self reproach overwhelms me again.

We've reached the harbour area and Martha tells me she and Bill are going to hang about down here until the boat leaves. They'll see us later.

I let the 'us' pass as well as my plan to leave on another boat and find a space on one of the benches in the shade behind the gift shop while I try to focus on what Raffy just told me. But the news refuses to fill my head. A boyish misadventure on a Greek island. A Saab skidding on the road out of Oxford. How could they be linked? I'm concentrating but I can't shut out the chatter of the people around me. What's wrong with me? I find it easier to eavesdrop than to focus on the news that my parents may have been murdered.

There's a voice coming through the chatter, English with an overlay that sounds familiar. A monologue on a mobile from the other side of the building. That slightly studied pronunciation. It's Lisa Dunmore.

I think he's up the hill right now. Don't worry. He won't get on a boat without me seeing him. But my guess is he's staying overnight.

There follows a long silence as she listens to the response, then *OK, will do*, and she ends the call. I hear her but I can't see her, nor she me.

I have to assume that this is about Raffy and his missing-on-arrival performance that first day on Kryptos. That conversation has yet to take place. The person she was briefing was not, I imagine, on the island but surely en route. Kurt? If he was still on Mykonos he could be here very soon. As for Raffy, I don't know why he's here on Delos, but he will have a reason. As for his present whereabouts, there seems nothing for it but to climb.

The sun is at its hottest now, but Mount Kynthos is a mountain only in the romantic sense – for the ancients a designer mountain with its small peak offset, freeing up the flat ground for sanctuaries and associated shopping opportunities, the lower slopes rising at just the right gradient for a stacked housing development leaving Zeus and Hera, the presiding deities, just enough clear air above the mortals without the need for too much marble-hauling. As the track gives way to steps I stop to catch my breath. I sit on a wall and rummaging in my bag find Marcus's handkerchief with the flamboyant Gothic M, stained with my blood and Gabriel's sweat. I mop my forehead and see Raffy suddenly silhouetted against a white hot sky, hands screening his eyes as he looks towards Mykonos from which direction comes the faint but steady drubbing of rotor blades.

I'm at the top, trying to intuit his reaction to news of a manhunt building below, when he turns and sees me and hovers for the moment on the brink of a spontaneous reaction. We stand there, the sound building around us as the helicopter tilts and starts to rise as it approaches the mountain. Then he grabs me and pulls me into what a glimpsed sign tells me is the Sanctuary of the Egyptian Gods and pushes me down behind the wall while he reaches for an overturned wheelbarrow, lifts one end and signs to me to crawl under.

He joins me. The circumstances preclude conversation.

I pass the time reviewing my life so far. How it led to this. That dealt with, I proceed to what I know of Aegean helicopters, their nature and their purpose. Benign, usually, I believe, and horizontal, dashing across cloudless skies dropping weekenders onto the apron between their tennis courts and their swimming pools, scooping up scattered wind surfers, women in premature labour and half-flayed holiday-makers who came off their hire bikes on a gravel bend while wearing shorts and singlet. This one may be an exception.

It hangs above our galvanised love nest as we experience the intimacy of shared shrinking tendons, seared shoulders, crushed knees and twisted spines, and when at last it moves off we crawl out incapable of speech, and lie there letting body parts creep back into place.

After some time we sit up. Raffy produces water and I offer the handkerchief. Far below the helicopter has landed on flat ground, close to the harbour and perilously close to a group of tourists who have scattered. Two men get out. They screen their eyes and stand looking up at the mountain. When they rotor stops turning they are set upon by the tourists.

I turn to Raffy to deliver my interrupted message.

Lisa Dunmore is watching for you. Down at the moorings. She spoke to someone who is coming here to find you. Maybe he just did.

There comes a puzzled silence.

Lisa Dunmore? I don't know what you're talking about.

13

Drinks anybody? Anna?

I open my eyes to legs the colour of butterscotch and, behind those, a sheet of moving water. I sit up. Diane puts an icy glass in my hand.

I'm on the deck of a yacht, they call it that, crossing at uncanny speed to Kryptos. In my bag is an unused ferry ticket to Tinos, in my head an aborted excursion leg to Karistos, but the Goddess of Expediency came up with a third solution and I have to say her way is better.

Raffy and I were sitting on the café terrace thinking our separate thoughts, a carafe of half drunk retsina growing tepid between us. Below us the last visitors were being reeled in by their waiting boats like a video interpretation of civilisation rewinding, the setting for the great epic from pregnant nymph to merchant banker now left lying for our sole instruction. And what was it telling us? I was grappling with that when the Texans arrived.

Oh look, it's Anna. Hi Anna! Alicia hailed me from the path below the café. Diane, Gregory and Steve were just behind.

It's OK, I told Raffy as they came up to join us. *Harmless rich Texans. Off a gin palace.*

Fresh from my practice in dissembling I introduced Raffy as Gabriel's brother, reasoning that since they hadn't known Gabriel was my brother-in-law there was no need for them to know that Raffy was my husband. Pointless perhaps but I was trying to cultivate the habit, and there was also the question of our marital status, at present hard to define. Which left them clear to offer me a lift home.

I was smiling, shaking my head, saying thanks but no thanks when Raffy accepted on my behalf. I looked at him. In his *loco parentis* voice – I remember that voice – he pointed out that the boats had gone. How else would I get home? The Texans took that as a yes and as we got to our feet he avoided my eye and nixed my non-compliance by accompanying us to the harbour, keeping the others between us, walking alongside Diane who, taking him for a Delos excavator, was telling him she just thought he had the best job in the world.

From the deck I watched him turn and walk away from my frosty farewell. Then, as the island shrank back to actual size, shrank him with it, re-focused and stretched out to rerun what had happened there.

With the helicopter gone Raffy and I had walked down from the mountain. Dishevelled (me), confused (me), subdued (both of us). The shift in our relative status – I an increasingly scruffy fake tourist, he a fabulous creature hunted by land, sea and air – did not lend itself to small talk. But over a carafe of retsina at the café we made a start.

First he told me what had happened on the night of his arrival on Kryptos. An hour into the journey he had been hailed on the tourist deck by a woman. To him a total stranger but according to her an old acquaintance of the family's from one of those long ago Kryptos summers.

She knew Claudia's name and Lucas's. She knew we boarded with Sophia. And she said she knew you. She said her boyfriend who was meeting her had texted to say they were to give me a lift to your place. You'd sprained an ankle and couldn't drive. You'd phoned to ask them. I thought it odd that you hadn't let me know that yourself, but then I thought perhaps you were sending out signals that you were in no hurry to see me.

We got into the boyfriend's car and it became clear we weren't going to Karistos. They told me there had been a land slip and the direct road was blocked so we had to go over the top of the island. We climbed up into the hills and we stopped at their house. She said she just wanted to drop off her travel bag then we'd be on our way. We went inside. She went off to another room and the boyfriend started to pour us some wine. I turned it down but he poured it anyway.

Nothing about it felt right. He was standing there with his back to me, doing things with glasses and a decanter. I got the idea he was going to spike my drink and I'd never get out of there. And then it came to me who she was.

Go on.

She'd told me her name on the boat but it meant

nothing to me. It was not the name that finally came into my head.

Which was?

Debby Donnachy.

So . . . Marcus was right.

Marcus?

I'll tell you later. Debby Donnachy is the person who is down at the moorings watching for you.

Well I walked away from her then and I guess I can do it again.

How did you do that?

Went to the bathroom and climbed out the window. Hid in an olive grove then walked back down to the port.

You said you remembered who she was?

Yes, well, I had just a vague impression of her, but that was enough to remind me who her boyfriend was. Her boyfriend that year.

And?

His name was Zac. He was . . . well, my father was away and he was hanging around my mother.

I remember him. He was the guy who took your mother to the party the night you went missing.

At which he stopped talking. Talking, moving, breathing for all I knew. And I saw what was up. What he'd been telling me came from fresh experience. The old stuff was secondary to that, relying, I thought, on buried recall. He'd started in on that buried stuff and Id bounded on ahead with a shovel.

Reproach dropped from the skies and hunkered down round our table. The shift from fluent, slightly feline, on top of nearly everything man I married to sullen stilted person with a problem was a speeded-up version of what had gone before. And what I felt then, and felt strongly, was my own disinclination, my refusal, to leave the world of sunlight for another visit to those Stygian depths.

I was letting this work through when a man came out of the museum and, seeing us, came over. He was the man Raffy had spoken to on the Sacred Way.

Jean-Paul, he said reaching out a hand.

Anna, said Raffy. No helpful tag, no *my wife*.

He was an archaeologist from the French School working on the island, he told me. Told me because I asked. Someone had to say something, but with Raffy muffled in non-communication obviously not a lot, and he respected that and left. And when he'd gone Raffy made an effort to pull himself together. He told me Jean-Paul was an old friend he was staying with on the island. From there, waxing practical like his brother the night before, he said he was sure he could find me a bed. But with the mention of that he became anxious again, and for my part I needed to put distance between us. I was already looking forward to sleeping on the hillside above the stadium, pleasurably anticipating the smell of baked earth and stone, the rustle of lizards in the grass.

And then, borne in on a propitious but aggravating wind, came the Texans.

Leaning against the rail I sip the icy cocktail Diane has handed me, something with pomegranate juice, mint leaves and gin, and return to the present. I glance at my watch. A bare ten minutes have passed. I'm facing portside and the view is a bit of a puzzle, Kryptos and its neighbouring islands end-on to the port side and getting no bigger while Tinos, when I turn my head, looms large to starboard.

I point this out to Diane.

Change of plan, she says brightly. *Greg wants to go to Tinos. You don't mind, do you?*

The Goddess Expedia tells me no, I don't.

Tinos is the home of the wind god, Aeolus, and at the moment he's not doing a lot. The sea is millpond calm, not a problem when you don't have a sail. Sail, no sail, it's all one to me. Had I been born a Viking I'd have been that Viking who dropped out and planted turnips.

On the other hand, the Ithaca mindset, who is not in thrall to that? The voyage for the voyage's sake, the ports to be entered for the first time, with such pleasure, with such joy. And when you're the one doing the entering, increasingly immoderate on the joy front, I'd have thought. The pleasurable perfumes, the Phoenician markets, the amber . . . the reward that is not the point . . . might it not go a bit wrong there? We're in a reward society now, how does that translate?

I'd guess, even for a Texan with prospects, it's those perfumes, those markets you carry in your head as you approach an island. But the Phoenicians have fled with the amber and the perfumes, the mother-of-pearl, the coral and the ebony, and now there are pizzas and postcards, so . . . anti-climax? Or just a new island to conquer. As the marina comes into sight with Russian oligarchs and Dutch financiers jostling for moorings are you the invader, the successful invader with the coolest ship, or do you just park and go and look for a drink?

I've no idea. And on the brink of stamping Greg as a guy with a boat instead of an imagination I see that this limp attempt to get inside one male brain is just another stab at the halfway house of Raffy

So. Tinos. Island of sculptors, pilgrims, dovecotes. Home of the wondrous icon of Panayia Evangelistria and her church. Above us the horned peak of Examburgo with its Venetian *kastro*. Below that the basket weavers' village of Volax. I met a man once in Volax, an old man, who told me how, as a child, he'd walk the long road down to the port with a consignment of baskets bound for Smyrna to become packaging for figs. That was an Ithaca moment. So Tinos, yes, I'm well disposed to Tinos.

We moor along the coast from the town, not in a marina. A taxi is waiting. Greg called ahead, Diane explains. He wants to go back to Pyrgos and look at a piece of sculpture he saw on his last visit. He's been haunted by it ever since, she says, and now he thinks he might buy it.

I volunteer to stay behind but Alicia has a headache and can't face the hairpin bends, so I squeeze in with the rest.

We're running along the spine of the island past isolated hamlets, rough tracks dropping off down to the coast while we head onwards and upwards, the islands around us building contours. We park on the edge of Pyrgos and walk quickly through, turning off from the square with its cafés and vast sheltering plane tree, Greg leading the way, anxious that he won't be able to find the workshop this time or that they will have packed up for the day. I'm happy to trail along, glad of an excuse to visit, in no hurry now to be on my own which will only throw up questions unanswered and unasked, the Cycladic figurine, the Lucas question, the provoking central mystery, and the question I never thought to ask: what has changed that made Raffy come here now?

Here it is! Greg pushes open a gate in a high wall which leads to a courtyard with plants, a sleeping dog, and outbuildings. The gallery at the far end of the main building has an open door set in an intricate carved marble arch. En route we pass a tall dusty window through which I catch a glimpse of the backs of two stiffly combed head, giants at a cocktail party going on inside.

A man in a leather apron comes out dusting his hands. He shakes Greg's hand, then goes along the line greeting each of us individually, saying his name, Aris, while Greg stands impatiently in the doorway, then leads us all inside.

Along one wall is a series of cropped marble arches framing openwork motifs – boats, birds, dolphins, a traditional feature of Tiniot front doors – in the centre of the room an intricately carved font, ready to go amongst its polystyrene packing, and ranged along the back wall chunks of unworked marble. Greg is gazing into an alcove where a small high window bends shafts of sunlight into the centre of the room to play on the font, leaving the alcove in relative shade, which leaves the thing in it to take shape slowly. A superb rendering of classical beauty. Classical male beauty and classical horse beauty. Alexander and Bucephalus.

How're ya gonna get it home, Greg?

Steve sounds hesitant, the others hang back. I'd guess Greg doesn't invite comment. Everyone is looking the other way, and while this is going on I'm thinking of the yacht which is, in yokel speak at least, a boat. Does it stay here, then? Or what?

Greg is pacing the floor looking at the piece from different angles. It is life-size but truncated, horse bust and man bust, horse neck arched, nostrils flaring, Alexander scanning the horizon, perhaps asking himself what mountains are those and whose land is this that he is about to add to his collection, and has he after all come further east than is altogether sensible.

If I had Greg's finances, depending on the source of these – regardless of the source of these – I'd buy it like a shot.

Greg is still pacing and frowning. I go out into the garden. A door to an outbuilding stands ajar and I push it open. A boy is in there smoothing off a rather creepy life-size marble hand holding a marble ball. A door knocker. He smiles shyly and I nod to him and admire the hand, but, through a window behind him, I can see across the yard and into a window of the giants' cocktail party room, where I catch in profile a familiar half-smile, a smile not fixed, a smile that I imagine arranges itself only when it is being observed. It's a *kouros*, near-twin of the one I saw in Marcus's house.

Aris comes out into the garden to smoke a cigarette and let Greg make up his mind. I tell him how much I admire his work and ask how many sculptors work here. In addition to the apprentices, he tells me, three others. Over his shoulder through a half-open door the *kouros* is watching me watching him. Aris stubs out his cigarette and Steve puts is head round the door. Greg is ready to do business. I follow Aris inside.

Where ya gonna put it, Greg? Diane wants to know. *Inside or out?*

Greg is still pacing, taking in all the angles. *Oh it's not for the ranch, it's for the boardroom. Beats the shit out of Rothko. It's saying* look, if we like the feel of your outfit don't squander whole armies trying to resist. *Plus it's art. Great horse. The pater's gonna love it.*

This resolved, Aris opens a fridge and brings out ice and a bottle of ouzo. He pours us all drinks.

To America, he says, raising his glass, *now that your cowboys have gone.*

Diane casts a nervous glance at Greg.

He also raises his glass. *To Greece*, he says. *Tighten up your public sector. Sack the lazy bastards. Then you'll be fine.*

We leave, the sun now lower in the sky, and meet a man coming up the path. It's Dimitris. We greet each other and he asks what I'm doing here. That's impossible to answer. *Visiting*, I reply. He, on the other hand will be buying things, I imagine, for his craft shop?

He takes time answering. *Some things, yes. Many interesting things Aris makes. Small things too. Ashtrays and weights for papers his boys make from cut-off of the marble. Is clever man, Aris.*

In the taxi retracing our journey along the backbone of

the island I'm wondering what our plans are. That is to say their plans, though I'm sure they'd like to think my views are being included. Another night is coming on and I have just the two tops, one stained, one crumpled, and no fresh underwear. I want to leave, want it so much now that I'm downgrading the risk factor of landing on Kryptos to something close to nil. The irritant of being with people not in the loop when you have unresolved problems to tackle is beyond vexatious. Which means, I think, that I've stopped running away.

Alicia is waiting for us, showered, changed, groomed, cocktails mixed. Steve is looking restless.

What's the plan, Greg? Back to Kryptos?

But Greg is no longer in sea-going mode.

Overnight Tinos. Kryptos tomorrow.

We're sleeping on the boat of course. They have room for me. Diane offers me a nightdress, a choice of tops and the run of her lingerie drawer.

Walking into town for dinner which, *pace* the Delos muffin, feels rather pressing, Greg wants to know the story of the famous church. He walks slowly, his posture softening to something approaching humble, in the guise now, I think, of earnest student. Perhaps he is hoping to find me the educator I am not, the second American to do that today. So I take a deep breath and tell him about the nun Pelagia in the Convent of Kekrovounia, whose vision of the Virgin telling her of her icon buried in a field resolved into one of the miracles of Orthodoxy when digging in the field turned up, not just the icon. but also the foundations of an early Byzantine church, the church of Panayia Evangelistria then built on the spot becoming – thanks to the icon and its history of miraculous cures – the premier place of pilgrimage in Greece. He listens attentively, not punctuating, not interrupting. And not putting out sceptical vibes.

As lovely and as haunted as is the island of Tinos, downtown at night has the feel of a busy commercial centre, and once we've put away *pastitsio* and *yemistes* at a crowded tourist restaurant I'm through with socialising. Fortunately Greg suggests an early night, and before long I'm climbing into a small but surprisingly comfortable bunk, weak lights flickering through the porthole, watery sounds shivering through the bulkheads. But once again I'm too strung up to sleep. Too much has happened too quickly. Too many places, too many people, too much information, not enough time to process it. The bed, the space, starts to feel claustrophobic, like a room in a multi-storey hotel between one journey and the next. I'm losing all grasp of my identity. And so I feel my way out into an open space that boat people will have a name for with doors leading off it, sleep sounds coming from behind them, but water sounds and a promise of starlight beyond. Barefoot I go up on deck.

The air is cooling at last and the pine-framed, pine-scented coast road has few cars passing at this hour. I settle into the space where the bows frame my back and, as the lights dance on the water and the Texans sleep below, let myself think about all that Raffy didn't tell me.

The night long ago when he went missing . . . that was plainly the start of it. But then not really the start of it, because I married a rational man, and only in the months around my parents' deaths, before and after those, did his personality change. So, something happened, something that brought with it a vow of silence and a duty to protect . . . whom? Lucas, Claudia, Michael, Gabriel?

Not Gabriel, surely. But then it was Gabriel who checked out an ordinary looking parcel and spoke the word *entrapment*. Who warned me against trusting. Who might have dealings, innocent or nor, with Kurt.

Not Michael, because Michael is always irrelevant due to being some sort of muscle-bound and unanswerable minor deity. But what do I know? That's ten-year-old stereotyping doing the talking.

Not Lucas, because I still like him and feel he wouldn't do wrong. Perhaps I need to look again at Lucas.

Not Claudia, because . . . because . . . because I find it difficult to think about Claudia.

I try to focus on the night he went missing but nothing marks it in my memory. It followed a day I've forgotten, a day that must have seemed like any other.

If not that night, then that summer? Lucas was away. Where? I was a child, I didn't question adult arrangements. He would have been looking at icons.

Zac I remember because, like Raffy and Marcus, I instinctively disliked him. But Claudia was following a different instinct. He was good looking in a louche sort of way, but perhaps that meant in a Claudia way. He flattered her. Many people did that and oddly for such a glamorous creature she was hugely susceptible. He flirted with her, quite flagrantly as I recall, my Puritanical eleven-year-old self rather disgusted with both of them. Raffy was hugely bothered by her behaviour in spite of his apparent detachment. She was his mother.

Raffy was different that summer. They all were, perhaps because Lucas was gone so long, perhaps because Claudia was being even less than usually motherly.

Gabriel corralled crabs and starfish, followed lizards, studied sea urchins with a particularly unwavering rigour while Raffy was gone for hours, exploring the unfrequented interior of the island. Late in the afternoon he'd turn up on the beach when the sky was turning to gold and we were about to leave, and so we'd stay on, following our promise to Claudia, while he swam far out, well beyond my father's notional life-saving reach. In the evening he'd be quiet, less than communicative. I remember that because it bothered me.

Where did his walks take him? I asked him once but got no clear answer. Just one route I know of because, walking with my parents one day, we saw him go up over the track past Aghios Konstandinos, the uninhabited monastery above Marcus's house and close to the house that was not to be Meriel's, close to where I met Lucas. I try to remember what lies on the other side. No tracks, no dwellings, just scrub, I think, and maybe a marble quarry. I don't believe I've been there.

Further inland on the central plateau there's a scant network of tracks and minor roads that branch out to the hill villages and connect with the seaward-tending routes that go to coastal settlements in less frequented parts of the island. Such as the track, recently a footpath, that leads close to Mavra Vrahia. I'm wondering now . . . had he seen something on one of those walks? Something he shouldn't?

I'm tired of speculating. I head for bed and sleep at last.

In the morning I'm desperate to be off. If they don't get going soon I'll catch a ferry.

Definitely, says Greg, we'll be leaving before noon, but now we are going to see this church and its miraculous icon.

So, this is what it's like to be beholden. Or am I just out of practice at group thinking? It's perfectly reasonable. He asked about the church, I told him and now we're going there. I'm the one who's out of step. His entourage must find it tolerable, attractive even, that he assumes his every impulse will be acted on. Perhaps he has a feudal sense of the plural self, as when talking up a Crusade or egging on the horde to see what lies west of the steppe. OK, he doesn't want to conquer the church, just look at it, but he certainly means that his friends should come along. Requires his friends to come along. I'm sure he thinks it's good for them, that they have no better ideas of their own, that he is a benign despot if a despot at all, but I'm equally sure the others know better than to disagree. Well, that's their problem.

We chat perfunctorily as we walk. The girls are friendly, but mainly want to know what's good to buy in the islands. Alicia says she liked the look of the shop I visited that day – Byzantiana? – and if they hadn't been called away she'd been going to look at it. Maybe she'll get another chance.

We're close to the port. Check out ferry times? I could do that. I'm walking between Steve and Diane when the idea becomes pressing enough to mention. Steve shakes his head. *Not a good plan.* Diane says that if Greg says we're leaving before lunch then we're leaving before lunch. *Unless you bug him*, says Steve. OK. Point taken.

Approaching the harbour which lies directly below the church, now dominating the waterfront from its hill, we see a small boat docking. On deck is a group of women dressed in black, remarkable after the bleached colour spectrum of Kryptos, their eyes raised towards the soaring white church on the hill. As we draw near some of them prostrate themselves on the deck, some make the sign of the cross. Greg is fascinated. He stops, which means we all do, to watch them disembark.

They are in an extreme state of emotion. One woman hands her bag to a friend and sinks to the ground. I don't want him watching this so I put my hand on his shoulder and turn him to face up the broad steep carriageway that leads to the church and, building on yesterday's attentive mien, start to talk about what he will see there, the pilgrims from all over Greece camping in the courtyard, the queues forming to see the icon. Another of those, I tell him, credited to Saint Luke.

It works. He crosses the road and as the others follow I tell him how on August 15th 1940, the day of the Dormition of the Virgin, the Virgin whose icon the church was built to house and in whose protection the whole Greek nation rests, the cruiser Elli was torpedoed by the Italians in Tinos harbour, prodding Greece into World War II.

He's listening. Quite raptly. Again a surprise. We're ascending slowly the broad steep avenue flanked by icon and candle shops and I'm running low on facts, but talking still in an effort to stop him noticing the strip of carpet that runs up the carriageway alongside the pavement. But now he's dodging back and forth between the icon shops and the faded but unmistakably upholstered strip of roadway. And inevitably, as we climb, he spots ahead of us a woman ascending on hands and knees. He speeds up then and slows just behind her. She is smartly dressed in a café-au-lait trouser suit with hair salon fresh and is no older than fifty. Her son in a well cut suit walks alongside carrying a man-sized candle and her daughter carries her bag. Greg walks behind them, fascinated.

Come on Greg, you're being gross, says Alicia coming up behind and plucking at his sleeve. He shakes her off.

Well I'm going ahead, I say and the other three join me.

Pilgrims are pouring into the lower courtyard, and up the staircase to the area in front of the church whose Italianate facade has a belfry and a frilly frontage of white marble. Blankets and pillows are spread out where pilgrims have passed the night sleeping or in prayer. Two christening parties are here, the children swathed in tulle and carrying tulle-wrapped flowers and candles. Only a few foreign tourists are about. This is the most Greek of islands. We pace apprehensively and at last Greg joins us, flushed, dusty and limping.

That's excruciating, he says. *My knees are all over carpet burns.*

*You **crawled**?* Alicia is aghast.

It's awesome. Heap powerful medicine.

Greg, you're in shorts.

I walk right away from them and go inside on my own.

Of course it's lunchtime by the time we get out of there. We descend again to the harbour front and Greg decides we'll eat where we ate last night. Under cover of washing my hands I go to a ticket office and find there's a boat to Kryptos at four. The yacht will be quicker if we don't delay but, acting on reasoned foreboding, I buy a ticket as insurance.

And after lunch Greg decides that we will visit the convent of Kekrovounia. No dilemma there. I've seen it. I tell him that, and say I will meet them when they come back. He does not respond but walks off with Alicia, heading for the taxi rank. Before they get there Alicia drops back to join me. She slips her arm through mine. *Greg's upset. He wants you to change your mind.*

What difference will it make to him if I stay here?

He doesn't like it when people split.

Really?

But there's something else she's trying to get out. *There's stuff he wants to ask you.*

Stuff?

You living here, he thinks you must know all about the islands. She gives my arm a squeeze. *Please? He's not too nice to be around when he has a setback.*

Oh for Christ's sake.

Greg holds the taxi door. I get in not looking at him. His phone rings. He answers, then moves away. When he climbs in his mood has changed. On the way up to the convent he doesn't talk but when we arrive and he again holds the door for me I catch him looking at me speculatively.

It's half past three. We're still at Kekrovounia. My need to get off the island is huge, all worries about what may await on Kryptos dwarfed by the desire to be out of here. The ferry leaves in half an hour. I see another overnight coming up. I'm ready to march up to Greg and tell him I'm commandeering the taxi when a thought strikes me. What if he's not a spoiled, self-centred, megalomaniac little rich boy who doesn't like to be crossed, or rather, what if, as well as these things, he is trying to keep me away from Kryptos?

More paranoia? Or a late developed instinct not to trust. Remembering what I told Raffy – *harmless rich Texans* – I think, what do I know? That they're American and over here. Like the Hollanders, like Marcus.

I think back to how I first met the girls. They were with Marcus. They said they'd just met and I took their word for it. Nothing in their behaviour made me doubt that. Their reappearance at the taverna next to Mavra Vrahia? That was a coincidence certainly, in no way connected to Gabriel and me. But was it connected somehow to Thanasi, Yanni, Michel?

I edge away from the others, step outside, and spot our driver standing, smoking. Finding the right face I tell him I've just had bad news. The plan now is that he drops me at the port, then goes back for the others. I scramble into the front passenger seat. We drive off.

Standing on deck looking back over open water as the ferry draws clear of the harbour I see a taxi hurtle along the waterfront and draw up at the quayside. I can't be sure from this distance, perhaps they are just passengers who missed the boat, but the people who get out, two men and two women, stand for a long time staring out towards the ferry and the open sea.

14

Michael, I'm thinking as I unlock the front door, drop my bag and grab a swimsuit. That's who Greg reminds me of. Not so good looking but every bit as unaccountable. (I don't want him in my head, he's just slow to leave.) Unaccountable because never called to account. Now why is that?

How he reacted to the supplicant on Tinos, a sight that people of sensibility deal with by not noticing, was grotesque. But insensitive? I don't think so. He was trying to get his head round it. Empathy? Hey! New thing! For him, a skill not there from birth. Could the same be true of Michael?

It's late afternoon and there's no-one on the beach. As I cross the crescent of crisp sand, narrowing my eyes against the sun, the sea tilts its polished surface towards me. I'm home.

I'm swimming parallel to the shore when a butterfly passes me heading out to sea. It's a butterfly not a goose, and nothing about it suggests resolve or forward planning or even a grasp of straight lines, not to mention this is summer and how long do butterflies live anyway, surely not long enough to be worth the hassle of migration. To be back on Kryptos is, after all, to be back amongst unresolved problems and avoidance tactics. It's thinking time. So . . .

The voice. The voice that began it. Peter Karpodinis. At Nico's party he had not identified me. If he was aware of a possible eavesdropper he didn't make the connection. And when he arrived at my house instead of my neighbours' he was recognising me from the party, not from the garden. But now? It may since have occurred to him that his subconscious pointed him into the driveway where he had stopped previously to answer his phone.

Lisa Dunmore, Debby Donnachy, whoever. She knows I'm Raffy's wife, has even used my name, but does her curiosity extend beyond the fact of my existence?

The butterfly. Does it know that it's at sea? The butterfly does not concern me.

Marcus. Coincidental, after all, and anyway incapable of the vulgarity of violence.

Rebecca. Transparently opaque would sum her up, but she is surely too good at what she does to be involved in anything shady.

The men on the boat . . . in the field, on the beach, on the track, those men. They shadowed me to the ferry. Happy to see me respond the call of my phone? Not those two. Doing the bidding of someone gratified by that. I can spare some compassion for those not noticeably happy men. Rather than fixing to drown me were they merely waiting for me to lead them – and him – to Raffy?

Which leaves Lucas. Whom I cannot sully with suspicion, not without spoiling this swim.

The neighbours, then. I spin to face our two houses, not expecting to see anything behind their hedge which is almost as dense as my own, but even as I scan it someone comes out of the gate. A woman. She crosses the road and starts to walk down through the field to the beach. This is interesting.

So OK. Lucas. Suspicious behaviour, Gabriel said, quoting Raffy. What could that be? And am I really so naïve as to believe that all three Hollanders, Lucas, Gabriel and Raffy, arrived here coincidentally? Yes. And I believe that still.

Lucas coming down the track from the derelict house near the monastery, turning me back towards the road, was that suspicious? I think so. Why? Because that location had been pin-pointed. But by nothing overt, just an overheard conversation that was allusive rather than specific. So not really suspicious? But then again there's an aura about that place, its proximity to the uninhabited monastery, to Marcus's house, to the track over the hill, and about Lucas too. These auras, perhaps, of my own making.

Thanasis. I must stop shying away from Thanasis. Name checked in the olive grove conversation, probably the architect of Mavra Vrahia, interested in Gabriel, interested in me, interested in everything.

And then Gabriel himself.

I pick up my towel, step into my sandals and after a quick scan of the horizon for a massing of migratory butterflies walk straight into my next-door neighbour.

Hallo? I stop in front of her.

Hallo. She is, after all, English.

I believe we're neighbours? She looks blank. *That's your house?* Blank turns to cautious as she looks to where I'm pointing – to our two houses, side by side, built for togetherness by a retired Athenian economist (theirs) and his now deceased brother (mine), their closeness looking from this distance and to my freshly appraising eye ill-conceived, defensive, panicky even, the empty fields drawn up around them, pressing them together.

I pull back from that. *I'm Anna.*

She looks at the hand I'm offering. *Oh. I'm Clare.*

She appears uncomfortable, in dress and in manner, out for a stroll, taken aback, perhaps, to find the sea so close, right here next the beach, and sand underfoot. Or has our common language startled her? Do I spell a threat to her privacy? But would that sensibly explain the not-at-home performance when I tried to visit?

Are you staying long?

We don't know yet. It depends.

Because maybe you'd like to come round for a drink? You and your . . .

Husband. Brian. He's away just now. I wait. Reassuringly she finds this flow of non-information hard to sustain. *Perhaps when he comes back. I'm not sure when that will be.* Days? Weeks? The flow has dried up.

I'll leave it with you then.

Certainly. Thank you. And off she goes along the beach, not a problem solved after all.

Back at the house I shower, wash my hair, fill a bowl with pistachios, then outside, picking a lemon from the tree, spot another sheet of sketch pad fluttering on the terrace, another graphic query from Rebecca. This one shows the musclemen swimming, crossed out, the nude on her towel, crossed out, me under my tamarisk, crossed out and Rebecca alone under her umbrella, eyebrows raised, shoulders raised, hands open in a where-the-hell-is-everybody? pose.

I carry it indoors, ignore the light on the answerphone, but am struck by an excess of tidiness. Papers in a neat stack, laptop closed. Odd. I left in a hurry. Remembering the figurine I go into its bedroom to make a better job of concealing it. It isn't there. And now the doorbell is ringing.

I usher in Clare now in a crisp linen dress and shake hands with Brian, tallish, fiftyish, white-haired, in a white ironed shirt with the folds from the packing still in place.

He came back, she says, *unexpectedly.*

He stands there looking like someone unexpectedly back from somewhere. If they are acting they are doing it well. They opt for G & Ts in tall glasses if I have those with not too much of the G. They would like to have accepted the ouzo, Brian explains, but they haven't finished quantifying their reactions to it which can be sudden and disconcerting.

We've all been there, I say and wave them out to the shade of the back terrace as the sun, slipping down the sky, is still radiating heat. Fixing the drinks I feel well disposed towards them. They came, after all, with alacrity, disconcerting alacrity, suggesting some spark of sociability. That or an urgent need to know what I'm about. They have the manner of people accustomed to certainty but currently a little short of the things that might keep that stoked. Whatever the truth of it, I find them unnervingly bland, offering no history or geography, leaving it all to me, and so I tell them of the day I tried to visit.

Really? says Clare. *We must have been out.*

I don't think so. It was three, maybe four evenings ago. You were setting out your garden furniture, so I was sure you would be there.

She turns for help to Brian. *Ah*, he says. *Conference call.*

Our business, Clare explains. *Online.*

Our company, Brian amplifies. *Classica.*

Music?

Art.

And with such pleasantries we occupy a full half hour until they make their excuses and leave.

When they've gone I tackle the answerphone. There are three calls from Lucas, one from Marcus, one from the electrician and one from Raffy. The Lucas calls express regret that he has missed me again, the electrician says reproachfully that he called yesterday, and Raffy tells me he is hitching a lift from Delos to Naxos, and hopes to pick up a caïque from there to Karistos and thence to the house.

There is one other call. It's from Claudia.

I go back and check the time of Raffy's call. This morning. Does that mean he will arrive tonight? I don't know. I do know that I shouldn't delay calling Lucas so I ring his mobile and he answers right away. He doesn't ask for an explanation but suggests we meet tomorrow, then maybe I could run him out to the chapel on the rocks. He has spoken to the key-holder. He would like to show me the icon. I hesitate – Raffy might be here – but, after all, vanishing is the thing he does best. *Fine*, I tell Lucas.

I call Marcus on the number he left. There's no reply. It's too late for the electrician.

So, what now? Take stock. Of the house, first of all the house. Former lust object, long time sanctuary and, these days, sadly neglected living space that even the thief who broke in to steal the figurine felt moved to tidy up, where a spider has spun a web between the bay leaves in the faux-Fabergé bonbonnière and the Georgian coffee pot on the counter, and where the *rigani* in the Doulton Toby jug is shedding pollen over two unwashed Coalport mugs. The fridge contains one egg and the remains of the Gabriel gastro-splurge. I need to shop.

Raffy will wait, so long as he can do that out of sight. I leave the back door unlocked and drive off quickly on a raid of the village shops – supermarket, greengrocer, bakery – and at the bakery run into Nico. He is pleased to see me but bridles at my haste. I switch back to island pace and immediately feel better. He tells me that British reporters have been on Kryptos covering the story of the murdered journalist, and their take on it is that he may have been working on an exposé.

Really? Exposé of what?

Anna mou, I can't believe this. What could be on our island, criminals or such, to make exposé? I think it is your newspapers, always looking for make good story . . . money, passport, not enough story.

I'm back at the house, unloading the shopping – some fresh feta, plump capers from the greengrocer's barrel, giant tomatoes, warm to the touch, short fat cucumbers, purple onions, a long loaf of white bread with sesame and a rough wholemeal loaf with aniseed – when the phone rings. It's Claudia.

Anna?

She sounds uncertain. It's been a long time, there have been a lot of people, and my voice has grown up.

Hallo Claudia.

My dear. She is inhabiting the Claudia persona again and I'm a graceless badly put together child. I remind myself that she's acting as she tells me in her familiar studied drawl that she's in Athens, in a cute little hotel off Syntagma. I'm absorbing that when she says she is so looking forward to being back on Kryptos. My silence, shocked, not artful, is clearly not construed that way, for her voice escapes its nicotine-weighted end of the scale to ask if I've heard from Raffy. She believes he might be on the island.

Raffy? I say. *Here? Well. I don't know, Claudia.*

I'm not here, says Raffy's voice behind me. I stiffen but don't turn.

Claudia? Sorry. Interference. No, this end. No, I haven't heard from him. The fact of his voice startled me, not the sound. Some good in that.

She gives me a number to call if I hear from him and tells me she will phone later when she knows when she's coming to Kryptos. I hang up and turn to face Raffy.

Close up and with nothing *noir*, no moonlit harbour or mountain with vulture, he looks newly met. The T-shirt he is wearing is two sizes too big and has a cartoon joke on it, a joke I'm not getting.

I let myself in. I imagine that's why you left the door open. He looks at the groceries laid out on the counter. *If you were about to cook something don't let me stop you.*

I reach for a bottle of homegrown wine and hand it to him, warding him off. *The glasses are on that shelf.* I'm not ready for this. Proximity. Proximity and strangeness. Complicating those, familiarity.

I was not about to cook, so you'll have to settle for a Greek salad. Later. First, I think, you should sing for your supper.

It began with Claudia, he says, fingering his wine glass and staring out into the darkness. We're side by side on the futon in the pergola, clear of the neighbours and also of the challenge of speaking face to face. No it didn't, it began with his walks in the interior. But for him it began with Claudia.

That night, the night of his disappearance, she had been invited to a party in the south of the island by the guy who'd been hanging around her – young, Londo Greek, the legendary Zac. Lucas had been away an she'd been bored out of her mind with the people wh were there that summer. Not the foreign corresponde and film directors of the first years, but school teach and bank managers. ***Small town*** *bank managers.*

captures perfectly the totality of her dismissal. ***Shop** keepers. From . . .* ***Denmark***. Their frisky little wives and great glowering children were also not to be tolerated. Zac was different. He knew people. All this Claudia had told the boys.

Gabriel didn't give a shit what she did, he'd made a world of his own, but Raffy was still looking out for her. A thankless task, that would have been, but fruitful for an acute observer. He had detected a difference in Zac's approach. *He was acting smitten, he wasn't feeling it.*

Because he had a girlfriend? Debby?

Maybe. I don't know. She was always working. I think they were more a team than a couple.

The party was at the summer villa of a Greek philanthropist and the guests were to include a party from a ship owner's yacht.

How would Zac have known these people?

I think he'd been useful to them in some way.

Claudia had told them she would be back late, she might even have to stay overnight.

They'd been put on their honour not to stray from their usual haunts. She handed out drachmas, kissed them goodbye, tossed a wrap around her shoulders and went off on the back of Zac's motorbike. And they spent the evening as they usually did, playing *tavli* in a backstreet café with some of the village men who'd taught them the previous summer. After that they strolled round the village stopping to talk to anyone they knew, eating *souvlaki*, drinking coke, watching part of a football match on the big screen at the café in the square, finally heading home via the harbour where some

fishermen, unloading their catch, hailed them. The boys, Michael included, had often been out on their boat and knew them well.

But the man who came walking along the quayside as Raffy laid down a box of mackerel was a stranger. He knew Raffy's name though. He told him he'd been sent to find him. Someone, someone Raffy knew, was in need of his help. *Looking back, of course that was crazy. I was eleven, not Greek, how much help was I going to be, but I wanted so much to be part of that community, they gave so much time to us, teaching us* tavli, *all that, more time than our parents, and, remember, we were living in Athens by then, I was beginning to feel Greek, Greek men were my role models.*

Raffy went with him through the back streets of the village, the narrowest of the winding passages where the houses were a donkey's length apart and the balconies on the upper floor almost touched. They came to a house that had a brass doorknocker in the shape of a hand and a canary in a cage hanging from the balcony.

The man beckoned him in. They entered a dim barely furnished room with a fireplace, a table, a fridge, an icon, and against the wall an old black and white TV which was on but with the sound turned down. The man poured himself an ouzo and gave Raffy a warm can of Coke. It felt odd. He hadn't introduced himself and he had offended against the laws of Greek hospitality by serving himself first. And no-one else was there. The man pulled up a chair and sat down opposite him. Raffy began to feel apprehensive. On the table was a knife. A serious knife. The man now seemed in some way familiar. He thought he had seen him on one of his walks.

The man picked up the knife. He held it in the air between them and turned it slowly, his eyes on Raffy's face as the blade glinted in the lamplight and the TV flickered in the background. Outside the canary began to sing in its cage as the knife was presented – ***presented***, *you know, as if to a crowd of worshippers before a sacrifice, the kind of thing they had in comics back then, the evil guy from the East and his drug-crazed devotees, very familiar to me and anyway it was that kind of knife, more like a dagger.* He laid it on the table and asked him to look at it closely, because an identical knife was at that moment in Zac's possession. Then he put it to him that he was no longer to go walking in places where he had no business to go, places in the interior of the island. That he was to forget any such places he'd seen on his walks and any people he might have seen in these places.

He said that Claudia was presently in the company of a dangerous man. Very dangerous. That unless Raffy swore on the bible – *he actually had a bible there, laid out next to the knife, which was weird since I'd never believed, and he, the guy, seemed to be investing it with a power he was sure I wouldn't challenge* – that unless he swore that he would cease snooping and disclose nothing of what he might have seen, Claudia would not be coming home.

And in case he doubted that this was for real he should know that Claudia's party date had been planned with this in mind. The man with Claudia, the man with the other knife, was not afraid to use it. It would not be the first time. And if Raffy had any illusions about how easy it would be to dispose of a body, he reminded him that they were on an island . . . that they knew the fishing grounds . . . that the chances of her turning up in a net were zero . . . and that they knew all this from experience. And if he were to think of telling anyone, the same rules would apply. *In triplicate. Her. Me. Them.*

He pauses. He is sitting forward, staring ahead towards the vines and olives, indistinct in the fading light, and beyond those the eucalyptus, the tamarisks, the road and the sea. He is seeing, I think, a knife, a bible and a TV set. A lot of his time will have been spent in that room, reconsidering his options.

He sits back.

What did you do?

Swore on the bible. And the guy said and don't think you will be safe when you leave Kryptos. We know where you live in Athens. We can reach you in America, all of you. So go home, boy, stay on the beach, stop walking, be silent. Go. *And he showed me the door.*

He has finished, I think. I'm still listening but this time he has stopped talking. He raises his glass, examines it, decides it's a wine glass all right, examines the wine, drinks some.

This is yours? It's good. Sweet, though.

I can see he believes he is establishing a degree of normality. He isn't. He reaches for a pistachio and starts to pull it apart. The sun has dropped behind the mountain and left the sky in tatters.

What happened? I say at last. *I mean now. Why are you telling me this now?*

Because, he says, *Claudia is here. Could we eat that salad?*

The strangeness of our being together has to be addressed and placated with small talk. Back at the marble table he fills me in on London life while I fix the salad. He is renting a flat in Fulham and spending a lot of time in the British Museum. He has seen a few of our friends but doesn't go out of his way to contact them. Out of awkwardness, mainly. And yes, most of them think I just walked out on him.

But all the time we're re-running his story. The graphics, the lighting, the sound effects. The pre-adolescent schlock horror world view. The improbability. The believability.

For total empathy I would have to become the child I also was. That doesn't happen. I feel motherly. Wifely. Detached. A person of now. A person of a different gender.

When we finally lay down our forks – he ate avidly, I lightly – we decide for reasons of privacy to carry our coffee cups back to the pergola where once again he picks up the story.

Of course, he says, *I didn't know what I was seeing. They could have let it pass. I was no danger to them. But after that I began to re-play everything – where I'd gone, what I'd seen.*

One day, when he had walked further than ever before, he came to a place where a dried-up stream, a winter water course, approached at right angles to the path and below it had formed a small ravine. A goat's skull complete with horns was lying in the ravine. He climbed down to look at it and, looking up from below the track, saw a space under the overhang above the path that looked like a small cave. He climbed back up, pulled himself up to the entrance and looked inside. It was quite shallow, with boulders supporting the roof at the back and in one corner was a small opening. Two torches and a storm lantern were tucked behind a boulder. He logged it in the back of his mind and went home.

But another day, taking a different path over the hills from Karistos, a path that was just a shallow cutting across a marble hillside with no real vegetation and little scrub, he came to a point about half a mile from where the other path led to the ravine and the cave. Towards the end of this path there was a splash of colour just visible under some thorn bushes. Two blue stripes in the rather crude azure that was then the colour of the island's doors and shutters had been painted on the marble of the hillside.

Later, on his longest walk, he found another set of the blue stripes on the inward-facing slope of a mountain whose far side stretched in rises and falls down to the barren coastal plain in the south of the island. This walk had joined up for him what he had been learning of the island's topography because it opened up a vista of the sea to the south west and showed him that the island, which had seemed infinite, was really rather small.

All these places where he had walked were uncultivated and uninhabited. Some had traces of old boundary walls and terracing, but they were steep slopes with thin unproductive soil. They opened up fresh views of fields and goat sheds, chapels, an abandoned monastery on a rocky height and the occasional solitary house, but they were not places where people walked other than the occasional man with a rifle looking for rabbits.

At least that's what I thought they were doing. The man who threatened me was one of them. I placed him afterwards.

When you say you saw nothing . . . does that mean you still didn't know what this was about?

Then I didn't. I soon found out.

Because, he says, he ignored the warning and continued his walks.

To begin with I went nowhere. I just kept running it over in my head. What happened, what I should have done. I tried to think what Michael or Gabriel would have done and it certainly wasn't that. Sitting there listening, swearing on the bible. Gabriel would have walked out on him and told someone and Michael would have picked up the knife and stabbed him through his evil heart.

Whenever he morphs into Captain America his voice changes. I see a Guns N' Roses T-shirt and a cowlick.

Not being able to tell anyone was the worst of it. I thought I might implode with constraint. But then I decided the way out of it was to find out what they were up to and do something about it.

And so one day I got up early, at first light, and went to the cave above the ravine. I picked up the torch that was hidden there and crawled into the opening at the back. The first thing I saw was part of the torso of a sculpture. Artemis, in a peplos. *Another large fragment was lying behind it. There was an almost intact marble* pyxis *– you know, a box* *with a lid – and a couple of loom weights. Of course I didn't know the names then, but they were finds, you didn't need an archaeology degree to get that. It was mind-blowing. I stood there holding the torch but inside I was freaking out.*

Had the things been dug up from in there, in the cave?

The cave was very small. They were using it as a store, I think, a temporary store. But the opening at the back continued into the hill. There were some traces on the floor – a flake of obsidian, I did know obsidian, and some pieces of coarse pottery that suggested other things had been stored there. So I started exploring further.

You went back?

Several times. I started looking for places where the ground was disturbed, where they had been digging, though it was easy to make that look like cultivation. If the blue marks were delineating the boundaries of where they had found stuff, then it had to be extensive. And then there was the time span. Of course I'm talking now from hindsight. From hindsight it was, or would have been, a site of major importance. One that might have answered a lot of questions. But from my state of total innocence it was just the ultimate adventure.

But surely you were afraid of being caught?

To start with, yes. But pretty soon I began to feel invincible. I was going to work all this out on my own, save civilisation, put the men behind bars. And then one night my mother came home with a black eye.

I remember that. She wore a black patch.

Yeah, and she had bruises. Those drapes she wore? She kept them hidden. She said she'd fallen down some steps but of course, knowing what I knew, I didn't believe her. She was scared. And then the guy stopped me in the street . . . took me by the shoulder, drew a finger across his face, diagonally across his face, and said for your mother, your beautiful mother. If you go again. *So someone had seen me. And after that I was just wiped out with remorse. I mean that was a big bucks operation they had going. Why would they not be serious?*

So you didn't go back?

I stuck to the village and tried to show I was just a harmless kid. But they saw to it that I didn't relax. There were reminders.

Reminders?

Sure. In Athens. One night when my father was away a guy came to take my mother to the theatre. A different type altogether. Suave. Articulate. In a suit. As they were leaving he turned and made a throat-slitting gesture behind her back. I wasn't getting it, I thought it was some kind of joke. He winked at me. Then he did it again. That was what finally freaked me out. That they might be anywhere. And mocking me.

For the first time his voice becomes unsteady. *There was no peace of mind. She knew so many people. She was so fucking reckless and undiscriminating.*

I know.

It might be wifely to lay on a comforting hand. Or motherly. I sit tight and let him get it together.

And so I decided to live my life as if the threat was actual and continuing and put the whole thing out of my mind.

Successfully almost.

Yeah.

Well . . . well done.

He laughs and squeezes my shoulder. Switches off.

We sit in silence. There's a lot to digest before I can formulate questions.

So, where are we now? Are you in the open?

Not exactly.

You're saying there might be men with knives closing in on us even now? I fling a showy glance round the dark fields. They're dark. They're close.

I don't think so. Not the reassurance I expected. *Claudia knows, sure, but . . .*

The whole story? You told her all that?

Minus those aspects that would totally undermine her self esteem. She says if the bad men come to get her that's fine, it will stop her ending up in a care home.

So . . . why did you tell me to say I hadn't seen you?

Because I wanted to tell you everything first. Also . . .

I thought there might be an also.

I think Lucas is somehow involved.

There's a long long silence while we let that sink in.

Not everybody is as straight as you think. Hollanders especially.

What?

That's what Gabriel told me just before he went back to Mykonos.

I think we'll leave that for tomorrow.

15

So now I have this date with Lucas. But first, breakfast with his son. It's time I got to know him.

Conversation falters – in the wake of last night how could it not? – but words need to be exchanged. I ask after London acquaintances, our old neighbours the Smithsons, their cat Alastair, their less memorable son. He counters with news of my former colleagues and at Estelle the obit editor, the frisson that might have been threatening now safely sandbagged, we pick up our coffee cups and walk.

It's pleasant touring the garden together. Bees buzz and warblers warble and there's an industrious background whirr from the washing machine, halfway through a 40 degree cycle with my Mykonos/Tinos tops, the T-shirt he was wearing last night and the clothes he travelled in.

Loading it, I felt married. He was pleasantly present in everything he'd worn except the T shirt, borrowed from Jean-Paul, which showed a man in owlish glasses scratching his head over something anatomical in a hole. This would be an archaeological joke. Context. I'm right out of practice with everything not solo, and I have washed no clothes but my own for longer than I care to remember.

Today he is wearing my baggiest shirt, a faded Liberty print, with the batik beach square worn as a sarong and one of my silk scarves wound pirate fashion round his head. This because his travel bag with his clothes was still in Kurt's car as he climbed out of the window. Anyone spying will think I got lucky in a beach bar. I avoid looking at him as the idea is quite persuasive.

But he is in executive mode. When I meet up with Lucas, he instructs me, I should tell him that I've had a call from him.

Say I called from Athens. Say I may be coming over in a few days.

Why am I doing this?

I need to know how he responds. The Adam's rib thing again, as if we shared a grasp of normal. *Then, too, it might make him act.*

Act? Act how?

I'll tell you if it happens.

Last night I hitched a lift to the past on the back of his souped-up recall. Once there we went our own ways, following the threads of our separate stories. His world was not my world, mine not his. We came together in our shared responses and in our sharp sensory recall,

So, we're cool with each other. But bonding in hyperspace does not slip into the warp and woof of marital chit-chat. And waiting their turn to be aired are a whole heap of things, few of them conducive to irony, bathos, or innuendo. We're never going to talk. And I would gladly cancel Lucas.

Remember I'll be bringing him back here. After we look at the icon. Where will you be?

Out of the way, don't worry.

Then from the chaos of unsorted stuff in my head a figure takes shape. **The** figure. No need to saddle it with that diminishing *ine*.

Before I go . . .

Yeah?

On Delos when we were talking the first time . . . on the mountain . . .

Yeah.

I said something. The words I used were your surprise parcel. *And you said* my what?

Well? What?

You didn't send me a parcel with an address label headed Byzantium Books?

Never heard of them.

With a note inside that said hide this*?*

He shrugs.

Then Gabriel was right.

Gabriel? What are you talking about? What was in the parcel?

A Cycladic figurine.

My God. Where is it now?

I hid it like you said. Or like someone who can copy your handwriting said. And now it's gone.

Since when?

Since I left for Mykonos.

And the note? In my handwriting? Has that gone with it?

As I leave he's sifting through coffee grounds, onion skins and peach stones, and I'm half way to the village before I remember that Kryptos is now recycling. It's paper. It's in the blue bin under the stairs.

Lucas is already at the café in the square. He stands up to greet me and the man he has been sitting with turns. It's Yannis. As Lucas pulls out a chair for me Yannis gets up to leave but I say *please, don't go,* and he sits down again.

So, I say, *you two know each other?* There is a short pause before they agree that they do.

In the old times, says Yannis.

Acting on an impulse to move on from those old times I say *tell me, was that your house that Lucas was leaving when I met him a few days ago? Opposite that little blue-domed chapel in the wood?*

Rather than answer me directly he glances at Lucas. It's Lucas who answers.

I was out walking when we met. I've been doing a lot of that. Actually I was looking to see if that path led up to Aghios Konstandinos. There used to be a very interesting icon there. I thought it would probably be locked but someone thereabouts could let me in.

Neat, but I don't believe him. *Only* – I'm addressing Yannis – *I seem to remember Meriel saying something about wanting to buy that house from you?*

A reaction there. But Lucas quickly cuts in with

Meriel? Meriel? I remember a Meriel a long time ago. She was a painter.

The Meriel I'm talking about does massage. Reiki. Facials. I haven't heard that she paints.

Excuse me, says Yannis and leaves.

Well, says Lucas, *coffee? And then we'll be on our way.*

I order a *metrio*, he asks for another *sketo* and we settle back into not quite the easy groove we found last time. He tells me he has been revisiting churches and icons all over the island in light of discoveries he has made in other places. I bite back a mention of my visit to the Panaghia Evangelistria on Tinos.

Are there any icon painters on Kryptos?

A very distinguished painter indeed, very old now. He is currently in the monastery of Aghios Theodoros but before that, before it was closed, he was in Aghios Konstandinos. His work was really outstanding, in many ways evocative of the early Byzantine paintings. And much in demand, as you can imagine, with church benefactors.

And he still paints?

A little. His eyesight is not so good now. But the icon we are going to see – deft change of subject here – *at the little church near your house . . . I'll be very interested to see that again. It's the farmer on the hill above who keeps the key. His wife is going to let us in.*

I was intrigued by what you told me. That they don't know who it depicts. When you're identifying icons I imagine you don't just go by looks?

There ***is*** *quite strong facial recognition. And there are characteristic poses. And of course names are often written.*

But there are traditions too, are there not? I mean even I know that George has a dragon and John has messy hair and Nicholas is the patron saint of sailors.

Certainly. Only this icon, as I remember it, was rather devoid of clues.

As Lucas talks I'm picking up the clack of *tavli* checkers, the ebb and flow of café voices, men's voices, and of these, one in particular. I'm angling my chair to look when Nico arrives in his role as messenger from beyond.

Anna mou . . . perhaps you have heard? The police have made arrest for famous journalist.

No. No I hadn't heard.

What's this? Lucas leans forward.

You wouldn't know him. An English newspaper journalist was killed last week in the street close to the port. Who did they arrest, did you hear?

Was two men, not from here. Maybe from FYROM, maybe Alvanoi, Voulgaroi. Only this morning I hear. My cousin tell me.

The pianist?

He is friend of Stelios, Stelios of police. They go in school together.

Well that **is** *interesting.*

Nico goes off to share his news at another table and Lucas decides we should be on our way. As we get to our feet I see that the group at the other table comprises Nico, Dimitris, Yannis, who merely changed places, and Peter Karpodinis. It was of course his voice I picked out. Kurt, surprisingly, is also there. Loose consortia indeed.

Walking to the car I'm too busy mulling over this to listen to Lucas's continuing iconography lecture. Nico's news has also to be picked over. So when a girl with grey eyes passes by and looks intently at us, she also comes in for scrutiny. I have seen her before, those eyes, that look.

The track that leads to the chapel meanders between a field of goats and an olive grove to the farm on the hill. We park in the farmyard and walk down towards the sea. The chapel clings to the apex of its promontory, its tiny forecourt straddling the rocks where the pious pirate struggled ashore to be followed at first light by the icon.

The door is open. The farmer's wife comes out and hands Lucas the key. I know her by sight, I realise, and she me. She gives us each a motherly pat and says she'll leave us to it if we'll lock up and return the key.

The chapel is tiny and freshly whitewashed, smelling of scrubbed stone rather than beeswax. Four windows set high in the dome supplement the light from the door. On the carved and gilded iconostasis the Virgin sits with the child, another tiny child-adult with the high forehead of an intellectual and an expression that remains inscrutable while you search it for purpose or opinion, a scrutiny that seems both lacking in respect and unavoidable given his maturity. Over there is John the Baptist with his straggly beard and signature wild hair. And here a grey-bearded man, possibly Saint Nicholas. And there in an alcove is an icon I can't see as Lucas moves to stand in front of it. When I have checked out the other rather undistinguished paintings I walk over to join him.

It's a man. Quite a young man, beardless but with a shadow following his lower face that suggests stubble and sideburns though the overall effect is of a well-tended self-aware rather modern look. Disconcertingly familiar. The background is rocky with a small hill. His garments are sepia coloured and above his left shoulder there is a slender column of something that has lost its outlines. First I see it as a bird, a familiar, perhaps an owl, and then I think it's the neck of a guitar slung over his shoulder. There is just a suggestion of flaked-off halo.

I look questioningly at Lucas. *Well now*, is all he says. From his ethnic document carrier he takes out a notepad and scribbles some notes, then he brings out a camera. He takes several shots in close-up then steps back to shoot the iconostasis, then the interior of the church and finally, outside, the church itself.

A mystery, he says. *Shall we go?*

He locks up and we stand for a while on the forecourt taking in the view of the lagoon. The coastline here is wild and uninhabited, ready to expire altogether in a headland that marks the northernmost extremity of the island. Coves interspersed with rocks, boulders and juniper clumps make occasional moorings for yachts whose crews prefer not to socialise. There is one out there now. In the other direction I have a partial view of the beach in front of the house where I can just make out Rebecca's umbrella and the fluttering candy-pink cover-up of our beach's nude habituée.

Returning the key to the farmer's wife we step around ogling turkeys and slinking cats. A dog unfurls and barks for just long enough to bring her out. A sign on the wall offers fresh vegetables and home-made feta for sale. I buy things for lunch and as we drive back to the house Lucas is silent, still deep in thought. He has made no further comment on the icon.

Raffy as promised has melted away. As I tackle sun-warmed tomatoes, elongated yellow peppers, short firm cucumbers and sweet purple onions Lucas goes off to explore the garden. He returns looking animated – did Raffy, perhaps, hang out his washing? – but he is holding out a pottery shard.

Yes. There are a lot of those. Under the olives. On the beach. I used to think they might be from an ancient wreck but if you examine the crumbly edge of the field further up where it's being eroded you can see a whole pottery layer.

He runs his thumb over the shard – it is one of the thicker liquorice allsort types – and lays it on the counter.

You know, the first summer we came here? He pauses, collecting his thoughts. *We chose Kryptos to avoid the crowds that come with a sight. Foregoing, a little reluctantly, the magic of such a sight. But that would have been . . . that is . . . magic for the many. It's the private magic that becomes addictive. The sense of what has still to be discovered.*

I hold my breath.

We avoided the crowds but I'm afraid we got hooked. Well now, is that lunch?

No revelation then. And why would there be? Nothing about Lucas shouts looter.

I know what you mean, I say quickly to keep us on track. *Every morning when I step outside there's a sense of impending revelation. Every afternoon. It's endemic.*

It's the context. You can't escape it. It's calling the shots.

He is making us passive in the face of that context and to an extent I'd go along with that.

Perhaps, I suggest, *if the context was more prosaic or the topography less ravishing or the distances less haunted or the islands differently spaced . . .*

Felicitous, says Lucas, helping to cool this down to guide book levels. *I think that's the word. The island. Its nature. Although* . . . a longer pause . . . *sometimes it tests us.*

A secret after all.

Anna. Have you ever found anything?

But on the point of possible illumination I am hijacked by my own ramblings. I'm extending some of this to people. To Raffy. The attraction of the never quite knowable.

Anna?

Oh. If you count shards, yes. Plants sit wilting while I root around in the hole. I hit marble and I stop and check it for chisel marks. I haven't found any, so no. Pottery, though. I have a whole box of fragments.

It's time we ate and brought this to an end. Lucas helps me carry dishes to the shade of the terrace. As we eat I feel some of the old rapport returning. It's safe, it's simple, it's lunch.

Perfect, he says, looking around and waving his fork. *All of this. Only one thing would make it better. If Raffy was here.*

Ah, I say, remembering my instructions and seizing the baton. *That too might happen. He phoned.*

He stops eating.

He did? When?

Yesterday. He was in Athens. He tailors a piece of feta to fit a raft of bread then lets himself look up. *And he said* – I load my fork with a little of everything, tomato, onion, pepper, rocket, cucumber, an olive, feta, go back to spear a caper – *he hopes to come here.*

Great. Great. Inelegant but immediate. *Did he say when?*

In a few days.

So, do you know where he's staying in Athens? Did he leave a number?

No. Sorry. I expect he'll phone again if he decides to come.

Right. Would you let me know if he does that? You have my number. He won't use a cell phone. I don't know why. I guess he just doesn't like to be too contactable.

I had told him to let me know when he wanted to go back to the village and soon after this he drains his wine glass and stacks his plates.

If it's not too much bother, Anna, I should be getting back.

In the car he's quiet. I've sabotaged the rapport by holding back on Raffy's supposed phone call. And only after I've dropped him does it occur to me that we never returned to the subject of the icon.

When I get back Raffy is on the terrace.

Where did you leave him?

On the edge of the village. He said he wanted to walk.

Can I take the car?

Of course. I hand over the key. *But isn't that rather reckless?* He has shed the pirate headdress and is looking very much like himself only in shades and a sarong.

I'll chance it. I want to see what he's doing.

I've hung up the washing and I'm tackling the lunch dishes when he returns. He leans on the counter and watches me, collects himself, picks up a tea towel.

While you were away I took a walk, he says, nodding towards the fields behind that, over the rise, spread out to bake through the span of another afternoon. *I met a friend of yours.*

Rebecca.

I don't know her name. She was sitting painting just off the track. I stopped to look. She seemed to be painting an icon.

Well now, she **is** *versatile. She's supposed to be working on a mural for a hotel. How did you find out we know each other?*

She asked if I was on holiday and I said I was staying with my sister. She said Anna? *I said* yes.

These disclaimers are becoming an issue. I dry my hands. *I think perhaps it's time for your sister to fill you in on what's been happening to her.*

So we move again to the shade and privacy of the pergola where Raffy eats the remains of the salad and I tell him my story from death sentence to dead journalist, rounding off with lost phone, fake message and possible attempt on my life. I have to say his consternation is gratifying.

Why didn't you tell me?

I've been rushed off my feet just listening. I doubt if you would have taken it in. Don't worry. I was dealing with it. Am still dealing with it. It's coincidental. Mostly.

How so?

Well, I only came out of my . . . how can I describe the happy and utterly engrossing isolation I came out of, engrossing, possibly bordering on reclusive . . . *I only became involved because I overheard that conversation. Which, after all, had nothing to do with me. And it was only because I reacted to what I'd heard that I was in touch with other people to the extent that I was. Provoking them, subsequently, to steal my phone, have a go at killing me, be stabbed after talking to me and the rest of it. Socialising, you see. I always knew that was dangerous.*

And have you thought about why you were at the port the night the guy was knifed?

To meet a boat. To meet . . . well it was you that time if I remember correctly.

Quite. Might he not have been there because you would be meeting me?

I sit back in the futon and consider. I rerun that night, the phone messages, my general state of alarm and denial, the feeling that everyone was acting in play for which I alone had no script.

He wasn't a gangster. He was an English tabloid journalist and a boring one at that. And the first time I met him I wasn't meeting you, I was meeting Marcus. Though he didn't know it.

If he was doing an exposé it might have involved Marcus. And if he'd been keeping tabs on him and he saw you go off with him it's not beyond the bounds of possibility that he turned his attention to you.

How would he know I was going to be there the second time?

I don't suggest that he did, but it's probable, surely, that he spent his evenings hanging around the port. It's easily the best place to watch the comings and goings. And when he saw you turn up for a second time he may have thought you were up to something.

But I wasn't. And hey, what do you know, I didn't kill

him. And he ***was*** *killed. Presumably by someone who did have something to hide.*

OK. But there's another possibility. If someone saw you talking to him as the boat was disembarking they may have thought he was me?

There's quite a lot to think about there. For both of us.

An hour later we're swimming. Not at the beach in front of the house but across the bay at the beach where we first met as children, just along the shore from the new hotel.

He swims far out and stays out there, catching up, I suppose, while I, rather as my father once did, check intermittently that he's still in sight, imbued now with a far greater sense of danger in this idyllic spot with its safe associations than I have felt so far.

As I swim I'm playing with a new idea, the notion that someone on this island, someone who knows me or knows of me, may have been watching me all this time in the hope of getting to Raffy. And the shadowy character of Zac has begun to haunt me. Might he now be here? Would I know him? And the man who threatened Raffy, nameless but surely local in origin, is he someone I see on the street as I stroll through the village?

And John Burnham, out of his depth and at a loose end on the island, might he not have picked up a scent and followed it as a reflex?

When he swims up alongside me he points along the shoreline and I tense, as I do now automatically, as I follow the line of his finger. But all he says is *the sheep rock.*

Silhouetted against a bright sky I see two small boys perched on the flat summit of a pulpit-shaped rock, the summit from which, at their age, we would watch a farmer push his entire flock of sheep, one by one, into the sea, obliging them to swim, offended but diligent, in a slow arc to the beach beyond through the cleansing waters of the Aegean.

16

It was when Jean-Paul called me I realised I had to do something.

The sun is going down and we're on the roof terrace with glasses of ice-heavy ouzo and a bowl of home-grown olives. The sea is making fretful splishing sounds and the tamarisks lift their branches and give them an experimental shake. A *meltemi* is coming.

He told me things were turning up here and there, often from reputable sources but with a shaky provenance. Shaky but tolerated. Several major museums had bought them. The source locations were given as different islands but he thought they might have a common origin. I had a strong idea what that origin might be.

Did you tell him?

That wasn't an option. I'd started getting reminders.

Started?

Of course. You didn't think I'd been fielding that crap all these years?

It stopped, then.

When we moved back to the States, that was the end of it.

And you hadn't told anyone?

Who would I tell? My mother? My father? They were still together. I wasn't going to be splitting them up. It was over, whatever it was. Closed.

So . . . what was it that started it up again?

If I knew that I might have been able to deal with it.

You got reminders . . . how exactly?

A pause when I picked up, then this voice . . .

Greek voice?

English . . . giving some banal detail of a train journey or a dentist's appointment.

They were still keeping tabs on Claudia?

They were remarkably well informed about where she was living but I guess . . . he reaches for an olive . . . *I guess they reckoned she had become expendable.*

Expendable? How?

He drops the stone into a Spode egg cup. *Nice, needs more salt, and to an extent they were right. I was ready to take a chance on going public. After the call from Jean-Paul I decided I would try.*

My olives are impeccably salted and I know these tactics. He is limbering up to be the one who knows best.

But then they brought you into it.

Yes?

They knew your schedule. They wanted me to know they knew.

They knew when I was having root canal treatment.

You lunched at a salad bar. He called from the next table. Detailed every item on your plate.

Bluffing.

I thought so. In the evening I asked you.

Don't tell me. He was right to the last radish?

He rustles up a smile and spreads his hands.

You didn't think of telling me?

I did. But as a first step – he looks me in the eye but can't sustain it – *I confided in your father.*

Ah.

He was the one to tell because, although he wasn't professionally involved in Greece, he knew it well. And he had the contacts. I fixed to meet him and told him the whole story up to and including the implied threat to you . . . which was containable so long as you knew nothing. He meets my sceptical gaze. *If you'd known, you would have done something.*

I am being cajoled retrospectively into letting the men handle it.

When I saw him again he had thought of a possible way in, though he didn't tell me what that was. The last time I saw him you and I were at their house for lunch.

That lunch. For me too the last time. *And then?*

He shrugs. *The accident.*

But . . . I still can't make the leap . . . *it* **could** *have been just an accident?*

No. They called me afterwards. And in the same call they told me they'd stepped up their watch on you.

I look away towards the many on-hand distractions, the sun two-thirds sunk behind the mountain, the sea more irritable, the tamarisks essaying a swish. I pull back from those, pull back from my father, my mother, my orderly childhood, my faith in the laws of probability.

And then I came here.

Yeah.

Sounding righteous now. For here, I'm guessing, is where he turned superhero. Of course he was already more than half way there, had been since the age of eleven, but this would be where he stepped out into the stratosphere, straightened up, and cut off earthly contact, ready to bind the demon in the desert, fly a plane into a skyscraper, hold still while a fox ate out his heart. Whatever.

I came here and – I'm seeing my actions through his eyes now – *I led a charmed life.*

Yes. Because I did nothing.

The Spartan option. Possibly the most difficult. He at least has no doubts.

I look out at the milky stripes and white crests now lining up across the grey waters of the lagoon. *Tell me, why didn't they just take* **you** *out?*

I may have been a bargaining chip for someone else.

Or they thought you'd already told someone? The more likely, the more sensible scenario. Negated, perhaps, by my parents' deaths.

The last sliver of sun is poised on the mountain top ready to disappear, a ritual that demands our observance. We watch it. It goes.

Claudia. She left her number in Athens. I'm supposed to call her when I hear from you. Have I heard from you?

Now might be the time.

But events here seldom come singly and as we make our way down from the roof terrace the phone rings.

Hi there! says a voice that is perky, drawling and not quite identifiable all at the one time. *It's Marje, honey. Remember me?* Marje. Gabriel's fashion editor. *Guess what? I'm here. I like your island, dear. I could settle I think, but that's getting ahead, I've been here five minutes. Look I'm going to see some houses with a real estate guy here in town. Maybe we could meet after?*

I glance at Raffy hovering in the doorway. *Hi Marje. Could you give me a second to check my diary?* I cover the phone and fill in Raffy who says *meet her, why not*, so I tell Marje I'll see her at the café at the port, the café of many meetings which is, bad karma or not, the easiest landmark for a person who has no transport and who doesn't know the island. And then I phone Claudia.

I tell her Raffy is arriving later today if he can get a boat. I'm not sure where he's coming from. She tells me she'll catch a boat tomorrow, she'll let me know the time once she has checked the schedules.

I hang up. In the garden the palms are swishing and through the half-open door comes the screech of an early owl. We carry our glasses out to the terrace.

Would you like to tell me exactly what you told Claudia?

First I have to fill you in on why I'm here now.

Because you're no longer protecting her. Because Jean-Paul is worried.

There's more. I had another call from the guy. Perhaps he was missing the bulletins since you'd baled out. He said he wasn't sure I understood how seriously they had me in the frame. For which reason a friend of his had gone to board with my mother in Cape Cod. He suggested I call her to confirm that. I did. I'd hardly said hallo when she was telling me about this charming Greek boy, so helpful, changing light bulbs, fixing the computer, feeding the cat, and very cultivated, they were going to art openings and concerts. I flew over there right away. She wasn't that pleased to see me. She may have been on the point of another relationship experiment. I should tell you she hasn't lost her looks. I made things difficult by being a devoted son so he had to give us space. Then I hired a detective.

He pauses. If it's for effect that's unnecessary. *You hired a detective.*

I told him I thought the guy was trying to con her out of her savings. He did some digging and guess what? He was illegal and wanted for questioning in London **and** *in Athens.*

And then?

I told her the whole story.

Which was?

He sighs and sits back as if he's finally free of a load. *You're right. I edited.* A car passes, throwing out music and voices.

The Zac relationship . . . that that was engineered to have a hold on me . . . I dropped that. I didn't entirely believe it anyway. And of course the rough stuff. She heard me out quite calmly. It spooked me, I have to say. She was compliant. Compliant with pzazz, but compliant. Then she really threw herself into it. Hugged me. Apologised. Said she'd been a bad mother. I protested and she said well of course not really but sometimes she'd been a bad judge of character and Zac was a case in point, the lodger being another. I told her everything might be coming to a head and I had to know she was going to be careful from now on. She did that maddening girly smile, you know the one? I told her, I want you to look at careful with new eyes. C-A-R-E-F-U-L. It's not just an adjective for boring people. She took that on board and said from now on she would be watching out for herself, giving up cigarettes and the company of men and cutting down on vodka martinis, possibly wearing a hair shirt if the hair came out of an alpaca. She said she would like to see you again.

She did?

She always liked you.

It didn't feel like it.

Well she resented you for being your age and for having claims on me but apart from that, yes. And she always thought you were good for me. And she realised that it was her behaviour after all that was the genesis of the rift between us.

She realised that? How did that come about.

I told her. And then I came here. And I don't know how but I guess they knew I was coming.

The reception committee?

I was thinking of the figurine. They knew they would have to try a different tack. Incriminating me was probably the best they could think of.

But I left it lying in the courier office for days. And then when I did finally pick it up we buried it on the beach.

We?

Gabriel and I. He said it had entrapment written all over it.

There's a long silence while he takes that in. *Did he now?* We both consider the role of Gabriel.

And he pointed out that the policemen who came to

search the house had probably come to look for it, but didn't actually seem to know what they were looking for.

The police came to search the house?

Sure. But it was on the beach.

OK. Let's take this slowly. How did it get from the beach to the house?

Once Gabriel had gone I brought it back.

I let that replay. How it sat there, floodlit, on the marble table, kitchen quality marble but marble, perhaps, from the same mother mountain, sat there with the dark behind it, a dark full of darker shapes, natural, native, some introduced, arching palm leaves, stretching branches, tumbling vine tendrils, all mobile but not moving, as if they were frozen in its presence. Its stylised, spine-tingling, wholly unnatural presence.

But if it was really sent for purposes of entrapment who was to do the entrapping?

They would have been waiting for me to arrive. And I wonder . . . when that didn't happen did they simply break in and take it away? It hadn't done the job it was scheduled to do. And it was worth a shitload of bucks.

There were no signs of a break-in. I remember the surprising and wholly agreeable tidiness. *Quite the reverse.*

Was anyone else here, here in the house after you dug it up?

Just Lucas, the day I got the call to go to Mykonos.

Lucas again. His name hangs in the air, and as the scarlet afterglow is blown away on a stiffening wind, the palms flapping furiously, the owl swooping past rocked in its course, with the evening cooling and with many more things coming into the frame than we can deal with now, I remember my date with Marje – a pointless diversion with the potential to be utterly infuriating. Raffy says he'll come with me as far as the port. *Then I'll leave you to it. There's something I want to check.*

You think it's safe to do that?

Safer.

Based on what?

Just a general fuck you feeling.

Based on nothing, then.

I guess.

Marje is there before me. This time she is wearing a Greek fisherman's cap, black with a peak and black braid, a scarlet silk poncho and a massive navel-scraping gold and enamel chain very like the one the Archbishop wears at the televised Easter service. I fear she may have mistaken an orthodox accoutrement supplier in Athens for an upscale souvenir shop.

Almost as noteworthy is her companion, the French estate agent Michel.

You two know each other, yes?

We agree we do. I want to add *slightly* but we don't do slightly on Kryptos.

Michel here's been showing me some cute little houses in town and a couple of scary studios right on a cliff edge. You open the door and you fall straight out onto the rocks. Two years later you're washed up in bits on Grand Cayman. I've told him I want a vine and a lemon tree and a bit of something between me and the edge of the world. I know lawn is a dirty word here. A dirt patch would do as long as it's big enough. I have a notion to plant things. I want to sit on my terrace and watch them grow, zucchini, cannabis, deadly nightshade, I don't care.

I look at Michel.

I have been telling her that old houses here don't have gardens unless they're Venetian mansions. Or old farmhouses with an earth floor. If you want some ground you have to build or buy new.

Perhaps you're thinking of showing her Mavra Vrahia?

He looks shocked. *Oh no, that is too far down the line. Much too far. There is much work to be done there first.*

Listen honey, I'm a now or never person. I've got the notion now, I buy now. Doesn't mean I want to move in now. I might not be this way again for a couple of years. And I'm not planning on packing up the job tomorrow. I'd give it five years from now. So tell me, what's this place Anna knows about?

It is a very new development, very different, very complex, very far from town. There is much rock cutting to do and the foundations are difficult because it is rock and we must have earthquake foundations. And water will be a problem. We are going to make a desalination plant. All this takes much time, much infrastructure before we start to build houses.

You're saying I'd be a first settler. You sure know how to get to a Yankee heart. We'll go tomorrow, yes?

As he takes his leave and before he lets go of my hand he makes sure I catch his very considering glance.

Well, honey, where's it to be? I'm done with pretentious. I want to eat moussaka and fries.

That's easy, then. Seafront or inner village?

Wind's getting up, isn't it? Let's do village. Something in a courtyard maybe?

I know just the place.

Marje at dinner is too big a serving for one. She knows that and sets about sharing herself around. We go inside to look at dishes cooked and grill-to-order, and despite a moussaka seething under a golden-brown crust and a heap of fries netted fresh from the virgin oil her eye is caught by a fish. It has a look of thwarted joie de vivre that might make one think twice about eating it, but as she stands there flirting with it I also think it's her habit to go against expectations, hence the Mavra Vrahia move. She asks its name and is told *lithrini.* She grabs my arm and steers me out to the courtyard where it becomes clear she is looking for a *lithrini* in the throes of being eaten. A Scandinavian family have two on a platter garnished with oil, lemon and parsley, one already down to the skeleton.

Hi, she says, standing over their table. *I'm a brash no-manners New York Yankee who hates to order what she's not going to eat. You folks are eating my dish of choice. My question is, is it as good as it looks?*

The Scandinavians rest their forks while they consider her and her question. The son, a six-foot pre-teen with a scalp showing pink through his over-cropped yellow holiday hair goes as far as to consider an answer. *It is very good.* She beams at him and lays a hand on his shoulder – *thanks honey, mind if I have a taste?* – picks a sliver off his plate, pops it in her mouth and mimes total bliss. Back inside she orders *lithrini* for two – she asked, I think, but possibly didn't wait for my answer. *And take some nice wine*, she tells them, *and a couple of cokes to that*

Scandi kid and his family and if you've got a gateau or something, maybe some icecream, add that on my bill. I'm not sure I have talk enough in me to get us through dinner, but maybe she only needs a listener. I would like to quiz her – subtly – about Gabriel but I doubt if subtle would get past her radar.

We sit down with a carafe of house wine and with the eyes and ears of the restaurant upon us and in her version of a lowered voice she says *Tell me now Anna, would you say this island has heart?*

I tell her that as far as I am concerned it is the best place on earth to live but if it's heart she's looking for she may not find it in Mavra Vrahia.

You think it's going to be over-chic?

Over-engineered, certainly. It doesn't actually exist yet as a place, so I suppose you could look for a biblical dimension. Someone may strike a rock and a spring will flow. Someone with a pile driver. It's embryonic. But with a good restaurant.

You're saying I couldn't have my garden.

For all I know they're planning to bring in tons of topsoil. In fact I'm sure of it. They may even lay a golf course. They already have a jetty. Michel will be able to tell you. I'm surprised he wasn't in a hurry to promote it to you. I'd have thought you were just the client he was hoping for, ready to invest but in no hurry to move in.

Our fish arrives, distraction enough, and when we've picked the last bone she gets to chatting with the French guys at the next table and the quietly amused elderly English couple on the other side. Soon both couples have joined us. We have wine, ice cream, little triangles of *baklava* and some complementary glasses of *souma* which I decline as I'm driving, something I'm anxious now to get on with. I said I'd meet Raffy at the car around eleven. It's ten to, but Marje seems reluctant to let me go. Although I decline she orders coffee and while we're drinking that a stylish couple come in under the pergola and move towards a corner table. Marje turns. *Well hallo there! You following me or something?*

It's Kurt and Shannon of the illicit rendezvous on Mykonos. Though they're plainly headed in the dim direction she beckons them into our light. Shannon looks defensive. *Kurt wanted me to see his island*, she tells her. Their obvious wish not to join us is not going to be respected. Marje waves at the chairs the English couple are vacating. *Sit. Sit. Eat the lithium. The fries too.*

The departing Brits have left their tabloid. I spot a headline, reach for the paper, stow it in my bag, and get to my feet. Kurt is standing right in my path. He waits till I know I'm being obstructed before he takes his seat. I signify, as I did not before. I thank Marje for dinner and leave her to them.

There is no sign of Raffy when I reach the car, but as I unlock it he steps from behind a pavement kiosk. *Drive*, he says. He tells me a man was following him as he came down towards the darker streets near the harbour. That apart he seems to have had a productive evening.

I've been checking out local planning politics. You can no longer build in places that have not traditionally been inhabited. And, anyway, not right on the coast. Which would make your Mavra Vrahia break all the rules. I think we should go there.

I tell him that Michel, with some reluctance, is to be showing Marje the site tomorrow.

Oh and Kurt showed up.

He is too preoccupied to respond.

Back at the house the answerphone light is flashing. I'm going through my avoidance rituals, drifting out onto the terrace to look at the stars and dead-head the geraniums, so it's Raffy who presses the PLAY button. There's a message from Lucas, a different sounding Lucas from the amiable world citizen of my previous voice mail. He wants me to call him right away.

Good, says Raffy.

Claudia has also called. She will arrive tomorrow afternoon. And, curiously, Rebecca has phoned.

That's strange. She usually communicates in pictures.

There is one other call. I don't recognise the voice but Raffy stares at the phone in disbelief. It's Michael.

17

This time we travel counter-clockwise. We bypass the port town and circle blustery coves with small beaches, tavernas screened against the wind, a couple of these with villages growing round them, shops, a café, a garden centre with starter palms and eucalyptus, thorny strands of bougainvillea stapled to a cane, rattan chairs to lounge in once the plants are up and running.

This is new, Raffy says. The road is climbing to wind across the south-western flanks of hills that rise close to the sea as the coastal plain shrinks to a ribbon and the centre of the island becomes compensatingly capacious. *The road used to follow the coast.*

It's a euro-road.

You can see right into the interior. I think I'm seeing my hillside . . . you know, with the stripes? if you could stop . . . OK, sod it, it's gone. If there's a track going left take it.

A track shows up sign-posted to the monastery of the Aghios Theodoros. I brake and swing off. We ascend briefly before it turns back on itself and drops to an area of level ground, poor-looking soil intermittently worked, ringed by low grassy hummocks.

OK. Stop. I pull off onto the verge and Raffy gets out to scan the undramatic landscape around us. *I know this. About half a mile back that way is the cave.*

You walked this far?

It isn't so far when you come straight over the hill from Karistos. We've quadrupled the journey. Look, I don't want to involve you here but I would like to have a look at the cave.

OK. I pick up my bag and lock the car. *I'm coming too.*

It's as drab and unfrequented a stretch as I've seen on the island, the sea shut off on one side and the inland slopes facing us as opaque and nondescript as back garden walls. Presently the lower rises fall away to our right and we can see across the inner plain to where the land dips and explodes into the dark greens, grey-greens and light greens of cultivation with white houses dotted here and there, massing into a couple of hamlets in the distance. Beyond these the mountains rise in their full grandeur to the highest summits of the island.

Raffy stops. *Here. This was the second track I followed. The one with the blue paint marks. The next track along is the one that leads over to Aghios Antonios.*

We walk on. And stop. A tall wire fence like a tennis court surround descends the hill on our left then runs beside us along the edge of the track. Signs in Greek tell us to keep out. The fence is going to separate the track from the place where Raffy expects to see the cave, but when we reach it the place is obscured by low structures like builders' site offices running across the face of the hill.

What is it? Are they excavating? Officially?

No. It's not a Ministry of Culture sign. It's monastic property. Property of the Monastery of . . . well now, not Aghios Theodoros. Aghios Antonios!

But that's miles away. Even by your reckoning it must be four miles. Would a monastery, an uninhabited monastery, own that much land?

It does now. Or seems to.

There's no-one in sight and we get out of there while luck is still on our side.

We can hear the rock-breakers at work long before we come to Mavra Vrahia. We draw in at the spot where Gabriel parked and, bracing ourselves against the wind, peer down at what can be seen of the excavations.

Back in the car and headed for the taverna I wonder if this is such a good idea. Does it no longer matter if he is recognised? But when we start down the track the parking space is empty. I look at my watch. It's going on one, still early for lunch in Greece.

There's a delicate lemon and coriander scent evocative of lightly cooked vegetable *mezedhes* coming from the kitchen as well as the whiff of conflagration that says *crème brûlée.* The tables fronting the virgin beach with the improbable flailing tamarisks are empty. The sea is tossing tetchily, back-tracking, coming on again, ricocheting from the rocks on either side.

Uninviting though it is we decide to swim. But first we should greet the *genius loci* and mermaid painter.

Simon? Hallo? No reply. *Dolmades, zucchini keftedhes, horta* and a dish of green beans are laid out under the glass counter, carafes and glasses stacked on open shelves, tablecloths and napkins in an open-fronted antique cupboard, a guitar propped against the wall. Fridge and freezer hum, there's a light on, but there's no-one at home.

Having a swim I guess, says Raffy, shedding his freshly laundered clothes under one of the more convincingly rooted tamarisks. *Before the rush starts.*

We're both swimming when the cars start to arrive, negotiating the steep turn from the road and crunching down the track. Raffy is far out, swimming close to the mesh fence that marks the boundary of the construction site, and I'm in front of the taverna. From the first car come Thanasis, Yannis and the woman who was with them on the day I came with Gabriel. The car is silver but I'm done with that. Thanasis looks inside and calls Simon's name before they take their seats at the same back table. The second car disgorges Michel and Marje. From the third comes Marcus with Rebecca.

Michel and Marje pick a table on the edge of the beach, Marcus and Rebecca opt for two along. From my viewpoint, half-drowned in choppy water, I see the groups greet one another but make no move to mingle. Marcus and Rebecca wave – they recognised my car – and I swim out further to where there's more of a rolling swell, but I'm putting a face on it, it's not a day for swimming, I wonder that Simon bothered.

Ten minutes of it and I start back. I see Marje get up and go into the kitchen. She comes out carrying three tablecloths. Treading water I watch the odd little transaction as she hands one to the woman with Thanasis, one to Rebecca, and drops a third in front of Michel. She goes back inside. I'm touching sand when she comes out carrying a tray and strikes a do-I-have-to-do-everything-myself here pose. Three majorly disinclined people spread three crisp cloths and Thanasis sends her a long stare, but she unloads glasses then takes up a Lady Justice stance, a carafe in each hand, and as I come into earshot she's saying *face it, the guy's not here, so which is it to be, the red or the white?*

I pick up my towel from the suspect sand and drying my hair become identifiable. From Marje, now filling glasses, comes a head toss greeting and from Michel the same charm-free acknowledgement as yesterday. Marje pushes back a chair and signs for me to join them, but I'm in a wet swimsuit and Rebecca is also beckoning, mime artists duelling for an audience of one. But my focus is on Raffy whose appearance may turn the actors into the audience. I want to see faces, Thanasi's in particular, when they spot him.

Thanasis turns and recognises me but there's a shout from the sea. Raffy is swimming in, swimming with difficulty, supporting someone – someone, I see as I swim back to help him, whose thick chrysanthemum hair fans out round a face that has a livid mark on its forehead. Simon.

As we tow him towards the beach the others scramble to help. Thanasis, Yannis and Michel wade in to take him from us. Yannis drops onto the dry sand beside him and begins the hypnotic and, it seems to me after an aeon or two, fruitless ritual. He has done this before. When he sits back. I think . . . *that's it then?* But Rebecca pushes past and takes over. Her hair slips from its knot and falls about her pale shoulders as she rocks back and forth. *Simon*, she whispers as she sits back on her heels. I think, *oh my god, they're lovers.*

Michel walks away and lights a cigarette. Marje is already smoking back at her table. I wonder how many of us spotted the wound on his forehead. Yannis takes over again and I catch Raffy's eye. We step away. *Where did you find him?*

At the fence. He'd been gripping the mesh. I think he'd just lost consciousness but he was being held up by the wire. It was embedded in his hand. I had to raise his arms to free him. There was someone there. On the other side. He dived under before I reached him.

Then it must have just happened.

There's a sound of retching, Yannis straightens, Rebecca crouches, speaking his name. The rest of us stand clear, letting him have our air.

When he can sit, Thanasis and Yannis lift him and carry him between them to the silver car. Rebecca says something to Marcus and goes with them. The Greek woman, now on her own, joins Michel and Marje at their table. Marcus follows. No-one is interested in Raffy. He and I dress quickly and join them.

Introductions are made. The Greek woman is Carolina Alifieri, she of the business card, an architect working with Thanasis on the development.

But we are edgy, bleak, purposeless and confused. There's none of the high octane buzz of a disaster survived because each of us, I guess, wonders if another might, at third or fourth hand, be implicated. Greeks have a word for this. Two words. Don't ask.

Marje gets up, goes inside, comes back carrying a salad bowl and lays it on the table. She rummages in her bag and puts a twenty euro note in the bowl. *OK folks, money up front, food to follow.* She waits while we do our distancing moves then says *the guy cooked the stuff, we're hungry, he's alive, he needs to earn, what's not to like?*

We start to turn out our pockets and she says, *Anna honey, a hand here?* and I follow her inside resignedly and slice bread into a basket as she decants the *mezedhes* into serving dishes. I find cutlery, she does plates, we load two trays and carry it all out to where the others have pushed together and re-clothed two tables. And so we create a pastiche of early Kryptos, a small beach, a small taverna, a few simple dishes, strangers introducing themselves, pushing together their tables. We eat and drink and chat after a fashion and the wind starts to howl and we are as relaxed as the sea that hurls itself onto the rocks.

It's evening. We've showered and changed and soon we must leave to meet Claudia, but that's not what's playing in my head right now. I've had a revelation.

The icon in the chapel, I tell my husband's uninterested profile, *the icon your father took me to see? Of the saint that no-one could identify?*

Mmm?

I know who it is.

He has dragged a deck chair into a corner of the terrace out of the wind that rattles the shutters and heaps faded bougainvillea petals into tinted drifts around his feet while he plans what I should say when I phone Lucas, something I must do before the odds increase that he will first run into one of his family in the street.

It was thinking of Lucas that sparked it. The spark lit up the gold and sepia images in my memory of the rock church, and then the other, hazier, image. The anomaly.

I know whose face it is. The face on the icon. It's Simon.

Raffy looks blank. *Saint Simon?*

Simon of the taverna. The Simon you pulled out of the sea. The owl, alas, must yield to the guitar.

I see. So the Simon I pulled out of the sea is – indulge me if I'm getting my faiths mixed here – the reincarnation of an obscure holy man of the early Christian period, now running a restaurant on Kryptos.

It was a different icon.

OK.

He was mesmerised by that icon, your father. Always was, he told me. He'd been talking it up from our first meeting. But when he saw it he went quiet. I was expecting a disquisition on iconography with possible pointers to the most commonly portrayed saints followed by contra-indications for each. You know your father. Instead he said something non-committal and took pictures.

OK. I'm with you. And he said nothing to you?

No. I wonder why not.

And we're off on our separate trains of thought.

Mine is that I now have a licence to cast off the reticence that clogs the brain of a non-believer in someone else's holy place. Icons, windows into heaven in the Orthodox tradition, which I've always seen as fixed and constant, as much a part of the place they inhabit as the frescoes and the aura, are not, after all, either of these things. They're paintings on wood. And round the back will be wire and picture hooks. Even those icons powerful enough to have a church built round them as well as the intemperate few that bleed or weep fresh tears and bring the ultra-devout along with television crews hurrying to towns and villages anywhere in the Greek world are three-dimensional objects painted by a human. And objects can be moved. Someone removed the older unidentified icon and replaced it with an icon for which Simon was the model.

Raffy is on a parallel tack. The mobility of icons. Global context.

The change I've seen in him . . . my father . . . the probability is . . . well, I think it's work-related. Because he doesn't really have a personal life. It's . . . there's been . . . a loss of spontaneity.

Go on.

People often ask him to authenticate icons. Date them, give an opinion on where they might have been painted. That usually means visiting a church or a monastery somewhere off the beaten track, often somewhere that Greek experts haven't been, but equally it might in the States. Greek communities have icons they brought with them.

OK. And?

These are icons in situ. Even the New World icons have their church. But there are others on the art market from private collections and that is more fluid and way more commercial. And not like my father at all.

But still legal?

Mmmm. But for him a diversion. I saw him once with quite a well-known dealer in no-questions-asked antiquities. I asked him about that. He claimed not to know him.

When was that?

Two years ago? Not long after I'd started getting the calls. It crossed my mind then that the same people might have a hold on him. Only I couldn't see them using my mother as a bargaining tool.

Look at it from his point of view, she's still the mother of his children.

He loosens up and lets himself smile.

You didn't think of broaching it with him?

God no.

I forgot. Hollanders don't communicate.

Communication wasn't the issue. Trust was. I had the feeling I couldn't trust him.

Any reason?

Just a feeling.

And you think there might be a link from the dodgy side to why he's here now?

That's my guess. He **is** *working on another book. That takes travel. But there may be some crossed paths along the way. There are the revelatory discoveries of lost icons . . . and then there's creative thinking. I mean an icon is an icon is an icon, but its history might . . .*

Unless it's a fake icon.

What do you mean?

The Simon icon. Replacing a mysterious depiction of an anonymous saint. Which, with that story behind it, would be worth a packet, wouldn't you say? And perhaps not too sadly missed in its old home. Perhaps even leaving the community quietly relieved.

I see what you're getting at.

Your father, of course, would be in the clear there.

All the same, the fact that he didn't say anything suggests at the very least resignation.

The Simon icon . . . of course I would have to see it again to be sure . . . but what I'm thinking now is . . . Rebecca painted it.

Raffy ponders this. I recall his walk past Rebecca's goat shed.

*She **is** very good,* I prompt him, *and didn't you say she was painting what looked like an icon?*

I did. Yes. Of a female saint, though. Or it could have been a hairdresser or a travel agent now I think of it.

And Simon is also a painter. And although she didn't react when I first told her about the taverna it seems obvious now that she was dissembling. They're an item.

She phoned you yesterday. Did she leave a message?

No, and I can't call her back, she doesn't have a phone. I think we need to see her.

Raffy looks at his watch. *My mother's boat gets in in an hour. We could go there first.*

There's no sign of her outside the goat shed and no reason anyway why she would be sitting out here painting in a head-on gale and in fading light except to take her mind off things. My first thought is that Simon is still in hospital and Rebecca with him, but when I call her name she comes out, still in street urchin mode, the ragged shorts and loose hair. She stands contemplating us, assessing and inclined to be reproachful.

He's not your brother, is he? OK. Come inside.

Raffy and I sit on the futon, Rebecca opens out a ripped canvas chair.

Can I trust you? She doesn't wait for an answer. *I hope that's a yes, because there's not another human being on this island I can tell and I've got to tell somebody.*

Outside the wind howls and the goats bleat. It's payback night for the good times, and for Rebecca who, I recall, sought permission from a nymph or a goat-god to settle here, perhaps more than that. She tucks bare feet under pale thighs, the canvas parts some more, and she tells her story.

She and Simon met at Art School. They got together in their first year, and after the degree exhibition, though they both wanted to travel, they had different ideas about where to go.

Simon was the one who wanted to go to Greece, Rebecca was set on India. So they went their separate ways agreeing to meet up later and take things from there. But they reckoned without the effect their chosen places would have on them.

Well, I knew. I knew India would blow my mind. And I knew I had to go there on my own. But Simon is more of a people person.

After India she started in on Indonesia until she began to suffer from overload. *I was storing it in my head and I was running out of space.* She came home and spent a year working from her sketches. She had called Simon's parents right after she got back, but he was still in

Greece, they didn't know where. A gallery gave her an exhibition and it sold out. She had funds to live on and when she called Simon's parents again they had a contact address in Hania, on Crete. She went there but he had moved on. Someone in the bar below the room he'd been renting mentioned Kryptos. *He knew Simon. He said if I found him I should give him a message. He pulled out a menu and wrote something on it.*

But she didn't go straight to Kryptos. When the ferry stopped at another island she liked the look of she got off there. She tried three islands before she got to Kryptos a few weeks later. And once again Simon had just left. *But this guy I spoke to in a bar in Karistos said he was sure he'd be coming back. He told me where he'd been staying. I took a room near there and I fell clean in love with Kryptos. And Simon didn't come back.*

She pauses to re-order her thoughts. *It was ages later that I ran into him in the street. He'd been back for a while, but by then I'd moved into the goat shed, and he was staying at the other end of the island. And that was it.*

We sit motionless, afraid to break her train of thought. But she does that herself.

Where was I? Cooking. Did I stay he'd started cooking? That's what he'd been doing to keep body and soul together. He'd been working in tavernas. Only I didn't entirely believe that could be all. I mean, I asked him, I asked what he'd been painting and he just shrugged and said no time for that. *Only later when I started nagging him did he mention the commissions.*

She stops as if retrospectively interrogating him. There's a hint she might not want to hear the answer.

Commissions? What sort of commissions? I'm trying to sound only politely interested but she has already decided not to go down that route

Anyway he said he'd always wanted to have a restaurant of his own and the chance came up with Mavra Vrahia. Thanasi's company built the taverna and the idea is they run it as a partnership until they see how it goes. By the way did I mention that we're not supposed to know each other, him and me? His idea. At least not before Kryptos. And then . . . then I remembered the menu. She sees our confusion. *The menu from Crete? That the bar guy gave me? With the message? I found it among some stuff and I gave it to him.*

When was that?

Last time I saw him. Two days ago?

And you'd had no contact between then and today?

She shakes her head. It's Raffy who thinks of asking how he is.

OK. Eyes on the floor, hair screening her face.

Rebecca, would you like to come and stay? Until things are sorted out?

Not possible, she says.

It's time to leave to meet Claudia. Raffy is pointing at his watch. I could stay, should stay perhaps, but she won't hear of it, indeed seems anxious for us to go.

Where is Simon now?

He's staying with Yanni. He's OK. I'm not worried. The doctor said he would be fine.

What actually happened, do you know?

He can't remember. She sounds as if she doubts that and we're half way to the port before it crosses my mind that she hasn't been alone with him since she left the hospital.

It's evening, the wind is howling and once again I'm at the port meeting a ferry. The associations are not good.

We cruise the waterfront looking for a parking slot and have to settle for squeezing between a hire car and the Apollo Surf Beach minibus two hundred yards from the ferry quay. As we approach along the esplanade, bent double, the wind hollowing our cheeks and flattening our clothes, the bay is empty of boats. Raffy stops suddenly and says he will grab the chance to buy some shaving things. He crosses the road to take a passageway to the inner village.

I watch him go, walking quickly in the shelter of the buildings, then struggle on along the seaward side, twisting to let the wind whip the hair back out of my eyes. I'm seeing us from the outside, Raffy lying low, growing stubble, myself forever pushing towards a new arrival and the hope of enlightenment.

The waterfront is strangely deserted, the port police not in evidence until I come upon them huddled in the lee of their office wall. Of course they're huddled here. There are no boats. The wind has topped eight Beaufort – topped nine by the feel of it – and the ferries are cancelled. I check. They confirm it. I know about wind and ferries. Why didn't I phone? Because my wits have deserted me.

And why didn't Claudia call us? The boat was due to leave five hours ago, she had ample time. Or did she? Did I check the answerphone? Do I now avoid even looking at it? I have allowed myself to think that things are normal again simply because I've been living, briefly, *à deux*. They're not.

The wind is pounding the palm trees of the promenade into the anguished attitudes you see in tropical tornadoes. Across the road the cafés and bars have wound down their windbreaks so that the whole hedonistic welcome-to-our-island waterfront of sky-blue chairs and scarlet geraniums is closed off behind a wall of juddering, glinting, creaking, thudding plastic. And still the sun shines weakly from a cloudless sky as it drops towards an empty, angry, red-gold sea.

Where is Raffy? I can't wait here in the wind. I look at my watch. Ten minutes have passed. Port police aside I am the only person on this wind-lashed side of the street. The hands creep round. I'm cold. Finally I cross the road and take refuge behind the plastic sheeting of the port café. I'll spot him easily when he crosses that deserted street.

The café reeks of thwarted travel, rucksack heaped upon rucksack, the air smoky, table tops crammed with cups and ashtrays. I find a place at a table with a Greek family and presently a waiter hurrying past with a tray stops for my order. It's the café owner. He recognises me. The recognition clouds his face. He has something to tell me, something he didn't tell the police. He glances round furtively then lowers his voice to tell me in English that John Burnham, the murdered journalist, had asked him who I was. He left him his number and asked him to call if I turned up again. He didn't tell the police because he didn't want to implicate me. I order Greek coffee, *metrio*, consider this, dismiss it, and take out my phone to call Claudia.

Turning it on, just before I remember she called me

on the house phone, I find I have three messages. The messages, all three, are from Gabriel. They say *Call me, Please call me*, and *I thought I told you to keep yr mthrng phone on.*

My coffee arrives and I thank the café owner for his discretion. It's a Greek solidarity thing this, every man a freedom fighter, even, it seems, if he's a woman, and a foreign woman at that. If I have to go on the run farmers may hide me and let me eat their goats so long as I awaken their inner *klepht.*

I call Gabriel but now his phone is off. I should text him. I settle for *Oops. Sorry. On now. Though yours is not*, then, suddenly desperate for communication as I wait increasingly anxiously for Raffy to go on not turning up, add *speaking of which do you know yr mthr is crrntly on way Krpts?*

Selecting SEND I try to think what Claudia would have done when she found her boat was cancelled. Checked back into her hotel, I guess. I drink my coffee and watch darkness fall out there beyond the plastic while here inside the smoke thickens and the travellers who aren't going anywhere move on to beer and ouzo and I move on to the certainty that Raffy isn't coming.

It's night, proper night, a small moon rising, and I'm back at the empty quayside. For an hour now I've been combing the village. Every café and taverna, many of the shops, most of the alleyways. Before I left the café I gave my mobile number to the owner to pass on to anyone who might come looking for me, remembering that Raffy, more cell phone phobic, even, than I, did not have it. *Anna*, I told him. *My name is Anna.* He wrote my details on the back of a menu which pointed me back to Rebecca. I decided to pay her another visit.

But as I reach the car I see Marcus. He stands close to but not quite at it, wearing a scarf and smoking, something I recall he claims to do only when stressed. My impression is that he has been waiting for some time, although of course his manner deftly dishes the notion. As the wind mauls my hair and flaps my shirt tails he huddles elegantly in a milky fleece which, while no doubt one hundred per cent polyester, manages to look like cashmere.

I saw your car, he says.

I wait, key in hand.

We need to talk. Are you going back to Karistos?

The lights of the town fall behind us and still my passenger is silent. *Well?* I say to stir the air a little. He tells me he'll keep it till we get there. There being his house.

My phone rings, and again I pull into a clearing. This time, in contrast to my surprise that it should ring at all, the thing has become a Pandora's box of possibilities that I'm afraid, by answering it, to let out, particularly in the presence of one who remains, despite our parodies of intimacy, a stranger.

It's Gabriel. He's amazed to hear that Claudia is coming and wonders why. I tell him I can't help there and that anyway her boat has been cancelled due to the storm. He says he'll come immediately to Kryptos. *How?* I ask. *Holy shit*, he says.

I would like to tell him about Raffy but my passenger's presence precludes that. I promise to keep my phone on, end the call, and drive off into a storm of self-righteous hooting and flashing before I turn once again up the track to Marcus's house.

The house, from outside, is as dramatic as designer up-lighting can make it. The giant white geranium is spot-lit in its amphora and the bougainvillea has its own light, deepening the shadows around it. As we near the gate the front door bathes itself in a golden glow and while Marcus hunts for his key the wind, which should be leaping and clawing at our clothes, fails to reach us. The hills are aligned to give us shelter – so much do I assume Marcus's mastery of his environment that I picture it that way round – as does a plantation of pine trees behind the house that echoes the thicket around the chapel below. But the steep dark fall of the hillside beyond marks the limit of this seeming sanctuary. A faint glow filtering through the trees comes, I think, from the Meriel/ Yannis/Lucas house, and across the pass that carries the road to the port I see the bone-white facade of the Monastery of the Archangels, reflecting weak moonlight, rising against its own hill. Above us and to the left the uninhabited monastery of Aghios Antonios also has a light showing – interior, electric, dim. Marcus unlocks the door.

The room is as beautiful as I remember, but now that I'm seeing it with more educated eyes I'm taking in less of the aura and more of the actuality. The abstract icons . . . might Rebecca have painted them? I look at the *kouros* rather then let it look at me. Why was he so quick to tell me it was a copy? This time he brings wine. And this time it is he who has a tale to tell.

I think you should turn off your phone, he says, sitting opposite me.

Sorry, can't do that.

OK, he says, *let's begin with your family.*

I think of my parents. *I have no family*, I tell him.

Your husband?

Ah. That family.

It is of course the Hollanders he wants to talk about.

I didn't know, he says, *when I met you before, that you were connected to them. Otherwise things might have turned out differently.*

He is sprawling conversationally, pale fleece shed, pale linen-clad elbow resting on pale upholstered sofa arm. When he straightens and squares his shoulders there's a thespian look to it. More so as he leans towards me.

There are things happening, he says. *Things that are not, perhaps, entirely above board.*

I raise my eyebrows sardonically but he is looking into his wine glass. *But of course that goes with the territory.*

He pauses in hope of encouragement then ploughs on anyway.

A place where nothing happens . . . that leaves no traces . . . no trash, nothing to covet or, I guess, exploit . . . that's a place with no history.

Our eyes meet for a second as mine skid away and his are brought into play. He is not, I imagine, given to monologues, and this is too studied by half. I think of a college-level Marxist preparing to justify revolution – omelettes, broken eggs, eggshells – the eggshells recalling to me the infinitely more interesting pottery shards, the fragment in the olive grove. I bookmark that for later and concentrate for now on being talked into a more sympathetic listening mode than he expects me to arrive at spontaneously.

When I first came here, he continues, *in my gap year, I just . . . flipped.* He pauses to let this bring me on board and perhaps into eye contact. *I mean, I did all the island hopping but this was the one I came back to.*

I'd been here a month or so when a man came up to me in the bar where I used to hang out. He started chatting, then he said I see you here long time. You like Greece? Maybe you like old things? *I wasn't sure what he meant but I guess I had an inkling. It's part of the package, isn't it?*

He wanted me to go with him to see something his brother had dug up. I said he should bring it there, to the bar. He said that was impossible. He had a pick-up outside and he took me to his brother's farm. It was a Cycladic figurine, the first I'd seen. The brother wanted five thousand dollars for it, the dowry for his daughter's marriage. Well, I was a student. And anyway there was no way I was getting into anything like that. He kept saying you rich American. I wait. You get money. I wait. *I finally convinced him I was not his man, but I couldn't get it out of my mind. Back then I got off on the whole notion of BC, no figures needed.*

He pauses to check and slightly soften his expression. Suitably sophomore, he presses on.

When I'd got to know a bit more and fixed the fifth century as the kind of Sixties of Greek civilisation I became more numerate. I spent some time in Athens educating myself timewise. The Thera frescoes, the Mycenean hunting scene dagger, all of that. The dates of those things – you know how that hits you the first time. When I'd seen a few more Cycladic figurines and discovered they were from the third millennium that was it. I was bound for Harvard business school, then after that my father's company, but that was no longer a possibility. So I . . . made the switch. To Art History.

He checks I'm still listening. I am.

Then . . . after I graduated . . . galleries, auction houses. Learning on the job.

I glance round the objects in the room.

You did well.

I did. Also my father died. He is showing me, I realise, his financial credentials. He has no need to be a grubby trader in under-the-counter ceramics. *Then I came here.*

To sell pictures of boats and windmills?

Well OK, as you guessed, that's only part of it. But I didn't come here to exploit. I just wanted to live in a grown-up country. With a history. And I didn't, I swear I didn't, know the extent of what is going on here. And he deploys, successfully this time, the blue eyes, which tonight look too compromised for purpose.

Which is?

I'm sure your husband has told you. He says this in a subtly altered 'look, we're both adults here' tone.

I'm sure my husband knows much less than you might think.

And that makes him hesitate.

Well . . . he checks to see that I'm not being disingenuous . . . *in that case you should know that there is an area of continuous settlement here that's never been excavated. Formally excavated. It lies in poor land that belonged to poor families. Related families, I believe. When they started to dig up the odd thing they just took it to where tourists hung out.* A pause to revisit being a tourist, hanging out. *And then some not-so-poor families got in on the act.*

As they do. To keep him talking. Because I don't know why he's telling me this.

And they were able to buy up the adjoining land. Another pause. This is way too much information for an impromptu chat. But I'm listening, and he has a point to make.

It was about this time they brought in a tame archaeologist. There was a boy whose family came from Kryptos and who had just graduated. I believe he was offered a fee that must have seemed very persuasive when they said it included a legitimate-sounding secrecy clause. Only, he was a shining paragon of recent graduation. He kept records. And when he realised the extent of what they were finding he called a friend in Athens. When the friend arrived he wasn't there to meet him. So I was told. Of course he may just have decided it was time to leave.

He looks away towards the *kouros*, then back again. *So the friend went back to Athens and after that they kept it in-house.*

They being?

You wouldn't know them. He shrugs. *I don't know them. Local people. Farmers, people with jobs. I believe they've become rather knowledgeable. And of course they feel entitled. It's their land, their heritage, why should it be outsiders who dictate what happens to what they see as their birthright? Although of course this is going back god knows how many waves of settlement. Anyway. They've set up their children and looked after their mothers, that's all. It's the marketing side that involves . . . people of higher profile.*

People I might know?

Sure.

And where do you come in?

Late and innocent, comparatively. I had contacts.

Back there you said as you guessed. *I didn't guess. You told me. That first time here it was you who mentioned antiquities.*

That's true. That's how recently I was telling myself it was all borderline innocent.

And now?

He spreads his hands. *It's too big. Just . . . far too big.*

For you? For them?

It doesn't concern me. For the people it does concern . . . well I'd say it's beginning to overwhelm them, judging by how they're reacting.

Which is?

With undue haste. There are people, you know, who might inform. For that reason they prefer off the island and out of the country in one move.

Yachts?

He hesitates. *Of course marinas are out.*

He's on a tack of his own. I wait.

Yacht owners are a breed apart. They're something else, they . . . He sees he's drawing a blank. *I mean they're careful. Of their reputations?*

Forgive me . . . are we talking of things that can't just be disguised as a crate of booze?

A sarcophagus? A statue that has survived in two pieces . . . that it would be rather a shame to break up further?

Good god.

Quite. And with the recent finds . . . well, you could say it was obsidian to ostentation in one tidy package.

He checks my expression and sees he's overcooking it.

And so, he hurries on, *when Thanasis decided to include a marina in his villa development it was suggested by someone, I don't know who, that he should include an inland access road. Include or allow. It's an unfrequented part of the island as you know, and boats will be coming and going with building materials.*

I try not to react to Thanasi's name. *They're thinking that far ahead?*

I'm told there is an embarras de richèsses. *And I mean* embarras. *A lot of people are privately wishing they'd never started. Gentlemen opportunists included.*

You're trying to tell me that Thanasis tears a chunk out of the island to build an export system for looted antiquities and still considers himself a dilettante.

No. No. It's not that way round. Thanasis is a megalomaniac property developer first and foremost and after that a Kryptos nationalist. He wants Kryptos to be a kind of Aegean Monte Carlo. It's his baby. And with the new airport he's well on the way to realising that.

The new airport being a result of his lobbying?

I believe he had a casting vote. But what I'm saying is his hands are relatively clean. He would have agreed to let his jetty be used by friends.

He can see I'm not softening, if that was his aim. He

still has some convincing to do, whether out of obligation to a third party or out of narrative exactitude I can't tell.

His concern is for the island. His wish is that the site had been properly excavated from the start. In fact, because it's turning out to be of such major importance, I believe he is exploring ways to make that still happen. And then Kryptos would truly be in the first rank of Greek destinations.

But . . . there's opposition?

Of course. Because, depending on how that might be handled, a lot of people could go down. Some relatively guileless islanders among them.

And where do I come into it?

Sorry?

Why did you decide to tell me all this now?

Because I believe your husband is in danger.

I see. And why now particularly?

Because he has come here, has he not, to blow this whole thing apart?

I'm set to voice a protest when I think well, yes, now that I hear it that way, that's why he's here. In essence. But as I sit here trying to digest all this it feels very far from the truth. And his now even more alarming non-appearance has a context. I can see that Marcus has stepped out of line, a line he professes not to be in, possibly to return a favour. I warned him of a plot against him, now he is warning me of a plot against Raffy.

Tell me, I say, *tell me honestly, who did you think might be plotting to kill you?*

I didn't believe that anyone was. I don't believe I know anyone who could order the kiss of death in so few words. He hesitates. *But because I was backing away – I was just latching on to the extent of it – there was always an outside possibility. And they might have thought I knew too much. Though I didn't then.*

The night we had dinner in Karistos . . . did you know then?

Not everything. I'd been given a hint of the possible extent of the finds . . . in an . . . in an attempt to persuade me to stay – to come – on board.

And when you heard about the journalist who'd been stabbed you thought he might have been mistaken for you?

No. That wasn't it. He had come to the gallery ostensibly to buy paintings for his new house, but he'd asked me a few questions that suggested he was onto something.

So . . . I'm back-tracking again . . . *when I overheard the phone call that mentioned your name and the guy said* kill him *he wasn't talking about you at all?*

It's unlikely.

Who then?

That would be someone not implicated. Someone in a position to shop us all.

I don't have to ask. And he said 'us'. But I also know that my husband's name did not cross the lips of the man in my driveway and on the phone. Marcus is hyping up the threat to Raffy by whatever means come to hand.

He gets to his feet and starts to pace. He walks towards the *kouros* but turns back as if fearful of drawing attention to it. He takes a cigarette from the box on the table. He asks if I've eaten. I haven't. He goes out of the room. I should use this time to make decisions but I'm distracted once again by the objects I'm sharing the space with, each of them now pulsating with possibilities. I stand up and cross to the window. The village, far off, twinkles behind thrashing trees against a sea that is lit just enough by the harbour lights to act out its spasmodic movements in black and white.

Raffy the avenging angel does not ring true. He came to find out, not to confront, which, anyway, would have been crazy. He had no idea of the scale. And the place where he would take his suspicions would be Athens, or perhaps – I don't know – London or Oxford. He has, after all, only his childhood discoveries to go on along with Jean-Paul's second-hand reports. All that balanced by his love for the island. But it's what people believe that dictates their actions.

He could not, as far as I know, name names. Recognition is all the other way. And who on the island knew he was coming here? Lisa Dunmore. How she knew I can't imagine and what use she planned to put that to is even less fathomable. Enterprising easily foiled kidnapper certainly, but a cog in the wheel of an island mafia? I think not.

If Raffy was always a projected target then I have to rethink the chronology. It was the day **before** his arrival that I overheard the conversation and went to meet the boat, the boat that Marcus came on. For Raffy to be the target then he would have been expected the night before he came. And who believed he was coming then? Not I.

Marcus comes back carrying a tray. He has heated some slices of *spanakopitta* and made green tea in a glass teapot. He is, in this more talkative and confiding mode, as ambiguous as before. More ambiguous because I believe he does nothing without a purpose, and the purpose of this frank, staged, almost certainly pre-planned confessional is not just Raffy's welfare.

I help myself to a slice of *spanakopitta*, noting wearily the inevitable lightness of the pastry and the panache of the antique onyx-handled serving gizmo. *What did you mean when you said if you'd known I was connected to the Hollanders things might have turned out differently?*

He smiles as he pours the tea.

Well now . . .

And then there are sounds outside. At first I think it's the wind changing direction, the wind god, perhaps, in a fit of pique signalling that you can soft furnish all you like but you diss the gods at your peril. And then the light in the forecourt brightens and the door starts to rattle as if someone is pushing at it. Marcus's expression hasn't changed but I can see he is putting something on hold. From just outside comes a gritty shifting sound, the sound of something unimaginable moving about on the paving stones. A sound of panting. Suddenly a blood-curling howl, an animal howl, and right after that and before I can dispel the image of a wolf on hind legs scrabbling at the door, a rifle shot.

Marcus lays down the teapot. He gets calmly to his feet and goes towards the door. I sit clutching my cup, my saucer and my plate, feeling like a bit player in some fifties rep production as he pushes the door half closed behind him. The scrabbling and the rattling have stopped. I lay down the cup, the saucer and the plate. I hear Marcus open the outside door.

There are voices, Marcus's, still calm, speaking

Greek, the words inaudible, and another man's, gruffer, excitable, raised. Marcus's voice moves further away, the other following it, its pitch rising. Then the wind pushes open the door of the room and a newspaper, a wall hanging, some lilies in a vase all animate as the smell of pine trees and salt and the distant noise of the sea force their way in.

The newspaper flaps a name at me but I blank it as I get to my feet and go out into the hallway. The door stands open and through it I see that the gate is also open. I edge forward, taking in a dark pool that is discolouring the paving slabs to the right of the door. I brace myself. I step outside. It's a dog. Or a wolf. It's dead.

There is no sign of Marcus and no longer any sound of voices. The wind is still yammering above and below the house and my car is still parked on the verge below the open gate. There is, it occurs to me, no sign of Marcus's car. Nor was there when we arrived. Seeing my car at the port, I imagine, he left his own and improvised.

I stand listening to the wind howl, keeping my eyes turned from the dog. Fear of the door blowing shut is now edging out the physical fear. My bag is in there. I should retrieve it.

Back inside everything changes. This is calming décor. I can't help noting that the vegetal green of the tea is picking up the colour of the lily stems in their vase while highlighting the darker green of the *spanakopitta.* I wonder if Marcus has programmed his sensibility to exercise mind control in his absence.

I should go and look for him, should I not? I'm so good at that. But then there is the problem of securing his house with its *objets d'art* while not locking him out, actions which seem incompatible. I can't stay here. Anything might happen. I sling my bag over my shoulder, glance again at the newspaper and step outside in time to see a car come quickly up the track and park behind mine. It's Dimitris of the craft shop, last seen at the sculptor's workshop on Tinos.

I go eagerly to meet him but he is looking past me at the scene of carnage which gives me the courage to look again. If it isn't a wolf it's a wolf look-alike, long-legged, short-eared, not designed to be lovable. Dimitris walks over and crouches beside it. I am touched and humbled that he is putting its welfare first, islanders not being known for their love of animals. He assures himself that it's dead then he picks it up and carries it into the deep shadow at the uphill edge of the garden where he drops it over the fence. It hits the ground with the unmistakable sound of a fallen body. He comes back, turns on a tap on the side wall of the house, rinses his hands, dries them on his jeans and comes towards me smiling.

How are you Anna?

A bizarre greeting in the circumstances. It makes my blood run cold. He looks at the bag slung over my shoulder.

Where are you going?

Well, I was going to look for Marcus.

Not necessary, he says and moves closer so that I step back inside the door. He closes it behind him and pockets the key.

I'm crouching on the hillside, deep in scrub, out of sight and out of reach of the wind. A moment ago I heard a car leave. Dimitris on his own would not be able to search in these conditions with the wind's roar covering all other sounds and only a sliver of moon for light. If it's important – and I have no views on that – he'll be back with help.

I'm close to the south wall of the Monastery of Aghios Antonios. The dim light I noticed is coming from a window on this side. I wonder whether it is left on to suggest habitation and so to discourage strangers from snooping. To me it looks only inviting. Bending low I edge out of the bushes and approach the south wall. Before I look for an entry point I should check all round the building. Still stooping I go along the back wall through heavy thickets of lentisk and between tall stabbing stands of acanthus. The windows on this side are shuttered.

The north wall is screened by a row of cypresses and on this side the ground has been tended. Between the trees and the track runs a high mesh fence like the one we saw by the cave, continuing out of sight to the top of the hill. The wall which faces the sea is high, clear and open. I look and listen before I step out of cover and walk close to it, feeling my way along its eerie almost phosphorescent pale stuccoed mass. In the centre of the wall is a door hung with heavy chains which have been left unhooked. I put my hand against the carved and studded woodwork. It moves. Inside may be more scary than out but I haven't that many options. I squeeze through the opening and into an entrance hall.

The interior is stark and unadorned, the starlight entering through a high window above the door amplified by the white walls. Over to my right a door is ajar, spilling a grudging sixty watts of artificial light. The wind outside is loud enough to hide the sound of my sandaled feet on the stone floor as I edge towards the room. From the doorway I can see the corner of an easel. I smell paint. On the wall by the window I see the subdued glitter of an icon. I step into the room. Before I have taken in anything of my surroundings a man's voice says *Kalos ilthate.* Welcome.

A tiny figure in black robes sits with his back to me before the easel, painting. From his lack of concern I'm sure that he has mistaken me for someone else. His fragility, his stoop, his bony hand, the wispiness of the long white beard tell me that I am far more likely to alarm him than he to startle me. I remember the old icon-painting monk Lucas told me about. Here he is, painting.

Forgive me, I say in Greek and move slowly round into his line of vision so that he can see I'm harmless, physically at least. Women don't belong in monasteries, but perhaps in an uninhabited one the rules are different. He stops painting and looks in my direction. He is not alarmed. *Good evening*, he says. *I thought you were the other one.* Ah, I think, Rebecca.

She is not here just now, I say. *Perhaps she will come later.*

She learns well. Very well. And you, do you wish to learn?

I who have not a scrap of talent for painting wonder

if to act out this strange charade may be my best hope of sanctuary and enlightenment.

If I may.

Then come to stand behind me.

Thankfully I step into the shadow behind his chair and look at the icon spread before him. It is a painting done by instinct by an almost blind man. From the rocks and the desert in the background I can tell that this is John the Baptist, John the Forerunner as he is known in Greece. But while the formality is Byzantine, the figure of the man who stands in the foreground, bearded and with wild hair, spills out beyond the clean stylised outlines of Orthodox iconography. It is an impressionist painting superimposed on a formal one and all the more powerful for that. He is painting the robes of the figure conventionally enough but it is the face that haunts me. This John expresses through asymmetrical features the travails and the doubts that have beset him in the wilderness. I am in the presence of the painter of the icons on Marcus's wall.

I'm still digesting this when I hear the wind grow louder. Someone has opened the outside door. But I am safer with this venerable man, surely, than fleeing across a dark hillside.

Behind me someone enters the room.

Kalos ilthate, says Brother Gerasimos.

Kali spera, says Rebecca's voice behind me. Good evening.

Hallo, I say. *I thought you might be coming.*

An hour has passed and I'm squatting under a thorn bush dabbing at scratches with Marcus's handkerchief. This is an inhospitable spot, steep and scrub infested, just above a quarry but with a view of Marcus's house. The wind is slackening. Free of its howling the hillside seems more exposed, certainly more receptive to sounds.

Rebecca is with me. Tired of being prey when no-one appears to be hunting us she digs out a bar of chocolate from her bag, breaks it and hands me half. The adrenalin is settling. I snap off two squares.

How did you get away? she asks, not lowering her voice. I have told her about Raffy's disappearance and sketched in what happened down there. When I got to the dog I got the first real response. *The Wolf Dog?* she said. *It's dead?*

You know it?

Sure. It lives up here. Eats rabbits. There are lots of rabbits in the monastery lands because no-one is allowed to shoot there. Brother Gerasimos likes to feed it. He believes it guards the monastery. But the farmers around here, they think it's a hound of hell. They've been after it for ages. So it's dead? That's sad.

Far below car headlights glimmer along the valley floor. They seem on a different plane from us. Up here we're sharing the intimate glow of the telecommunications mast on the mountain across the bay, looking from this altitude like a tall floor lamp seen across the sweep of a high-ceilinged penthouse, with the monastery dominating the mezzanine. There are three layers to the island, I think – the upper world we're in, strung out in space between the light on the mountain, the monastery and a plane winking across the sky, then the middle world – the headlights delineating the valley floor and the people down there – and below that the third layer I'm working my way down to, the underworld, source of all troubles, full of shards, pediments, images of deities, flints, ores, skulls of pygmy elephants, Cyclops heads, foundations of things decayed before they're guessed at, beetles, bodies, bones.

Well? says Rebecca. *How did you?*

When Dimitris locked the door and signed to me to go back into the room he was avoiding my eye. Avoiding sending out signals. I thought am I a prisoner? *Because the gesture was not hostile. But the key in the pocket was. So yes. Whose prisoner being a whole other question.*

So then I thought, sow confusion. *I went back to my chair, dropped my bag, picked up the tea cup, the saucer and the plate, unwrapped the fork from the napkin Marcus had laid out on the tray, spread the napkin on my knee and began to eat the spinach pie. And it did have the effect I meant it to. He was so thrown by my behaviour he believed I was a total innocent.*

Or just bad mannered.

That's also possible. Anyway after a few forkfuls I excused myself to go to the loo and I climbed out of the window. Like Raffy.

Wow, says Rebecca and squeezes my arm. In my bag I find some water which I share with her. It's very girlie this, the two of us on the run, but with bags.

Your turn, I say, and we settle ourselves into a more comfortable position while she tells me how she found that Simon had become involved in an icon faking scam in Crete.

Icon ***faking****?*

Yeah. He was painting them in good faith, painting to commission, using old wood and old techniques. He didn't know the guy was passing them off as genuine antiques. But of course someone latched on to it and the guy who commissioned him professed to know nothing about it. According to him it was all Simon's idea. So he got out of there. Crete, that is.

And started cooking?

Yeah. Buried himself in kitchens. No-one knew about his painting.

Until you came?

Right.

She breaks off to eat the last square of chocolate. *I was painting from the start. When I'd finished a few things I took them to Marcus. I'd seen his gallery. He liked them. He told me I could get much higher prices for them than I was asking. There are some seriously wealthy people here now, you know. He's got me several commissions.*

Like Thanasi's hotel?

Oh no. That had nothing to do with Marcus.

That's not the story he told me.

She considers that. *OK, maybe everything is up for revision. Anyway Simon and I were being careful. We were acting like we just met, and so far as everyone on Kryptos knew he was just a food guy. Then I gave him that menu that the man in the bar on Crete gave me. I guess he must have called the number.*

Do you remember what the message was? On the menu?

Just a name and a number I think. Maybe something written. It was Greek. I don't know Greek.

So, you think the man he knew on Crete, the man who gave you the menu, came here?

No. No, there was hardly time for that. The guy on Crete must have contacted someone who was already here.

Far below we see the glint of car headlights descend the track from Marcus's house to the road, the car we saw arrive just as we were leaving the monastery. We watch it go then get to our feet. The air is still fresh but tinged now with the emerging scents of crushed mountain herbs.

I should tell you I have seen your Simon icon.

Really?

In the chapel.

What?

You mean you didn't know? It's in the little chapel out on the rocks beyond the beach where we swim.

Bastard, says Rebecca.

18

It's mid-morning, the wind has dropped, and Lucas is facing me across a table in the square. We're eating *galaktoboureko* and drinking *frappé*. My idea, I called him.

Lucas sits in a canvas director's chair wearing a stonewashed grandfather shirt with the sleeves rolled to just on the elbow. His *faux naïf* document carrier sits on the chair next to him. His hair is freshly washed. He looks like a lecturer in intelligent design, a cosmetic surgeon, a psychotherapist or a financial adviser to the stars.

After we've discussed the weather for a bit I say *you must be very happy.*

He smiles and chases a syrup-soaked pastry curl round his plate.

All your family coming here?

Surprised but controlling it, eyes on his fork.

Perhaps you know something I don't?

Well, Claudia . . . didn't she tell you?

Claudia? Coming here? No. When is this?

Today. I assumed you knew.

Which is not quite true, not true at all in fact. His surprise slides smoothly into calculation – I'm noting to order for Raffy – then less smoothly becomes something else, something too intimate for me to sit here observing.

Does she know I'm here?

I don't know. This **is** true. Another aspect I hadn't considered.

Well – he is looking, quite reasonably, for an explanation – *perhaps it was Gabriel who arranged it.* Gabriel who, with the boats running, texted to say that *for tribal reasons* he would probably turn up.

Or Michael. I sit here wincing as I mete out the blows.

Michael?

He's coming to compete in the Windsurfing Championships.

Those were the two messages on the answerphone when I got back last night. Claudia and Michael.

Lucas is digesting my news. I let him do that for a bit.

Claudia is coming for that? I see how his mind is working. Long hours on a windy beach in a headscarf doing penance for missed school sports days. *How did they come to have your number?*

I expect Raffy gave them it. I recall his own attempts to find me and realise that, for whatever reason, Lucas is out on his own.

A moment's pause, then he looks unreservedly delighted. *Of course. I'd forgotten. You two are communicating. Tell me, have you heard from him again?*

Yes. He's here.

A hand trails across my shoulder – *family*, purrs Nico, passing – so that I miss his reaction, then catch *Here? Now? Raffy? That's amazing.*

That accomplished, what do I do for my second trick? I have put Raffy on Kryptos but I have this other, dud, card up my sleeve. I have mislaid him. I am not enjoying this but someone has to keep the show on the road.

Claudia, I tell Lucas, is arriving in the afternoon. As for Michael, he didn't say when he was coming. I expect he will be travelling with other surfers.

Well my dear, I have to hand it to you for holding the family together. I tend not to stay in touch when I go off. Perhaps I should rethink that. What time is Claudia arriving?

A quarter to two. That's the schedule. I imagine you'd like to come to meet her?

He smiles. *Of course. Thank you.* He stands up suddenly. *But if I am going to do that there are some things I have to deal with first. Anna, would you excuse me?* He puts his hand in his pocket.

Don't worry. I'll see to it.

When he's out of sight I get to my feet and, *frappé* and flaky thing unfinished, drop some money on the table. The café owner, edging past with a tray of fresh *baklava*, stops, appalled, to ask what's wrong with his pastries. It takes a full minute to reassure him before I can hurry in pursuit, but when I spot him again he has no phone clamped to his ear nor is he heading out of the village in the direction of the mystery house. He calls in at the chemist and comes out carrying something in black and silver packaging. Aftershave. Then he heads into the tangle of streets that form the upper village, the area where he told me he was renting a room.

Back in the square I stop to buy a newspaper. Something among the indoor racks catches my eye. Alongside the Greek name-day cards is a very English display, glossy, Constabley, Hogarthian, Landseerish. I pick one up. Blank. For your own greeting. On the back, the name of the imprint. Classica.

When Rebecca and I crawled out from under the thorns last night, we picked our way across the hill, and found Marcus's house in darkness. The car was where I'd left it. The dog had gone. I pictured Marcus lying bleeding on the hillside. I pictured him crawling through the undergrowth with a head-torch and a knife in his teeth searching for me. Neither hunted nor hunter seemed a fit. Finally I pictured him asleep between unbleached linen sheets in a room whose walk-in cupboard had garments in every shade of pale and, content that I had imagined him into wellbeing, drove off. Before I dropped Rebecca I asked how she had got to the monastery. *Walked*, she said. *Across the fields. Like I always do.*

Back home, adrenalin dispersing, it was the pastoral world that stayed with me.

Now, driving home to check again for messages – I'm clinging to the idea that Raffy is in hiding and will soon be able to reach a phone – my mood is unshakably upbeat. This is the Aegean, I tell myself, not Hackney or Harlem. Something will happen, something beyond our inept tampering. The thing will implode or, in the Greek way, a creative solution will be found.

I look round my barely lived-in living room and, in expectation of an influx of Hollanders, do some quick and overdue tidying. I'm replacing a book on the shelf, the book I carry around but fail to read, when something catches my eye. A post-it note is stuck inside the back cover. I put it back on the coffee table to check out later then spot the newspaper, unread and unremembered, sticking out of my bag, sibling of the one I saw in Marcus's house. It's a tabloid, rival to the one that showed the second Mrs. Burnham bereft on the Kryptos quayside. This one can say exclusively that the couple had already split. Rancorously and for real. She was never coming here.

The port café, now milling with yesterday's thwarted travellers, has the adrenalin levels of Bank Holiday Heathrow. It's the edgy time anyway, early afternoon culturally subsumed into forenoon. Something, some attempted armistice with the natural world, a sort of make-shift civic amulet, delays the onset of noon until everyone can get home. They're shutting shops, closing offices, scrambling towards the deadline of eat and sleep, but until then ratty, preoccupied. What they call afternoon begins in the evening. What we call afternoon they placate by blanking it.

What we call afternoon is *mesimeri*. Mid-day. Once it was Pan's time, the countryside his to play with, to seed with his sensed terror, and now, as they head off like lemmings to oblivion, I think they're still handing it to him on a plate. Right now, though, at going on two hours after noon, it's the mid-day of the working world. The café owner slams down two cappuccinos with puddles in their saucers.

Lucas too seems slightly dimmed and it's hard to speak above the sounds of taxis and cars dropping people where they shouldn't, the whistling, the hooting, the shouting.

How long is it, I ask, *since you last saw Claudia?*

I don't know. Five years?

That long? I thought Gabriel mentioned a family reunion.

Sometimes, yes. Some of us.

I wonder if the separation with its amicable exchange of text messages is quite as clean and accommodated as it was described to me.

A boat has rounded the headland. Travellers slap money on tables and drag their luggage across the road. We follow.

Claudia, amongst all the people disembarking, is unmistakable. Straight-backed, swathed in an off-white pashmina, she emerges, looks about her, then comes down the ramp like a swan among scuttling ducks. She can do that because she carries no luggage. The man disembarking alongside her is carrying her case, leaning proprietorially towards her. At my side I hear an intake of breath.

Two men move out from behind us and go towards the ramp. They're wearing the light blue shirts of the real police. I recognise Stelios Kritikos and his second in command who searched the house. As Claudia and her companion step down onto the quay they move forward and stand in front of them. There is a brief exchange and then they are being escorted through the crowds towards a police car. I hurry forward to catch Claudia's attention and let her know that I'm here. Stelios Kritikos looks up and acknowledges me before he waves me, quite amiably, away. Claudia's eyes meet mine as she dips gracefully into the back of the car. She takes the time to flash me a dazzling smile.

When I turn to speak to Lucas he has vanished.

I'm walking. Walking in the *mesimeri*. Lethargy crushes the oxygen from the air and its place is taken by something more hallucinogenic. As I walk I think about last night. Was I being . . . how would you describe it . . . held? As a bargaining tool, perhaps, for Raffy? And, if held, held by whom? Marcus? The participle surely offends against his ethos. Delayed, then. And Dimitris, where did he come in?

The track lifts me from sea level into the ironed-out empty place that lies behind my house. From here the mountains that form the core of the island stand aloof from the accretions of habitation, the village, far off, looks separate and defined, and the few houses climbing the lower slopes look ornamental rather than the start of an infestation. All signs of human meddling recede as the view widens to take in the mountains of the next island across the strait.

There's no-one in sight. The goats kneel in the stubble or stand motionless, only their yellow eyes alert. When I pass the farmhouse the dog, sleeping by the barn, gives a token bark then lets it head drop back onto the baked earth.

Rebecca is not there. I walk on towards the other, east-facing, shore enjoying the boundlessness of all this, not to mention the personal space created by all these disappearances. At the next small farm even the dog is asleep.

Approaching the coast, stands of juniper thicken up right and left, and the track turns from baked compacted earth, to earth and sand, and finally to loose sand as it reaches the junction with the other even less defined path that meanders along the eastern shore and is dominated from across the narrow strait by the bigger neighbouring island.

A sudden surge of laughter, male laughter, comes from the juniper thicket ahead. A camper van, customised, hand-painted in azure sworls on darker blue, with a roof rack designed for surf boards, is parked beside the track above a cove that preludes the start of the surf beach. The strait ahead is gaudy with the sails of wind-surfers idling on the flat water, tacking in search of a stray puff of wind.

Michael is coming. Perhaps he's here already. Perhaps across that hedge.

I turn right, away from the surf beaches, along the rocky coast that borders the fertile plain. Up ahead where the coast draws nearer to the foothills of the central mountains the land becomes less fertile, more picturesque, turning its owners into hoteliers and restaurateurs who arrange their tables to face the rising sun, the icing sugar town and the soaring mountains across the strait so that their guests sit gazing at that other island, no longer attuned to the land around them. But here, where the soil is deep and the path a pencil line between the blue of the sea and the blond of the corn stubble, people still work their land and turn their backs to the view. And here also live, or lived, those spirits of place that police country people and test them, visiting afflictions on those who stray or forget to practise self control. Do they, I wonder, evolve? Keep up with the newer sins? Might they, even now, on this idle afternoon be picking up the scent of the windsurfers?

Michael of all the family is the one I know least. Back then I thought I bored him, that everyone bored him. Now I think the disability was his, his remoteness a symptom, not a pose. Girls watched him, boys made sporadic attempts at mateyness to which he responded readily enough but never for long. Perhaps he knew his limitations, knew to keep changing friends – for him the choice was endless – so that no one would find him out. How did that transfer to the adult world? And how did he feel about Claudia's liaisons? Also, because I can't recall it, what was his relationship with Lucas?

Lucas. All round good guy. If what Claudia asked of life was to be desired and entertained, Lucas expected to be liked. Seduced you into liking him, or rather seduced you into wanting him to like you. Talking to him, he gave you all his attention. But, now I think about it, he never had to keep that up for long. For his family and friends the summers on Kryptos were always coloured by his imminent departure.

A rabbit bounds out of the field and vanishes into

the rocks as a gunshot close by displaces air. Seagulls rise squawking and a slow and steady tinkling drifts across the fields. The goats are moving out of harm's way. Is it safe to be walking here when men are out hunting and women presumed indoors and asleep? Ahead of me I see a man come out of a farmhouse gate with a rifle in his hand. Behind him a woman's voice is raised. He shouts back and heads out across the fields. As he pauses and glances round he sees me and stops. For a moment it seems he will go back into the house, then he continues across the field.

Did Michael ever join Raffy on his walks? Not that summer. The year was notable for absences, Lucas off hunting angels and icons, Michael house-partying in France. So we were told. And Gabriel? Here, certainly, but doing his own thing, blanking out all of them, Raffy included.

And I, with curiosity already highly developed, avoided over-analysing the Hollanders. Because they were already central to our lives? Partly that. Because I was content for them to be stereotypes? A lot of that. I took them home like snapshots to remind me of how it felt to be in Karistos in the summer. Too much diversity would have blurred the picture, change would have defiled it. They couldn't change. They were an aspect of my sense of self.

Just as I can't recall a group photograph, so, in life, I believe I never saw them all together. Their present untidy dispersal is pretty much how it always was.

A second gunshot echoes across the fields. A second rabbit. Then a familiar drubbing fills the air and gathers to a point above me, a helicopter firing sunbeams as it descends. It's Friday afternoon, arrival time for Athenian weekenders, amongst them the extra-affluent who can bypass the ferry. The seagulls skid off over the sea and I clutch my ears, my hair, my dress as the dust swirl rises around it. This one is not bound for a millionaire's clifftop eerie, though, it's going to land in this field. I turn and run for the shelter of the juniper, the Delos helicopter in my mind. When I come out further down the track and look back, all I see is two guys in shorts and singlets heading towards the surf beach. The helicopter is already taking off. Windsurfers, it seems, may also be affluent.

And now Rebecca is there, seated at her easel. Approaching from this direction the dog gives no warning of my arrival. She has positioned herself with the sun behind her so I come up on her blind side and stand for a while watching. She is beginning an icon, the icon of a female saint, her halo in outline angled like an Ascot hat. Last night I saw her rendering of a Christ whose face blazed with a conviction that was in outline Byzantine and in essence twenty-first century alpha male. Who is commissioning these things?

She looks up. *Still alive then?*

Yeah. You too?

Seems so.

From the juniper thicket comes a whoop as the newcomers arrive.

Surfers, says Rebecca. *From all over. They've got some competition coming up.*

What's the news of Simon?

She goes on painting, shadowing the fall of a robe. *I don't have any news of Simon.*

He's still with Yannis?

Who knows?

You mean you haven't heard anything?

Yannis said he'd bring him over. He hasn't.

Are you worried?

She lays down her brush. *I'm scared.*

And an hour later we're crossing last night's hillside on a mission to demystify everything: flickering lights, glimpsed shirt sleeve, overheard fig tree, disputed property ownership, all the coincidence and proximity and made-up miasma we have separately constructed out of the Yannis/Meriel/Lucas house.

When we slide down into the clearing that surrounds the house I can see that the light that shone through the pine trees last night comes from a naked bulb above the back door, still burning in daylight. The windows are shuttered. We edge round to the front of the house facing across its little levelled plateau to the Monastery of the Archangels on the mountain opposite and I can see right away why Meriel wanted to buy it. It's the perfect organic Cycladic house, rough blocks of island marble plastered over, a stone wall seat stretching from the door into the shade of a shaky chestnut pergola with an unpruned vine dropping a dense curtain around it, and, set off to one side, a well, a lemon tree and a fig.

I finger the shutters tentatively, Rebecca tries the door. By knocking on it. I hold my breath. No-one comes. She puts her shoulder to it and it flies open. It wasn't locked.

Inside it is as Meriel described, the earth floor, the tiny living room with its corner fireplace, sepia photographs, homemade table and two stools, and the bedroom still with tarnished brass bedstead and mouldy sagging mattress as if its occupant had been gathered by her maker from the travails of a rainy winter. Behind the bedroom at the back there is another space with a different door, incongruously new and shiny. This door has a steel handle and a padlock and chain. When I try the padlock it is, of course, locked.

Let's look round the back, says Rebecca. *This might have a window.* At the sound of her voice there is a faint noise from behind the door. *Simon?* Rebecca leans closer. I grab her arm and haul her outside as a car crunches up the track. We just have time to pull the door behind us and get back into the thorny cover above the cutting where the house stands when the car appears.

It's blue. Thorns stabbing where thorns stabbed yesterday we crouch behind a bush and watch as the engine is cut and a man gets out, a tall, gaunt, at first unfamiliar man who, closing the door, stops to answer his mobile, ring tone In the Hall of the Mountain King. It's Peter Karpodinis. Beside me I hear Rebecca's sharp intake of breath.

Talking, he pushes open the door of the house, and disappears inside to the sudden accompaniment of The Dance of the Sugar Plum Fairy. I wrench the phone from my bag. It's Gabriel.

Anna? Why are you whispering?

Call me in ten minutes, I whisper back.

Ten minutes later Rebecca and I are in the clearing by the blue-domed church.

Why did you think that was Simon?

Know. Why did I know.

OK. She has that look.

When I go to the monastery I see torch lights. I've always thought they came out of the ground like trolls. I thought maybe they'd taken him to their troll cave.

My phone rings – it's Gabriel again – and to my surprise and considerable relief he's here on Kryptos, at the port. His voice sounds gritty and no-nonsense, which is a good sound right now. *Where are you?* he wants to know.

I struggle to describe the location but he knows it immediately. *OK I'm at that café-bar sunset place. On the roof.*

I don't have the car.

Then flag down the bus. I start to explain that though there are indeed buses their schedule is sparse. Then I see one and flag it down.

Rebecca won't come with me. As the bus pulls away she is already walking back along the road to Karistos. The window gives me a new perspective across the valley, and as the bus starts its climb over the pass, the ordered rows of olive trees giving way to vineyards then to dried grasses, all overseen by the Monastery of the Archangels, this recent sample of the voice of Peter Karpodinis, this time beefed up by the sight of him holding a phone, trips another switch.

The voice on my answerphone . . . the voice I accidentally erased on the day that Raffy failed to arrive . . . **that** voice. It was trying to reach a Mr. Hilliard. Would Mr. Hilliard call him back. It was urgent. Urgent was the word he used, but the voice was too lacking in animation to convey much of that and, calling a wrong number, not my concern. Though slightly familiar.

And now I'm wondering . . . all those no-message messages left around the same time, the silences and bleeps punctuating the other familiar voices . . . was he behind those? I thought my address put me in danger. Perhaps it's my phone number.

Gabriel, barely recognisable in white polo shirt and linen slacks, is sprawled in a rattan chair, glass raised, legs stretched, brow furrowed, hair 1950s Wimbledon blonde, straight and heavy, hint of racquet to hand, a style change hinting at days spent on the very surface of things, so now wholly hacked off with all but traditional fashion and, with any luck, his addiction to being obscure. He is a Hollander in the hand, one of one. He will listen. He will help. But not yet. He needs to get something off his chest.

Narcissus, he says, *the boy I was telling you about? Who's been posing that for me?* I struggle to look interested but he is plainly enthralled.

I'd made him this pool. It was in a . . . well, close enough to a . . . woodland glade. Anna?

I hear you. A woodland glade on Mykonos.

***Made** the damn glade.*

Oh. OK.

***And** the pool. With a broken mirror and, I don't know, maybe twenty-four bottles of Loutraki – no, I guess it took thirty-six . . .*

I'm not too into this.

The kid had been gazing into the pool so devoutly and for so long it was beginning to freak me out. I mean I'd stopped directing him, I just circled and shot. And then – I still can't believe this – a woman came down the hill to milk a goat and she called out to him. His name . . . his name was Narkissos!

Count yourself lucky he didn't drag you in.

I can't be charmed, haven't the time, he notices and so I tell him everything. And as we rip at the gauze and the mirror partly clears I feel that as well as breaking the spell I am, this time, committing us to action.

He wants to go immediately to the police station and there is a lot to be said for that except that I'm fearful of putting Raffy and Simon at risk. Claudia, I point out, though probably fraught and furious, is at least safe.

We're at a rooftop café-bar designed and named for the sunset, still an hour off. Non-Greek pre-sunset music is playing, piano classics and ska, not so loud we can't hear each other but too loud for our voices to carry. Which is important. I want him to come clean now.

Entrapment, I say when the waiter has gone. *Why, when you knew nothing of what was going on, did you suddenly come up with that?*

Ah. Well. Serious time, huh?

I think so.

So, what do you want me to tell you?

It's not what I want to hear, it's what happened. Facts. Anything that's relevant.

OK. That would be my father. Back in the bad old days when we were still together. He had a credibility crisis. That's how he put it to me.

Where was this?

Athens. When we were living there. Between Athens and here.

And?

He wanted to give my mother a bit of a scare.

And that was . . . why?

She was seeing some dodgy people. Men.

I thought he had come to terms with that.

Does anyone? I don't know that there was that much to it, maybe not much more than an ego boost, but an ego boost for her was an ego crash for him. Anyway he wanted her to see what this particular guy was really like. So he paid him to scare her.

How?

I don't know the details. But afterwards the guy turned it around. He blackmailed him into authenticating a fake icon that was going to an American collector. Later when he realised there was a major scam going down he was ready to tell someone. They got wind of that and planted a real icon in our apartment. Then they told the police. That would have been the end of his career and his reputation. He wanted me to know how he'd got into all this so that someone in the family would understand if it all came out. Of course he couldn't tell Claudia. And Michael would have killed him.

But what happened with the police?

*Police***man***, it turned out. He let him know they could come to some agreement. In fact I think he was one of theirs.*

He catches my expression. *Cheer up. No-one died. He dealt with it.*

I would have sworn he was absolutely on the side of freedom, truth and the American way.

And so he might have been if he hadn't been married to my mother.

He stops talking. He takes the lemon slice from the rim of his glass and starts to weave a toothpick through it, in and out. He contemplates the puckered lemon slice, dumps it in the ashtray. A waiter swoops down with a clean ashtray.

He was young when he met her. Just graduating. She was slightly older. Also slightly pregnant. With Michael.

Ah. Holiday snaps. How little we see of what lies behind them.

I don't think, I say, copying the lemon and toothpick trick, *it was all over just as easily as that. I think he might still be involved.*

Really? Oh OK. Whatever you say.

Look, you lived with your damn family, Gabriel. You're one of them. You must have some ideas.

On the contrary. I've taken great care to expend none of my insight or imagination on my family. This trip has been very messy in that regard.

So I tell him about the Simon icon and the Simon incident, and then I have his attention. And we sit watching the idlers on the esplanade until their vapid demeanour pisses us off so much that we know it really is time for action.

The waterfront is seething with people and cars as we set off to find the police station. A ferry has just docked. Passing the quay we're stopped by a stream of disembarking cars and lorries. An acid yellow customised van with surf boards on its roof pulls out in front of us. I catch a glimpse of two guys with wide shoulders and sliced-off hair and I remember the thing I forgot to tell Gabriel.

The guys in that van, I say pointing as it disappears, *one of them might have been Michael.*

He doesn't respond. He stops walking, looks confused. Raffy is approaching, strolling along our side of the street. I stop too. When Raffy sees us I half expect him to turn and run, but he smiles as if he's just run into two old friends on a High Street.

He looks from my face – disbelieving, accusatory – to Gabriel's – reproachful, hedging his bets – then reaches out a hand to each of us.

Hey. Loosen up. I can explain.

I walk away.

It's quite a time before they catch me up. I'm heading for the car park on the edge of town before I remember I don't have the car.

He can explain, says Gabriel.

But more often, I point out, *he chooses not to.* And then I remember the stick I have to beat him with. *Your mother . . . she's been arrested.*

I know, he says. *I fixed it.*

When he walked away from me, he tells us, on the night of the storm, he was stopped in the street by someone who said he recognised him from the old days. We are sitting now, the three of us, at the café in front of the church. It sounded genuine, he said, spontaneous, although of course he'd just been handed the profile of the very person to avoid. *With hindsight*, he says. *At the time I was rather pleased.*

He wanted me to step inside a shop just by where I met him to say hallo to his mother. It was one of those sewing shops, embroidered tablecloths, lace curtains plus needles and cotton, all that. I could see an old woman behind the counter so I thought OK, I won't remember her, but I'll make the gesture. I stepped inside and they grabbed me, two of them, and bundled me into the back shop. The second guy pulled a knife, the first one had a cell phone. He dialled a number and handed it to me. A man's voice said good evening. *I said* who is this? *He said* a friend from the old days. Perhaps you don't remember me. My name is Zac.

Gabriel starts to realign the sugar bowl, the menu holder and the flower vase.

He said he was in Piraeus. With my mother. He glances at Gabriel to include him in joint ownership of Claudia. *He put her on. She was rather economical with her greeting. He took the phone back and I imagine he moved out of earshot when he said he'd be bringing her . . .* ***bringing*** *her . . . to Kryptos tomorrow. That's yesterday, I believe, though I'm beginning to lose track of time. He said he looked forward to meeting me. It was hard to be sure on that crackly line – he may have been my London caller.*

They locked me in the back shop. I could hear the old woman's voice raised in protest. I guess she may really have been his mother. They were telling her she was going to close early. Then for a while I could hear the men talking and lighting cigarettes in the front shop. I was foraging for something more effective than a darning needle, or more incriminating. I did find a book on the archaeology of the Cyclades.

The back shop had a small high window but it was barred. Much later when the streets had quietened I could hear the guys arguing about whether to take a chance on leaving me. I guess they reckoned I'd be safe till morning. In the early hours I managed to gouge out the lock with some rather specialised craft kit. The front shop took a little longer. Then I went to the police station.

He sees my raised eyebrows. *I was right out of patience. There were just two junior guys there. I tried to persuade them to call the man in charge but they were not impressed, so I sat there with them till morning.*

Doing what?

Listening to rembetiko. *Looking at girlie mags. Drinking utterly revolting frappé.*

You didn't think of calling me?

They wouldn't let me. Finally the senior guy came in.

Stelios Kritikos?

That's the one. I had started to outline what had happened when he stopped me and took me into his office. Closed the door. I told him everything. The thing when I was a kid, the threats along the way, the thing with my mother, all of it. He was good. We went to meet the ferry. You saw what happened.

You were there?

In the back of the police car so I could point them out. I saw you but he wouldn't let me speak to you. I've been at the station ever since. He didn't want to let me go. Someone is coming from Athens. But I'd given him a statement and I told him this was no way to treat a friend of Greece who was, after all, assisting him in inquiries he hadn't even made yet and who could also call on the back-up of the US of A if his liberty was infringed. Then I walked out. I was just going to call you.

And what's happening now?

They've got Zac in custody.

And your mother?

Checked into a hotel with a policewoman. I don't suppose she slept much.

And you?

Expected right back. But I'm not making that mistake. I'm going to get Jean-Paul over from Delos. I'll go back when I'm ready.

19

It's morning. I'm at the harbour meeting a boat.

As I cross the road from the café a fresh cast is throwing itself into the re-enactment of what it takes to get here. Stacked and smudged across the horizon other islands wait their turn, all the islands kept functioning by the toiling boats.

Waiting in the wings are the things that take over when islands empty. On days when the lure of the island seems to me oppressive and senseless, almost unhealthy, when I want to fight it or at least try harder to work out what it is, the veil twitches and I see that the charm of islands is a survival tactic.

Today our island is particularly charming, its peaks outlined sharp against the sky, its monasteries rising sheer and white from its heights, and a healthy consignment of toned and tanned people is pouring off this boat.

Today it's Jean-Paul I'm meeting, Raffy lying low,

the beads, bandana and wrap-around shades designed this time to throw off passing police (who on this island of reinvention would spot him, I think, while respecting his look) as we head back in time to the place he remembers as the gateway to the underworld of island history.

Gabriel is not with us. He has hired a motor bike and gone shopping.

Last night we took a taxi back to the house. A modest milestone there, I thought, two Hollanders under one roof. So I cooked pasta, stripped a basil plant, made pesto, watered the plant, decanted some *vin du jardin*, lit candles, and only when we'd eaten a semblance of a family meal told Raffy the story that Marcus had told me. Economical with the dog and leaving out Dimitris and the copycat window escape, I brought in Rebecca and the monastery but left out our flight through the undergrowth.

As I talked I was avoiding eye contact. This from instinct. Vindication would be in there but also a perfect storm of complex reactions, among them something like – this was my ungenerous thought – pique. After all the years nursing his secret, spinning complexity upon complexity, here it was in outline, slung together and articulated by someone else. But when he started to speak I was reassured. He was already revising his approach.

OK. This changes everything. We can't let the police charge in. It's too important. If they feel cornered they might decide to destroy the evidence.

Charging in, I thought, would not be the style of Stelios Kritikos. *Destroy it? How?*

What's out there is out there. It's what remains that's at risk. If this guy is right, if they're ready to rethink the whole thing, stampeding them would be counter-productive. They might decide to dynamite the site.

Oh, surely . . .

They have the means and the cover story. When you hear blasting, it's a marble quarry. And they're opportunists, not archaeologists. Put yourself in their position. You might think that counting your blessings and saving your skin was the sensible option, maybe even the decent one.

I couldn't share that view. Would you dynamite your own history? *But it's out of your hands now, is it not? What could you do?*

Your friend Marcus . . . why do you think he was telling you all this?

To ease his conscience? To put on record that he wasn't one of the baddies? In fact he said it was to warn me that you were in serious danger.

And did you believe him? That that was his motivation?

Not entirely. But we were interrupted. I think he was going to put some proposition to me.

I still don't get it, said Gabriel. *You don't get told that stuff and live.*

He's hardly a natural born killer. You've met him.

It's not his intentions that matter, said Raffy. *If anyone knows what he told you, you are, or would have been, in deep shit.*

Would have been?

If I hadn't spoken to Kritikos. The angel back on my case, then, hovering in guardian mode. Why did that feel oppressive?

Of course it all depends what he's done with it . . .

In the kitchen making coffee, the silence from outside was leaden. When I carried the tray to the terrace even the cicadas were on layoff. It was Gabriel who attempted to lighten things. He pointed out that there seemed to be two factions, foreigners and islanders. But the foreigners didn't really cut it as a faction. All they had in common was their foreignness.

We talked about that, and got nowhere. Raffy was silent, brooding over his coffee.

Nor did the islanders necessarily hang together, I said, any more than Captain Hook and the crocodile.

Gabriel volunteered to check out Lisa Dunmore now that he knew she ran the antique shop in the hill village that I'd stopped him visiting, and Raffy stood up and began to pace the terrace.

It's a hoax, he said.

What?

He was using you.

And suddenly I was spitting mad.

Sarcophagi . . . half statues . . . it's not possible. They're setting up a scam.

You're saying I'm so gullible they picked on me to spread disinformation. Why? What would that do?

They're trying to flood the market with fakes on the rumour of a secret find. You've already seen a fake kouros.

Look, you don't know Marcus. He was scared. He was acting cool but you could see the effort. He's as risk averse as you are. More possibly. And not a team player.

But however I painted this he wasn't going to be swayed. And once we'd called it a day I lay awake allowing this new possibility to spread and develop. If he was right then all my recent dealings were open to revision.

Promise me this, I said over breakfast. *Just don't infect Jean-Paul with your scepticism. Not before you've seen the site.* And he agreed.

So now Raffy, Jean-Paul and I are off to see the cave. We take the same route as last time, heading south then turning inland rather than risk one of the tracks closer to Karistos. We leave the car in the same clearing and once again approach on foot, confident in Jean-Paul's anonymity, Raffy's beach boy look and my own disguise. I am a British tourist in shorts, money-belt, trainers and easifold straw hat.

It's a beautiful day. There are scents of sage, *rigani* and wood smoke. Raffy stops from time to time to discuss with Jean-Paul the lie of the land. The gate in the fence by the huts is padlocked and there's no-one in sight. Opposite the gate the track is banked above a field which has a sporadically ploughed look to it, the familiar look of a halted development where the diggers have been in but the builders gone elsewhere, letting weeds sprout on turned soil and heaps of stony subsoil contaminate the look of undisturbed earth.

Raffy and Jean-Paul slither down the bank. They are approaching a recently turned earth heap when Raffy stumbles and falls. He sits up and pulls his left foot out of the ground. Jean-Paul squats beside him. They scrabble at the soil which has been heaped loosely over some tarpaulin-covered planks. Back in the direction we came from I hear the sound of a car. I call down a warning to them and as they dive for cover I start to amble along, lone tourist style, staring around from time to time with a look of diligent rapture.

The car comes up behind and I step onto the verge, turning to smile at the driver as he passes. The car slows and stops. It's a roof-down beach buggy.

Good morning. Greek-accented English, whiff of aftershave. *I think you are lost. Maybe I can help you.*

Not lost, I tell him. *Walking.*

He leans an elbow on the window and smiles at me, one of those long-running smiles that goes with an engine idling in a practised sort of way, hot metal smells, sun, all the time in the world, time to take in the bone structure, tastefully crumpled button-down shirt collar and sleepy charm. All this is standard. Perhaps just a little more than that.

Where you from?

I am not going down this route. *Excuse me*, I say. *I want to keep going before it gets too hot.*

I can take you somewhere. Where you want to go?

I want to walk, thank you.

This road goes nowhere. There is nothing to see.

Well that's all right, I'll keep going until there ***is*** *something to see.*

Is that your car?

Car? Where?

Back there.

I look along the road in the direction he is indicating where the car is out of sight.

I don't have a car, I say. *I'm walking.*

But already I know this is not going to work.

Another car is coming up behind. I look towards it with some relief. The driver calls out in Greek to ask what the trouble is. The beach buggy driver tells him I am refusing a lift. The second driver gets out and comes over.

This is private road, he says. *Verboten. I must ask you to go with my friend.*

I shrug and get in looking huffy and implacable. I refuse to converse until he drops me back on the coast road beside a bus stop. Shortly after he speeds out of sight a bus comes into view headed south. I wave it down and get off at the Aghios Theodoros sign. I climb back up the track and start down the other side. The car is where I left it and Raffy and Jean-Paul appear from a neglected olive grove. We get in, reverse and drive back to the coast road where we head on south and compare notes.

They ducked in under the bank by the road, Raffy tells me, and there, under a tangle of thorns, spotted the little ravine from which he had first looked up at the cave. Once the two cars had gone they climbed down into the ravine and saw that it continued, shoulder-width, under the road. They squeezed through, coming out into a drainage ditch immediately below the fence which, from their viewpoint, straddled the final narrow angle of the ravine. They crawled under it, under the hut, and found themselves looking into the mouth of the cave.

And?

Domestic things, says Jean-Paul. *A* rhyton *in three pieces with a bird. Piece of a marble* kandili. *Also a brooch of ivoire, many shards, and some . . . traces.*

Nothing mind-blowing?

The fact of it is mind-blowing, says Raffy.

The spread, Jean-Paul amplifies.

Aha, I think. But say nothing.

There were sounds, Jean-Paul says, under the cave, perhaps from a passage leading under the road. But all the time they're speaking we're heading further south and soon we'll arrive at Mavra Vrahia, a destination devoutly to be missed. I pull into a lay-by and put the case for north.

Below the monastery of Aghios Konstandinos, I tell them . . . *in that house on the hillside, the uninhabited house I told you about with the well and the pergola and the lemon tree, where I met your father* . . . I'm laying it on a bit because everything I have on this place is flimsy . . . *well, Rebecca says she has seen lights there and heard voices. She has this idea that Simon is a prisoner there. He's supposed to be staying with Yanni. But maybe we should check it out?*

A fresh location and the chance to change things. Because the other is too old, too cold, too complex. No place to spend a sunny afternoon. And ultimately, I think, not in a foreigner's remit.

The chivalric possibilities excite Jean-Paul, coming from an island frozen in time, so I put my foot down and, when we reach the turn-off, drive straight up to the door. In the silence when I switch off the engine everything is different. The sun is brighter here, the air softer and kinder, there is the song of a lark, the buzzing of bees, the background hum of traffic and the grumble of a boat, all the din of living occupation. Also a pregnant pause. It's familiar, this pause. What has this to do with them, emissaries of the past? This was my idea. The guys will be hanging back.

The front door is still unlocked and the inner door with the padlock looks as it did before.

Simon? I'm addressing the crack in the door. *Simon?* The restive shifting sounds come from Raffy and Jean-Paul distancing themselves outside. I try a knock, exploratory, reassuring, righteous, a knock by Walter Scott or Baroness Orczy. I hear larks and bees, the sound of my breathing. Another knock. The chain drops. The door swings open. There's no-one there. But stacked on shelves hidden under canvas drapes there are rather a lot of icons.

At the goat shed we find Rebecca and a paler, thinner Simon. He nods to us. He is eating bread and cheese.

I bought a bolt cutter, says Rebecca. *At the hardware store. Then I walked along there and cut the chain.*

So now we're sitting on the ground outside the goat shed, the centre of a circle of goats. They're hobbled. From time to time one of them sets off in a lopsided rush towards a fresh clump of something, then rejoins the chewing circle that is using us as a diversion from the effortful pulping of stringy grass, a sort of goat TV dinner. Goats acting domestic. Happy endings. A cloud crosses the sun.

Simon is confirming Rebecca's supposition. He called the man on Crete whose number was on the menu card because, well, because there was no reason not to. *I just knew him from this bar I used to go to. He asked what I was doing now and I told him. Next day I went for a swim. End of story. Nearly.* He inclines his head in Raffy's direction.

You mean you can't remember what happened?

His shrug tells me to back off and lighten up. Well, tough.

Who was the guy in the bar on Crete?

The owner. Greek, fortyish, five eleven, thirteen stone, clean shaven, mid-length dark hair, penchant for old swing classics, I don't know, just a bar owner.

Was it he who commissioned the icons?

No. That was a half Dutch guy.

His name? Inquisitorial suddenly – they all look at me – because to know is, after all, an imperative, without which the unknown I'm so hipped on would have no base-line.

Peter something.

Karpodinis?

Possibly. Why? You know him?

I'm beginning to. If it's Peter Karpodinis, he's here.

OK. Look no further.

I just can't imagine him swimming.

I'm seeing him as I did at the party, no sunlight on his skin, you'd think, ever. Of course he didn't have to swim. He had someone to do that.

So . . . what happened when you left the hospital?

OK. That would be when Yannis took me back to his place. Nice house, nashy steel and smoked glass furniture.

And?

He was kind of abstracted. The hands-off host, you know? Perhaps I'd like to lie down or maybe make myself some coffee. He showed me the kitchen, where things were. He was going out – something to check out, he said – but I should stay indoors for my own safety. Pretty soon I needed to buy cigarettes. I mean I haven't smoked for two years but there were no books in that house and have you seen Greek daytime TV?

Was the door locked?

It ***was*** *rather hard to open.*

So you got out?

I bought twenty Karelia Lights and a box of matches from the kiosk in the square. I hadn't even lit one which is why I'm happy to say I'm still smoke free.

When what? Hadn't even lit one when what?

Sorry. Can't help there. I was taking a short-cut round the back of some houses when . . . you know, hand over mouth and nose, short struggle, next thing, headache, dark room, door seriously locked. And a whole lot later Rebecca.

OK. Not Peter Karpodinis. Someone working for him.

Simon considers. Around us goat jaws work and goat eyes keep watch. *I wonder when he came here?*

I'm watching Rebecca. She is watching the goats. *I thought . . . didn't* ***you*** *meet him once? Didn't he come here?*

I told you. I'm not good with Greek names.

When he came to my house he gave me one of Thanasi's cards. But maybe that was just borrowing an identity for the day. If he'd been in with Thanasis surely he would have known where Simon was. I re-run the few clues I have. *His voice was on my answerphone. It was a wrong number.*

On Crete he was living in an old converted arhondiko *in the mountains. He'd built on a gallery. There was a guest lodge. He was quite high profile. Drove an old open-top sedan. Wore a panama. Picked people up from the port, potential buyers I suppose. He seemed like he'd got it made.*

Whereas here, I say, *he's keeping his head down. He's part of a group that meets at the café in the square. Older, retired, time on their hands. If he was trying to set up a respectable profile that would be a way to do it.* I remember his visit. *As a cover he's taking on house conversions. He may actually be doing house conversions, he needs to live.*

Whatever. Simon, like Rebecca, seems anxious to move on from The Flying Dutchman. But he hasn't been exorcised, only evaded. They may after all have been deeper in than they care to remember. Then I have a practical thought.

Simon. What is your surname?

Hilliard.

Aaah.

Well I like it myself but I don't usually get that reaction.

Hilliard, Hollander. He called the next number in his contacts file. Which means that I'm in there too. Or my name is. **Their** name. Hollander. *But if he had your number all along why did it take your phone call to Crete to tell him where you were?*

Old number, old phone.

He knew you were here, he just didn't know where. Tell me, did you leave the island? A fortnight ago, something like that?

I went to Athens to order up some stuff for the taverna.

Which boat did you come back on?

I was booked on the Apollon Express but I ended up catching the Sea Jet from Rafina.

Then **you** *were the person I meant to save. Not Marcus. I just didn't catch your name.*

I don't know what you're talking about but I certainly appreciate the gesture.

My phone rings. Gabriel is back at the house wondering what's happened to us. I tell him we're on our way. It strikes me as we get to our feet that we are becoming rather numerous, a diverse gathering of the forces of . . . well, if not the forces of righteousness then surely the forces of quite nice. For the final struggle against what? Planning abuse, misrepresentation, detention, a bit of GBH, deviant shop-keeping, looting from your own land? A missing archaeologist. A dead journalist. And perhaps two other unexplained deaths. If I believe that. Which I have been inclined not to. Very much inclined. Allowing me to stand back as always and play the wry observer, non-judgemental, absolutely not vengeful. And absolutely no longer appropriate. So not to be pursued. For now.

I'm on safer ground with motives. What is driving all this? Money. No mystery there. The sources of the money, those are more of a mind-bender. Real people, but people who have mastered the art of remaining notional, one here, one there, possessed not only of wealth but also, one imagines, of learning, of finely honed aesthetic sensibilities and, unless *nouveaux riches*, of preferences, Greek over Roman for a start. Enough of them in their ones and twos to sustain forward planning and to justify the lengths to which those other less shadowy people will go. Do I know these people?

They're not in my sphere. But behind the people, buyers and sellers alike, animating them, activating them, is the thing itself. The place, the island. And that I do know. You could, if you wished, blame it all on the island, its past, its present, how it looks, how that affects us all. Love of place, especially a place not your own, a stronger stranger thing, sometimes, than love of a person. And so much less examined.

Look, I say to Rebecca as she walks with us up to the track past the dog, the guard turkey and the escort goats already gathering right and left. *The icons? I don't want to pry but are you doing this . . . well, under duress?*

No. No. I love doing it. I was really just helping out Brother Gerasimos. That's how it was put to me. I didn't have a problem with that so long as they didn't. I mean they might have thought a foreign woman was some kind of contaminant in that sphere. But no. And they pay well. It's just . . . when they asked me to copy an icon I imagined it was my copy that was going to be sold.

I really think you two should come with us.

Hang on. I'll get my sleeping bag.

20

O manavis!

The voice, the revving engine, the blasting horn shatter the glassy calm of early morning. I'm on the roof terrace, barefoot, leaning over the parapet watching a yacht manoeuvre into the still waters of the lagoon. Still and shallow. It shivers to a stop.

O manaaaavis!

I find my sandals and go down to the greengrocer who has turned, staring, silenced and transfixed. At his call my barren tract is spontaneously repopulating. Rebecca and Simon unfold, wraithlike, from the futon in the pergola while from the front terrace lopes Gabriel tying the sash of a kimono, and from behind a palm steps Raffy in shorts and from the olive grove Jean-Paul, already dressed in chinos and a light blue shirt and carrying a pottery shard. Silent and improbable they float inexorably towards him.

Kalos ilthate, he shouts suddenly, nailing them by

force of personality to this dimension, and throws open his van. Whatever happened here let us not dwell on it, let us just sell vegetables. I buy two kilos of everything – wraithfood – but when he hurtles off throwing up gravel, turn myself to practicalities. Breakfast. Which of us can safely go out into the world to buy bread? Jean-Paul gets the job and the car keys.

Which leaves far too many people still standing about, people who, given half a chance, will bond, interact, chatter, and drive away my half-formed ideas as well as the wholly formless thing that lives here and keeps, unless provoked, bad outcomes at bay.

But then Gabriel steps forward. Last night we saw him unload a box labelled *Byzantiana* from his hire bike. Now he carries it to the marble table and starts to unpack it in the manner of a Silk Road trader unloading his camel.

You bought the ***typewriter****?*

It's an early Olivetti. OK, but look at these. He pulls out a piece of old embroidery on silk. Then a rag rug, a woven bedspread, a toast rack, a portrait of a senior citizen in a gilt frame and a naïve painting of a sailor sitting on a bollard smoking and talking to a girl with ribbons in her hair. *And this.* He is holding what appears to be an ancient and very covetable icon.

Simon leans forward and takes it from him. He studies it, turns it over, and reads from a label on the back: *Painted in the Monastery of The Lesser Saints, White Mountains, Crete. Now, how did that get here?*

You know it?

I painted it.

It depicts two halo-ed holy men with a passing resemblance to Kosmas and Damianos, the penniless saints.

Can I ask what you paid for it?

She wanted seven hundred. I knocked her down to five.

Blessings on you, gracious patron. Steep mark-up from one-fifty, though.

A mishmash of cultures is coming out of this box. Trading styles jump aeons, civilisations clash with vogues. My head spins, and something small is calling me from the final layer. I reach in and draw out a Cycladic figurine, the one which, when I picked it from her shelf, Lisa, formerly Debby, took from me and told me was not for sale.

You ***bought*** *this?*

That one I stole.

I think it's genuine.

So do I.

Raffy takes it from me and studies it. *This is from her shop?*

He is thinking as I am that this would seem to upgrade her from kidnapper of unknown motivation to someone in the swim. But that's not possible. A little shopworn, a little compromised, neither a mother figure nor a Madonna, her place would be on the outer, courteously dealt with but not indulged, fringes of island society. They would not trust her. A rogue icon commissioned by a shady person not of this island and passed off as old might be no great surprise in the chaos and bad taste of a foreigner's junk shop. But an antiquity . . . ? The explanation awaits.

Anything else?

Just this. He holds a parcel swaddled in wrap which unpeels to reveal a raspberry pink bubble glass bowl with smaller pinker drinking vessels dangling from its rim.

Don't run it down, says Gabriel. *It's thanks to this lovely piece which I insisted the lady wrap for me that I was able to pick up that.*

Raffy takes the discarded wrap and folds it round the little figurine as Jean-Paul appears wreathed in bakery scents and bearing four varieties of loaf, a brown paper bag and some news.

I have seen a man, he says. *In the* boulangerie. *A man I have seen before. He was suspected of certain thefts from museums. I was not sure at first so I spent some time in the shop. I bought many things.* He lays out the loaves on the marble table, perfumes of yeast, sesame and aniseed mingling, and opens the bag. *See! I have found* pains au chocolat*!* Pains au chocolat *in Greece!*

Don't celebrate too soon, says Gabriel. *They're Greek* pains au chocolat.

This man, he also bought many things. Eight loaves, some paximadhi *and several portions of* tiropitta.

Who was he? Why will no-one stay on track? *Did he see you?*

He does not know me. His name is Müller. Kurt Müller.

Kurt. Often glimpsed, always suspected, not much considered. Gabriel is re-packing his box and I'm handing out plates and knives plus a Rockingham bowl filled with the peach jam last year's glut forced on me.

Lisa Dunmore. She's some sort of fence then?

Looks like it.

But otherwise basically a shop keeper.

In this incarnation. Can't shake the taste for bad guys, though.

A taste shared by Claudia, I recall. Inappropriate was Lucas's word for them. Zac was summer holiday appropriate, though obviously not for Claudia, but perhaps didn't travel well. Kurt would be more of a global but grudging deployer of charm. He wouldn't waste it where he didn't need it to work.

Some time ago – Jean Paul has started in on the *pains au chocolat – in a museum, I will not say where, but in a museum in Greece, there was discovered a, you know,* ***switch****. In place of a certain piece, quite an important piece, there was a copy. The copy was good. After this all museums were advised to check. There were some surprises. Not just in Greece, in several countries. In France also there was one surprise. Kurt Müller came into the picture because of a suspicion of complicity of members of staff.*

Female members of staff?

I believe so.

Kurt, Kurt and Shannon, Mykonos. I look at Gabriel. *On Mykonos*, I tell him, wondering whether this is fair, *I overheard a conversation between Kurt and one of the fashion assistants, her name was Shannon, that seemed to be about you. As if – it wasn't clear – they had some arrangement with you. Or designs on you.*

We all watch him.

Well now, he says. He is heaping quite a lot of peach jam onto a hunk of sesame loaf. *He was trying to find you.* He looks at Raffy. *You're famous, baby brother.*

And?

He was planning a little extortion to discover your whereabouts.

How? says Raffy, amazed. *Using what?*

An indiscretion.

We avoid his eye and wait.

Yeah?

I was indiscrete.

And did you? Shop me I mean?

No. I'm comfortable in my indiscrete skin.

Gabriel, then, is one of the blessed. Like Michael, like Greg, the happy possessor of the gift of making himself unaccountable. Unlike Raffy, unlike me. No unaccountability fairy came to our christenings. I don't know whether that's good or bad.

How does it feel, I wonder, to be too cool to question? Like Lucas, now I think of it. Like all the Hollanders except Raffy. Particularly Lucas, Lucas of the engaging manner and floppy hair, when there always accessible, but often not there, and, when not there, unimaginably occupied, flying against the sun to the countries east of west, to the winged sandalled men, the swordsmen, heathen-tramplers and dragon slayers of the Constantinople diaspora. And perhaps, from Gabriel's account, with something to hide. You would need that, I think, to get your money's worth out of being unaccountable.

Which brings me back – the yacht moored on the lagoon might, I thought, be his – to Greg. Greg especially inviolate thanks to his combative kind of cool. Greg who came here to do what? I have no idea. What do rich boys come here to do? Windsurf? Dive? Spearfish?

Jean-Paul is passing round the *pains au chocolat*. I decline and, still on track, follow Greg underwater. It's a still day . . . a still afternoon . . . this summer or perhaps last, with the yacht scarcely stirring at its mooring and the seabed magnified through the lenses of his goggles as a fish swims into range and he sites his harpoon and sees, perhaps, lurking behind it, an amphora. An amphora raising its barnacle-encrusted shoulders out of the sand close to the reef. Would that not blow your mind even if you weren't fresh out of Texas? Greg who listened with that disconcerting and childlike gravity to the tale of the wonder-working icon and then crawled up the carriageway. A man if ever saw one in the early grip of the Greek passion. How long before he becomes a stop-at-nothing collector? And why am I assuming . . . the money . . . the yacht . . . the unaccountability . . . that he's not there already? Because I thought I wouldn't know these people. Because I still have a lot to learn.

The sound of a helicopter brings me back to the here and now. It's landing nearby, on the field behind the beach.

Raffy, bringing fresh coffee, reminds us of Claudia, now weighing on his conscience, possibly still in protective custody.

She was a victim after all, he says. *Potential victim. Not that we need to use the word to her. She was a witness, though, and in my experience they like to keep their witnesses in-house.*

Anything less than five star custody, says Gabriel, *and I'd say she's out of there.*

Raffy and Jean-Paul have decided to work out a

clear-headed and non-attributable outline of what Marcus told me to be delivered to Stelios Kritikos in confidence. Nothing in writing. They seem to see it as a monologue, two monologues, subject to conditions they feel are theirs to impose. It will be voiced as rumour and disquiet amongst the wider archaeological community that a site of major importance may exist on Kryptos which they feel should be investigated properly.

I think, Raffy says, *that once it's out in the open the notion of looting might become unpopular. Unpopular rather than reprehensible. The guys disapprove. If the excavations can be thought of as recent and hailed as positive – great discovery, knocks the other islands for six – a quick brush under the carpet might be enough for a clean start. I think, if they decide to play it carefully, some of the finds might return to base. That's how I would handle it. We can only suggest.*

How much more, his words imply, if we were calling the shots. If this was our country, if we were lords of the island, ministers of its past, present and future. If we could appropriate this country's much more interesting history as a version of our own. Centuries of precedent there, a longing for lapiths and centaurs, ziggurats on our skylines, sphinx fragments in the fishing nets. Perhaps it's now imprinted on our greedy chilly genes.

A bike roars out of nowhere and the engine is cut. We look up, all of us, and watch to see what bearer of bad news will come round the corner. He's tall with heavy dark-blonde hair and a red bandana. It's Michael.

Hi guys, he says.

Yo bro, says Gabriel. *What gives?*

Hi Anna. House party, huh?

He stands there, just sort of occupying his spot. He has biceps. The physicality that used to emanate from his entire person seems to have got localised in these two bulges that make me think of bouncers flanking an empty night club. *Hi*, I say faintly.

So, when did you get here? Raffy asks.

Yesterday.

And when are the championships?

Start Friday.

Have you got a chance? asks Gabriel.

Hey man, I'm number three in the States.

I sense a little tension building, then a woman's voice calls *Michael!*

Shit. My mother.

She was entangled in the pillion housing but now as she turns the corner of the house ahead of Michael and spots strangers she straightens up and stalks towards us without missing a beat.

Anna! She hugs me. She is wearing a perfume of the past, something I can't quite put a name to, Patou's Joie or Guerlain's Mitsouko. Raffy is introducing her to the others. *How?* Gabriel mouths at Michael. Michael taps his phone. I'm six feet above it all, staring down.

An hour later we're on the beach. I've lent Rebecca a swimsuit and a sarong. She can't take too much sun. Claudia declined the offer. She is not planning to swim. I can't recall that she ever did. Michael has Speedos, the others, assorted man pants. Together we have the flung-together look of a tour group, and the two men climbing aboard the helicopter now preparing to take off from the field close to where the yacht is moored pay us no heed.

Partly to escape the group, mainly to follow my slow-burn yacht recognition hunch, I swim as close to it as I can without leaving the semicircle of the beach. It looks to my disaffected eye very like the yacht that took me from Delos to Tinos, and even the helicopter seems familiar. The yacht has a name. I think I'm reading *Alamo* in the moment before it rocks away, but even if it's *Anemos* its crew are talking American, twangy heated American, and I'm heading away from there as smoothly as I can. I don't know if helicopters have names but as this one swings out over the sea, churning up a small storm in front of the chapel I note that it's the same yellow, on the daffodil side of sulphur, as the Delos helicopter and the one that dropped off the surfers.

Back on the beach I go to sit with Claudia. I ask how she is feeling after the stress of the past two days.

She balks a bit at *stress*, not a Claudia word. *Really*, she says, *it was all a misunderstanding. There is this man I knew on Kryptos many years ago. Greek but brought up in London. He was very charming, rather amusing and a fabulous dancer. Anyway I ran into him again at Piraeus when I was boarding the ferry, before the wind got too strong for us to leave. We got talking and after they told us the boat wasn't going anywhere he suggested dinner.*

The Claudia reality. I must be very careful what I say. And indeed she tells the story as a rather gripping and amusing anecdote so free of knives and death threats that I'm ready to believe it really did happen that way. She agrees, though, that he seems to have some sort of record for which reason the police were waiting for him when they landed.

The first small breeze is starting and traffic is passing on the road behind us. The starkers sunbather has arrived and staked her territory. I'm still edgy, perhaps because we're on the brink of rather too tidy a denouement, perhaps because I have decisions to make, decisions about the future, but mainly because I have a premonition of things pending beyond this hedge of chattering people.

When Rebecca decides she has had enough sun she and Simon go back to the house. Gabriel is hungry and keen to get creative with the fresh produce. He and Simon will do lunch. Claudia also wants to get out of the sun. Raffy goes with her. Jean-Paul, done with picking up pot handles on the beach, has walked out to the little islet to look at its traces of Cyclopean walls, and Michael is swimming as far out as Michael can. I decide to stay on for a bit and watch the yacht.

Now there are just the nude and I on the beach. An egret takes off from the island and lands on the water. A bell rings. On the forecourt of the chapel I see the farmer's wife in silhouette pulling on the rope.

The Simon icon. Who put it there? The person who removed the other, I suppose.

Lucas. Where is he?

From the yacht comes the sound of raised voices. An altercation. Someone dives from the deck and starts to swim in this direction. He comes on towards the beach and walks ashore, sloughing water from T-shirt and shorts, a sullen pretty boy with curly wet blond hair.

Kurt. He takes off his T-shirt and wrings it out, slings it over one shoulder and is about to head up the track that leads to the road when he sees me. He stops. He comes over and drops down companionably beside me so that to a casual observer we would seem friends.

Well now, he says. *Here you are again. I did not think when I saw you on Mykonos that you were of any interest. But I did not know then what I know now. Now I know you are doubly interesting. And I am ready to make your acquaintance.* He holds out his hand. I ignore it.

You will please tell me where is your husband. Also his brother who has something of mine.

How am I going to play this? Adrenalin stirs and my brain clicks into gear. He thinks I'm alone. He does not, after all, know where I live.

Actually, I say, *I'm due to meet him in the village for lunch.* I pause to let him think the initiative is his. *I was going to walk back there, but if you have transport . . .*

He does not look surprised, easily re-absorbing the coercion that was in his voice in the belief that his charm is more effective.

Certainly. You want to go now?

Why not? I smile and get to my feet, picking up my towel and strolling alongside him, asking trite questions to cover the fact that I have no bag, no clothes. At the end of the beach as we step around the nude lying as always with her eyes closed, *chink chink* sounds spilling from her ears, I scoop her wrap-around dress from the stand of beach grass where she leaves it and as we walk up the track tie it around me, talking all the while, as we head towards the *deux chevaux*.

It's evening, and the cast has reassembled. My hunch to hang around the shoreline paid off. The yacht was Greg's, and though the link with Kurt is only circumstantial it validates my hunches. As we sit here resting our forks, the taverna agreeably busy, the *mezedhes* plates almost clean, Michael and Jean-Paul are filling me in on what happened after I left the beach with Kurt.

I was headed to shore when I heard it, Michael says. *Scream like a fisher cat.* He shakes his head. *Louder.*

Cri perçant, Jean-Paul confirms.

So I got my ass in gear – I'm seeing the not quite Olympic class freestyle as, behind him, a man come into the square – *and there was just this all-over orange person with a growing out Brazilian, flapping her arms at me and shrieking.* He looks round the table to include everyone though I must be the only one who hasn't heard this. The man stops, looking towards us. Looking towards Michael. *She wasn't bleeding. She wasn't fibrillating. I thought maybe a scorpion or she trod on a sea urchin. She kept shouting* forema, forema. *I couldn't recall that particular word.*

Dress, says Gabriel. *You never knew it, man.*

The thing I remembered, the Greek thing, was ti na kanoume? *They used to say it all the time. It's, like, a question? I thought it meant* what's up? *Gabe tells me it's not that, it's more* like what can we do? *with the answer being basically fuck all, but what the hell, that's no reason to slap me. Anyway, finally Jean-Paul got there.*

Fortunately, says Jean-Paul, *I was wearing a shirt. Very often I wear a shirt. I took it off and gave it to the lady.*

The man is close now. Raffy turns and stiffens as he comes into our sightline. It's Vasilis, Kyria Sophia's son. A girl runs into the square, the girl with the grey eyes.

That nice blue shirt, says Claudia leaning solicitously towards Jean-Paul. *Gone forever, would you say?*

She wanted to make a rendezvous but I told her it was a gift.

He has stopped, facing Michael, whom Raffy now leans towards. Claudia is looking round for the waiter. I'm watching the girl with the grey eyes as she runs up calling out *Vasili! Vasili!*

He is holding something. A gun. Raffy has Michael by the wrist and is pulling him forward but he resists and turns. The man shouts *Dolophone!* Murderer. Murderer in the vocative. The gun goes off. Michael slumps forward. Claudia screams. The man walks away. The girl stands staring, her hands over her mouth.

Maria's son calls the ambulance.

What happened to me was this. I went to the village with Kurt and led him to Maria's taverna. He ordered wine. Time passed and I acted irritated, as if Raffy's failure to show was a familiar problem. Not as irritated as Kurt, but irritated enough. I wasn't worried. Something would happen.

He demanded I phone Raffy. I told him he didn't carry a phone and neither did I. He asked where he was staying. I said I didn't know, we were separated.

He called Lisa. And whatever it was she said it made him mad. You wouldn't have to search for reasons, but among them might be rumours of Zac or of Shannon, or just an overdue disinclination to get in any deeper.

Then Nico came past. He greeted me but didn't stop – he'd taken a long hard look at Kurt – and when he'd walked on a bit I called *Oh Nico?* He stopped walking and I went after him. Speaking loudly enough to be heard I said *could I use your phone? I don't have mine.* He gave me it and I called the house. Raffy answered. I told him what had happened and as I was talking Kurt got up and walked away.

I stayed at the taverna until Raffy and Jean-Paul picked me up, then we drove straight to police HQ where Stelios Kritikos heard them out with a mix of courtesy and brisk dispassion that said he was already well up on things. Someone, perhaps, had begun to leak his own version, and he may also have been aware of the rumours but not, till now, the facts. And he had, it turned out, been warned about Kurt. Police in several divisions had suspicions about him, while Zac was wanted by Interpol and would soon, once the escort squad got here, be on a one-way ticket to Athens.

Which left John Burnham. I asked, and yes, the men arrested for his murder did indeed sound like my shadows.

Hire people, I think you call them. They work for money. They are not intelligent. Only clever enough to tell us nothing.

So, did the person who hired them to kill John Burnham also hire them to follow me? And there I censored myself because now that they're in custody and I am no longer in the picture, I have, or should have, peace of mind.

Congratulations, I said. *Quite a clean-up.*
Today the Gods were on our side.

21

The doctor at the island medical centre has never been asked to remove a bullet. He is young and quite up for it and the bullet accessible in Michael's upper arm, but when he calls Athens Athens says no. They'll send a helicopter.

I hear this second-hand from Raffy, who went with Michael and Claudia in the ambulance. Hear it via a cell phone. He bought one. Disgorging his story seems to have left space for new things. He tells me that Claudia is going with Michael in the helicopter to Athens and that he will be back shortly.

I hang up and return to the front terrace where I'm drinking mint tea. Gabriel, Jean-Paul, Rebecca and Simon have taken a carafe of my rosé up to the roof, freeing me to tune in again to the pulse of the dark garden and its once indulged possibilities. Then, out of this promising hiatus, a police car turns into the drive. Stelios Kritikos gets out, glances round the garden, up at the roof, down towards the sea. He walks across to the *pythos* and flicks it with a fingernail while his partner pauses to take a call. Finally they come up to where I'm sitting under a dim moth-encrusted light. Kritikos pulls out a chair. His partner lights a cigarette and walks away through the oleanders. I see the glow of the tip flare and point towards the neighbours' wall. I think *what fresh hell is this?*

Your neighbours, says Kritikos conversationally. *Of course you will know them now?*

Not really.

He raises his eyebrows.

They're British. So am I.

Ah. Your famous reticence. Have you talked with them at all?

Once. They came for drinks.

And when they were enjoying those drinks they told you, perhaps, of their business, their business established in England which they plan also to run from here?

Now I'm worried. With so much on his plate – more criminality, surely, than an island paradise should expect in a couple of rough decades, more than this island will have seen since the era of the pirates – how has he time to think about my neighbours?

Not really. Some sort of marketing enterprise I believe.

Your source for this?

A guy who came here. Wrong house. It was them he was looking for.

And do you know the name of this person?

My equanimity is beginning to unravel. The thing that began all this, the man who began all this, have I really managed to forget him?

Peter Karpodinis. He gave me a card.

There is a palpable slackening of tension across the table. I'm still waiting for a context.

Art business? he says encouragingly. *Greetings cards and other small reproductions?*

He says this looking off towards the neighbours' unlit garden, inviting me to add something. And it's not that I'm unwilling. I've seen the cards and *other small reproductions* sound a neat fit for the people I met. But a scam? If that is right then I have to re-think tucked-in shirts and ironed-in creases as a method of character analysis. Ironed-in creases even in their shorts, mind you.

But now I'm seeing log fires and tinsel. On his aborted visit here my nemesis spoke of Christmas cards. Had he – uprooted, under-occupied and possessed of many icons – been struck by a eureka moment? Prompted (wild guess) by a business flyer left on a café table by the aspirant purveyors of fine art stationery next door? The provenance of Christmas cards . . . who would check? Small business acumen, High Street values, a tidy turnover till the heat is off. Icons in bumper packs, printed with season's greetings, bringing an essence of eastern orthodoxy to the mantelpieces of Britain. Paving the way, perhaps, for the real thing. My neighbours' rather stilted furtiveness imposed on them by their new associate. My visitor is waiting but I'm tracking the them onwards into drinks coasters and fridge magnets.

Down among the oleanders the partner stamps out his cigarette and Kritikos gets to his feet. I remember Simon up there on the roof.

Has he done something? Peter Karpodinis?

Following information from a reliable source I arrested him this afternoon.

For?

He turns away without answering, stops again to turn and shake my hand.

All these arrests! In one day! He can't leave it like that.

I hope to have no other like it. Still in departure mode. *After this my hope is only to pick up motorcyclists.*

I wait.

Our own people – he will hang on till he gets this off his chest – *our young people who will die before they wear a helmet. Then the Italians who like to drive and talk with a friend each side. Then the Germans who are right even when they are wrong and the British who hope by example to convert us all to drive on the other side.*

You arrested him. On suspicion of what?

The theft and the counterfeiting of Byzantine icons.

Simon on the roof a potential witness – should I speak up? – but perhaps only at the risk of incriminating himself.

May we leave our car here?

What?

We would like to speak to your neighbours. Their gate, we find, is locked.

This visit, then, perhaps not much more than their answer to a parking problem. And I almost shopped Simon over it. And with him, no doubt, Rebecca. Which must rank with ironing one's shorts in *savoir faire.*

The neighbours' gate clatters. They're climbing over. A cat strolls past. Raffy returns. He walks over to where I'm sitting. Laughter is coming from the roof, voices from across the wall. He sits beside me. We watch a bat circle on the edge of the light and a shooting star flash and die. This is familiar. We sit without talking, absorbed in the pulsating blackness of the garden, the far-out throb of a ferry, the rustle of the hedgehog, the shout of a lone cicada.

22

Thanasi's house stands on a hill, the Hill of Aesclepius. Its bookshelves speak in two languages of his ruling passions: art and history; the history of art; the art of history. The furniture is island antique, the paintings by a well-known Greek naïve painter and we are eating lobster mayonnaise from plates whose faded glitter evokes an extinct European royal household. They're telling us, I think, that Thanasis is king of the island. But beyond its cliffs and beaches he holds no sway.

I was told as much this morning by Carolina Alifieri, architect and business partner, who stopped me in the street after I dropped Jean-Paul at the port. She knew this dinner was planned.

Thanasis, she said . . . *he is, I think, the Prospero of Kryptos. If the island had a voice he believes it would be his. For your husband he wants that the island should repair him. You understand?*

I did. Her meaning and her word.

And you can trust him, she continued, *but you cannot depend. He will make things all right here on Kryptos, but many people are involved outside of here. Many debts are owed. He is only a man of the island. There*, patting my shoulder, *I have said all I can say.*

And he has, at short notice, rustled up a sense of occasion, though perhaps at the expense of warmth and spontaneity, normally at the heart of Greek hospitality. The evening drags and the lack of substance in the conversation so far hints at a heavy wrap-up speech to come.

I am not at ease, and from Raffy I sense antagonism and a general disinclination to sit up and behave. When Thanasis finally lays aside his fork and looks portentous, we are not encouraging.

In these islands . . . he begins and pauses, waiting for us to listen up. With neither of us meeting his eye he tries again. *In these islands . . . for most of our history . . . which as you know is a long one . . .*

He gets no further when Raffy interrupts. I know what he's thinking. We are being steered towards the under-the-carpet solution, the one he visualised, hoped for even, only two days ago, when the outcome was theoretical and he didn't see himself in the role of dust. Soon a florid epilogue may render any mention of an event that, on the day, came at him, cloven-hoofed, from the dark side, nitpicking and ungracious.

The man with the knife, he says. *I think you may have heard this story?*

Thanasis looks opaque.

The man many years ago . . . who threatened me with a knife? My mother was also threatened.

Uncomfortable but holding out.

A knife . . . he fingers his antique silver fish knife, picks it up, holds it – presents it – then lays it in the centre of the table, pointing away from him . . . *a knife such as you might use to slit the throat of an animal?*

Ah yes. Changing tack now. *Mr. Kritikos told me. The youth.*

Youth?

The Ritsos boy. A well-known trouble-maker. Long ago he was sent off to Australia.

I was a boy. This was a man.

Thanasi's face shows only disapproval: a breach of manners, his look says, breaking the *don't ask* code as well as the rules of guest etiquette. He waits, but keeps his eyes averted. This is a mistake.

The look he is avoiding I can only guess at. Thanasis is opposite us, Raffy sits on my left, rock still. I can read the text of his silence, Thanasis could hardly avoid it. The past is not past. Without acknowledgement it lives on as a dangerous present. Particularly dangerous, I think, because it has just moved out of my comfort zone.

He is receding, I think, drawing on the impressions of that day . . . becoming small . . . letting the man, the bible and the knife grow large, shrinking into the boy, and from there growing to confront Thanasis as something more than the man.

The knife lies there, pointing at Thanasis. I don't know that unmoving posture. Stiff-winged is the phrase that comes to mind. I can't see into his eyes from where I'm sitting but Thanasis, when he finally turns his head, can. He shifts in his chair and looks away again.

Presently their eyes lock and for an aeon or two they sit without talking. When the wings finally relax a profile I know takes shape. The expression I can't see turns to something which Thanasis recognises as a green light and so he begins again.

In these islands, he says, avoiding Raffy's gaze, but principally addressing him, *we have dealt always, you understand, with our own problems. Sometimes we come together to fight a common enemy, in the last war, of course, and before that against the Turks – not the Persians, on that we were divided – but many times throughout our long history we have united. But because we are small islands in an unpredictable sea we have been, throughout our history, each island independent.*

Adrenalin has made me not the guest of choice. Passive reception of a speech preparing to paper over cracks is beyond me. My own crack-papering job is too raw. These last days I've had a sense of the ground stirring. Earth shifting. Nothing so crude as their grave opening, but although my increasingly restive parents are far too restrained to behave like Claudius's ghost, they mean that I should take note.

To drown out their voices, theirs and Thanasi's, Thanasi's claiming ignorance in Raffy's case while also coming up with a name, I reprise our current state of play. Which is that Michael will live. The bullet removed from his left biceps had lodged superficially. It winged him. The gun was old and faulty or Vasilis was shaking with emotion, possibly both. And this morning, when Raffy called London and accessed his answerphone, he picked up a message from the detective he'd hired in

America. He called him and found that Claudia's lodger, a small-town guy from northern Greece, was a cousin of the Zacharias now en route, under escort, to Piraeus. Rather than take the rap for a relative with a criminal history he had spilled out the story as he knew it. An enterprise, Raffy's source said, principally client-led. You want it, we'll get it. Meanwhile you might like to know about a few things fresh on the market.

For most of our history, Thanasis continues, *we grow and catch, each of us, what we need to live, the wheat, the wine, the oil, the fish. The same with our laws. We make the laws we need, our own right and wrong. Each island, when a thing is wrong, we deal with it. When it is not so wrong, not hurting anyone, more a – what do you call it, infringement, a rule from outside – we do not have so long experience of that. But times change and we move with those times.*

Raffy is now putting on a formal display of attention. He will be leaving on the night boat for Athens to keep an appointment with the Ministry of Culture. The air no longer crackles. Particles are settling. The lobster was good, our plates are empty.

Somewhat unusually for a Greek man Thanasis is now taking care to address his remarks equally to me. He is greatly inhibited in what he can say, he explains, by an agreement with Stelios Kritikos, but he can tell us that regrettably some criminal elements on the island exported certain goods using networks established by foreigners for certain illegal imports. Their methods were of that trade and nothing a true man of Kryptos would have anything to do with.

This needs a token dissenting murmur. Casting around for or something to sully his whitewash I remember Mavra Vrahia, its jetty, its access roads, its disproportionate ambition. I mention my two visits, my surprise at the scale of the undertaking. Why, I ask. Why there?

Ah. He seems pleased I asked. *Always my dream was to build in the impossible place.*

This is unexpected. I don't have to press for reasons. He is telling me.

You have been, perhaps, to Santorini? Those terrible cliffs, that black sand. But which island do you see most often in pictures of our beautiful Cyclades? Kryptos with its beautiful small beaches and golden sand, with its olive groves and orchards and pastures beneath our kind mountains? No. It is Santorini.

Then there are the places of the holy men, Meteora, The Holy Mountain, also in Lousios and Vikos gorges, all these are beautiful and famous and impossible, of course, because for the holy men the impossible place was closer to heaven.

He is talking himself into the ultimate hubris. He sees that and veers off. *Also in Italy there is the Amalfi Coast, in Provence, the beautiful villas of the Corniches, the west coast of Corsica, The Algarve, cliffs, rocks, etcetera, I love this landscape, very good for pictures. In Mavra Vrahia we will make an impossible architectural masterpiece.*

He almost convinces me. And then the phone rings. He excuses himself and goes into an adjoining room. As he goes he calls *Zenobia!* and the pleasant-faced woman who showed us in comes from the kitchen to top up our glasses and clear our plates. She responds only hesitantly to our attempts at conversation – she is not Greek – and we are able to pick up some of his conversation. It's hurried and in Greek and we don't catch all of it. We're pushing breadcrumbs around our florid plates, fidgeting with the heavy crystal stems of our wine glasses, setting separate clocks for Raffy's departure for Athens. But as Thanasis ends the call he says something that makes us look up quickly and seek each other's eyes.

Excuse me. He returns to the table looking grave and makes no move to sit down. *A situation has come up. A serious situation. In my business, you understand. I am afraid I must deal with it immediately.*

We get to our feet. He apologises profusely but our anxiety to be gone must be evident as he steers us towards the door and wrings our hands abstractedly, edging round Raffy with a brief grip to his shoulder rather than glance at his face. Then he reaches again for my hand. He grips it and looks me in the eye. He means me to see, and I do see, vision, effort, responsibility.

The land, he says, *was the land of my grandfather. The poorest land on Kryptos.*

I'm convinced.

Out in the night on the dark hill an owl shrieks and the cicadas draw us back into the real world. The door has closed behind us. We stand there taking in the immense indent of the bay below outlined in lights. Headlights separate from the moving ribbon tracing the shore lights and a car climbs the hill towards us, past the pillared gate and the glowing garden, an old car, window down, island music spilling from it, the Greece we know. But it's

Thanasi's last words to his caller that are echoing in our heads.

Did you hear that? Raffy asks, lowering his voice.

The house behind us discourages elaboration but none is needed. Driving back down the hill towards the harbour I am replaying the words in English and in their unguarded Greek.

I have to go. The boy is here. He's here with his wife.

Too early for the ferry, too wired to sit at a crowded café, we stand on the dark quay-side locked in our separate thoughts. Mine are simple. He was always coloured by that experience. Only for the first summer of our acquaintance was he the untroubled person he might have been. How he is now – not entirely fluent, not entirely formed – will change, starting perhaps in Athens, telling the tale, righting the wrong. But first acquaintance counts. And it was in that first summer of sharp instincts that we came together.

As the boat comes into sight I recall the other thing I overheard. That Yannis is missing. I'm on the point of telling Raffy this when I recall that he has never met him, and it's in that checked, distracted moment of irrelevance that he turns to go, turns back, plants a careful kiss on my cheek and turns away again.

Kalo taxidi!

If he hears me he doesn't react, already lost in thought. And I too have moved on, chasing that loose and tantalising thread.

The streets are busy, the cafés and bars crowded with the late night party set, music spilling out right and left as I walk through the town towards the car park. I'm passing a curtain of creepers that screens a piano bar when someone hails me. It's Dimitris. He is sitting on the terrace with someone in deeper shadow.

Anna. He jumps to his feet and pulls out a chair. *Please. Come and join us.*

I stop where I am and in weariness and disaffection, strengthened rather than assuaged by soft piano jazz, the scent of jasmine and designer up-lighting, meet his eye and let him feel the chill of my stare. Then, with the shadow solidifying into Marcus, I take the chair from him and join them.

The talk is of nothing, local gossip. In the Greek way we avoid all that might be, that surely would be, difficult. A little above the category of gossip is the news that the newer, bigger airport might not after all be built. The spiralling estimates, the case against, the availability of funding in a recession, all these are working against it. Dimitris, always on the side of the anti-s, is pleased.

What we have here is special, is it not? Tell me, Anna, you come here from your own country because it is special, yes? You don't go in Spain or in big island with fly from London. You come for special, yes? He assumes a yes and leans across to shake my hand, then gets to his feet and bids us goodnight. I watch him walk away then turn and come back. He stands behind me, squeezes my shoulders, then vanishes into the crowds. He too knows that things suppressed need some acknowledgement.

You were saying, I say to Marcus, *when we were interrupted?*

I don't believe I remember.

Because I thought back then that things were, in some way, touch and go?

A crowd of young Athenians swings past in a mass mock embrace singing a florid ballad of thwarted love. He waits for them to pass.

For a moment, so did I.

Is it really a copy?

He takes time to answer, long enough for me to feel that not everything has been resolved.

Made by a sculptor on Tinos. I commissioned it soon after I had a house to put it in.

And it never gave you ideas?

I assure you . . . the progression was all the other way.

I saw one like it. On Tinos.

It may have given other people ideas. The sculptor has no part in that. He works to commission.

And the icons? They were painted by Brother Gerasimos?

This I **am** *happy about.*

Unable to settle in his new home, Marcus tells me, it had become the venerable icon painter's custom to break for freedom whenever he found the chance and cross the hills to his old monastery and studio. Marcus, Dimitris, several local ladies and latterly Rebecca began to take him meals and do his laundry, and the good brothers of Aghios Theodoros no longer came to round him up. Recently, acting as his agent, Marcus has sold a couple of his paintings. The money is going to pay for a housekeeper with any further proceeds to island causes.

We contemplate this happy outcome. On the point of leaving I ask: *will you stay here?*

Of course. Will you?

But I don't know the answer to that.

23

Next day is a lost day. I tidy things, water things, swim briefly and without pleasure from an empty beach and back home try to read in the shade of the palm tree. But I can't disengage. Rather, I can't find a comfortable perspective from which to disengage. Presently my mother then my father join me under the palm tree. Sorry, I tell them, I didn't believe it. Still don't.

The palm fronds droop like a skirt around me as I reach for the person I was, the people they were. You brought me here, I tell them. Look what your vacation choice got us into.

So sweet and so straight, Gabriel's words, waspish but fair. Mine was the childhood Raffy imagines he would have chosen, my parents the parents he might have picked, unreliably cool but always accountable.

But not superhuman. My mother a tactful and long-suffering passenger, my father a head-in-the-clouds driver. More than capable of driving into a tree. More capable of that than is Raffy of letting go of his view of things. That his caller, hearing of the crash, might have moved to cash in on it would not have occurred to him. Though perhaps it occurs too readily to me.

So . . . can I now absolve myself of the sin of deferred mourning? Perhaps. From the start Raffy was in there, dealing with police, doctors, registrars, excising the fate from the fatality, the tough luck that's just about acceptable from the finality that is not. Making me distrust my own reactions. And all that zealous people-handling – with hindsight, of course, to assuage his guilt – left me without a role. Sweet, straight, confused, redundant, insufficiently bereaved.

I'm not that person now. And I still rate my view above his. Some way above it. Though not enough to cancel his out. Hedging my bets, then, I should open my mind to the untapped joys of vengeance or, if not vengeance, blame. But the man I glimpsed carrying Claudia's hold-all down the ramp of the island ferry seemed too slight to carry such weight, as do all the bit players along the way. No-one, so far, has that status. Only the island stays in the frame.

As for the phone call, I overheard it, followed it up, went from eavesdropper to voyeur to half-hearted tangler in other people's affairs. Nothing singular there. A spark of curiosity and we're off, Persephone, Pandora, Aurora, all of us, no option to spit out the seeds, slam the lid, ignore the spinning wheel. You do what you're programmed to do.

The sun is going down. I'm tired. As I drift off to sleep the book I never read slips again from my hands.

When I waken it's raining, the first rain for months, heavy sullen drops out of a dark sky, good for the garden and the reservoirs, bad for tourists and windsurfers, freak unseasonal rain, for me a reminder of a life lived not entirely out of doors.

Once again I'm alone in the house. It feels strange. I make coffee, slice bread, spoon out the last of the peach jam, and turn on the television news. I'm not sure how long it is before I realise that I'm looking at the harbour of Kryptos.

A man wanted by the police, says the newsreader, escaped from an armed guard on a ferry taking him from Kryptos to Piraeus, and was yesterday found dead off the Aegean island of Lesbos. He had fallen overboard from a cargo vessel bound for the Turkish port of Ayvalik. Police identified him as Zacharias Triandaphyllou, wanted by police in several countries.

Raffy. He has a phone now. He hasn't called me. But neither the possession of a phone nor the use of one has any place in how I'm seeing him. I think of him now and I see wings. I focus on that and they start to stiffen. Soon I will hear them beat.

Minutes have passed in which I've spilled coffee, hit the standby button, played music, thrown open windows, made more coffee, spilled that. The rain stops. Stays stopped. I pick up my coffee and carry it out to the garden. The plants are steaming, the air sultry and stifling, clogged with insects. A buzzard circles, a giant grasshopper crashes from a creeper and lies writhing at my feet. Ants grow wings and start to swarm.

The phone rings. I think about leaving it but I can't do that now. It's Gabriel in Athens. Michael is fine, he tells me. Well I wasn't that worried, but I'm more than glad to listen to Gabriel telling me, sotto voce and sardonic, that Michael would like me to take a message to his friend Josh at the windsurfers' camp where they must all be devastated wondering what happened to him. I find a pen and write it down. And by the way, adds Gabriel, he has no idea why anyone would want to shoot him.

Well I do. Vasilis had a sister, a small slight girl with a pale oval face and a mass of kinked black hair, still at school but helping out her mother in the holidays. I remember her. Raffy remembers her. When the ambulance left we talked about her. Michael perhaps does not remember girls. He would certainly not remember their brothers, in particular Vasilis who went out every day to take his dead father's place in the fishing fleet.

We heard, one of those early summers, that Vasili's sister had died. They didn't like to talk about it but Kyria Drossoula, our landlady, told my mother what had happened. *She flied*, she said, spreading her arms. *Flied from a cliff.* She was pregnant. Was that the summer that Michael joined the house party in France?

As for the girl with grey eyes, as she ran into the square the years fell away and I recognised her. Vasili's girlfriend from back then, another schoolgirl, perhaps now his wife. I remember how she too would watch Michael, helplessly and hopelessly. How they all did. How he stirred not a feather to charm, engage or entertain. How he just was.

I shake myself back to the present. Gabriel is telling me that Claudia will stay on with Michael in Athens until the hospital clears him to go, possibly in a couple of days. He, though, will return to Kryptos tonight.

There are things I should fix, he says. *Should have fixed.* He doesn't amplify.

When Marje calls I'm still in need of distraction. She's looking for Gabriel. He doesn't answer and she wonders if he has already left for New York. I tell her about Michael and she tells me that the wrap-up island yacht trip promised by Kurt is happening tomorrow, and if Gabriel wants to join them he should call her. They can pick him up on Kryptos. Kurt, then, still in business. Using Greg's yacht. Thoroughly distracted now I miss the next bit and come back to . . . *had to hold a gun to the guy's head but he finally agreed to take a deposit. Anna honey? You with me? The house. That weird place in the rocks. It got to me. I'm thinking Plymouth Rock. Founding Mother. Without the biological obligations of course.*

When she hangs up Raffy is back in my head. I can't settle to anything so I drive into the village to check my mail. In the post office I find Nico the centre of a group of people, very exercised, questioning him repeatedly. When they see me they stop talking. Their eyes flash *foreigner*. I haven't seen that for a while. I go to open my box and Nico sees me.

Anna! Many strange things are happening, we are confused. Yannis – you know I think? – he is missing. On the hill near a little house he . . . he had an interest in . . . an old house, you won't know, a dog was whining, one of those loose dogs, digging in the ground. Some people went to see. They thought: Yannis is missing, many terrible things are happening, maybe another terrible thing. They dug in the ground and they found a body. The body of a dog! The people then, they thought that dog was looking for the other. But beside the dog they found some opening, maybe some secret passage, and in this was a holy icon! They think now maybe this dog was bringing them there, to this icon. The people are wondering what is intended here, maybe we should show kindness to such dogs? What is happening, Anna? What is happening to our island?

Back at the house I consider foreignness. I don't give enough thought to foreignness.

What is happening to our island? Nothing happens to the island. Things happen to people on the island. For those of us who carry a foreign passport the amulet of another reality twinkles through the perfumed smoke of this one. To reach for it would seem to break a contract, infringe the terms on which we live here. But there are times when you just have to grab it. Dive back into your gene pool. Emulate Alice. When is a secret passage not a secret passage? When it's an excavation. When is an icon not an icon? When it's a picture.

Still in need of distraction I remember Michael's message but can't find the note. Rummaging on the phone shelf I dislodge the receiver. When I replace it it rings immediately. I grab for it, drop it on the floor, pick it up.

Anna? The voice seems to come from the ocean bed.

Lucas! Where are you?

Right now I'm in Istanbul. I just want to apologise. I realise you must have been worried.

Lucas in Turkey. Lucas for whom the Aegean is a backyard, who will hop on a cargo boat as soon as catch a ferry.

A little worried. More puzzled.

It's quite simple. I ran. When I saw them together . . . Claudia and that bastard . . . I . . . Anna?

One moment, Lucas.

I grab a cushion and slump on the floor, covering the mouthpiece until I can get myself together and absolve Raffy. Lucas . . . he is right in the picture. It was Lucas after all who named his sons after avenging angels, perhaps even the son who wasn't his. And now Lucas himself, in my mind at least, is transfigured.

Are you all right? Is she there? Claudia?

She's in Athens. They all are.

I need to cool this down while I think, although what I think is never going to be voiced. I tell him in some detail about Michael and over the line hear a release of breath and a silence, and imagine the huge adjustment from metaphysical time to family time. He too remembers Vasilis, Vasilis and the beautiful sister.

Michael, you know . . . there's something missing. Claudia never saw it.

Never saw it, perhaps, because she is also lacking.

He doesn't understand the effect he has. He's just not capable of understanding. Mother and son, I think, perhaps both less culpable than they seem.

I have to tell him. Talk simply. Keep to the facts. I say that when Claudia stepped down the ramp of the ferry that afternoon, walking so close to Zac, it was not of her own free will. I tell him the whole story.

From the ocean depths comes the sound of a sigh. The silence that follows goes on and on. Lucas, if instrumental, a mere instrument of fate. I let that flicker around him and wait for the silence to end, then break it myself when it occurs to me that he might finally have made himself irresistible to Claudia.

She's coming back here. Shall I tell her you'll call?

Yes. Yes, I . . . may come back. After Trabzon I ***will*** *come back. Oh Anna?*

Yes?

Tell them – Raffy, Gabriel, I think they'll know what I'm talking about – what I'm doing now, have been doing lately, some calls I've been making, other things . . . it's restitution.

I hang up and think about that. The details don't matter. The idea does. It was Lucas who turned in Peter Karpodinis.

And when the phone rings again it's Raffy. He has had a first meeting. It was constructive. I tell him about Zac. He'd heard. I tell him about Lucas and he is silent for a long while, digesting. I try to read from his voice how things might be with him. I read in my listening self the indulgence of that. The pleasurably distanced husband once again hanging out there. The unknowability of who will return.

He too has news. The graduate archaeologist, possibly alerted by a relative on Kryptos, has come forward with his records. The body count lightens. And like me he has been thinking that, in the matter of

Vasilis, Michael might be persuaded to put the case for leniency.

Who knows? he says. *He might decide that himself.*

The clouds are lifting and the sun brings out the fresh-start smell of baked rain-washed paving stones. I pick up Michael's message to the windsurf fraternity but my bag is crammed with the detritus of the past days. Here is Marcus's handkerchief stained with my blood and Gabriel's and Raffy's sweat. I shall wash it, bleach it, perhaps even iron it and return it. That's a resolution within my reach.

And here is the second tabloid with its banner headline updating us on the Burnham marriage. I lay it beside the first tabloid and the unread book and, remembering the note inside the back cover, open it. Above a scrawled JB and a phone number the man at the next table had written: *Drinks some evening? Call me.* Life, people, so often so much simpler than I realise.

When I set off to walk to the windsurf camp a stiff breeze is blowing, but when I reach the dip in the fields by the goat shed it falls away. The dog barks. Rebecca is there, painting. Perhaps she is finally working on the hotel mural, the modern take on a classical theme. So many possibilities. So much omnipotence, so much vengeance, so much hubris. For the walls of an aspiring resort hotel so not anodyne. But then a Greek resort hotel. Hence, with reservations, apt.

So . . . not Oedipus. Not Iphigenia, not Electra, none of that family. No Phrygians, Myrmidons or

Persians. No-one from Troy or Thebes, no frogs or birds. Mythology? Ah. I see Dionysus in shorts and shades, see him home in on a girl on the beach, see her turn from the empty horizon, look up from the boring book, step away from the flaky boyfriend. See them all the time. Poster boy and girl for a Greek island holiday. I wave. Rebecca waves back. The goats line the track and watch me pass.

I take the path that leads beyond the juniper thicket to the windsurfers' camp. Two guys are sitting at a driftwood table drinking beer. *Josh?* I say. They wave out towards a strait clogged with crossing sails.

Could you give him a message? From Michael?

Hey, says the nearer one. *He got shot, huh? Cool.*

I lay the note on the table and watch them take it in as they return from another reality. There are many realities on Kryptos. I pick up a stone, weight it, and walk on.

The cliff-top path stretches ahead. I walk for a bit between the corn stubble and the sea, letting the *mesimeri* drift up and settle round me, heavy with those things I brush against but have no wish to understand.

A man comes out of a house carrying a gun, the man I saw before. He sees me and stops. He comes across the field and stands by the track. When I come alongside he addresses me in English.

You are wife, he says. *That boy, he did good. Are bad people on Kryptos* – he gestures off towards the centre of the island – *but most good.* He indicates the fields around him. *Here, good.* He shakes my hand, shoulders his gun and goes off.

What am I to make of that?

I turn and let the sun sear my other shoulder as I head for home. As I walk there is a stirring in the air and the grasses of the verge start to ripple, shadowing my path.

It's local, then. Is that what he means? The land hereabouts has no buried antiquities. The people here have not splashed out on cars and houses. Or the people here, mindful of all that's on and in and under their land, know better than to disturb it.

Today the yacht left the lagoon. I stood on the roof terrace and watched it go.

I don't know why John Burnham was killed, whether from mistaken identity or to stop a foolhardy one-man exposé attempt.

I don't know who took the figurine, who spent those nights on my roof, who beamed a message to my phone.

Not knowing is good. To be among things not known . . . that is essential.

If that first summer we had taken a ferry to Dieppe, had passed our summers in a sleepy French enclave where the postman cycling past each day with a fresh baguette was the indelible image, life might have taken a quieter turn. I see long dappled avenues of poplars leading to remnants of visible centuries. But we touched down on a highway roaring with vanished traffic, traffic travelling in two directions, to the past and from it. You can pull up sometimes and feel it float or thunder past, and in the lull of afternoon see shapes solidifying in that silent vortex, but there is no option, ever, to turn off.

The electrician has called. He may come tomorrow.

There are voices across the wall. I don't know who the neighbours are but already, whether or not they know it, the island is processing them.

If Raffy and I have a future it will be decided on the island as our first meeting was decided.

Under an olive tree a pottery shard is waiting. The soil is baked hard and will resist me but I'll dig for a while and see what comes up.

END

A Note on the Author

Deirdre Chapman is a journalist and short story writer, occasional reviewer and travel writer, and contributor to several books on writing and place. Born on the east coast of Scotland, she now divides her year between the city of Glasgow and a house on a Greek island.